A WOMAN'S NEEDS

"It's very beautiful." Her voice trembled. But the white man's world—its boats, its buildings—made her feel so closed in. It had no fresh air, no smoke holes for the stars to peep in and wink down at her. There was no sense of the familiar world on the other side of a thin piece of hide.

The mugginess of the night air, the confinement of her new clothing, and the animosity during supper combined to push her over the edge. She began to shake.

Grady put his arm around her and drew her close. "I know all this is new and not easy."

The fact that he understood and didn't think she was overreacting took away a bit of her homesickness. Sighing and moving a tiny bit closer, she whispered: "No. I was warned."

Grady took her hand in his, his thumb moving tenderly over the soft skin of her inner wrist. "You are a kind, gentle, giving woman. If others cannot see what I do, then that is their problem—and their loss."

His words warmed her, as did his tender touch. She needed both like a starving man would need the nourishment of the *Maka* and the warmth of *Wi*. And standing beneath the carpet of stars, Star was suddenly very afraid of needing much more.

White Dreams

Susan Edwards

LEISURE BOOKS   NEW YORK CITY

A LEISURE BOOK®

November 2000

Published by

Dorchester Publishing Co., Inc.
276 Fifth Avenue
New York, NY 10001

ISBN 0-8439-4790-X

The name "Leisure Books" and the stylized "L" with design are trademarks of Dorchester Publishing Co., Inc.

Printed in the United States of America.

Butterflies and Angels

The free-spirited butterfly,
Dancing on a warm summer breeze,
Flitting from flower to flower,
Touching, caressing, moving on.

Wings of chiffon, God's creation
Appears each spring, vibrant, wondrous.
Life is short for this fragile being,
Whose beauty soothes, inspires.

For it starts out not so worthy,
Cannot fly, not very pretty.
Yet a great service it completes,
As it grows, transforms, emerges, flies.

Sally embraced the universe,
With arms outstretched, heart full of warmth.
Like the elegant butterfly,
She gave, cared, nurtured, blessed our lives.
Though her time on earth was cut short,
She brought us love, joy, happiness.
To all her family and friends,
Sally was special, the Lord's own.

She's in Heaven, has earned her wings,
She's taken her place, high above.
Finally at peace, free of pain,
Among angels and butterflies.

ACKNOWLEDGMENTS

Heartfelt thanks to Tom Dewey at the Jefferson National Expansion Memorial in St. Louis for all his help and time spent researching and answering my questions about early St. Louis. Any historical errors are mine and mine alone.

Prologue

Late summer 1856, Nebraska Territory

Insidious, like a snake slithering through the tall prairie grass toward its unwary prey, the vision came in the dark of night when her mind was at its most vulnerable. It hovered at the edge of consciousness: a swirl of color, a whisper in the mind, a thread of awareness. Without further warning, images of events to come struck, obliterating her peaceful sleep.

Star Dreamer moaned and thrashed, trying to wake and ward off the unwanted vision. But it seized her mind and will with swift savagery. Across the back of her closed eyes, the kaleidoscope spun, bringing with it a familiar sense of nausea until, with crystal clarity, a scene formed.

She stood in the middle of a battlefield.

The night sky glowed with yellow, orange and red flames. Smoke filled the air, making her gasp even in her sleep. Her hands rose to cover her ears in a vain attempt to blot out the war cries as warriors battled to the death. On and on the scene raged, until just as suddenly as it had begun, it stopped. The eerie silence frightened her more than the battle cries and left her shaking. She backed away and tripped over the fallen body of a warrior.

She scrambled to her feet as the ground turned red. Blood red. All else faded but the red sky, red dirt and the pale body of the fallen warrior whose life's blood drained from his body. Crimson pooled on the soil and flowed away from her, a dark, glossy river absorbed by the *maka*, from which all life sprang. Moving in slow motion, she reached down and touched him, felt his coldness. Felt *death*.

In the night sky, the bright, round face of *hunwi* slid from behind a cloud and sent a beam of white light to illuminate the fallen warrior. Vulnerable, unable to fight what she did not want to see, Star bolted upright on her pallet of furs, her eyes wide open yet unseeing, hands in front of her as she struggled to free herself from the grip of the frightening vision. Hunching over, knees drawn to her chest, she covered her head with her arms. "No," she whimpered, her fingers pulling and clawing through her hair.

Look, the traitorous voice in her vision commanded. *See the face of the newly dead.*

"*No!*" The sound of her own hoarse shout tore Star from the clutches of the nightmarish vision. She woke bathed in sweat. Frantically, she reached out beside her, needing the comforting reassurance of Two-Ree, her husband.

He wasn't there. The mound of furs beside her was empty and cold—as cold as that lifeless warrior in her vision. The last vestige of the vision fled, leaving her wide awake, shivering and apprehensive. Her chest constricted, her throat tightened. "No," she moaned, over and over, denying what she knew to be true. She'd seen her own husband's death.

Her gaze swept the tipi, hoping it wasn't too late to warn him, but it was. His weapons were gone. With frenzied movements, Star untangled herself from her bedding and dashed out into the predawn light. She ran between tipis, past solemn warriors and weeping women, searching frantically.

Near the edge of camp, a handful of warriors gathered on horseback, the paint on their bare torsos and faces standing out in the faint light. Relief that the war party hadn't left yet spurred her forward. It wasn't too late.

Star scanned the men gathering to ride to war. Where was Two-Ree? He wasn't with the mounted warriors. Behind her, she heard the approach of horses and spun around. Two warriors rode toward her: her brother and her husband. Relief left her knees trembling. She wasn't too late. Two-Ree had painted his torso and face with wide slashes of red and black, and he wore a quiver of arrows slung across his back. In his hands, he carried his bow, shield and lance.

Pride warred with fear. Her husband had been chosen to accompany her brother, Chief Striking Thunder, on a raid against their enemy for the murders of their people earlier that day—including Meadow Lark, Striking Thunder's young wife.

Star stumbled forward to stop her husband, to warn him of her vision and to plead with him not to go, but denial and doubt stopped her. What if the fallen warrior in her vision had not been her husband? It could have been anybody. In that short space of uncertainty, both men rode past in stoic silence to join the rest of the war party.

Star ran after them. Whether or not it had been him, she needed to share her vision. Before she could approach her husband, the shaman, an old man with long, flowing white hair, stepped forward with arms outstretched. In a loud chanting voice, he evoked the Spirits to go with the brave men. Star watched, helpless to intervene. When the wise man finished, the air came alive with shouts and chants from warriors and tribal members alike. Revenge would be theirs.

Two-Ree glanced back at Star. Their gazes met and held as he lifted his lance high and let out a long war cry. Tears streamed down her cheeks. To approach him now, to speak and ask him to remain behind would shame him before all. He was a great warrior and, as such, it was his duty to protect his people. Yet he was her husband, the father of her children.

A small, warm hand slipped inside hers. Star glanced down at Morning Moon, her young daughter. The child's eyes held a hint of worry. Together, in silence, they watched the warriors ride off.

A week later, Star woke once more to the sound of screaming—her own. Oblivious to her family rushing in, she rocked back and forth. She didn't need anyone to tell her that her husband was dead.

Chapter One

Spring 1857

Star Dreamer watched her people rejoice in the marriage of Chief Striking Thunder to Emma O'Brien through troubled eyes.

In the center of the village, women moved about wearing dresses exquisitely adorned with beads, feathers and dyed quills. More feathers and beads decorated their long, black hair, which gleamed in the firelight. The men, not to be outdone, had painted their bodies and wore their best breech-clouts and moccasins.

Orange-red flames from a large fire leaped high into the sky, casting a warm glow over the dark-ened camp, showcasing male dancers. Some wore impressive bonnets made from sacred eagle feath-ers they'd earned with their brave deeds, while oth-ers waved coup sticks in the air as they shuffled, twirled and danced around the hot flames.

Infectious laughter competed with the chanting of dancers, voices raised in storytelling and the happy shrieks of children running among the adults. She spied her five-year-old son, Running Elk, tumbling and somersaulting with other boys, and smiled. Like most children his age, he loved to stay up late and play in the dark. Though it was mid-March and the night air held a bitter chill, no one minded. It was a night for everyone, young and old alike, to lose themselves in the simple joy of being alive.

Star ran her fingers through her shoulder-length hair—a reminder in itself of her recent loss—and her reasons for avoiding the crowds. She yearned to be happy and carefree, even if only for one night, but shame at failing her people held her back. The fast and furious beating of drums accompanied by the loud, rhythmic chants of the drummers rose in pitch and tempo.

Death. The words came at her, echoed loudly in her mind as the pulse at her temple reverberated with the loud, pounding drums, driving her farther into the deep shadows between the tipis. Peace, harmony and contentment would always be denied to her. Like her deceased grandmother, Star possessed the Sight. But unlike her grandmother, who'd considered the ability to see into the future an honor, Star felt cursed.

She hated the uncertainty of never knowing when the visions would strike. She dreaded losing control of her mind to a force unseen and unfelt by most. Most of all, she was tired of being afraid. Tired of taunting glimpses into the future. Tired of being torn by the knowledge that each time she failed to heed or understand the warnings of her dreams, she put her people at risk. Death lay on her shoulders, bowing them under the weight of guilt, leaving her feeling as though she lived in the dark shadows of the Spirits.

Walking around the perimeter of the outer circle of tipis, she spotted a group of girls trading beads and necklaces. Morning Moon, her daughter, sat among them. Watching the girl laugh and play with her friends, Star wondered how long it would be before her daughter began suffering the same fate.

Morning Moon already has the Sight.

Prickles of gooseflesh chilled Star's flesh. She rubbed her bare arms. She'd been sure that her daughter had been spared, that once again a generation had been skipped. Morning Moon, knowing how her mother felt, had hidden the truth from her.

Tears trickled down Star's cheeks. Despair engulfed her. *Please, not my daughter, not my sweet child.* Morning Moon was only eight winters—an innocent child—too young to understand. Just knowing that one day her daughter would experience this same torturous pain as her mother made Star want to fall to the ground and curse the Spirits for their cruelty.

"Why does my sister hide in the shadows and walk alone?"

Startled, Star jerked her head up. Striking Thunder, her brother, stood before her, arms crossed, a fierce frown upon his stern visage. He looked every bit as intimidating as their father when displeased. Unable to look him in the eye, Star averted her own gaze.

How could she join in the happy celebration when it was her fault that many present tonight had lost their loved ones? Since her own husband's death, she'd felt so lost and alone. Two-Ree had been her anchor when her world spun out of control. Hugging herself, she turned from her brother. "I wish to be alone." Forcing herself to smile and act as though nothing was amiss was more than she could manage.

Striking Thunder's fingers, warm and firm, stopped her retreat. He turned her gently, forcing her to meet his frustrated gaze. "You still blame yourself for your husband's death. When will you accept that you were not to blame? If you do not stop torturing yourself in this manner, you will make yourself ill."

Concern roughened his voice. His gaze slid down her body. Even in the shadows, her weight loss was noticeable, as were the sunken hollows below each cheekbone, the pallor of her skin and the sharp jut of bone beneath his fingers.

"You must eat, build your strength, *mitanski*, my sister. I know you are troubled. You fight your gift, but someday you will fulfill our grandmother's prophecy."

Seeing her brother's hard features soften with worry made Star uncomfortable. It would be so easy to bow her head, agree and grasp at the hope he offered. But she couldn't. Not any longer. "*Hiya!* You are wrong." Star squeezed her eyes shut against the stark truth and yanked herself free. She didn't want to remember their grandmother's words, her promise that the Sight would one day save their People.

Star's visions used to be filled with vague images or impressions she couldn't interpret and could easily shove aside or discard. And once she'd had her children, they'd visited her less often. But over the last year, messages from the Spirit world became more frequent, lasted longer, the images far too powerful to ignore. They warned of evils she couldn't—and didn't want to—comprehend.

Only her grandmother could have understood the panic Star felt when her vision darkened and control was taken from her. Only Seeing Eyes could have known how it felt to have one's mind caught in the grip of a spiritual force.

"My gift is not strong—not as it was with our grandmother. Only births are clear to me. But I cannot see or prevent death. The visions either come too late—like the death of your first wife— or they are not clear enough to be of use."

Except for seeing your own husband's death in battle, and that you did nothing to prevent. Already seeded in her soul, her guilt sent its roots deeper.

Striking Thunder held out his hands, palms up. "This is not true. Did your gift not prevent me from killing Emma's father? You knew he was not the enemy. Had I attacked, it would have brought the wrath of the soldiers upon us and destroyed our people. Did you not save our people that day?" Her silence lent frustration to Striking Thunder's voice. "What of Wolf and his wife? You warned of the danger surrounding them . . . and yet you still believe you have no power?"

"I could not see the danger clearly. It took you and our father to know where the danger lay. Look what happens when you and my father are not around. People die—like your first wife. Many died last summer because I could not warn them of the attack. I saw death and did not understand what the Spirits were saying." Her voice broke on a sob as she recalled her sister-in-law's brutal murder. "You lost a wife—and a child—because I refused to listen to what the Spirits were trying to tell me." For the first time Star spoke of the unborn babe none but she had known about. She revealed her knowledge not to hurt her brother, but to prove to

21

him how terribly wrong he was, how dangerous it was for him to put his faith in her.

Striking Thunder's only reaction was a tightening of his jaw. "You speak nonsense! You are not to blame for the death of my first wife, nor of any child she might have carried." He drew a deep, shuddering breath. "It was not meant to be. I know this as do you."

"Then why did I see it? What was the point if the outcome could not be changed? I can't bear the thought that more of our people will die because I fail to understand the messages of the Spirits." Star angrily brushed the tears from her face. "The Spirits took my husband, left my children without a father's love and protection."

"You are not responsible for your husband's death. Do you think if he'd known the truth he'd have stayed behind like a fearful old woman? No! Your husband—my friend—would have gone with me that night, no matter what you told him. Had he known he was riding to his death, he'd have done so with courage." Pride tinged with sadness filled his voice.

Star froze, reliving that one brief moment when her husband had ridden past her. One word. He'd have stopped. He'd have listened. And though part of her acknowledged that her brother was right, that her husband would have ridden to war that night regardless of what she'd said, she'd denied him the choice. Perhaps the knowledge would have made him better able to protect himself.

Fear of dishonoring him had kept her from sharing the vision with Two-Ree. What good was honor to her now? It didn't provide for her family or come home each evening to be a loving father to his son and daughter. And honor was a sad substitute for the friend she so greatly missed and grieved for.

Striking Thunder glanced behind him. A slim, red-haired woman dressed in a bleached deerskin dress came forward from the deep shadows. Six months before, Emma had been his white captive, but now she was his beloved wife and Star's newest sister-in-law. Striking Thunder brought her forward. The love in his gaze was reflected in an answering adoration in hers.

"The Spirits took one wife but gave me another. Who is to say this is not the way it was meant to be? Who is to say there is not another husband for you?"

"*Hiya!*" Star shrieked. There would be no one else, ever. Never again would she risk seeing the death of a mate. It hurt too much. She backed away.

"I'm not worthy of our people's respect and honor. I failed—failed you as my chief, failed my family, my grandmother—my people." Anguished, Star spun around and ran away from the tipis, away from the warm circle of light, away from the happiness of those people she loved—people who might one day die because of her own inability to use the Sight.

From where he stood, Colonel Grady O'Brien watched his eldest daughter ride away from the village with her new husband. Inside, he still harbored mixed feelings about her marriage to the young Sioux chief. Did she truly desire to remain here among the Sioux rather than return home with him to St. Louis?

It went against his fatherly instincts to leave her out here where life was harsh. Here illness wiped out entire villages, and war with other tribes or soldiers was a gruesome part of life. He longed to wrap her in his cloak of protection and keep her safe from harm, shield her from the ugliness that made up this world. He could have insisted she return with him.

Maybe he should have.

With his soldiers, he had the power to forcibly take her away. After all, it could be argued that after her ordeal of being captured first by Yellow Dog and his band of renegade Indians, then rescued and held captive by the man who was now her husband, she couldn't possibly know her own mind. But deep down, he of all people understood the power of true love.

And he had no doubt Emma loved her husband. Or that Striking Thunder loved her. No matter how much he worried, Grady would not deny his child the chance to follow her heart. Some would whisper he'd been too ashamed to bring her back to polite society, that she'd been ruined by her time spent in captivity among the Indians, but he knew the truth. It was love that tied her to this land, to her husband. It was that love that would give her the courage to embrace a life so different from the one in which she'd been raised.

Glancing up into the bright, shimmering heavens, Grady thought of his late wife, Margaret Mary. With a sigh, he spoke to her. "She's all grown up, Maggie. Our baby has flown the nest." Though some found his habit of talking to his deceased wife strange, when he spoke aloud, carried on conversations with her, he felt as though heaven and earth weren't so far apart.

Even after nine years, he still missed her. His wife's sunny smile, her laughing green eyes and her love of life had made his own life complete. When she'd died, colors faded, joy ebbed and part of him shriveled and died too. He was now a mere shadow of the man he'd once been. He knew that, but what was to be done?

"I'm leaving her behind, Maggie. Watch over her." Adjusting his gloves, he spun around, away from the black emptiness into which Emma and Striking Thunder had disappeared. At least he wasn't returning home alone. He still had his youngest child. And speaking of his other daughter, he realized he hadn't seen her in hours.

He set off in search of her.

He had no difficulties moving about the camp. No one stepped forward to block his path. His easy grace and commanding presence—Grady was well over six feet tall—had always served him well among both soldiers and Indians. Not that any of the village's inhabitants would have a reason to stop him. Although there was always some tension between the Sioux and his soldiers—not without cause, he realized—the wedding celebration had done wonders for that. And he had ordered his men to be on their best behavior.

As he searched for his daughter, he observed the men under his command. So far, they had put their best foot forward, but he knew temptation could weaken even the strongest of men. Spotting one soldier walking alone with a young Indian maiden, he beckoned him over. "I believe it is time to return to our camp, soldier."

"Ah, Colonel—"

"You heard me. I will tolerate no improper behavior."

The man looked as though he would protest, then thought better of it. "Yes, sir." And with that the soldier took his leave.

Satisfied that all was in order, Grady again turned his attentions to the whereabouts of his youngest daughter. Where had she gone? A flurry of movement near the food caught his attention.

"Ah." He might have known she'd still be rooting through the leftovers. The child ate enough for three people.

Deciding to spend some time with her, he headed her way. Before he reached her, she and her young friend, Morning Moon, ran off toward the river that was a short distance away. Frowning, he wondered what she was up to. She knew better than to leave the safety of the village at night. But since when did rules apply to her? he thought to himself wryly. Renny being herself, as he'd discovered, tended to act first and think later. With a rueful shake of his head, he followed.

Though he dreaded to learn what mischief she was caught up in, he chuckled softly. "You'd have loved this one, Maggie. So full of life and spunk." He hesitated. "Maybe a bit too much."

Raising this girl would be difficult, not half as easy as the military career to which he'd once thought he'd escape. But life, and luck, had brought him back. The last time he'd seen Renny, she'd only been a few days old, an infant with big blue eyes and a thatch of golden fuzz covering her tiny head. How difficult it had been to leave her, especially with his wife's sister, Hester Mae, trying to take control of both his children. He thanked his stars that his sister Ida had agreed to raise his daughters.

But now his youngest daughter was nine, full of rebellion and resentment and not in the least bit happy to have him back in her life—especially when it meant leaving the sister who'd raised her to return home with a father she'd never known.

Reaching the river, he paused, listened, then followed the sounds of hushed whispers. He found the two girls kneeling near a small cluster of rocks. "Ranait! What are you doing out here?"

Startled at his bark, Renny dropped a large rock back on top of the pile. Standing, she placed her body in front of it. Beneath the light from the moon and stars, she looked guilty as sin. His gaze narrowed when she hurried to stand before him, hands behind her back.

He refrained from looking toward the piled rocks and gave her his complete attention, saying nothing. Years of dealing with his soldiers had taught him that silence often broke down barriers, whereas questions frequently brought forth lies and excuses.

After several long seconds, Renny squirmed. "Nothing. Just playing. What do you want?" she asked, her tone sullen and resentful.

"Don't take that tone with me, young lady. I gave you orders to remain within the boundaries of the camp. Return to the village immediately. It's not safe for you to wander so far." Hearing the harsh command in his tone, he winced, fully aware that his actions were much more authoritarian than loving. Her glare of resentment reminded him that he had a long way to go in learning how to speak to a daughter.

"I'm safe here." She pointed. "Lone Wolf stands guard, just over there." Her words ended on a smug note. Behind her, Morning Moon remained silent and watchful.

Drawing himself up, he held up his hand, palm out. "Do not argue, Ranait. As your father, I'm ordering you to return. You are not to leave the safety of the village at night again."

Renny's lips trembled but she didn't cry. She glared at him, her small arms crossed over her narrow chest, furious defiance in her eyes. "My name is Weshawee. It means Red Girl."

Staring into defiant eyes the same blue-gray shade as his own, he felt as helpless as the day he'd cradled her in his arms and named her. She'd been so tiny, so fragile. And with Mary Margaret gone, with everything changed . . . he'd been afraid of her, afraid of failing both his daughters without his wife at his side to guide him. The same fear of failure assailed him now, but this time there wasn't anywhere to run.

What if I can't do this? Maybe she's better here, with Emma.

A soft wind caressed the back of his neck. *No. You know what is right. The two of you belong together. You won't fail.*

The voice in his head was familiar, so like that of his beloved wife—giving him the courage he so desperately needed.

Frustrated with his silence, Renny stamped her foot when it became apparent he wasn't going to argue or plead with her. "I wish you'd stayed away." She backed away, her eyes glittering with unshed tears.

"I hate you! I want to stay here with Emma." She grabbed her friend's hand and pulled. Both girls ran back toward the circle of tipis behind him.

Grady's shoulders sagged. After months of sleepless nights and long days in the saddle searching for his daughters, his body felt close to collapse. Running a hand over his bearded jaw, he wondered if things would ever be right between them.

"She's confused. In time, she'll understand."

At the sound of the soft, husky voice, Grady shifted and glanced over his shoulder. An Indian woman stood several feet behind him, her face pale and drawn beneath the gentle sweep of the moon's glow. It was Star Dreamer. An emotion stirred deep within him. He owed this kind, gentle woman more than he could ever repay. She'd befriended both Emma and Renny, and had been instrumental in saving their lives.

He bowed politely in greeting, removing his hat and holding it behind his back. "She'll never forgive me for abandoning her and her sister . . . and it's no more than I deserve." His words were spoken coldly, matter-of-factly. He had little tolerance for those who shirked their responsibilities, and this was his.

"You are here for her now," Star pointed out.

"Yes. Yes, I am." There was truth to her words. He was trying to do right, to make amends. But would it be enough? "I fear my reentrance into her life has come too late."

Star shook her head, sending silky strands of black hair swinging across the tops of her shoulders. "You must not believe that. From what Emma has told me, it was Weshawee's need to find you that made her leave home to come in search of you. Weshawee needed you then, and she needs you now. You are her *ate*, her father."

"Ah, yes, she needed me. But it seems my headstrong daughter has changed her mind."

Her gentle laugh filled him with a strange warmth. "It is easy to wish for things, but when we get what we wish for we must accept the change that comes with it. That is always hard to accept, even for a small child. Give her time. She's frightened of the unknown." Star reached out and touched his shoulder, then walked past.

Grady pivoted, his eyes tracking her. He didn't add that he too was scared of the changes in his life. The thought of leaving the army—it had provided a haven from his feelings, from his responsibilities—to venture back into the chaotic civilian life he'd fled now left him feeling as though he walked along a narrow ridge, high above a deep chasm. One wrong step either way and he'd plummet into oblivion.

Grateful for the Indian woman's wise words, Grady replaced his hat and prayed that in time Renny would come to regard him as a beloved father. So much had happened in the last six months, since Emma and Renny had first disappeared on their way to Fort Pierre to find him. His well-ordered life had turned to shambles and beneath it all, he craved what he'd once known with his wife: happiness. Peace. Joy.

He squared his shoulders, determined to salvage what he could of his family. If he had to work harder, perhaps that was only what he deserved. Renny had a right to be angry with him; he should have been strong enough to overcome his pain at the loss of his beloved wife. He should have realized the army was not an answer, but an escape. And most of all, he should never have betrayed Margaret Mary by fleeing from her legacy—her two daughters.

Determined to do the right thing, he trailed after Star. He watched as she knelt down at the stream to cup water in her hands and drink. She sat back on her heels, silent and still, lost in thought, his presence forgotten. Her head fell back.

Transfixed, Grady couldn't take his eyes from the slim column of her neck and the sharp jut of her jawbone as she lifted her face to the silver light of the moon. Her hands slid up her throat, over her jaw and into her hair. Tiny dewdrops of water glistened along her throat like pearls. Thick black lashes smudged her pale face, and her lips parted briefly as she drew in a deep breath.

His own breathing turned ragged. Though only seconds ticked by, he felt as if time had come to a stop. Then she tipped her chin back down, her hair swinging forward, hiding her face as she stared out over the misty stream.

Moonlight turned her black locks silver. Unlike the other women in the village, who wore their hair in long, thick braids, Star Dreamer wore hers short—a sign of her recent bereavement. Yet even in her grief, her hair shorn, Star Dreamer remained strikingly beautiful. An aura of fragility surrounded her, adding to her allure. His protective instincts rose. This woman drew him, made him want to ease the lines of grief from her face and put a smile on her lips.

He was attracted.

It horrified him, yet a plainer and simpler truth didn't exist. It didn't matter that it was against his will, or that he'd vowed to never love again. There hadn't been another woman in his life—in any capacity—since the day he'd buried Margaret Mary, and he'd sworn there never would be. He would not feel that pain again.

But like a caged, starving animal, desperate for a morsel of food left just out of reach, a strange hunger tore at his soul.

His hand lifted, needing to touch this woman, wanting to pull her hair back from her face so he could gaze upon her moonlit beauty. He yearned to trace the taut flesh of her throat from the hollow where a hidden pulse beat, and kiss the soft skin beneath her chin as his hands skimmed upward to cradle her face in his large hands. Was her pale, golden skin as soft as her voice? Would a kiss ease the trembling of her full lips? His blood quickened, and the feel of it in his veins shocked him out of his foolish fantasies.

Grady angrily shook off his physical reaction. He was no better than the soldier he'd ordered back to camp. Taking a step back, he tried to convince himself it was gratitude that drew him to her, or maybe it was the sadness cloaking her. Or maybe he'd been out in the wilds of the western frontier too long.

He blamed his momentary weakness on the air, the marriage of his daughter and the bright moon and stars overhead. Grady backed away, intending to leave Star Dreamer to her solitude. He remembered his own need to be alone in the months following Maggie's death. The howl of a lone coyote and the buzz of crickets near the water's edge broke the silence. Suddenly she stood and joined him.

Uncomfortably aware of his body's weakness, he sought a distraction. His gaze slid to the pile of rocks with which his daughter had been playing. "Perhaps it's in our best interests to see what our girls were up to down here."

"Where your daughter is concerned, that is a wise choice." Humor once more threaded its way into her tone.

Star joined him as he lifted a flat-bottomed rock off the top of the pile. Together, they peered into a deep, dark cavity in the mound. "What the—?" Reaching in, Grady pulled out several pouches.

Star opened one. "Food."

"Same here." He dumped a bunch of dried chokecherries into his palm. Each pouch was stuffed with provisions: nuts, berries, dried meat. Now he understood why she seemed to have an abnormally large appetite. She was hiding food.

Star looked puzzled. "Why are they storing this? Winter is over."

The full weight of parenthood dropped onto his shoulders. He released a long, drawn-out breath. "It's my guess that my daughter will go to any length to avoid returning home with me—including running away.

"I thought to give her some more time here, with me, so she could get to know me before I took her away, but it's not working. As long as she's here, she won't give me a chance." He paused. "I can't risk having her run off. We'll leave tomorrow."

"I will be sorry to see her go. She brings a spark to us and to our lives." Star helped him put the pouches back into the cairn and accepted his hand.

Staring down into Star's upturned face, Grady longed to smooth the lines along her forehead, bracketing her mouth and nose and etching her pale golden skin. He took a mental step back. He had enough problems without taking on anyone else's. "Shall we rejoin the others?"

She turned, every line in her body stiff and unyielding. He felt as though he'd suggested she walk to her own execution. Again, understanding flowed between them. She was no more eager than he to return to the sounds of gaiety floating on the night air. Yet he couldn't remain out here for much longer, no matter how much he enjoyed gazing at her. There was too much to do in order to be ready to leave at first light.

Even so, he hesitated. His daughter's new sister-in-law looked as though she needed a friend. And from deep inside him, that starving, lonely creature he recognized as his own soul cried out for companionship. What harm could it do to remain with Star Dreamer a bit longer? After all, this quiet woman posed no threat to his heart. He was leaving tomorrow, and when next he saw her, she'd probably be remarried. He ignored the twinge that thought caused.

Surprising himself, he waved a hand at the meandering stream. "Would you care to join me for a walk instead?"

Chapter Two

Star considered the colonel's offer. She'd come out here to be alone, to avoid having to pretend all was well. Yet solitude invited morbid contemplation of the future, guilt over the past. Perhaps with the colonel, she would find safe ground. He seemed a kindred spirit. Both of them wore their inner torment like a cloak. Each had lost his mate, each worried over his children and neither knew how to throw off the tangled veils of pain and grief.

"I'll understand if you'd rather return to your family." Grady waited patiently for her to decide.

Star smiled weakly. Though her family meant well, her emotions were too raw and she felt too close to breaking to face more of their well-meaning concern. "I'd like to walk. But don't feel you must remain out here with me. I will be safe on my own."

Grady indicated the path before them. "I'd be

honored to have your company this evening, Star Dreamer."

Star smiled at his formality. Emma's father was such a nice man. It was hard to believe he'd abandoned his children when their mother died. The love he felt for his daughters was plain to see. It emanated from him, as did his lingering grief, and she knew only too well how grief could eat at a person and change her.

They walked in companionable silence with neither feeling the need to talk. They followed the winding river away from camp. Star measured her steps a bit slower so she could watch him. Tall and handsome, he was so different from the men in her village and the trappers they occasionally traded with. He wore an air of authority with the ease most wore their clothing. The man was formal, polite and dignified, yet there was a savage wildness about him as well.

Unlike the men in her village, he sported a bushy beard that hid his jaw and chin. The facial hair, a shade darker than the bright waves of red hair that fell to his shoulders fascinated her.

He slowed his steps so they were walking side by side. Nearly a head taller, Grady's large frame could easily have frightened or intimidated her, but instead, in his presence she felt protected, safe. She gave him a grateful look and felt a wave of pleasure pass through her.

Though she couldn't see his eye color in the darkness, she knew—she'd stolen glances at him over the past few days—that his eyes were the warm, gentle blue-gray of a lazy summer day. When he was worried or displeased, the color changed; the gray became sharper, like the bite of the cold breeze that crept into her tipi during long winter nights.

Frowning, she realized she'd spent a fair amount of time observing this Grady O'Brien since his arrival. Their shoulders bumped, startling her. She stumbled. His arm reached out to steady her, his touch warm but impersonal. So why did her heart leap to her throat?

Uneasy with the thought, Star noted the position of the moon in the night sky. It was time to return and collect her son and daughter from their play. They'd been up far too late already. A few more minutes, she promised herself. She just needed a few more minutes.

"It's a beautiful night. I shall miss seeing this vast array of stars when we return." Grady's low voice drew her from her thoughts.

"You cannot see the stars from your home in the city?"

"Not like this. Here I feel so close to the heavens. Emma is fortunate to be able to enjoy this. I hope she will be happy among your people." He paused. "It doesn't seem right to leave her behind when I take Renny back to St. Louis."

Star took the poignancy of his tone as an excuse to look at him. His expression was tortured, revealing again how deeply he felt toward his daughters and what they'd suffered. She gave him a pointed look. "Emma is loved. She is a wonderful friend and sister and is cherished here. She has given my brother—and the rest of us—much, as has Renny. Renny is—" How could she describe the young, energetic child? "Renny is Renny," she finished on a laugh. "She brings joy to all."

"Joy and a bit more," he agreed good-naturedly.

Star tried to find the words to reassure him. His child was stubborn, but beneath that, Star knew the girl desperately wanted to believe her father loved her. But words wouldn't be enough. Renny needed proof of her father's love—and that would take a strength that Star knew Colonel O'Brien had, though it had long gone unused. Still, she felt sure it was only a matter of time.

Star sighed, wishing that was the case with herself and Morning Moon, but time was her enemy. As Morning Moon grew and matured, the girl's visions would grow in power and frequency, as Star's own had. She closed her eyes. *Please*, she begged the Spirits, *please spare my daughter this. I will do whatever you ask, but spare my child.* In her blind supplication, she stubbed her toe on a large stone in the path and cried out.

Grady caught her arm. "Easy, there." He led her to a large boulder near the river and coaxed her to sit. "Are you all right? You seem troubled." Before she could answer, he continued. "I want to help you. Surely there must be something I can do in return for all you've done for me and my daughters."

Ignoring the pain in her foot, Star's mouth trembled. Without thought, she blurted, "No one can help me. I'm cursed."

Kneeling before her, Grady grasped her cold fingers. "What?"

His hands warmed hers, eased the anxiety from the pit of her stomach. Tears trickled from Star's eyes as she gave up; it was no use trying to keep her feelings inside. If anyone would understand, it suddenly seemed that it would be this man with the soft blue gaze. "It's true. While time is your friend, Colonel, it is my enemy. . . ." And then the words poured out. In short, halting sentences, Star told him of her gift, of the torment that came with it, and how she'd failed in the past. Then she told him of Morning Moon.

The dam burst; Star's fear over the future over-flowed. "She can't be allowed to develop this gift. I'd hoped it would die with me, but now . . ." Now she longed to jump up and run from it, hide and deny its very existence. Yet the gift was a part of her, a part of the land and the Spirits around her. She stared into Grady's confused eyes. He didn't understand.

She gave herself an angry shake. Well, of course he didn't. How could he? He wasn't one of them.

Grady opened his mouth to speak, but as he did, she felt a pounding in her head. His voice faded into nothingness. His image blurred, his red hair darkening, filling her vision. Then he was gone and she was alone, trapped on a narrow, rocky ledge, teetering against a buffeting wind.

Another vision. Too weary, too exhausted mentally and emotionally to fight, she watched herself plunge off the ledge into nothingness.

Star gave a cry, but as she did Colonel O'Brien again appeared—this time on the ledge far above. He jumped, came after her. She heard the deep resonance of his voice as he shouted for her to grab his hand. She tried, but he was too far away.

Then his voice changed, became the shriek of an eagle. His hands lengthened and became wings. He arrowed down past her, spread his wings wide and caught her in his soft embrace.

All at once they were one. The pair of them were soaring through the air, across a brilliant blue sky, through wispy clouds, following the course of the sparkling rivers below. They dipped, turned, and flew toward the sun before banking to float on a warm breeze.

Star saw what the eagle saw, felt its exultation as they flew through the heavens, leaving their grief and pain behind. Far below, her brother's village faded as the eagle carried her off, away to some wonderful new world.

Then anxiety washed over her. This was not the first time she'd flown with this eagle. The memory returned, her riding the great bird, watching as another dived past. A hawk! But what was its prey? Oh, yes, that had been the vision that had warned her of the danger to Emma. But this time there were no dark overtones. Only the ringing echoes of laughter. Star turned her head to see where it came from. To her surprise, she saw Renny and Morning Moon riding on her back—the eagle's back. And their eyes were bright with joy.

What did this mean? As suddenly as it had come, the vision fled. A sense of peace filled Star, even as she collapsed.

The eagle.

Twice now she'd flown with this eagle in her dreams. The first, the great bird had turned out to represent Colonel O'Brien. She'd realized it the first moment she'd seen him ride toward her—handsomely dressed as he was in his bright blue uniform. He had been the answer to that dream; he'd helped save his daughter from her cowardly kidnappers. But this time, what did the vision mean? What was she to do?

The sound of Colonel O'Brien's worried voice drew Star back to reality. . . . "Perhaps we should head back."

She opened her eyes. "I'm all right," she reassured him. And she was. In fact, she felt relaxed, calm. It was something she hadn't felt in so long, she'd forgotten how it felt. If only all her visions could be so soothing.

Staring up into the colonel's worried face, it

wasn't hard to recapture the feelings and emotions of her vision. As usual, the effects of the Sight stayed with her. Sometimes they lingered for a few minutes, sometimes for hours—days. And right now, all she felt was secure, safe.

Grady held out his hand, his brows drawn together as he watched her.

Star accepted his help up and didn't protest when he turned them back toward the village, his hand lightly holding her elbow as he guided her toward the fading campfire. His touch was comforting, and suddenly she felt very close to this man. Even though he didn't understand her gift of sight, he hadn't shied away from her.

Like most whites, he couldn't comprehend the close ties her people had to the land around them. Earth. Sky. Air. Water. Those were *waken*, sacred. And because her people lived as one with their surroundings, the Spirits had given them special gifts to help them survive.

She shoved aside her fears of not being able to live up to her village's expectations, her sense of failed duty. Putting her own problems aside, she thought of Colonel O'Brien's plans to leave in the morning. "Renny and Morning Moon will miss each other."

Grady sighed. "I know. Renny would rather stay with you than return home with me, her own father. I'd wished to give her more time . . . but that is impossible." He smiled ruefully over at her. "Please forgive me my moment of self-pity. Renny's attitude toward me is no more than I deserve."

Star came to a sudden stop. The colonel's words swam in her mind. In her vision she'd flown with the eagle—away from her village. Away from everything she feared. And she'd felt safe, free. A soft breeze caressed her face. She inhaled deeply as her mind latched on to the whisper of Spirits.

Clear as the sky had been in her vision, Star knew this man was the answer. If she and her children left with him—flew away—perhaps her daughter wouldn't be able to develop the Sight. The gift came from the Spirits. In a great big city filled with noise, wooden buildings and a life so different from that which she knew, the Spirits wouldn't be able to find either of them. The more she thought about it, the more she knew leaving was the answer.

But would the colonel take her and her children to the city with him and Renny? He had to. She moved in front of him. "Renny and Morning Moon can stay together."

His brows lowered. "I don't see how. I wish it was possible, but I cannot stay—and I will never leave the child again." He drew a deep breath. "She'll miss your daughter and Emma. When we get back to St. Louis, I'll hire a woman with a child her age to watch over her and run my house. Perhaps then she won't be so lonely."

Star drew herself straight and took a deep breath. Her idea would work. "Morning Moon and I could go with you. I'll care for Renny. Now you will not have to hire a stranger, and I can stay as long as you and Renny have need of me." Her gaze latched on to his, and inside she willed him to agree.

Surprised, Grady rocked back on his heels. "I appreciate the offer, but I couldn't ask you to leave your home and your people."

Afraid he wouldn't let her explain, that he'd turn her down, Star reached out and grasped his hand, drawing on his warmth and strength to give her the courage to do what she must. "You said earlier you wished you could do something for me. I'm asking you to take us with you."

Grady rubbed the back of his neck and shook his head in confusion. "I don't understand. Why do you want to leave your family and friends?"

Star glanced toward her village. "I will do anything to stop my curse from destroying my daughter's life. Leaving is the only way. If you will not take me, I will take her away on my own."

Grady removed his hat, ran a palm over his hair, then replaced it. "What of your family, your parents?"

Hope flared in Star. He hadn't said no. He was considering it. "It is my decision to make," she said. "Perhaps I will eventually return. You will take me?"

Heartbeats ticked by. He gripped both hands behind his back and regarded her intently. "You're serious."

"Yes."

Star held her breath.

Finally, Grady nodded. "I will take you. On two conditions." He paced before her, each step measured. His movements were precise, and she admired him quietly as he thought. She held her breath, excitement running through her.

This was the answer! She would do anything he asked, for it would save her daughter from the anguish she had known.

Grady stopped before her, and briefly Star found herself noticing the way his uniform was stretched across his broad shoulders. She had little trouble understanding how this man had become an officer; he seemed to exude power.

"First, as you will be in a foreign land, you must allow me to oversee your well-being and safety. And second, even though you are related to my daughter by marriage, I will not take advantage of you by allowing you to labor without compensation. I insist on paying you a fair wage for taking care of my daughter."

Star opened her mouth to accept. He held up his hand.

"Here you do not need money, but it's a different matter in the city. There, I'd have to hire someone to run my household and watch over Renny. I'd much rather entrust them to you. Also, this way you will not be beholden to me. When you choose to leave, you will have the means to do so."

Star didn't hesitate. It didn't matter that she'd never been to a city and had no idea what running his household entailed. It didn't matter. She'd do whatever it took to protect her daughter. "I accept." With that, she turned and hurried back to the village and her tipi. There was much to be done before tomorrow.

Flat on their bellies, Renny and Morning Moon watched their parents walk away. Renny lifted her head to peer over the top of the grass, but ducked when her father hesitated and glanced back over his shoulder. Her heart hammered, but eventually her father moved off.

She breathed a sigh of relief, but just for good measure motioned for Morning Moon to remain still. Finally, she lifted herself up onto her knees.

"It's safe. We can talk now," Renny said, bouncing in her excitement. "Did you hear them? My dad is going to bring you and your family back to our house! Your mom is going to take care of me, and that means we get to be sisters. And Running Elk will be my brother," she whispered excitedly.

Morning Moon sat up and crossed her legs. "We should not sneak up on adults and listen to what does not concern us, Weshawee." She glanced around nervously.

"But it does concern us. See, now we don't have to run away. 'Sides, how else will we learn stuff? Grown-ups never tell us anything."

Seeing that her friend still looked uncertain, Renny tossed a handful of grass at her. "You worry too much. I *never* get caught." She giggled. "You should've heard what some of Aunt Ida's friends used to gossip about. They never knew I was hiding in the parlor. I have lots of hiding places back home."

Relaxing, Morning Moon rolled her eyes. "You won't be able to do that anymore. Your father is a wise man. He'll catch you."

Renny fell back and chewed on a new blade of grass as she stared up at the stars. "He won't. I'm smarter. 'Sides, he won't do nothing."

Shaking her head, Morning Moon leaned forward. "If my grandfather or grandmother caught us, we'd have to listen to a story meant to teach us proper manners. And if my uncle were to find us, he'd shame us."

Renny shuddered, then rolled over to peer into the darkness to be sure no one was coming. "Your people punish very strangely. I think I prefer being sent to my room." She'd only been publicly scolded once, for carelessly knocking over a bowl of ground nuts. While she'd immediately apologized, Striking Thunder had *suggested* she stay and help the old woman grind more nuts to replace those that had been ruined. Renny had to admit, though, she'd learned to appreciate the time and effort it took to produce even the smallest quantity of food.

Actually, she hadn't really minded the punishment too much. The woman had been nice. Morning Moon and the other girls had even joined them, and they'd had fun. But at first it had been humiliating, especially having the chief speak so sternly to her in front of everyone. His words had been very effective. She'd felt bad, so the next day, Renny had offered the woman a rabbit pelt she'd been given to show how sorry she was. No, she sure didn't want any more *shamings*.

Still . . . "No one will find out, so quit worrying."

After a moment of silence, Morning Moon grinned. "We will be sisters."

"This is going to be fun. I'll even share my room with you."

"And you'll show me all your hiding places?"

"Yep, but you can't tell anyone," she cautioned. "That's why they are my secret places, 'cause no one knows about them."

Stretching out on her stomach, Morning Moon rested her chin on her fisted hands. "It will be fun living in a big wooden house with so many rooms. My uncle Wolf's cabin is small, and it has a bed in a loft. It's fun to climb the ladder and sleep up there. Do you have ladders to get to your sleeping areas?"

"No, silly." Renny giggled. "We have stairs." She grew serious. "This would be perfect except for *him*. Maybe he'll get bored and leave. Then it'd be just you and me and your mom."

"*I* think your father is a nice man."

"Well, I don't. He doesn't love me. He's just pretending—so Emma won't worry. He says he doesn't blame me for my ma's dying, but I don't believe him. If he didn't blame me, why'd he leave?"

Morning Moon put a protective arm around Renny. "My grandfather says we should always look to the heart for answers."

Renny snorted and jumped to her feet, answering her own question. "No good reason, 'cept he didn't want us. Come on. We better get back." Though she spoke bravely, she didn't want her father to come looking for her and learn she'd left camp against his orders. He scared her. He was big, and he never smiled.

The two girls headed back, shoulders bumping. When they reached the camp, they skirted the tipis, walking around the outer perimeter. Renny's mood lightened and she alternated between walking and skipping. "You know, I don't want to leave here, but it won't be so bad with you and your mom and brother coming with us."

She ground to a halt and frowned. "Hey, what if your grandfather or uncle won't let your mother leave with you? What if they change her mind?"

Morning Moon stared up into the bright heavens, her face somber. "She won't change her mind."

Chapter Three

Morning brought the promise of a storm. Overhead, dark, menacing clouds gathered. Gone was the week of warm, sunny spring days. Winter had returned for one last show of strength.

Camped a short distance from the Indian village, soldiers dismantled tents, hampered by strong gusts of wind that attempted to wrestle the canvas from their gloved fingers. Despite the weather's quick deterioration Grady's men moved with practiced efficiency as they saddled horses and loaded gear.

Compared to the activity of the soldiers' camp, the Indian village was nearly deserted. Most of its inhabitants had opted to remain inside their warm, cozy tipis. Those outside in the brewing stormy weather spoke in hushed whispers and avoided the large tipi near the center of the village, where the sounds of arguing could be heard.

Inside of it, a storm of a different sort had just

broken. Shouting could be heard throughout the camp.

"Enough discussion. You will not leave! I will not allow it!"

Inside her parents' tipi, Star Dreamer met her father's furious glare. "I *am* leaving," she stated quietly, avoiding Striking Thunder's eye. Somehow, her brother had learned of her plan and had returned early to add his protests to that of their father. As soon as her father had learned of her plan, he'd commanded a family meeting. For the last half hour, her family had been trying to talk her out of her decision. Even her youngest sister, White Dove, seemed to have taken up against her— and Dove was the most rebellious of all her siblings.

Golden Eagle paced from one side of the tipi to the other. He stopped at the closed flap of the doorway, flung it aside and stared out into the gray mist of morning. The air thickened inside despite the cool air rushing in. Leaning out, he growled something beneath his breath. Squeals of fright followed. Star watched several children take off running—Renny and Morning Moon among them. They had obviously been eavesdropping.

Turning, he dropped the flap, blocking out the dismal day and children. "You have not thought this through, daughter. The white man's city is no place for one of our people."

Star lifted one brow in perfect imitation of him. "I do not seek the permission of my family, only understanding. I carry my mother's white blood— as do my brothers. They have each been to the cities of my mother's people. I choose to visit as well."

Pain mingled with disbelief in her father's features. Star didn't dare peek over at her mother, fearing what she'd find there. For the first time in her life, she was rebelling against her parents. She might be twenty-five winters, but right now, she felt sixteen.

Biting her lip, she wished there was some other way. She didn't want to hurt them, but during the long, lonely night, she'd thought hard about her decision. And in the cold light of the morning, it seemed her only option. Her plan to accompany Renny and her father to St. Louis seemed the perfect solution.

After all, she'd had not one but two visions of flying away from her village and her people with the eagle. Hadn't she felt safe with the great bird? Free as she'd never felt before? Yes. This was meant to be. There was a purpose to the arrival of Emma to their village as predicted by her dreams—one look at Striking Thunder's happy union was proof of that—and so it made sense that the girl's father would also play a role in her life. Grady O'Brien was the eagle of freedom.

The vision had been a sign from the Great Spirit that she was meant to leave. Though she didn't expect to find peace or happiness for herself, she prayed that this was the reprieve for which she had begged the Spirits. Her daughter would not know the torment that plagued Star's own life.

She kept her hands folded tightly in her lap.

"Why, daughter? I do not understand."

Star sought the right words. "You cannot understand, my father. You do not fear waking each day because something might happen that you should have prevented, yet failed. When you go to bed each night, your dreams do not haunt you. Flashes of future events do not leave you frightened and confused and waiting for the worst to happen. You do not have your vision grow black as control is taken from you."

Golden Eagle spread his hands wide. "I *do* understand. As chief for many years, I too felt the same worry and the same fear. But none of us can know the future for certain. Only the Great Spirit knows. Many times I have feared failing our people."

Star shuddered and squeezed her eyes shut, fighting the tears. "You have never seen your own mate's death," she whispered.

Golden Eagle moved to his daughter and lifted her chin, forcing her to meet his dark gaze.

"True. I have never had visions as you and my mother have, but I've lived with the fear that my decisions would cause unnecessary death. I've been responsible for the lives of our warriors—I too have afterward wondered if I could have done something differently. You are too hard on yourself." He looked to his wife, frustration filling his features.

Star cupped her father's hand in hers. "It's not the same. I have the gift. I should be able to use it to help our people, but I can't. Many have already died because of me." Her tears broke forth, her control finally overcome.

Golden Eagle stood and paced. "None of us can know the intentions of the Spirits, but I do know our people need your gift—as much now as it was needed when your grandmother walked the *maka*. Did she not learn how to use her gift for our people? She saw many times the approach of our enemy and warned us to move. Your own power will improve with time. You just need confidence."

Star sighed. They'd had this same conversation more times than she could count in the past. "My gift is not strong like my grandmother's." It hurt deeply to admit to her parents that she was a failure, but it was the truth. Only luck had enabled her to save her brothers' mates, and now her people were beginning to get a false sense of competence about her. Nothing had been clear in those visions—just a sense of danger.

A clear vision meant seeing the death of a parent or child, and having no way of preventing it—and she wanted nothing to do with that. In a weary voice, she addressed her parents. "No matter what you say, I know I will never have the ability of my grandmother. But my leaving isn't just for me. I will do everything I can to prevent my daughter from developing the Sight. I do not wish to see her suffer, as I do."

Golden Eagle frowned. "If she is to have your grandmother's gift, then it will be so, no matter where she lives."

Star wrapped her arms around herself. If that were true, then what was the point in leaving? She hesitated, then strengthened her resolve. She had to believe there was hope for Morning Moon—hadn't her last vision promised freedom? "The Spirits are strongest among our people. They are part of our world, they inhabit this land from the blue sky above down to the ground below. We live among the Spirits, we take our life from them, they are *waken*, and so I will take her to a different world, one where the Spirits cannot find her, cannot talk to her. There she will be free to grow up among my mother's people."

Staring into the burning embers before her, Star shivered despite the warmth rolling toward her from the smoldering fire. "I have decided." Her words were desperate. She had to escape the deep, dark pit her life was slowly becoming. If she didn't, she'd lose her mind; her daughter would have no one. Star's breathing quickened with panic.

Unable to face the prospect of another long argument, afraid she'd buckle and give in, she glanced over at her brother. He had remained silent so far. His eyes, filled with worry and doubt, held hers for a long moment before he glanced over at Emma. His wife was biting her lower lip, torn between what her husband wanted and her father needed.

With a start of surprise, she realized Emma's father also had much to lose if she decided not to go. He needed her for Renny, as much as she needed him for Morning Moon's sake. He'd admitted that. Her presence would make his slow reconciliation with his young daughter that much less strained. Emma knew that, obviously. Smiling weakly at her, Star strengthened her own resolve and grasped at the one bit of power left to her.

Reaching over to take her brother's hand in her own, she clutched it, willing him to understand. "Is not the father of your wife trustworthy?"

"That has nothing to do with this." Agitated, Striking Thunder tried to pull his hand free.

Star tightened her grip. *"Is not the father of your wife trustworthy? Can he not be trusted to watch over me and my children away from our people?"*

Striking Thunder closed his eyes, a sign of imminent defeat. If he admitted that Grady O'Brien was trustworthy, he'd eliminate all the reasons why she should not go. And if he said no, he'd risk angering and hurting both his father-in-law and his wife. She sat back and waited, satisfied she had finally found the words to stop his protests.

"Yes, my wife's father is trustworthy—"

Star rose to her knees. "And will I not also be helping Weshawee, your new sister-in-law, as she is reunited with her father? Does not the child trust me and have need of me? Is she not a sister to my own daughter?"

"You have been very good to—"

"And would your own wife not have peace of mind knowing her young sister has left happy, and willingly, instead of being taken against her will?"

Striking Thunder glanced at his father. Both men bowed their head in defeat.

Star glanced around the tipi. Her mother and Emma looked pleased. She held Dove's gaze until her sister gave her a small nod. To her father and brother, she said, "Then I must do this. I will go and help Emma's father and sister. In return, the colonel has promised em-ployment," she stumbled over the new English word. "I will not be alone, and I will have a safe place to live."

Golden Eagle asked, "What about Running Elk? You will take him away as well? All heard his loud protest this morning. He has no wish to leave."

Star sighed. "My son has asked to stay with his other family, but I cannot leave him. He will go with us." Honestly, she'd actually considered allowing him to stay behind as he wished. All Indian children were given a second set of parents to keep the birth parents from spoiling them. In times of hardship or death, there were always others to look after a child's best interest—especially with her own large and loving family. Yet her son belonged with her. Didn't he? Wouldn't the city be a good place for him to learn about the changing world?

Star thought of Wolf, her twin brother. Before their birth, their grandmother had forecast twins who would each use a special gift to serve their people. Wolf's gift was knowledge. At twelve winters, he'd been sent away to be educated in the white man's boarding schools, and his learning was still widely respected.

But at first there had been difficulties. She recalled her brother's despair over his forced separation from his family and people. He'd suffered many injustices at the hands of the whites and had finally run away. But at last he'd found his way, discovered his purpose.

In fact, by this summer's end, Wolf and his wife, Jessie, would return to the cabin that had once belonged to their mother. There they planned to run a boarding school for Indian children, to educate them in the ways of the white man.

Still, remembering how her brother had fared among the whites gave her pause. Would her son feel the same anger and pain at this forced leave-taking? All during the long winter, Running Elk had spoken of nothing else but learning to shoot his bow and go on real hunts with the other boys his age.

He wanted to become a great warrior like his father, uncle and grandfathers. Could she subject him to what his uncle had gone through? And what would happen when and if they returned? Would he have to prove himself to his own people all over again, as Wolf had?

Emma spoke up hesitantly, interrupting her thoughts. "Running Elk is welcome to stay with us." The woman's offer earned her a frown from her husband; Striking Thunder clearly did not see the separation of mother and son as a solution.

Emma shrugged. "You cannot stop Star from leaving, and I for one think she should go if that's her desire. Though I will admit my reasons are selfish." She cast an apologetic look at her husband. "Renny will do so much better if Star and Morning Moon are with her. And one must follow one's heart. Star Dreamer obviously needs to go."

White Wind nodded her head, although somewhat more sadly. "I agree with my new daughter. Does the separation between mother and son have to be forever? Running Elk with be well cared for among our people . . . though it is of course my daughter's decision."

She held up a hand as both her son and husband started to protest. "Why not set a time? A trial period. Emma's babe is due at the end of summer, and I'm sure Emma's father will wish to return and see his daughter and grandchild. Why not ask the colonel to bring Star back to us at that time? And if it is her wish then to remain in the city, we will decide on Running Elk's future."

Neither Golden Eagle nor Striking Thunder looked pleased with the compromise, but there was little else to be said. Star had made her decision: She would go to the city.

But what about the fate of her son? Parting mother and child was never an easy decision, even though Running Elk had begged to be left behind. Her mother and Emma smiled at Star with understanding, but White Dove still looked worried. As Star glanced about, she saw the men still wore varying degrees of frustration on their faces. She had to act fast. "My mother is wise. I accept my sister's offer to look after my son until I return . . . if it is still his wish to remain here."

Her stomach churned. Would her son decide to stay? It wouldn't be fair to take him away if he truly did not wish to go, but a part of her wished that everything could remain as it had. But it couldn't. She needed to get Morning Moon away from here, away from any chance of pain, and if her son would be happier here . . .

White Wind rose gracefully to her feet. "Then it's all settled."

Striking Thunder rose as well and met Star's teary gaze. "I will choose a handful of warriors. We will accompany you to the fort."

White Dove jumped to her feet, her frown of worry gone. "I will make ready."

Striking Thunder and Golden Eagle frowned again. "Make ready for what?" Star's father demanded.

White Wind lifted a pale brow. Her lips curved with wry amusement. "Does my husband truly need to ask?"

The once-great chieftain let his shoulders slump. There was little use in arguing once these women of his clan made up their minds. "There is no need for us all to ride out. I would have my wife remain here to await her husband's return." He folded his arms across his chest.

Star's mother just smiled sweetly. "Yes, dear, I'm sure you would." She grabbed a plain leather pouch hanging from a nail in one of the poles of the tipi while White Dove grabbed up an empty water pouch and her weapons. Both women exited the tipi. Then White Wind stuck her head back inside. "Are you coming, daughter? We must make sure you and the girls have all you need for your long journey."

Star hurried out, smiling with relief. Not only was she going, but her mother and sister would see her off. Her heart lifted at the thought. She'd miss them. A fresh wave of tears obscured her sight.

Emma rushed after them. "Wait for me! If you are all going, then I'm coming as well." Behind her, Striking Thunder called out. Emma hesitated.

Star laughed and grabbed Emma's hand. "Come then, sister. My brother will cease his bellowing soon enough. We women stick together and our men understand, even if they do feel they must protest."

At her words, the bellowing ceased.

* * *

Grady surveyed the large group of soldiers and Indians assembled on horseback before him. They had finished their preparations in less than an hour. A cold breeze found its way past his woolen scarf and down the back of his neck, making him shiver. Pulling up his lined collar, he readjusted the scarf, then shifted his mount so the gust blew against his back.

Now that everything was loaded, he was eager to leave. His trained eye roamed over the group of waiting warriors, then shifted to the women, huddled around Star as she hugged her son and said her good-byes.

He shifted, impatient. He blamed the adverse weather conditions for his mood, but if he was honest, he'd admit his eagerness to be gone was in part due to his fear that Star Dreamer might change her mind and not accompany him and Renny to St. Louis. Watching her with her son, he felt selfish for taking her. But he needed her—for his daughter's sake.

Two scouts with identical matted gray beards and long, stringy hair hanging past their shoulders rode up to him. The buckskin breeches, shirts and coats they wore had seen better days.

The one named Zeb removed his dirt-encrusted hat and scratched his ear. "They's all comin'?" He indicated the group of Indian women mounting their horses.

Next to him, his twin brother, Zac, copied the motion. "The whole durn family?" Zac made a face, which caused his dark, leathery skin to pucker and wrinkle his wrinkles. Two sets of deep brown eyes waited for their commanding officer's answer.

Grady's lips twitched. "Should be an interesting journey back to the fort," he commented, shifting his mount slightly to the left. The two men before him were trappers. And though they looked as old as the hills—and smelled as if it had been at least a decade since they had last bathed—they were the best to be found. Grady didn't complain; he just tried to stay downwind.

"Ain't never seen a squaw with bow and arrows," Zeb muttered, eyeing White Dove warily. The brothers each pulled a large silver crucifix from beneath his shirt and kissed it.

"We's gonna head out, check the lay of the land." At their colonel's nod, they rode off, muttering in low tones.

Anxious to leave, Grady nudged his own horse forward. As he neared the women, he hesitated. Star Dreamer was still on her knees, talking softly to Running Elk and running her fingers through his jet black hair while tears streamed down her cheeks. He frowned. How could a mother leave her child like this?

How could a father abandon his children?

Grady felt guilt wash over him. He'd left his girls, much as Star was leaving her son. Though she planned to return, so had he. But once gone, it had been easier to stay away. Less painful. Somehow, he'd managed to convince himself he was doing what was best, that Emma and Renny hadn't needed him.

His discomfort grew at the thought of helping Star Dreamer to leave her people and son. But deep down, her desperation as they'd walked along the river had ensnared him. She'd looked so distraught, so vulnerable, he'd have done anything to ease the haunted look in her eyes and bring a smile to her lips—something he'd not seen very often. The young woman was far too sad. She deserved laughter and happiness. Maybe because he would help her, she would find it, or at least find peace within herself.

But now the weight of responsibility for her well-being rested squarely on his shoulders, and he knew he could not allow her to repeat his own mistake. He would bring her back at the end of summer, back to her people, back to her son, where she belonged, as her father and brother had asked.

His gaze strayed from the woman to his own child. Renny sat atop one of the horses she had been given, with Morning Moon perched on the other. His lips tightened at the memory of his daughter defiantly informing him that the two animals belonged to her and that she was taking them to St. Louis.

She hadn't asked, had even assumed he'd refuse to allow her to bring her horses, and it hurt to know she regarded him as an unfeeling monster—despite the fact that she had every right to be distrustful of him. It was still painful to bear. And for that reason, no matter how cowardly it made him feel, he was grateful that he wouldn't have to be alone with her for the next six months. Renny felt the same, he was sure. If Star Dreamer and Morning Moon weren't going with him, he'd have had to drag the child away kicking and screaming.

Fighting his impatience to head out, Grady rode over to his oldest daughter and eyed her with a worried parental eye. "Are you sure you should be riding?"

Emma leaned forward and placed her hand on his arm. "The babe is fine, Father. There's no need to worry."

He sucked in a deep breath, then stared out over her head, sudden guilt making him unable to meet her eyes. "I know I don't have the right to worry, Emma. I'm sorry."

Her voice turned tender. "Father, we've been through this. I've forgiven you. Let the past go."

Grady closed his eyes, grateful. Her forgiveness for leaving them so young was something he'd never feel he'd truly earned. He gave a small smile and looked over at his youngest daughter, who was giggling with Morning Moon over something. Would she ever come to love and accept him? Would she ever forgive him? Turning back to see Emma gazing at him worriedly, he reached out and caressed one cold cheek. "I love you, Emma. I always have."

His daughter's gaze strayed to Striking Thunder; her husband was heading toward them. "I know, Father. Now that I have a husband whom I love dearly, I understand the way you felt when our mother died. I don't know what I'd do if anything happened to him."

"You've been blessed, Emma. Not everyone finds true love."

"I know, Father. I know." Her voice softened.

"I will take good care of your daughter," Striking Thunder assured him, making it obvious he'd overheard them.

The Sioux chieftain reached out to trail his fingers down his wife's cheek. The tenderness the big, fierce-looking warrior wasn't afraid to show brought forth painful memories. Grady remembered how it had felt to do the same to Emma's mother and see her soft answering smile, that secret longing in her eyes that made his blood flow faster.

"If I didn't believe that, I would not have permitted the marriage." Grady stared at his son-in-law as he spoke, and he could see that his words had been understood. He glanced over his shoulder, then, as he heard shouts of farewell. Star had finally mounted. They were ready to head out. The Indian woman rode past, sitting tall and proud, flanked by her mother and sister.

Grady lifted his hand and gave his men the command to head out. He watched the unit fall into formation, then sought Star's figure on horseback.

The Sioux beauty knew the pain of losing a loved one. That alone—the shared anguish of loss—made him feel uncannily close to her. And now she was being forced to leave behind her child too.

The thought made Grady remember his own leave-taking, the sight of his eldest daughter standing on the porch crying as he rode away. But Emma had since forgiven him. Perhaps Star Dreamer would find a similar reprieve at the end of her travels. And as for now, she would be with him for six months.

Chapter Four

"Je désire faire la cour à toi, Madame Olsen."

I want to make love to you. The soft, cultured voice simmered with unspent passion and sent shivers of anticipation skirting along the length of Hester Mae Olsen's spine. Her hand fluttered to the brooch pinned at her throat—a gift from her lover. Suppressing her moan of frustration that they were in public, she patted the tight bun at the nape of her neck, making sure none of her dark, auburn tresses had become loosened.

Unable to publicly acknowledge the man deliberately standing so close behind her that she felt the press of his lean thighs against her backside, she handed over her basket of fruits and vegetables. Around them, people crowded and shoved, pressing them together. The heat of her lover, along with that of the other customers, surrounded her and intensified the womanly urges raging through her body. Overwhelmed by the furious longing welling inside her, Hester Mae reminded herself that she was forty, not some lovestruck young fool. She tried to move forward to put distance between them.

A low chuckle confirmed that Leodegrance Dufour was well aware of what the intimate contact did to her. There came another naughty suggestion whispered in her ear, and his breath teased the nape of her neck. Hester Mae struggled to remain impassive as she waited for the vegetable peddler to add up her purchases.

After paying the greasy-haired woman for the produce, she exited the stall and merged into the flow of humanity moving from one stall to the next in the Soulard Market.

"You want me, no?"

Leo's voice, velvet and silk trimmed with a wonderful French accent, left Hester Mae weak-kneed and on fire with need. She glanced over her shoulder and up to meet his gaze; their eyes were nearly at the same level as she was as tall as most men. Leo's height as well as his dark good looks were just two things that endeared him to her. She met the wicked lust in his eyes with her own hungry gaze. Oh, yes, she wanted Leo—badly—but it wouldn't do to let him know just how he affected her. "Mr. Dufour, we are in public." She rebuked him, quickening her steps.

"Ah, but everyone is too busy to notice us, *ma cherie.*" Leo deliberately closed the distance between them so he could reach down and squeeze her buttocks unnoticed.

Gasping at his boldness even as it excited her, Hester Mae said, "Mr. Dufour, I must insist—"

"Oh, yes, *ma cherie*, do insist." His smile turned

seductive as he bent his head to whisper another idea in her ear.

Her heart raced, but only the tremor in her voice betrayed her growing desire. Her lapse was short-lived, though. She sobered when she caught strangers staring at them. "Leo, you are taking a terrible risk. If anyone sees us together, they will tell Baxter." As much as she longed to be with Leo, she couldn't risk angering her husband. The man controlled her purse strings—and he was stingy enough as it was.

A couple in front of her stopped, forcing her to take a different route through the milling crowd. To her dismay, she spotted Irma Hamburg, the city's biggest gossip, coming toward her. "Oh, no," she groaned. She darted into a stall, slipping past two gossiping women to hide. She ignored their gasps at her rudeness as she pretended to peruse the vendor's selection of pastries and sweets.

From the corner of her eye, Hester Mae watched the matronly Irma pass by. In a moment, the woman had waylaid some other poor, hapless sop. Sighing with relief at the close call, Hester Mae merged back into the crowd and searched for Leo.

When she found him, he winked at her. She shivered, her body again beginning to spark with lust. Having the man she loved so close yet so far away was sheer torture. If only Baxter would hurry up and die!

Twenty years her senior, she'd never thought the old bastard would live to see fifty, let alone sixty. It had even begun to worry her, for he showed no sign of taking to his deathbed any time soon. The thought depressed her. She was tired of being tied to a man old enough to be her father. If only they'd had children, perhaps her life would have some purpose, but the old goat had failed to produce any in their past endeavors.

As usual, the thought of children brought her beloved nieces to mind. They were all she had in the world, really, and she hadn't heard from them since they'd set off on that crazy search for her brother-in-law. What had the girls been thinking to go off alone like that? Her lips tightened. When Emma returned, she planned to have a few words with her eldest niece for taking off on a wild goose chase.

Imagine! The girl hadn't even bothered to inform her own aunt what she'd planned on doing. Hester Mae had learned of Emma's plan to find her father when she'd gone to the house to visit them and found it empty. In the time since, there'd been no word from either Emma or Colonel O'Brien. She'd dutifully made sure the house was maintained. It was the least she could do.

Fearing for the safety of the beloved girls, she had gone down to the wharf each day to see if anyone traveling up or down the Missouri knew of her nieces' whereabouts. So far, no one had seen or heard anything. She felt herself grow tense. If anything happened to those girls, she didn't know what she'd do. She'd already lost her parents, and Margaret Mary, her sister. She couldn't lose Margaret Mary's precious daughters.

Forgetting about the danger of talking to Leo in public, she turned to him and asked, "Has there been any news about Emma and Renny?" Leo was employed by her husband to oversee his shipping business, based in St. Louis, and he had promised to see if he could find out what had happened to her nieces. He had many contacts and important connections.

Leo shook his head sadly and adjusted his hat. "*Non.* But you must not fret, *ma cherie,* I am sure they are safely reunited with their *papa*."

Hester Mae sighed, as much from his reassurances as his endearments. No one had ever before made her feel beautiful or cherished. Leo did both, though she knew she wasn't attractive. Too tall and thin, she'd been so ever since she had been a young girl. Even calling her a plain child would be kind, unlike her tiny, petite sister, whose beauty had drawn the attention of all. "Thank you, Leo. You are so kind. I don't know what I'd do without you."

Leo took her gloved hand in his and kissed her curled fingers, ignoring her gasp of protest. "*Non*. I am not kind. I am in love." He sighed dramatically when she snatched her hand away.

"I have to go." She turned sly, hungry eyes back to him. "Baxter left this morning for another trip south. You will come tonight?"

Leo smiled, his eyes hooded. "Of course, *ma cherie*. I would not dream of missing such an important day as your birthday. But alas, I will not be there until quite late. Business, you understand. I have an important shipment I must see to. Wait up for me. I have a very special gift for you."

"You remembered!"

"Ah, you wound me, Hester Mae. How could I forget?"

She preened under his adoring gaze, thrilled that he'd remembered her birthday. Baxter, damn his miserable, sagging hide, was as soft as the bark on a tree. He'd never understood her feminine heart, or desires. From him, she'd received a dozen plain linen hankies with her initials embroidered in one corner.

But Leo understood, and he was generous where her husband was stingy. She eagerly looked forward to the expensive gift with which he was sure to present her. "I'll be waiting, Leo. Don't keep me waiting too long," she breathed, touching the brooch at her neck. As she moved past him, she boldly brushed her fingers along the front of his pants, sure the movement would be hidden by the crush of people and their closeness.

The smile faded from Leodegrance's features the moment Hester Mae disappeared into the crowd. His expression changed from one of lust to annoyance. That woman's nieces would never come home. He'd learned from one of the captains who piloted a paddleboat up and down the Missouri that the colonel's daughters had been captured by Indians, and the colonel himself had spent months searching for them.

His reason for keeping that information to himself was purely selfish. He had plans for Hester Mae Olsen. Many plans.

Spring was Star's favorite season. It brought the return of warm sunshine, bright blue skies and gentle breezes carrying the scent of new grass and blooming wildflowers. Seated on a blanket beneath a tree, the stream's gurgling mingled with birdsong in the treetops. Grazing across the green land, herds of elk and antelope wandered. In the distance, she spotted a large dark mass—a herd of buffalo.

Across the stream a safe distance away, several does kept their wobbly-legged young close, ready to bolt for safety should the humans pose a threat. A flash of brown to Star's right caught her gaze as a rabbit and her young darted through the grass and down a hole. The land teemed with life.

With the harsh winter behind them—the storm that had been brewing as they'd made ready for this journey had miraculously passed without unleashing its fury—and the hard work of summer yet to come, now was the time for her people to reflect, rebuild and to make plans for the future. They would embrace this day. Embrace life. Bear witness to the miracle of rebirth, how nature took what appeared dead and desolate and brought it back to life. The sight gave Star a sense of hope, of new beginnings for all—including herself.

Leaning her head back against the rough bark of the cottonwood, Star smiled at the sight of her strong, fierce-looking brother hovering over Emma. His wife was drinking from the stream a few feet away. That was another new beginning; her brother embarked on marriage and parenthood. She noted the gentle swell of Emma's stomach and smiled secretly as she watched Striking Thunder lead his pregnant wife to a blanket spread out not far from where Star sat. Star suspected the frequent stops both the colonel and her brother ordered were more to make sure Emma didn't overtire herself than to rest the horses.

A harsh chattering from above drew her attention upward. Bits of bark and leaves showered down on her. Peering at her from a thick bough of the tree, a bushy-tailed squirrel scolded her in protest. Star's smile faded. If Running Elk were here, he'd have drawn his bow and arrow and tried to shoot the small animal. Thinking about her son, guilt, worry and uncertainty swept through her. She missed him desperately. If she felt this way now, after just a few days, how would she make it for six months?

Once more, niggling doubts assailed her. Had she made the right decision with regard to Running Elk? For the first time since losing her husband, she realized just how difficult it was to be an only parent. All decisions rested on her shoulders, which right now felt far too fragile to bear the weight. She sighed, closing her eyes as she prayed for the Spirits to watch over her son. If anything happened to him while she was gone, she'd never forgive herself.

Breaking her out of her reverie, White Wind, White Dove and the two little girls suddenly plopped down next to her. Star welcomed the distraction of Renny's chatter.

"What are these called again?" the child asked, touching a small purplish flower blooming among the bright green grass.

"*Hokshichekpa wahcha,* or twin flower," Star answered. "It is the earliest bloomer each spring." She leaned forward and separated one plant from the others. "See how most bear only two flowering scapes? When the head ripens, it turns white and bushy, like the head of an old wise man."

"I wish we were going to be here to see them turn white." Renny lay on her stomach and checked the hairy plants around her to see if all of them were twins.

Star reached out to reverently cup one small purple flower. "There is a song our children sing when they see the twin flowers blooming across the *maka.*"

"Really? Will you sing it for me?"

Smiling, Star nodded. "Let me see if I can think of the English way to express our words." After a moment, she began:

> I wish to encourage the children
> Of other flower nations now appearing
> All over the face of the earth;
> So while they awaken from sleeping
> And come up from the heart of the earth
> I am standing here old and gray-headed.

After listening once through, Renny and Morning Moon sang the song several more times, with the adults indulgently joining in.

When the girls fell silent, Star turned to Emma. The woman had come over when Striking Thunder left to see to the horses. "Tell me more of your house in the city."

"Let me, Em," Renny interrupted. At her sister's nod, the child raised herself up on her knees and held her arms stretched out to her sides. "We live in a big house and it has lots and lots of rooms." She ticked off the rooms on her fingers: "A den, sitting room, my mother's parlor, kitchen, dining room, morning room, bedrooms, cellar, attic—"

Star's jaw dropped. How could a dwelling have so many chambers? "It cannot be so big," she interrupted.

Emma chuckled. "I'm afraid Renny is not exaggerating. It is a big house, three stories tall."

After explaining the purpose of each room, Renny dropped onto her hands and leaned forward to whisper, "I'm not allowed to go into my mother's parlor"—her grin turned conspiratorial—"but I sneak in there anyway. That's where my mother's portrait hangs, and sometimes I went in there just so I could look at her." She sounded wistful.

Emma reached over and hugged her sister.

Star frowned. "Why would you not be allowed in the—parlor?"

Renny stuck a blade of grass in her mouth and giggled. " 'Cause I might break something. You're not supposed to run in the house, but sometimes I forget."

At the sound of Emma clearing her throat, Renny shrugged. "Okay, I forget a lot."

Emma rolled her eyes and Star chuckled. How

could anyone even hope to contain the energetic child in such a fashion?

"You'll like our house, Star," Renny said.

Despite her uncertainty of the future, Star looked forward to seeing the house where Emma had once lived. But no matter how hard she tried, she just couldn't imagine living in a house with many rooms larger than her entire tipi. Nor could she picture a whole floor of rooms above her head let alone two floors! The only wood house Star had even set foot inside was the small cabin that had once belonged to her mother before she'd married Golden Eagle.

She remembered being taken there, climbing up to the area beneath the ceiling where her mother had slept. Star had found the height uncomfortable. She found herself hoping that her sleeping room in Colonel O'Brien's house would be on the bottom floor, so she wouldn't have to climb up a ladder to go to bed each night.

"I guess now that Father is coming home, I won't be allowed in the den either." This time, Renny sounded resentful.

Star wrinkled her brows. "The den belongs to your father?"

"Yeah. Aunt Ida said he used to sit in there to work during the day, and smoke his cigars and drink brandy at night. There's not so much stuff to break in there, and I go in to read or play sometimes."

"But why go there when you have your own sleeping room? Is it not big enough?"

"Oh, no, my bedroom is nice and big—big enough for both me and Morning Moon to share if she wants." Renny's lower lip jutted out and trembled. "I used to go to the den to be close to Papa. At night, when Aunt Ida and Emma were asleep,

I'd sneak down there and sit on the couch and watch the stars. Sometimes I'd wish really hard for him to come back, then I'd sit and pretend he was there working, and that he wanted me to come and keep him company."

Star's heart contracted. "Your wish is coming true, is it not, Weshawee?" Off to her right, she noticed the colonel talking to her father and brother. With his legs planted apart, his hands clasped behind his back and his shoulders pulled back, she couldn't help but again appreciate his fine male form. Though fully clothed in tight-fitting trousers tucked into black boots that came to his knees, there was no doubt the colonel's thighs were as powerful as those of any warrior from her tribe. An unexpected warmth overcame her.

Star had a sudden urge to know what the colonel looked like clad as a Sioux warrior. Heat rose to her face. Grateful for the little girl's chatter, Star tore her gaze from the colonel.

Renny frowned, glaring across the way at her father. "It's too late. 'Sides, I just know he won't let me go in there anymore." She jumped to her feet, tossed her head, sending the leather thong at the end of one braid flying. "But I don't care. It's dark and stuffy and boring." With that, the young girl ran off before Star could stop her.

Her decision whether or not to give chase was a short one. A moment after the girl had fled, Star's brother returned and gave the order to mount up.

Instead of rising to her feet, Star found herself lost in thought. With her own world in such a confusing state, would she be able to help Renny overcome her resentment and accept her father back into her young life?

She felt a hand on her shoulder. Turning, she found it was that of her daughter. "Don't worry,

Mother. Weshawee's father *will* let her in the room." As Star stared at her daughter, the child didn't smile. Morning Moon looked uncertain, hesitant, as if gauging her mother's reaction.

Star's heart tugged. "How do you know?"

"I have seen it." Morning Moon gave her an odd look as she spoke, but excitement leaked into her voice. "I've also seen the room I'll share with Weshawee. It is the color of the sun rising in the morning. And the windows have white coverings that look soft as clouds."

"Curtains?"

"Yes. Like my uncle Wolf has, but different. Weshawee says she hates the pink and white fluff and ruffles."

Star tried to smile but couldn't. Her daughter seemed to have no problem seeing future events clearly. What was the extent of her gift, and was she herself doing right by trying to separate her daughter from the Spirits who bestowed it? She longed to question the child, but feared her answers, so she changed the subject. "Do you think you'll like living in such a big house and sharing a room with Weshawee?"

"Yes, Weshawee is so much fun." Morning Moon giggled, then sobered.

"What is it, daughter?"

Morning Moon bit her lip and eyed her mother warily. "Nothing."

Her daughter's obvious reluctance to talk—and Star had to assume it was about her visions—was a stab in the heart. But it was her own fault. Morning Moon had kept her developing gift a secret because she'd known how her mother would react. Even now, it was hard for Star to accept her daughter's power. But it was time, past time, they talked about it.

Before she could pursue the subject, Renny's father rode up to them, leading their horses.

Star frowned when Morning Moon took advantage of the interruption and rode off to join the other women, who waited at the head of the trail. The reason for her daughter's quick escape wasn't lost on her. She understood, and vowed to make it up to her.

"What's wrong?" Grady asked, dismounting, drawing Star from her dark fears. He reached across and removed a small twig from her hair.

His touch, brief and impersonal, warmed her. She accepted the reins he held out, then mounted. "I acted too late. My child . . . the visions have begun."

Grady tilted his head back, revealing a strong, bronzed column below his red beard. "They don't seem to be affecting her any." He pulled his hat off and swiped an arm across his forehead.

Star brushed bits of grass from her skirt. "She's too young to understand. I do not want her childhood tainted. She should be free to laugh, play, dream and enjoy being young—she should not have to worry about being an adult too soon."

Grady slapped his hat against his thigh, startling his horse. He turned pain-filled eyes to her. "You want for Morning Moon what I took away from Emma."

Yes. And what this curse took from me. She met his sad gaze squarely, again feeling an overpowering sense of closeness with this man. "I want what's best for both Morning Moon and Weshawee."

Replacing his hat, he swung into his saddle. "Together, we shall give out daughters what they need." He paused and squinted against the glare of the sun overhead. "You are giving up much for us, leaving behind so much. . . ."

Her breath caught in the back of her throat. The colonel's eyes, clear blue-gray, held hers. Yet it wasn't the color that fascinated her as much as the sensitivity, the glimpses into the man behind the uniform. For reasons she didn't understand, she was able to see past the stern commander, past the appearance of cold aloofness. Hidden deep inside, she saw the lonely, scarred man who by a cruel twist of fate had lost his wife in gaining a daughter.

Death renewed by birth. Endings lead to new beginnings. The words floated in her mind; they had been taught to her by her people and she knew she should believe them. But things were so different, so painful.

She and Grady O'Brien shared so much. Each had lost a beloved mate, had a daughter they loved, carried a soul full of guilt. She glanced over at him again and, seeing that he was thinking similar thoughts, she glanced away. An awkward silence fell on them, and they spurred their horses after the others.

Star sought a change in topic. "Tell me about your home—not what it looks like, though. Weshawee has already described the rooms. Explain what my duties will be. My mother has taught us many ways of the white man, but I fear there is much I still must learn. Especially cooking in a kitchen and using a stove."

Grady glanced over at her. "You will not have to cook—or clean. I will hire others to do those duties."

Absently, Star rubbed her mare's soft neck. "Then what is it I will do?"

"You will watch over my daughter."

His answer surprised her. "That seems so little." Star couldn't imagine having others around to do the work that she expected went with raising a child.

"You have lived with Renny for the last six months. I believe you will find watching over her in the city much different from living out on the plains. White children cannot roam freely as they do out here, in the open. I dread learning what mischief my daughter will land herself in without some guidance . . . and perhaps with it."

He smiled at Star and began regaling her with some of Emma's exploits as a young child, when she was younger than Renny. Star turned her head and watched him as he spoke. Sunlight glinted off his hair. The shade of red reminded her of a warm fire crackling in the night. Like the rest of the soldiers, his beard and mustache needed trimming, and his hair fell past his collar.

She wondered what he would look like without the hair on his face. Realizing she was acting like a maiden seeking the attention of a brave, she forced herself to concentrate on the soothing quality of his voice. Her shoulders relaxed, she laughed at his stories, and without her even being aware of it, some of her tension fled. All of her earlier doubts were replaced with a sense of rightness. She had seen death; she was ready for her new beginning.

One day from the fort, Grady sent three of his soldiers on ahead. He had no idea if anyone was still at Fort Pierre, as the installation had officially closed. As soon as he and his party arrived, though, he planned to send word of his return to Fort Randall, where most of his men had been reassigned. Then he'd wait for the next steamboat to make its way down the Missouri, resign his commission and hitch a ride home to St. Louis.

Home.

He hadn't allowed himself to think of it in years. Home for the last nine years had been wherever the

77

army sent him. A year here, six months there. He hadn't spent much time in any one place, and only now did he realize he'd missed having a place to call his own.

His sister had been right all those years ago when she'd accused him of fleeing. He'd spent the last nine years believing that if he never went home, he'd never have to face the pain that came with knowing he'd never see his wife again. Though time had dulled the crippling pain, smoothed the sharp points of anger, he still felt the horrible sadness that had followed his wife's death.

He prayed that by returning to the home he and Maggie had once shared, he'd finally be able to let go of the past. He needed to put his energy toward rebuilding his future—and that of their daughter. Despite his misgivings about returning home after such a long absence, he felt at peace with himself— something that had eluded him since losing Margaret Mary.

His gaze fell on Star Dreamer. She had moved off to the side with the rest of the women, and he watched her as she rode. She wore her black hair parted in the center and loose. The strands fell around her face, framing it in a drape of black silk. With each movement of her head, the shiny strands spilled forward, drawing attention to the gentle curve of her jaw, her slender neck and narrow shoulders.

The temperature outside was moderate, and she'd removed her leggings, revealing long, slender limbs the warm color of honey. Once more, he found himself staring, his gaze roaming her body appreciatively. Shifting on the back of her horse, Star rolled her shoulders and leaned her head back, exposing her throat to the kiss of the sun as she worked an apparent stiffness from her muscles.

Grady sucked in his breath, his body yearning for one such kiss, one taste of her sun-warmed skin and sweet mouth. His gaze lingered on her throat, traveling down over her loose-fitting top to where the fringe on the bottom of her skirt brushed against her knees.

He shifted against the sudden uncomfortable tightness of his trousers against his pulsing manhood. Damn. He tried scooting back in his saddle, but his body was on fire. Somehow Star had achieved what no woman had since Maggie: she'd brought his body back to painful life.

But what could he do? Surely once he returned to civilization he would be able to find a way to slake his newfound desire, but he had a feeling that any cure he found would be temporary. Only Star could give him the sweet release his body cried out for.

Recriminations for his wanton urges left him feeling lower than a snake. This wasn't some doxy to be ogled; she was his daughter's sister-in-law—and, he hoped, his friend. He could not risk behaving in a manner that might destroy their bond. He needed her.

Halting his mount, he leaned forward, resting his arms across the pommel as he breathed in deeply. He felt rejuvenated as he took in the bright blue sky and sweeping green prairie. Once more, he looked toward Star. How would she fare in his world? He tried to imagine her in a proper dress and hat.

His eyes went wide. "Lord, clothing!" She couldn't arrive in St. Louis in buckskins—no matter how soft they looked. Hell, she had to have something else for the boat ride home.

Emma's trunk. He snapped his fingers. He'd left orders for his possessions to be cared for. If the fort had been abandoned, surely his things would have been transferred safely to Fort Randall.

Then another thought struck as he considered their arrival in the city. He rode over to the women.

"Sorry to intrude, but there are some things we must decide before we get to St. Louis." He looked at Star. "I cannot introduce you into society as Star Dreamer."

"Why not?" The woman looked puzzled.

Uncomfortable, Grady cleared his throat. "Don't take this wrong, ma'am, but I'm thinking it might be easier for you in St. Louis if we give you a last name."

"Very wise, Colonel," White Wind agreed, her blue eyes narrowed as she gave the matter thought. "What about the name I used before my marriage? I was once known as Sarah Cartier."

Grady had heard the story of how Star's mother had come to live among the Sioux. She was proof that a white woman could find love and peace in the land of the Sioux—and she was one of the reasons he'd consented to allowing Emma to remain. "As there are a large number of French citizens in St. Louis, that should do nicely. I believe Star will suffice for a first name if we drop Dreamer."

Star wrinkled her nose and tried it out. "Star Cartier." The words sounded strange on her tongue.

Star Cartier. Silently Grady repeated the name. "As beautiful as the woman," he mused. Shocked to find he'd spoken aloud, he coughed and glanced away, but not before catching a speculative look from White Wind. The mother lifted a brow thoughtfully but said nothing.

Instead, she eyed her granddaughter. "I'm afraid Morning Moon will need an entirely new name."

"This is fun!" Renny looked at her father. "Can *we* pick her name? I can help her."

It was clear she expected him to say no, so he surprised her. "All right." The brightening of her face, and her wide smile warmed him inside, but as the two girls rode off to to talk about it, a voice in his head warned that he might have made a mistake. Giving Renny free rein was like opening the floodgates to trouble, but he didn't have the heart to call them back.

The others laughed. "I'm afraid what those two will come up with," Star murmured, echoing his own thoughts.

"I'm sure we will find out soon enough," he said with a small grin.

As the afternoon wore on, Grady stayed near Star. Emma, Dove and White Wind had joined the two girls to guide them in their name choice, and intermittent squeals of laughter from that group left everyone feeling light of heart. Even Striking Thunder and Golden Eagle joined the merry game.

Star chuckled. "I am not sure if the children or the adults are having the most fun."

Her soft laughter wrapped him in a cocoon of happiness. Grady enjoyed listening to her laugh and realized that over the last few days, she'd both smiled and laughed many times. Already, the strain was fading from her face and she looked rested. Even the shadows under her eyes had lifted.

"It's not often children have the opportunity to change their names," he said.

"My people often change their names as they grow older. When boys become warriors, they earn the right to take on a new name. My daughter is excited to do the same."

Silence fell, and along with it an easy companionship. It was something he appreciated in Star. Usually he felt awkward when in the company of women. The silences were thick and tense. But not with this woman. Between them, there wasn't the need for constant chatter.

Grady removed his hat to rub the grime from his face with his handkerchief. Dusty and sweaty from the journey, he longed for a bath. But before he could get too engrossed in such a fantasy, he heard the swoop of wings and saw the shadow of a bird growing larger on the ground in front of him. He ducked. "Damn!" He was too late to avoid the razor-sharp talons that grazed the top of his head.

"Goddamn bird," he shouted as several strands of hair were yanked painfully out of his head by the root.

The commotion of flapping wings, the raven's harsh cries and his own shouts, startled his horse, who sidestepped and half-reared. Using one hand to ward off the diving bird, Grady struggled to retain his seat. Another swooping attack and painful tug at his head followed, then another sideways jerk of his horse. One foot came loose from his stirrup, and he felt his whole body shift out of the saddle. He fell, landing flat on his back. The black bird soared high into the sky with a raucous shriek.

Thankfully, a thick cushion of grass broke the worst of his fall. Lying still, he attempted to catch his breath and salvage his pride. The raven circled above him, its cries sounding like gleeful laughter.

"Colonel, are you all right?" Star's worried features appeared above him.

He blinked. "Damn bird—going to end . . . in a pie," he wheezed, struggling to rise.

Gentle hands held him back. "Wait. Catch your breath first."

The feel of her hands roaming over him in search of injuries left him breathless. Beneath her probing fingers, a strange weakness invaded his limbs. Tenderly, her hands skimmed over his shoulders, down his arms, over his head and along each leg. His insides shook. He tried blaming his reaction on his fall, for to admit his paralyzing weakness from this woman's touch was not an option.

"Father, are you all right?" Emma ran up to him.

Grady grimaced at his daughter's worried tone. She too peered down at him. Swearing beneath his breath, he pushed himself up from his undignified position despite the women's protests. Emma and Star each took an arm to help him, but he shook them off and stood on his own, feeling stupid and embarrassed. "I'm fine."

Star stood and handed him his hat. "Just bruised."

Grady jammed the hat down on his head, then tucked in his long hair. One step confirmed he had a bruised backside, yet it was his ego that had taken a more severe beating. He glowered at the two women.

Emma's lips twitched. "I'm so sorry, Father. Black Cloud does like red hair, I'm afraid." As if to prove her words, the raven flew down and landed on Emma's shoulder. He cocked his head before gently pecking at Emma's long red braid.

Knowing he had presented a humorous sight fighting off a bird, he glared at both women, daring them to laugh. Being unseated by an animal was not something a man in his position found amusing. "That bird will be mincemeat if he tries that again." Grady's voice turned gruff. The raven sat calmly on his daughter's shoulder—not a sight seen in the city—which only served to remind him just how little he knew his eldest child. The knowledge that she fit in perfectly with the life she'd chosen made father and daughter seem miles apart.

Renny stormed over to him, tearing him from his contemplation. "Don't you dare hurt Black Cloud," she shouted, planting herself squarely in between him and Emma.

"Renny," Emma cautioned, grabbing hold of her sister's arm. "Father isn't serious. Now hush."

The girl yanked herself free and folded her arms across her chest. "Then he shouldn't say things he doesn't mean. That was one of Aunt Ida's rules, and you always say we have to follow rules."

Humiliated by his undignified fall and hurt that Renny continued to think ill of him made Grady lose his temper. "Addressing your father in a respectful tone is also a rule, and one you seem to have forgotten! Or you never learned it . . . and if you do not want to be confined to your room, you will remember it!" He glared at her.

She glared right back. "That's because I never had a father."

Striking Thunder's arrival, with Grady's horse in tow prevented him from answering, which was a good thing. Allowing Renny to rile him to the point of anger wouldn't win him her love and trust, although allowing her to be so outspoken with her elders went against the grain. But he realized allowances had to be made—for now.

Grady accepted the reins to his horse and remounted. The women wisely moved off to reclaim their own happily grazing horses, leaving him and the young chieftain alone.

"I'm afraid my bird is drawn to hair the color of fire." He smiled, pointing to Emma. The bird had climbed from her shoulder onto her long braid and was flapping his wings to keep his balance.

"Don't take offense when I say I won't be sad to leave your pet behind." Grady gave the winged menace a dirty look, but despite his aversion to the bird, he had to admit it made a funny sight—as long as the bird was perched on someone else's shoulder! Cautiously, he removed his hat and touched the top of his head. The sting of his finger scraping over a cut made him wince. "Damn, does he have to use his talons?"

Without warning, the bird let out a loud cry and took to the air. A moment later, a burst of gunfire rent the air. "What the hell?" Grady whipped his horse around.

Over the gentle swell of land before him, Zeb and Zac crested a small rise. The two were riding hell-bent-for-leather straight toward them.

Chapter Five

Something was wrong. Grady fired his own rifle into the air. The pounding of his horse's hooves sounded as his soldiers fell into position, their rifles poised for whatever danger pursued the scouts. Striking Thunder quickly positioned his own warriors with bows drawn to flank both sides of Grady's contingent of soldiers.

Glancing behind him to check on the women, Grady noted that White Dove had an arrow nocked, her bow drawn tight. Alongside her, three of his best-trained men were ready to give their lives to protect his daughters.

Zac and Zeb reined to a halt before him. "Arikara, sir. Lots of 'em, and they's armed."

"Get the women out of here. Keep them safe, men."

"Yes, Colonel." The two scouts galloped away.

Grady waited. When a single, wide line of warriors crested the hill, he tasted fear. His girls—what if he failed to protect them? Staring at the enemy, his mind went blank. The fearlessness he'd always known in battle fled, leaving behind a father who could only think of the danger to his children.

Striking Thunder spoke sharply. "Wait for them to make the first move." Grady glanced at his son-in-law. Striking Thunder was a true warrior. Hard. Focused. A force to be reckoned with.

"The women—"

"Will be safe. The Arikara are no match for the Sioux—or soldiers under the command of a great white warrior. We *will* show them." Silent assurance filled Striking Thunder's eyes.

Unconsciously, Grady drew himself up, becoming once again the colonel who had earned the respect of his men and fear from his enemies. His military training took over. He would deal with this threat in the manner in which he was trained; he had to trust others to keep the women out of danger.

Loud shrieks rent the air as the enemy flew down the hill on their horses. As Striking Thunder drew his bow, Grady lifted his hand. "Steady. Steady, men. Let them come to us," he shouted. A barrage of arrows and lead balls from their enemies' old muskets flew toward them, falling short. At the downward slash of Grady's hand, his own soldiers commenced firing. Several Arikara fell, but still they came.

At the slightest pressure of his knees, Grady's horse leaped forward. His men charged the enemy. Striking Thunder and his warriors let out blood-chilling whoops as they too surged ahead, riding without the use of their hands, their arrows flying one after another. Grady spared a moment to appreciate and give thanks that the Sioux were his allies, not his enemies.

Then the air filled with gunfire, shrieks of war and screams of the fallen. Grady saw one of his men fall, then took aim at the Arikara warrior who had slain him, watching with satisfaction as the enemy flew off his horse to land on the bloodstained earth. The brave's wild-eyed animal bolted for safety.

Sweat dripped down the sides of Grady's face, his blood pumping furiously and his heart pounding in his ears. Adrenaline raced through his veins.

Some of the Arikara had split off to the right to flank them, but Striking Thunder and his warriors wheeled to head them off. Under the relentless gunfire from his soldiers, the main body of the Arikara—their number smaller now by half—turned tail, riding back the way they'd come.

At the sight of the war party blocking their path, Renny moved close to Emma. Her older sister's face had paled dramatically. Terror seized her as the memory of another Indian attack closed off her throat. Last time, her protectors had been killed, allowing Yellow Dog to take her and Emma captive. He'd been mean to them, especially to Emma, and he had traded Renny to another band of Indians for horses. Renny swallowed convulsively. Was it going to happen again? What would happen to her if these Indians killed the soldiers and Striking Thunder's warriors? Her father? Her stomach heaved. "Emma?"

She glanced over to see her sister's grip on her reins tightened, her knuckles turned white. "It's all right, Renny. Fathers' men have better guns than they do." Her voice lacked confidence.

"So did Capt'n Sanders's men." Renny's voice broke off with a squeak. Her eyes grew wide at the sight of the approaching enemy. Their shrill cries were the stuff of old nightmares.

A hand reached out to calm Renny. It was Star Dreamer's. "Do not worry, little one. No one will harm you ever again."

Zac and Zeb motioned them to ride. "Let's git outta here. Colonel's orders."

Renny gladly obeyed the order to turn and flee. Her horse churned the ground up behind her, sending rocks and clods of dirt into the air. Her heart lodged in her throat and her mouth felt dry. She glanced over her shoulder and whimpered. A handful of Arikara had split off to the side from the Sioux warriors and soldiers. They were now closing in on the fleeing women.

An arrow whizzed past. Renny screamed, jerking on the reins. Her horse faltered.

Zac rode up alongside her. "Lay low and ride, li'l lady," Zac shouted. He glanced behind them, then swore.

Looking back too, Renny nearly fell from her horse. Two Indians were closing in on her. She froze, unable to think beyond her fear.

Zac reached over and grabbed hold of her, pulling her in front of him, shielding her body from arrows too close for comfort. Renny's scream caught in her throat as her horse veered away. Afraid to look, she held on to Zac for all she was worth. No one needed to tell her the Arikara were close.

Renny gulped air into her lungs as the sound of battle raged behind her. Peering around her protector's arm, she spotted soldiers, with her father in the lead, cutting across the prairie to intercept the small group of savages that was chasing them. Her father lifted his rifle and fired. Behind her, one Indian fell, leaving only one gaining on Zac. The rest veered away, and a group of soldiers broke off in pursuit. Her father continued forward to save her.

He bent low over his horse, eventually pulling up alongside their pursuer. He smashed the warrior with the butt of his rifle. The Arikara savage slid to the side of his horse but did not fall. Instead, he used the steed for cover as he drew a wicked-looking tomahawk.

Horror washed over Renny, but before she could scream or call out, her father leaned low and pulled a knife from his boot, then threw it in one smooth motion. She let out a yell of support.

"He killed him, Zac! Papa killed him."

The scout who held her glanced over his shoulder, then slowed his horse. "Yahoo!" His yell joined hers.

When their excitement faded, Zac rode back to where the groups were reassembling. The enemy had been thoroughly vanquished.

"Look, Emma!" Renny cried, waving to her sister. "We're saved."

Emma smiled weakly. "That we are, sweetie."

Morning Moon rode up too, shouting gleefully: "The Arikara run like the cowards they are!"

Colonel O'Brien appeared next. "Everyone all right?" His stern gaze swept over his daughters before moving to check on the rest of the women.

"We're fine, Father. None the worse for the scare," Emma said.

Renny glanced at her father with new respect. "Wow. I didn't know you could fight like that." *Her father* had saved them. "Papa saved us, Em! He didn't let those awful Indians get us."

Her father lifted his brow. "No one will ever harm you again, child. Now, come along. Let's go find your mount while we wait for your sister's husband to return."

For the first time, Renny remembered her horse. She glanced around, then sighed with relief when she spotted the animal grazing a short distance away, unconcerned. When her father held out his arms, she went to him, allowing him to settle her in front of him. With a slow flick of the reins, he urged the horse forward into a walk.

With her father's arms securely on either side of her and his large, hard body behind her, Renny felt safe. Maybe he loved her after all—even if only a little bit. She asked him what had happened to the attacking band of Arikara.

She expected him to act like most adults and give her a vague answer—they never wanted to tell kids the truth. To her surprise, he didn't.

"Well, Renny, sometimes people die," he began, then offered up an account of the battle itself. As he spoke, Renny felt an inkling of trust, and she was glad he was taking his time reaching her horse.

It was a weary group who arrived at Fort Pierre the following afternoon. Star, Morning Moon and Renny entered the large room they'd been given to sleep in until they boarded the next steamboat bound for St. Louis.

Star stared. The barracks were stark: four dirty walls, a plank floor, one small window cracked and so crusted with dirt that she couldn't see through it. And along the wall there were several strange pieces of furniture, each with two lumpy, misshapen mattresses.

Renny dumped her bedding in one corner, then climbed up the side rails of one of the metal contraptions. "Hey, look how high up I am. Come on up, Morning Moon." She glanced down at Star, then at her sister and White Dove, standing in the doorway. "This is fun! I'm sleeping up here. Hey, Em, maybe you can sleep in here too. There's lots of beds."

Morning Moon giggled and scampered up the end of the bed to join Renny. "She can't. My uncle will want her with him."

Emma brushed past Star and sighed with longing. "A real bed." She rubbed her lower back with one hand and her abdomen with the other. Sitting, she tested one of the mattresses, then grimaced.

"A feather bed it's not, but better than the hard, cold ground. Striking Thunder will have to manage one night without me," Emma decided, laying flat with a satisfied sigh.

Star copied her sister-in-law and sat gingerly on the bottom bed nearest her. It wobbled from the girl's movements above her. She jumped off and smiled weakly at her mother and sister, who had come in.

White Wind's blue eyes sparkled with mischief. "It's been a long time since I've slept in a real bed." She too tested a straw-stuffed mattress. "How about if we all bed down here tonight? We shall declare tonight to be a woman's night."

Star eyed the bed her sister climbed on. The frame creaked and rocked with each movement. "Perhaps I'll sleep outside."

Emma slid out of her bed and grabbed Star's arm. "Oh, no, you don't. It's not that bad. Besides, as soon as my trunk is brought in, you have to try on my dresses to see if they will fit." She glanced over at Renny. "We also have to see if you have anything for Morning Moon to wear."

"I have lots of dresses." She frowned. "Hey, we

should start using Morning Moon's new name so she gets used to it," Renny suggested, leaning half over the bunk bed, her red hair streaming down.

"That's a very good idea, Renny," Star said, eager to take her mind from the prospect of bedding down on one of those strange pallets. "Does that meet with your approval, *Matilda?*" Her daughter's face lit up and the girl nodded shyly.

The arrival of several soldiers carrying Emma's trunks brought forth a flurry of activity. Gasps of delight followed when Emma opened the trunk and started laying out dresses upon the bed. Not knowing how long she'd be gone from home, she'd brought more than enough garments for a long time.

When her sister-in-law lifted out the last dress—her best Sunday-go-to-meeting dress in a powder blue with lace and ribbons trimming the sleeves and neckline—Star's jaw dropped. She'd never seen anything like it. She reached out to rub the material between her fingers. "It's so soft," she murmured.

"And it will be perfect on you with your black hair." Emma's voice softened. "I was going to wear this the day we arrived, but—well, I have no need for it now. It's yours, as are the rest of the dresses. Try it on," she urged.

"I cannot wear this." Regretfully, she handed the dress back, unable to take something so beautiful from her friend.

"Why not?" Emma rubbed the swell of her unborn child. "I certainly cannot wear it. Besides, when I needed more suitable clothing to fit into your lifestyle, I accepted what you gave me."

Star acknowledged the gentle rebuke with a small smile. "Yes, you accepted, however unwillingly. All right. I will wear this beautiful dress."

Emma narrowed her eyes. Star hid her smile, remembering how Emma had refused to give up her own tattered dress until Striking Thunder had finally taken the choice from her—ripping the garment and rendering it useless.

At Emma's urging, Star removed her deerskin skirt and tunic and let the woman drop the dress over her head. Yards of material slid over her naked body like water sheeting across her skin. Her admirers' soft gasps filled the room. White Dove, sitting on top of another bunk bed with her legs crossed, wore an expression of awe; White Wind wiped tears from her eyes, and the two little girls sighed and stared down at her.

Emma clapped her hands. "I think it will fit, once we put on your petticoats and corset."

"And drawers, Em."

"You're right, Renny."

Star frowned when Emma tossed several strange bits of clothing onto the nearest bed. In short order, her dress was removed and she was attired in what Emma called a shift, drawers, several petticoats and a front-lacing corset that left her barely able to breathe. With the dress back on, Star felt as though the clothing was grabbing her with each step.

"I can't wear all this," she moaned, pulling at the bodice of her dress, fighting the constriction of the corset.

White Dove shook her head. "I am certainly glad *I* don't have to be trussed up like a stuffed prairie chicken."

Star sent her sister a baleful glare.

Emma sat back and frowned. "I can let out the seams of the dresses so that we don't have to tighten the corset so much, but otherwise, I'm afraid you'll just have to get used to it."

White Dove snickered. "Yes, Star. When Emma came to us, she adapted to our ways. You, dear sister, must do the same—unless you've changed your mind and wish to return with us?"

Star bit back a sharp retort, refusing to give in to her younger sibling's goading. "No. I will learn to dress like a white woman."

"Be thankful that this is one of the newest corsets with elastic, not whalebone. Those were horrid," Emma admitted. "Now, let's try on the rest. We haven't got much time to make the alterations, and I heard my father tell Striking Thunder that a steamer should be back down the river within the week. There is much sewing to be done."

Indicating the gown she wore, Star frowned. "I have this. Surely one dress will do?"

Renny giggled and hopped down from the bed. "You can't wear just one dress, Star. You have to have lots or people will talk and think you are poor. 'Sides, our stuff don't last as long as yours."

"Our stuff *doesn't* last as long," Emma corrected.

"Yeah." Renny sighed, looking at her own hide dress with regret. "Guess I'll have to get used to wearing my old clothes again too. Come on, Matilda. Your turn."

Eight days after they arrived at the fort, Grady's soldiers finally found and flagged down a steamboat traveling down the Missouri River.

Grady greeted the captain of the steamboat *Annabella* as he rowed ashore—there wasn't a suitable docking area for the steamboat close to the fort. The small, rotund man had a thick black beard and lively eyes the color of the muddy Missouri River, and he kissed Grady on both cheeks in greeting. Grady found himself smiling at the Frenchman's enthusiastic hello.

"Colonel, it is good to see you once again." He stepped back, looking concerned. "Your daughters? Please, I pray zat you found zem, and zey are back with zeir papa?"

"Yes, Captain Billaud. Emma and Renny are both safe. In fact, I was hoping that you have room on the *Annabella* for us."

"Ah, for you and your lovely daughters, I will make room." The Frenchman rubbed his plump hands together. "Zere is none who knows zis river like I do. We are like lovers, zis river and I. I know her moods and her wily ways. Do not worry, I will see you and your family safely back to St. Louis."

"Thank you, Captain. We should be ready to board within the hour."

"I will prepare cabins. Lucky for you zat we are not full."

Grady quickly sent word to the women to make haste. Ever since they had been installed in the barracks together, they had become a giggling gaggle, and their laughter had been heard long into the night. Though Striking Thunder and Golden Eagle had expressed anxiousness to have their wives back on their own sleeping mats, the women had remained inseparable for the past seven days, and Grady knew that at least the men would be glad to get things back to normal.

While he waited for the others, Grady saw to the loading of his personal effects and ordered his soldiers to report to Fort Randall, farther upriver. With them, he sent the letter of resignation that he had penned the night before.

At last, all was set. He was just waiting for the women to finish with their tasks. In the midst of pacing impatiently, Zac, Zeb and their younger brother Zeke—he had waited for his brothers' return at the fort—shuffled up to him. His heart grew heavy at the thought of saying good-bye to them.

They'd been together for many years now—ever since he'd rescued Zeke from what could have been a torturous death at the hands of the Blackfeet. Since that day, the three brothers had followed him from one wilderness post to another. With a start, Grady realized they'd become a substitute family.

Zac, Zeb and Zeke looked as miserable as he felt. Zac, the eldest, scratched his ear. "If it's all right, Colonel, we thought we'd go with ya to St. Louie. Ya might need some help protectin' them women, ya know." He broke off and stared at the ground.

"And mebbe ya might need some help gettin' settled, or . . . somethin'," Zeb added, pulling at his beard.

Zeke kicked a rock. "Truth is, Colonel, it won't be the same out here without ya. We promise not ta get in yer way."

The sight of the three—men who looked as though they sprang from the mountains and could tackle a bear and emerge the victor—wearing woebegone expressions, touched Grady deep inside.

Truth to tell, he liked the idea of having these three devoted men to help watch over Star and the girls. Space was not a problem, either. He'd had his home built a few years after Emma's birth with the hope of filling the vast number of empty rooms with the sound of children's laughter. But that had never happened.

Now his house sat empty, much as his heart had been all these years. But surrounded by friends and his daughters, the barren cavity of his heart was slowly filling. Apparently, so was his house.

Realizing that the three brothers were anxiously awaiting his answer, he grinned. "You are all welcome to come with me and to stay as long as you like." He vowed to help the men find employment in St. Louis for as long as they wanted to stay. Surely he had connections that would be helpful in doing so.

The men gave hoots of relief, and they hastened off to gather their piles of possessions.

"That was generous of you, Papa," Emma said from behind him, making him start. She approached, and he could see tears trailing down her cheeks. Was she really going to miss him so much?

Grady opened his arms.

She ran to him. "I'm going to miss you."

"And I you, my sweet Emma. My princess . . . thank you for coming to look for me." He tightened his hold, his fingers buried in her hair at the back of her head as she sobbed on his shoulder. After a moment, he gently held her away and wiped her tears with a clean handkerchief. "You'll never have to do that again. I'll be back. I promise, I'll be back."

"Oh, Papa, I know you will."

"Emma, are you sure this is what you want?" He knew the answer, that she belonged here with her husband, but he needed to hear the words one last time.

Emma smiled, her eyes softening. "Yes, Father. I'm sure. Very sure."

He nodded. "I will take good care of your sister."

At this, Emma's lips curled into an amused grin. She wiped the remaining tears from her eyes and chuckled. "She won't make it easy for you."

Grady sighed at the truth of her words. Renny would continue to test him. Lord only knew if he would pass or not. For the past week, whenever he felt he was making headway, she had turned on him. The return of Captain Billard halted their conversation.

"Miss Emma. Miss Emma!" The young woman was pulled into a hug by the Frenchman.

"Captain, I am so sorry for the worry I caused you." She pulled away. "And for the coach that was destroyed."

The riverman waved aside her apology. "Not to worry. I am just so relieved to see you have not come to harm." For the first time, he noticed her Indian garb and her rounding figure. He flushed.

Grady intervened. "Emma will be staying behind with her husband." He indicated Striking Thunder, who stood several feet away, a watchful and loving eye on his wife.

"Zat is your husband?"

"Yes."

Billard's brows lowered in fatherly concern. "Do you love zis man?"

Emma laughed softly. "Oh, yes, Captain, with all my heart."

A wide smile split his face. "Zen I wish you all ze best, Miss Emma. All ze best. And where is ze little one, your sister?"

"Here she comes." Emma pointed.

Grady glanced across the compound. Half a dozen soldiers were carrying two trunks and other assorted baggage. Renny and Morning Moon ran ahead of them, White Dove and her mother following. Grady assumed Star was following behind.

Renny skidded to a stop in front of the river captain. They too exchanged greetings, then she introduced Morning Moon. Though Grady saw questions in the Frenchman's eyes, the man didn't say a word or blink an eye. He greeted the two girls, charming them with his easy manner.

"Are my horses on the boat yet?" Renny asked eagerly, scanning the loading process. "There are two of them and they are mine." That last bit was added defiantly.

The captain's bushy black brows slid beneath his

cap. "Ah, mademoiselle has her own horses now, does she?"

"Yes, she does," Renny stated.

"Zen you must go check on zem."

Renny started to do so, then turned to her sister. Her lower lip quivered. Emma held out her arms and Renny ran into them.

"Emma?"

"What is it, sweetie?"

"What if there are attacks by the Arikara again? Things happen that are bad. . . . Morning Moon—I mean Matilda—lost her father, and . . . What if something happens and I never see you again?" The little girl's anguish made Grady's stomach twist and bunch, but his daughter bravely fought back tears.

Emma wrapped her arms around Renny, holding her tightly. "In your heart, you must believe that we will see each other again. If we worry too much over dying, we would never leave our homes. It is a part of life, death is. And we must live every day to the fullest—no matter where we are or who we're with."

"But six months is an awfully long time to be gone." Renny bit her lower lip. "You won't forget me, will you?"

"Of course not! The time will go quickly for both of us." Emma let go of her sister, then reached up to untie something around her neck. "I want you to have this." It was a beaded necklace.

Renny's eyes grew wide as she was given the beaded medallion. It depicted two stick figures—one tall, one short—and Grady realized they were her and Emma. "Hey, this is the necklace Morning Moon gave you when Striking Thunder first brought you to his village," his youngest daughter exclaimed, tracing the rows of beads.

"Yes. She didn't want me to worry about you and thought this would help me have faith that I'd find you again. Whenever you are worried, wear this and have faith that we'll see each other again."

Renny slipped the necklace over her head and cupped the beaded circle in her hand. She looked happier. "Thanks, Em."

"Come on, Renny. You'll see your sister again soon." Morning Moon, who'd already said good-bye to her family, put an arm around her friend. A moment later, the captain followed to see them personally aboard.

Touched, Grady strode over to Striking Thunder and Golden Eagle. He cleared his throat. "We must be going. Where is—"

He broke off when he spotted Star coming slowly toward him. She was wearing a dress of pale blue, and sunlight glittered in her eyes, Her mouth curved into a shy smile.

Her hair had been twisted and put up, calling attention to her slender neck, the smooth line of her jaw and the delicate hollows below her high cheekbones. Grady blinked and sucked in his breath and stared at the exquisite figure coming toward him.

Unlike the shapeless doeskins he was used to see-ing Star wear, the bodice of her new dress hugged her curves, revealing the gentle swell of her breasts and the narrowness of her waist. He knew just by looking, he'd be able to span it with his hands.

Before, she'd looked young and fragile, but now she looked as if the slightest breeze could sweep her away. All his protective instincts rose, as well as a few others of less commendable nature.

With a start, he reminded himself that she was coming with him to help him with Renny. He'd promised her a safe haven. She was off-limits. But the attraction he'd felt before again sprung to life, leaving him no doubt as to what his body desired.

She stopped before him, and the sudden appearance of a mischievous twinkle in her eyes left him reeling. Was she enjoying his sense of shock?

"Will this do?" Star spun around. Nervous but doing everything she could to hide it, she released her breath, relieved. She'd already endured a goodly amount of good-natured teasing from her brother and sister, though her parents had assured her that she looked beautiful. Surprisingly, she *felt* beautiful. She felt different, stronger, in control. But her racing heart still sought this man's opinion.

Grady cleared his throat. "You are truly a sight to behold, Mrs. Cartier." He took her hand in his, bent his head and lightly kissed the backs of her fingers.

Star looked confused for a moment, then grinned sheepishly. "I'm not used to being called by my new name," she said shyly. Or having her fingers kissed. The strange custom sent a warm glow through her hand and up her arm. She liked that manner of greeting.

Grady released her fingers. "If you are ready, we mustn't keep the good captain waiting."

Star turned to her parents, sister and brother. They hugged, cried and said their good-byes one last time. Then she and Emma embraced.

"I shall miss you, my sister. I'll take good care of Running Elk."

Star smiled sadly. "I know you will. I miss him already."

Her sister-in-law sobered. "I hope you will find what you seek." Emma wiped the tears from her face. "Watch over Renny and keep her out of mischief."

That released some of the tension, for both knew the task would be nearly impossible. Star laughed. "I will return in time for the birth of your babe." A sudden buzzing filled her head as an image of Emma nursing a baby flitted across her mind. An instant later it was gone. It confused and bothered her. How could she see the births of future generations from her brothers and sisters so clearly, while other visions were so vague and unsettling? Once again, she railed against the unfairness of her gift.

But at least she knew her brother's wife would deliver a healthy child. "You will make a good mother, my sister," she said. "I shall miss you."

Emma stepped back as Striking Thunder gathered Star in one last embrace. "Come back to us, my sister."

Attempting to lighten the heavy atmosphere, she sniffed back her tears and forced a brave smile to her lips. "I'll be back for the birth of your . . . *child*." She deliberately paused, and as she'd known would happen, Striking Thunder's brows rose.

"Wait! Before you leave, tell us—what is it, a boy or a girl?"

Star laughed and winked at Emma, then accepted Grady's arm. "I would not dream of spoiling your surprise, brother."

Striking Thunder spluttered, but Star took Grady's hand and got into the small wooden boat waiting on the river bank. A short while later, Star had left all she knew and loved behind for dreams of a new beginning.

Chapter Six

Star entered her appointed cabin on the second deck and felt as though she'd stepped into another world. The small, sparsely furnished room held two beds and a small table with two chairs. Plush red carpeting covered the floor, incredibly detailed flowers scrolled up the walls from midway to the ceiling and wood paneling covered the lower half of the walls. Lamps and mirrors edged with gold were hung as well in decoration.

"I do not have many passenger cabins, Mrs. Cartier, not like ze new steamers. I mainly haul cargo up ze Missouri, but zis is my finest room." Captain Billaud took the few steps needed to cross the room to open a door she hadn't spotted. "It even has a water closet," he said proudly. Stepping back into the corridor, he shouted for the men with her trunks to hurry.

Star peered into the small enclosure he'd just pointed out, wondering what exactly a water closet was. Behind her, Renny and Morning Moon tested the two beds, chatting excitedly.

Beneath Star's feet, vibrations from the high-pressure engines rumbled, and noise from the upper deck wound down to the one below, along with an assortment of odors, most not so pleasant. At last, two men arrived with the trunks. They were followed by a young boy.

"My cabin boy will see to your luggage for you."

The boy slid past the Frenchman's bulky form to pull open another door concealed in the dark paneling. Star was shocked to see a long rod and drawers set into the wall. With a wide smile at her, the cabin boy began to lift the lid of her trunk.

Realizing what he was going to do, Star rushed forward. "This isn't necessary, Captain. I can unpack my own things."

Renny giggled and flopped over onto her stomach. "Uh-uh, Star. That's not done. Servants do the unpacking."

"Quite right, madame. Zere is a promenade galley on zis deck for my first-class passengers, along with a newly redone salon in ze center of ze cabins. Rest, and I shall see you at supper." With a salute, the captain left.

Speechless, Star watched the riverman leave. Emma had said nothing about servants, nor had Colonel O'Brien. He'd only mentioned hiring a cook and cleaning staff. Sitting on the edge of her bed, she felt awkward—and embarrassed—at having a young boy handling her clothing, especially when she was perfectly capable of seeing to her own things.

Lifting her two Indian garments from the trunk, along with an assortment of leather pouches that held sewing, herbal and other supplies, he sent her an awed look. "Yer a *real* Indian!"

Renny and Morning Moon giggled, causing the poor boy's face to redden. "Girls!" she admonished. "Yes, my daughter and I are Sioux." He appeared only slightly older than the two girls.

"Gee, I've never met a real Indian before." He started in on the second trunk. Minutes later, done, he hesitated, as if he longed to strike up another conversation, but a sudden bellow from the hall had him scurrying out the door.

Star glanced over at her daughter, who was staring around her. "What do you think, daughter?"

"The bed is so soft!" Morning Moon's eyes were wide. She looked toward the closed door. "Do we have to stay inside and rest as the captain said?"

Laughing, Star jumped up and smoothed her skirts. "Absolutely not. Who wants to go explore with me?"

Both girls shouted at once.

"I can show you everything," Renny cried, wrenching the door open. "I've been everywhere on this boat—when Em and I were going to the fort."

Star followed the girls out, her excitement nearly as high as theirs.

Grady escorted Star into the ship's small but adequate private dining room. It boasted half a dozen tables covered with snowy-white cloths, gleaming silverware and sparkling glassware. The ivory walls were trimmed with gilt, and the large mirror at the end of the long, narrow room gave the impression that the room went on forever.

The captain came toward them. "Ah, *monsieur*. I hope you found your accommodations adequate?"

"More than adequate, Captain. I suspect you take more passengers than you let on."

Billaud's eyes twinkled. "Ah, ze money in zat is good. But not too many passengers want to go north on an old ship that has seen better days. Alas, most prefer to go to New Orleans on ze newer, more luxurious steamers."

Despite what the man said, from what Grady had seen, Billaud was managing nicely. Though the ship was small, it was well maintained and lacked nothing to make her passengers feel at home. "Come. You must join me at my table."

Grady motioned for Star to precede him. Like her daughter's, her eyes were wide with wonder. If she thought this grand, wait until she saw his house. His lips twitched. He chafed at the two months it would take to arrive home. He was eager to show her his home, and his city.

At the head table, another family had already been seated. "Ah, Colonel, may I present Mrs. Smith and her children, Bobby and Jane? Mrs. Smith is traveling from Canada to St. Louis to join her husband." Captain Billaud then introduced Grady and his party.

Star smiled shyly and allowed the captain to seat her at his right.

As Mrs. Smith looked from Grady and his uniform to Star, her gaze hardened. The woman stared at Renny then at Morning Moon. Star Dreamer's daughter stared back with dark, solemn eyes.

Mrs. Smith set her glass of sherry down and smiled tightly. "Captain, surely you do not plan to seat this squaw and her offspring at this table?"

Her high, fluttery laugh grated on Grady's nerves, as did the condescending looks she bestowed on Star and the children. "Is there a problem, Mrs. Smith?" he asked before the captain could intervene. He stared at her distastefully and she stiffened.

"Well, it's just not done," she said. "The *common herd* have their own facilities. I pay well to keep my children away from riffraff and those who are below our station. And you must admit, having your"—she paused—"this woman and her offspring sitting at this table is simply not proper. Appearances are ever so important, don't you agree?"

Grady rested his palms on Star's shoulders, silently cursing Mrs. Smith for her rudeness. He felt Star tremble. "It is my opinion, Mrs. Smith, that manners are much more so." That said, he swept his gaze over her with an air of dismissal.

She gasped. "Well, I never." She turned back to the captain. Billaud stood silent, his big hands on Renny's shoulders, obviously stilling her desire to protest the woman's rude behavior.

"Captain, I insist you intervene. I cannot share a table with heathens."

Captain Billaud nodded. "Quite so, Mrs. Smith. I would not wish you or your children to be upset." He motioned one of his servants over.

Mrs. Smith preened and shot Star a gloating look. "Thank you, Captain."

"See to it zat Mrs. Smith and her children are taken to zeir quarters and served zeir meal there."

The woman gasped in outrage, but the captain gave her an oblivious smile.

"I hope zis meets with your approval, Mrs. Smith. Come tomorrow, I will see zat you and your family are seated at ze table in ze back of ze room to assure your comfort."

After the woman had huffily stamped away, Grady sat beside Star. The captain seated the two

young girls opposite, placing Morning Moon beside him. Grady nodded slightly to show his
thanks, then set about coaxing a smile from Star
by regaling her and Billaud with a story about his
men that had never failed to be entertaining.

But though Star smiled and laughed, the excitement had dimmed from her eyes. Taking a sip of
his wine, Grady cursed people like Mrs. Smith.
He'd hoped that Star would enjoy her time with his
people, but they had gotten off to a terrible start.
He glanced down at her plate, noting that she
hadn't eaten much. Even now, she was just pushing
food around with her fork.

Across from him, he caught the stubborn set of
his daughter's jaw and knew she was busily plot-
ting something. She too saw how much damage
Mrs. Smith had done. He sent her a silent warning.

She lowered her eyes and gave herself over to
eating, but Grady felt certain that his daughter had
hardly given up her plan. Some perverse part of
Grady sided with Renny and looked forward to seeing what she intended.

He had the feeling this trip was not going to be
a dull one.

Renny and Morning Moon crept from their cabin.
Their shadows, long and grotesque, wavered along
the interior of the *Annabella*'s dimly lit walls. Below
their feet, the wooden floor beneath the worn carpeting creaked, making Renny cringe. After pausing she led the way, moving stealthily with her back
against the wall. At the end of the long corridor,
she stopped and peered around the corner. "No
one's coming. We have to hurry and do this, then
get back to our cabin before your mother comes in
to go to bed."

"Your father will be angry if he learns we have disobeyed." Morning Moon glanced nervously over her shoulder.

Renny whipped her head around, a deep frown marring her forehead. "Shush! Not so loud. And quit worrying. He won't find out. He's probably in bed 'cause he gets up so early."

Morning Moon sighed with resignation and followed. "I don't know why we're doing this. The soldiers are with your horses. They are safe."

Renny narrowed her eyes. "Jake yells too much, and he uses a whip on his horse. No one is going to be mean to mine."

They peered down the stairs leading to where livestock was kept. Renny froze. Deep male voices were echoing up from below—her father's and Zeb's. Wide-eyed, she gauged the distance behind them back to safety. They'd never make it in time.

Unwilling to face her father's wrath, she yanked on Morning Moon's arm. Testing the door of the room on her right, she found it unlocked. Billaud had said the boat was practically empty on its return trip to St. Louis, and Renny thanked Heaven for that. She ducked inside, pulling her friend with her. Closing the door silently, she pressed her ear to the cool wood surface, listening for her father's voice. "We'll just wait here until he's gone, then we'll sneak back—"

Morning Moon pulled on her sleeve. "Renny . . ."

Renny rolled her eyes and motioned for her friend to be quiet. "Shush! Gosh, you worry a lot."

"Renny!"

At the sound of desperation, she glanced at her friend. A sinking sensation hit her stomach at the sight of the girl's look of horror. Slowly, Renny turned to see what Morning Moon was staring at.

"Ah, is there a problem, *mademoiselles?*"

Renny jumped, squealed in surprise and flattened her back against the door. She groaned, as much from dismay as at the stab of pain from the doorknob jabbing her in the back. Oh, Lord. Of all cabins to duck into, trust her to pick the captain's. Her mind racing, she kept her fingers wrapped around the doorknob in case they needed a quick escape. "No. No problem, Captain. We just got . . . lost."

The sound of male voices outside penetrated the room. Captain Billaud steepled his fingers and rested his chin on them. "Ah, I understand." His eyes twinkled with amusement.

Heaving a sigh, Renny released the doorknob. "I was just going to check on my horses one more time, then go to bed," she muttered defiantly.

He nodded. "Yes, having animals is a responsibility. But you should not go down zere alone, little one. One cannot guarantee ze nature of every man on board. If you will not ask your papa to take you, zen I will accompany you."

The captain was a busy man. His offer made Renny feel guilty. "That's not necessary, Captain. I apologize for disturbing you. I'll just wait until tomorrow. I'm sure they are fine." But as much as she wanted to avoid putting him out, she did want to see the horses.

Billaud shook his head, his eyes full of understanding. "I think you will not sleep unless you see with your own eyes zeir well-being. Come. Sit and allow me to finish my entry. Zen we shall go down."

Renny and Morning Moon moved to the two chairs on either side of his desk. When he at last finished logging his daily entry, he set his journal and pen aside. "I am happy zat you found your papa. You and your sister had yourselves quite an adventure, no?"

Renny grimaced. "Some of it was fun, but lots of it was scary."

"Now you are returning home."

Swinging her legs, a wave of sadness washed over her. "Yeah, but not Emma. I wish I could stay with her."

"It is hard to leave family. But zat is the way of life. Someday you will fall in love and leave your papa, too."

"Maybe. But Emma gets to keep having lots of adventures—without me."

"Ah, little one, adventure is always around ze corner. You have to make your own."

"I always get in trouble when I do that."

"Well, no harm done zis time. In ze future, you might want to consult with your young friend. Sometimes our actions also affect others."

That was true. She could have gotten her friend in trouble too. "I'm sorry, Morn—Matilda."

"My uncle says you are a wild spirit who hasn't found a home yet." She grinned. "But I like that."

Relieved that her friend wasn't mad at her, Renny turned her attention back to their surroundings. The cabin was much like the one she shared with Morning Moon and Star Dreamer, but more cluttered. Trunks and boxes lined the walls. The sound of squealing drew her attention to a small cage on a sideboard beneath the curtained portal. "What's in there?" she asked.

The captain stood and brought the cage to the desk. "Zis is Tillie. I got her from another captain who assured me she'd make a nice pet. However, he did not tell me she would be a mama so young!"

Renny stared down at a large brown rat and her

babies. "Someone gave you a rat? For a pet? Wow! My aunt Ida was always trying to kill them. I didn't know you could keep them as pets."

"You cannot just take a wild rat, little one. You must start with a baby. See?" He reached in, and the mother immediately abandoned her furry young to scamper up his sleeve to perch on his shoulder. The bright-eyed animal licked its tiny paws and washed its face while eyeing the visitors with interest.

Renny stretched out her arm cautiously and held her breath when the rat planted its paws on her palm. Long whiskers tickled her wrist, then Tillie decided to remain where she was and sat back on the captain's shoulder.

Studying the small babies who climbed the sides of the cage, looking for a way out, Renny giggled, mesmerized by their beady little eyes, big ears and skinny tails. The captain reached into the cage and scooped one light brown rodent into his hand and handed it to her.

Thrilled, Renny held the baby rat and gently touched its soft head. "Look at this, Matilda."

A knock at the door interrupted her before she could ask the captain if she could have one for her very own.

Billaud called out, "Enter."

"Excuse the interruption, Captain, but I'm look-ing for—"

At the sound of Grady O'Brien's voice, Renny groaned and whirled around. As he saw her, her father's brows pulled together in a fierce frown. He advanced until he stood towering over her. Biting her lower lip, Renny waited.

"Ranait! Matilda! What are the two of you doing in here? You were told to remain in your cabin. It's late."

"I wanted to check my horses really quick." She stroked the rat's soft fur to avoid her father's furious look.

"And I distinctly told you that you were not to go down there without me or one of the scouts."

"Captain Billaud said he'd take me down. *He* thinks I'm being responsible!" Her voice trembled. She didn't dare mention that she'd been on her way down there on her own before the captain made his generous offer. She avoided Billaud's gaze.

Her father closed his eyes and his lips moved silently. When he spoke, his voice was tight with restrained anger. "Renny, the captain is a busy man." He glanced at Billaud. "I apologize on behalf of my daughter."

The riverman waved his apology aside. "No harm. It's not every night a lonely old man receives ze pleasure of two beautiful girls paying him a visit. Zey are welcome to visit any evening. I find your daughter very entertaining." He put Tillie back in the cage.

Grateful for the distraction, Renny put the baby rat back so that it could nurse with the rest. "What are you going to do with the babies?"

The captain rubbed the side of his nose. "Well, zis I have not decided."

"I could take one. And Matilda might want one too."

"You must first ask your papa, little one."

Renny's heart sank. She turned to her father. "He won't let me have one, I know he won't. He probably hates pets—like Aunt Ida who said they were too messy."

Grady sighed. He reached out and turned her to face him, a funny look on his face, as if he were in pain. "Try asking, Renny. I like animals. If the captain is willing to part with one, you may have it if

114

you like. But Matilda will have to ask her mother's permission."

Morning Moon shook her head. "I don't think I want a rat." She shuddered.

"Ze babies are not ready to leave zeir mother yet. But you may come back and choose ze one you want and play with it, to get it used to you." He stood and walked them to the door.

"Oh boy!" Renny whooped.

Her father smiled tenderly down at her, then tweaked a lock of her hair. "Now, off to bed with you two."

She glanced toward the stairs leading down and sobered. It seemed she couldn't check on her horses after all. She and Morning Moon trudged back the way they had come, but her father's voice stopped her.

"Wait." He let out a loud sigh of resignation. "I shall take you down to check on your horses. Then you and Matilda will return to your cabin. Understood?"

Renny whooped again. "Thank you, Papa!" She grabbed Morning Moon's hand, and together they ran for the stairs.

Star's new beginning left a lot to be desired. Though Striking Thunder had warned her about the attitude of whites toward Indians, she hadn't thought it would be so bad or start so soon. Somehow, donning Emma's beautiful blue dress and adopting a foreign hairstyle had made her feel different. She'd felt white, not Sioux. In dress, she was no different from the other two women on board. But at supper she had learned just how a person's skin color and features could influence others.

Gripping the wooden rail, she stared down into

the inky blackness of the Missouri River. Yes, this was a rocky beginning. Would all of St. Louis be like this? Or worse?

How would she cope? And what about her daughter? Star thought again of her brother Wolf. Would Morning Moon be forced to endure the same treatment that he had received at the hands of whites?

No. Star would keep her daughter home if need be—away from cruel, insensitive people like the mean-minded Smiths. She tried taking Grady's advice to forget the dinner incident, that fretting over what happened was pointless. He was right. She couldn't reason with ignorance.

Still, she also couldn't help the deep-seated hurt and anger seething in her.

Depressed and feeling lost, she followed the rail around the ship. Every so often, she plucked at her gown. Dealing with new people and new situations was bad enough without suffering through this hated corset and these yards of material, which hampered her every movement. She longed to slip into her soft deerskin dress and feel the breath of night air on her arms and legs.

Tipping her head back, she let her mind roam, soaring freely across the night sky, lost among the bright, twinkling lights and the silver-white moon. Though where she was had changed, the sky, with its vast array of stars, was the same. That one small consistency soothed and calmed her. Too bad she couldn't sleep out here beneath the comforting heavens.

Sighing, she left the rail to return to her cabin. The girls should be asleep by now and, proper or not, she was going to wear her Indian dress to bed. Passing a dark shadow, she paused. A fowl stench issued from it. Her heart froze, until she realized she was in no danger.

It was Zeke, one of the three scouts Colonel O'Brien was friends with. Exhaling, Star decided to talk to Grady about instructing the men on the art of bathing—especially if he intended the brothers to share his home.

Home. Farther along the deck, she paused once more at the rail to stare out the way they had come. She couldn't see the *Paha Sapa*, the Black Hills. Night cloaked them, but they were there, as was her family, her son—awaiting her return.

"Where's lover boy, *squaw?*"

At the sound of the scornful voice, Star whirled around. Before her, Bobby Smith, the son of the woman who'd insulted her at dinner, was close behind, a leer on his face.

His gaze fastened on the gentle swell of her breasts. "You sure are a looker for a savage. I thought squaws were fat and ugly."

Star backed away. "I suggest you leave, Mr. Smith."

He grabbed her arm. "You can't tell me what to do. You're a nobody." He stared down the front of her bodice. "What's the matter? Aren't I good enough for you? Judging from them clothes you're wearing, you must be real good on your back."

Shocked by his vulgar behavior, Star yanked her arm out of his sweaty grip.

"Hey!" the Smith boy said. "Don't you get uppity on me. Show me how good you are and I'll treat you really nice—nicer than that old man." He reached out to grab her again.

Suddenly, something spun him around. Zeke! Her assailant yelped as the scout's thick fingers dug into the material of his shirt collar, his large knuckles jamming into his windpipe.

Zeke lifted the boy off the ground with one hand, until his feet dangled a foot off the ground.

"The *lady* don't want nothin' to do with horseshit like you," the scout said, then glanced at Star. "You okay?"

She took a brief, perverse enjoyment in the Smith boy's terror as Zeke fisted his other hand and held it in front of his face, then said, "I'm fine, Zeke."

"I should toss yer worthless hide overboard."

"No," the boy gasped, his voice cracking beneath the pressure on his throat.

"Apologize to the lady." Zeke gave him a rough shake.

"I'm sorry. I meant no harm," he wheezed, his hands flailing at his sides.

And then, suddenly, Grady was there. "Release him, Zeke," he ordered, his voice cold.

Star stepped forward when she saw the fury glittering in the Colonel's eyes.

"Grady—"

"Are you all right?" He pulled Star close, looking down at her with an intensity that made her shiver.

"I'm fine. He didn't do anything."

"Not for lack of tryin'," Zeke growled. "It's a good thing you ordered me to be out here, sir. Can I hit him, Colonel?"

"Hitting might be too civilized for the *boy*."

"How 'bout we take him down below? Maybe we can leave him with the roustabouts. Bet they can teach him some manners."

The Smith boy's eyes grew wide and his face paled. Star opened her mouth to protest, then bit her tongue. It would do no good to try to stop Grady; she knew the colonel would have his way in this matter.

118

Also, she felt a strange pleasure at the thought of the boy being punished. Bobby Smith needed to learn that he could not go around grabbing women and treating them like this. And the sooner he did, the better.

She watched Grady clasp his hands behind his back, staring down the youngster. He was every bit a commanding presence and it made her heart flutter. "Not a bad idea, Zeke. Is that what you want, boy?"

Smith shook his head, almost in tears. The terror on his face was plain. Grady relented, "Let him go, Zeke."

The scout dropped Bobby to the deck. The youngster would have gotten up, but Zeke pressed his huge foot into the boy's groin—obviously anxious to make sure that he got the message.

Grady spoke again. "If you catch this boy anywhere near Mrs. Cartier again, you have my permission to do as you please." He paused. "I think he's learned his lesson. Now, let's help him up."

The two of them lifted up Mrs. Smith's son, holding him between them. Star watched as Grady let go and reached out to straighten the boy's collar and cravat. "He just made a mistake, isn't that right, boy?"

"Y-yes, sir."

"I thought so. See, Zeke? He's young and just forgot his manners." Star had to strain to hear as Grady lowered his voice. "I wouldn't forget them again, though, Mr. Smith. I might not be around next time—and I'd hate to see Zeke take your John Henry before you get old enough to figure out the right way to use it. You get my meaning, *boyo?*"

Bobby covered himself with his hand, shivering. He nodded vigorously.

"Good. So glad that we could resolve this rationally. I do hate violence." The colonel relaxed and stepped back. "Now, it's quite late. In case you've forgotten where your cabin is, I'm sure Zeke here will be more than happy to escort you to it. Isn't that right, Zeke?"

"Uh, no, that won't be necessary, Colonel," Bobby squeaked.

Grady nodded. "But I insist."

Star chuckled as the scout wrapped a bear-sized arm around Bobby's shoulders and started chatting about the various ways the Indians tortured outsiders who violated their women. To anyone observing them, it would seem as if the two were simply in earnest conversation.

"Thank you, Colonel." Star wasn't sure whether to laugh or cry, but she was grateful. Between Zeke and Grady, Bobby had gotten what he deserved. "He didn't do any real harm."

Grady tipped her chin up, forcing her to meet his gaze. "He frightened you. For that he should be horsewhipped."

"No." She paused. "He didn't frighten me that much. He mostly shocked me." Her voice trailed off and she glanced away. "I guess I have much to learn about your world."

"I don't believe he will bother you again."

Star shook her head and grinned. "No. With you and Zeke out here, he may never leave his cabin again until St. Louis."

Grady shrugged. "Good. Boys like that should be . . ." He trailed off and held out his arm. She accepted the invitation and allowed him to lead her around the promenade galley. "Why were you out here alone? It's late. You must be tired."

Star didn't point out that she hadn't been alone, that Zeke was out here—apparently on Grady's orders. He was making certain to protect her, and for that she was grateful. "It's so noisy, and the cabin is too hot. I didn't think taking a walk would cause problems." She blinked back tears of frustration.

Grady patted her arm in understanding. "The cabin is a bit small, I'm afraid, and not what you're used to."

"It's very beautiful." Her voice trembled. The white man's world—its boats, its buildings—made her feel so closed in. It had no fresh air, no smoke holes for the stars to peep in and wink down at her. There was no sense of the familiar world on the other side of a thin piece of hide.

The mugginess of the night air, the confinement of her clothing, and the animosity during supper combined to push her over the edge. She began to shake.

Grady put his arm around her and drew her close. "I know all this is new and not easy. Between that boy's mother's behavior at supper and this, I wouldn't hold it against you if you changed your mind about accompanying me to St. Louis." Compassion laced his words, but his tone, deep and low, reassured her.

The fact that he understood and didn't think she was overreacting took away a bit of her homesickness. Sighing and moving a tiny bit closer, she whispered, "No. I was warned."

Grady took her hand in his, his thumb moving tenderly over the soft skin of her inner wrist. "You are a kind, gentle, giving woman. If others cannot see what I do, then that is their problem—and their loss."

His words warmed her, as did his tender touch. She needed both like a starving man would need the nourishment of the *maka* and the warmth of *wi.* And standing beneath the carpet of stars, Star Dreamer was suddenly very afraid of needing more from Grady than was wise for either of them. She'd lost her husband, and would never risk taking another. She would never allow herself to foresee the death of another mate.

Grady lifted his hand, stroking the edge of her jaw. "We whites are so caught up. . . . The pursuit of wealth and position clouds so many minds and hearts to true beauty—to humanity. It seems like we spend all our days seeking more money, more possessions. We've forgotten the simple truths in life."

His gaze turned inward and sadness filled his voice. "My parents might be alive today had they not been more concerned with their social position . . . and offending those in power."

Star heard the anguish and regret in his words, tinged with anger. She could not help but ask; "What happened?"

He glanced down at her. "It doesn't matter. It was a long time ago."

The pain in his eyes compelled her. "I'd still like to know."

Staring out into the darkness, Grady fell silent. Then he spoke, his voice low. "My parents were invited to spend the summer at the plantation of a wealthy businessman my father knew. My mother was thrilled; this family was in a social circle much above our own. But I didn't want to go. The last thing I wanted to do was spend a season acting the perfect son while attending round after round of parties with my parents. While they thrived on such things, I, as a child, did not. I wanted to go fishing, boating, to take trips upriver with my father. I faked an illness to get them to stay behind, but they went anyway, leaving my sister to care for me. Ida was ten years older than I."

He paused. "Ida didn't mind. The one man she loved, and had been engaged to, had eloped five years earlier with another woman. She had no more desire to socialize than I did, to go out and know that our every movement was being watched and judged."

Grady smiled briefly. "Now that I think about it, I think my parents were glad to leave me in her care. To tell the truth, I was rather a wild child." He rested his hands on the rail and hunched his shoulders. "Somehow there was a house fire at the plantation. My parents . . . well, you can guess the rest."

Star rested her palm against his white-knuckled hand. "I'm sorry. That's an awful thing for any child to live through."

He cut her off, anguished. "If only they had never left. Like I did."

"But Grady, you didn't leave your children for the same reason."

Twisting around, he took both her hands in his and held them as if she were a lifeline. "No. But in the end, I am no better than they. Had my parents stayed, had they not changed their plans, they might still be alive. Had I stayed home and not run back to the army, my children would not have been forced to seek me out—and put themselves in danger. I was just as selfish. I've just been luckier, so far."

Star wanted to point out that if he had never left his children, they would never have met, but the implications seemed more than she wanted to examine. "Your actions since the first day we met interest me more. When Emma and Renny needed you the most, you were there for them. Not to mention agreeing to take me and my daughter home with you. Those are not the actions of a selfish man."

"Ah, Star. Don't make me out to be the saint I'm not." Grady ran his thumb over the sensitive flesh of her inner wrist. "Bringing you back to St. Louis with me is purely the act of a selfish man. I need your help with my daughter. And I ignored the fact that in my world there will be many who do not see that all of us are the same underneath. . . . There will be many like the Smiths." He stopped speaking and looked up at her. "I would not think badly of you if you changed your mind. It's not too late. We can leave the boat in the morning and catch up with your family."

Star considered, but then she recalled her reasons for leaving her tribe. Her way of life. For Morning Moon, she could endure the Smiths of the world. The girl would have a life, a childhood without the burden of the Sight. It was the least she could give her daughter.

"A true warrior does not run at the first sign of trouble. He studies his enemy and learns from him. This I will do with the Smiths of the world. I only hope that my presence does not cause you trouble, Grady."

He turned her face toward his, his fingers sliding up her cheek, his touch gentle but firm. "Thank you." His eyes seemed to say so much more. "And I promise not to ever leave you alone again to face what you did tonight."

His protectiveness made an odd sensation flare to life within her, a sensation she knew she must fight. "That is kind of you, Grady, but you cannot follow me around each day. I will learn to handle this on my own."

"All right. But know that you will have help if you ask for it. And if that gleam in my daughter's eye was any indication, she's planning something—though I don't know if it will be helpful. Mrs. Smith had best be on her guard."

Star chuckled and started walking again. She too had seen the warning signs in Renny. That child always acted first and thought later. And though Star had already talked to her—and her own daughter—about letting matters go, part of her wanted to see what the child would do.

Grady offered her his arm. "How about another turn before we retire?"

Resting her fingers lightly on his outstretched arm, Star fell into step beside him. No words were needed as they strolled slowly from one end of the ship to the other. And though she kept telling herself not to see him as the man he was but as the way to give her daughter a better life, Star couldn't help remembering how it had felt to be one with the eagle.

Leo approached the wharf area, driving a wagon. The clip-clop of his horse's hooves striking the cobblestone street sounded loud in the night. He glanced around, then drew his hat low over his head. Stopping the team, he waited. Behind him, he heard a moan. He glanced around, feeling exposed.

When the light from a nearby gas lamp went out, bathing the area in total darkness, Leo lit his pipe and searched among the deep shadows for the man who had arranged to meet him. A deep voice came out at him and he jumped. A bearded man appeared from the gloom.

"You have my cargo?"

"Yes." Leo stepped down and led the man to the

back of the wagon. He lifted the canvas covering. "All there." *This was not a man he wanted to fail.*

The bearded stranger nodded and handed him a pouch of coins. "Good work. Get them unloaded."

Leo did so, transferring the wagon's contents to the ground. The sounds of clinking chains and his own now-full purse made him smile.

Chapter Seven

"Are we nearly home?" Renny asked, standing at the rail.

Grady reached down and tugged a wayward strand of his daughter's hair. It never failed to amaze him how quickly her neatly bound hair became unruly. It was like her personality—one minute subdued, the next wild and untamed. "Soon, my little magpie. Soon. Asking the same question each day won't get us there any quicker."

Renny sighed dramatically. "There's nothing to do."

"You can practice your numbers."

She scowled. "That's not fun."

"Tell you what: After we eat, I'll take you down to groom your horses."

She brightened. "Okay."

Grady met Star's amused gaze. He'd found one way to his daughter's heart, horses. Since that night nearly six weeks earlier when he'd caught her in the captain's cabin and had taken her down to make sure her beloved horses were well cared for, she'd warmed to him a little more. She still rebelled and disobeyed, but the small bit of progress gave him hope that his daughter would eventually accept him fully into her life.

Around them, other passengers strolled along the deck. The *Annabella* had picked up more passengers during their slow trip down the Missouri River.

"You promised to take me riding in the park at home. You won't forget, will you?" She looked worried.

"No, Renny. I won't forget."

"Hear that, Matilda? We get to go riding, just like we did before Papa came."

"I want to see the stores and market too." Morning Moon's face shone with eagerness.

Grady smiled indulgently. "And so you shall, Matilda. There will be many new sights for you and your mother to see. And me as well. I'm sure much has changed since I left." He tweaked her nose and she giggled.

Renny's excitement dimmed. "I wish Emma was with us. She would know everything to show you. I miss her."

Star knelt before Renny, her arms encircling the girl. "Your sister is always with you, Renny. She is in your heart, and in your memories."

Memories. Grady wished he himself had more of Emma. As he watched Star with Renny, he vowed to make sure he and his youngest child had memories—good ones.

"It's not the same as being able to talk to her." Renny sighed, resigned.

Morning Moon spoke up. "You will see her often, though, Renny."

Grady watched worry lines mar Star's forehead at her daughter's calm words. He had the sudden urge to pull her into his arms, to reassure her that all would be well.

"You've seen this, my daughter?"

Star tenderly tucked a strand of black hair behind Morning Moon's ear, her hand lingering, drawing Grady's eyes to her long, slender fingers. They were so gentle, so tender. How would it feel to have Star's hands on him, sliding up his chest, over his shoulders, her arms wrapped around his neck, her fingers threading through his hair as they were now combing through her daughter's?

Giving her a worried look, Morning Moon rested her hands on her mother's shoulders. "Yes. I have seen this."

Grady frowned. How would he see his eldest daughter often when they were so far apart? He didn't understand. And why were this woman and her daughter convinced they could see into the future? It was on the tip of his tongue to ask Morning Moon how she knew what she did, but then, thought better of it. His question would upset Star.

The Indian woman hugged each girl, then stood, and Grady saw she was careful to keep her feelings from the children. But he saw a bleakness lurking in her eyes. The look she sent him was filled with confusion and fear. Changing the subject, he asked Star what she'd like to see or do first.

She smiled, understanding his ploy. "I'd like to see the market too. And your churches."

"I'll ask Charles Manning, my solicitor, where the best clothing stores are."

"Uh-oh," Renny said suddenly.

Grady scanned the deck behind him. "What is it, child?"

Renny unconsciously leaned against him. "Um,

I just remembered that when we left to come find you, we told Uncle Charlie, but we didn't tell Aunt Hester. She's going to be very angry when she finds out Emma isn't coming back." She grinned.

Grady frowned. "Why didn't you tell her you were coming to find me? She might have found someone to go along and protect you!"

Kicking the wooden rail lightly, Renny shrugged. "She kept trying to make us go live with her. She and Emma used to fight when they thought I wasn't around. We thought she would just try to stop us from going."

"Emma fought with Hester Mae?" Grady remembered his difficult sister-in-law only too well. Margaret Mary hadn't trusted the woman to . . . He'd had no idea she had tried to interfere with his daughters. Before he left, he'd made it clear he didn't want her to try and raise them. So when and how had the woman interfered? Neither his sister, Ida, nor Emma had ever said a word about the woman in their letters.

Renny continued. "Aunt Hester said Emma was too young to raise me, that I needed discipline. Before we left St. Louis, they had a big fight after she came to see me for my birthday. Emma made me go up to my room. I snuck down the stairs to lis—" Renny broke off abruptly.

Grady sighed and tugged on a lock of Renny's hair. Amused by his daughter's sudden guilt—as was Star, who smiled—he gave her a stern look. With his attention torn between Renny's story and the sweet curve of Star's mouth, he addressed his wayward daughter. "Continue, child. I already know you're an eavesdropper, so you might as well tell me what you heard."

"Auntie threatened to ask a judge to give her custody of me. She said Emma was allowing me to run wild. Emma told her to leave and never come back." Renny grimaced and looked both sad and confused. "That's when Emma said we were going to go find you."

Grady recalled the desperation in Emma's last letters to him and shame filled him. She'd begged him to come home for Renny's sake, had told him that his younger child needed him. But he'd thought she'd been exaggerating. Why hadn't she told him about Hester Mae and her threat?

Did it matter now? He'd failed Emma. He never should have expected the girl to raise her sister. At the very least, he should have returned home as soon as word reached him about Ida's death. Emma's letter had taken three months to catch up with him, and he'd even missed his sister's funeral. He'd meant to come home after completing his last assignment, but he'd been needed at Fort Pierre.

As usual, he'd put his military career before his children's needs, and it had nearly cost him his daughters' lives. For that, he could never forgive himself.

Furious with his own selfishness and his troublemaking sister-in-law, Grady planned to have a word with her as soon as he arrived in St. Louis. It'd be a cold day in hell before she got her hands on any child of his. Both he and Star reached down to reassure Renny at the same time. Their hands touched. Both looked startled at the unexpected warmth and awareness that came from the innocent contact.

He cleared his throat. "Don't worry about your aunt. I'll deal with her."

"Okay." A muted squealing came from inside Renny's dress. She reached inside its deepest pocket and pulled out two baby rats, who yawned and started washing their faces with tiny paws.

"Anna and Bella are awake. I'd better take them back to the cabin to feed them." She hurried away, trailed by her friend.

Silence fell between the adults after the two girls left. "Looks like I have a lot to make up for," Grady said, staring out toward the riverbank. There, white-topped wagons and clusters of people camped. They were nearing Westport, another jumping-off place for immigrants heading west. Days before, the *Annabella* had passed St. Joseph.

Grady pointed to the crowded bank. "If my daughters had not left St. Louis to come find me, I'd be at Fort Laramie, protecting immigrants like them as they headed west."

Star shuddered. "We were there, at Fort Laramie, last summer." Her voice held traces of fear.

Grady had heard the story. Star's twin brother, White Wolf, and his wife Jessie had suffered an ordeal near the fort with a trio of hardened outlaws. That had been the time Star had helped her family with the Sight.

Though believing in something like seeing into the future went against everything Grady accepted as real, for some reason he couldn't entirely discount Star's strange ability. After all, her visions had been instrumental in saving Emma and Renny's lives. And possibly his own. He recalled that moment of tension when he and his soldiers, out searching for his daughters, had come face-to-face with Striking Thunder and his warriors.

If not for Star, the two sides would surely have battled, each believing the other was responsible for the senseless killings that had been taking place.

Still, like her, he hoped that she wouldn't have any of her strange visions while in St. Louis. He wasn't sure how to handle them. Now that he thought about it, he wasn't sure how to handle her either.

Watching the scenery pass, he drew in a deep breath. They were nearly home and he was eager to reacquaint himself with the city he had once loved. And now he could show it to this beautiful woman at his side.

He looked over at Star, and she turned troubled eyes to him. "I did not know Renny and Emma had an aunt. Would she not be a better choice to help you with Renny?"

Grady shuddered. "No. Don't ever think that. That woman has always been trouble in one form or another. I'd hoped that once she married, she'd settle down and have her own children to keep her busy, but as far as I know, she never did. From what my daughter has said, I guess she's never given up on someday raising her sister's children."

"Why?"

Grady's features turned grim. "Hester Mae was always overly protective of Margaret Mary. She was six years older and thought she knew what was best for everyone. Even when we married, the woman refused to let her sister live her life. From what my wife told me, no one paid the elder girl any attention, so Hester Mae gave all her love and devotion to her young sister. As they got older, Hester Mae took on almost a mothering role. But it became suffocating. Yet Margaret Mary never said anything to her. I think she always felt sorry for her.

"We tried to include Hester Mae in our family events, but when Emma was born, I could tell Hester Mae's visits were becoming too much for my wife. I wanted to limit them, but Margaret Mary wouldn't hear of it. Said Hester Mae had been ignored all her life, and she wouldn't do that to her, too. So we endured her visits and I kept silent. But on the day of Margaret Mary's funeral, I learned just how unstable the woman was. She accused me of killing my wife. She even took Emma from the house."

"How frightening! What happened?"

"Luckily, Hester Mae's husband intervened and brought Emma back. He was the one who suggested I leave the girls with Ida and not Hester Mae when he learned I was leaving." Grady shook his head. "Luckily, I listened to him. Though it appears she still tried to meddle in their affairs."

"She sounds lonely and unhappy," Star mused.

Grady had never considered what made his sister-in-law act the way she did. It was true that Hester Mae had never seemed to be a very happy person. "Whether she's lonely or not does not excuse her behavior."

"No. But it allows us to understand her. She *is* Renny's aunt."

Not wanting to think about Hester Mae until it was necessary, Grady held out his arm. "Let's not talk about her anymore. It should be about time to eat. Are you ready to fetch the girls?"

Star nodded and rested her fingers on his arm.

Grady matched his steps to hers, enjoying her company and the comfortable companionship they'd fallen into. She made no demands on him, yet gave so much. He stole a glance at her, pleased by the changes the last six weeks had wrought. With him watching over her, making sure she ate and rested, the sunken hollows beneath her prominent cheekbones had filled out, and the pinched look around her mouth had faded. Her skin glowed with health, and she'd put on a bit of much-needed weight.

And yet, when he looked deep into her eyes, he

still saw the pain, fear and uncertainty with which she lived. His gaze skimmed down her simple pale yellow day dress. It didn't suit her nearly as well as the powder blue outfit he loved on her, or even the pink one she'd worn yesterday. One of his first orders of business would be to have a new wardrobe made for her. He glanced down at his uniform. It was threadbare in spots, and torn in others. All four of them would need new clothing.

Though his pay from the army hadn't made him a rich man, he hadn't spent much, sending most of it home for his family. And combined with the inheritance from his parents, he had become in his own right somewhat wealthy. He looked forward to spending some of that money on Star.

Out of habit, he peeked down at her feet, disappointed to see the tips of her shoes. But come nightfall, when they once again strolled the deck before bed, he knew she'd be barefoot and several petticoats lighter.

It amused and amazed him how much he looked forward to catching sight of her bare feet, her toes. He had to be crazy to find her shoelessness alluring. But he did. Unbidden came the thought: *If she dispenses with her shoes and petticoats during our evening strolls because she says they're restraining, what other items of clothing beneath her dress are also left in the cabin?*

Grady felt ashamed. Star Dreamer was in his care, under his protection. He had no business thinking of her in such a way. But he couldn't help it. His body wanted her. Her smile. Her touch. Her kiss. Her love.

The shock of that admission sent his heart reeling. Love? Was he ready for that? Even now, after so many years? He didn't know, but he knew one thing: This woman wasn't ready. She had her own demons to fight. Asking for her to love him would be like asking to hold the moon or stars.

The stars? Hell. The only way he'd have her was in his dreams.

Star Dreamer.

She was aptly named, and that only served to remind him of what he couldn't have.

It was their last night aboard the *Annabella*, and Star and Grady returned to the deck after tucking their excited daughters into bed. Come morning, they should see the St. Louis harbor. Star wasn't quite sure what to expect, then. Captain Billaud had informed them that sometimes ships were strung out for miles, waiting for space to dock. Unsure of what the next few days would hold, Star planned to enjoy her time alone with Grady. For the past few weeks, the highlight of her days had been the evenings spent alone with the colonel as they strolled around the deck or sat in chairs and talked. She planned to savor that tonight.

For after tonight, all that might come to an end. Tomorrow, Grady would be back with his people and his way of life. He wouldn't need to spend so much time with her. He'd spend his evenings with his friends or in his den.

The den. She smiled to herself. It seemed fitting for a man's room to be likened to that place where wolves and bears made their homes. Thinking of Renny's wish to have her father invite her into his den to be with him, Star found herself wishing for the same thing. After spending nearly every evening with Grady, she knew she'd miss his easy conversations, his stories of army life and his insight. But she could not expect him to entertain her once they reached his home.

Star gave herself up to the beauty of the night.

She reveled in the warmth of the colonel's arm beneath her fingers.

Suddenly, a soft curse from Grady made her snap to attention. She glanced around, then groaned when she spotted Mrs. Smith making her way toward them, her features twisted with anger and determination. Star peered down quickly, thankful that, even without a couple of the petticoats, the gown still hid the fact that she wore no shoes. She smiled to herself. By wearing a shawl, she'd left some of the buttons of her dress undone, also making do without her corset.

"Sir." Mrs. Smith stopped in front of them, forcing them to stop by planting herself solidly on the deck. She tipped her nose in the air, her voice rising. "I demand you take your daughter in hand!"

Grady positioned himself slightly in front of Star. "What seems to be the problem, Mrs. Smith?"

"*Rats*, sir! Pets indeed. I've never heard of such an outrage. I can't imagine why you encourage such disgusting behavior. She nearly frightened me to death when one of them shot out from beneath her door and into the hallway. That child of yours probably set it loose on purpose."

The woman eyed Star with a large dose of distaste. "She runs wild—like a savage—and I surely put the blame on this woman and her daughter's bad influence. I have heard that this woman is your governess, but you really should hire someone with more experience. Someone who will teach that girl proper manners!"

Star narrowed her eyes. She'd had more than enough of this loud-mouthed, rude, obnoxious woman, and she was going to do something about it. The gleam in Grady's eyes stopped her. What was he going to say?

"Mrs. Smith, may I suggest you worry about your

own children's lack of manners. The next time your son tries to accost a woman, he might not get off so easily. The newspapers might hear of it, ruining a certain young man's name and respectability."

Mrs. Smith paled, confirming that she knew of her son's run-in with Grady and Zeke. "Be warned; I plan to make sure my acquaintances in St. Louis are aware of your son's lack of respect for women." Grady then named off several families that Star didn't recognize but assumed were influential.

Star watched the woman back away, then turn and hurry off.

Grady folded his arms across his chest. "She won't bother us again." He looked smug. "Are you ready to turn in? Tomorrow will be a big day."

"I—"

The sound of a loud blast coming from another steamer leaving St. Louis, pulling alongside them as it turned to head south, cut her off. She waited for it to pass before continuing. The boat was old and decrepit looking, and a lot smaller than the one they were on. It was another cargo boat. The white paint had faded to gray and in the growing dusk, it reminded her of a shadow passing through the night.

Staring at the boat, a sudden chill swept through her, tugging at her mind and holding her in its cold, clammy grip. Her vision went black, but no images formed. There was nothing. Then she felt despair— and it was endless. There was also biting cold, and death.

From the foggy recesses of her mind, she heard Grady calling her name. At last, the gray steamer had passed them, and Star's sight returned. Consciousness returned with a suddenness that left her trembling. Grady wrapped his arm around her, and she sagged against him, grateful for the support and warmth.

"What's wrong?"

Star tucked her arms between her body and his and closed her eyes. A trickle of tears escaped. "Death," she whispered, frightened by the intensity of the vision. Since boarding the *Annabella*, she hadn't had a single vision and had hoped they were truly gone. She shook, trying to shut out the cold, desolate feelings she'd just encountered. It wasn't just death. It had been more—much more.

"Where?" Grady held her tightly.

Star couldn't bear to look upon it again. "On that steamboat."

"You had a vision?"

"I felt . . . something. Something terrible." She didn't mention that everything had gone black for a moment.

Grady stroked her hair, his lips touching her forehead. "Bodies of the deceased are oftentimes transported back to relatives for burial. You're so sensitive, that's surely what you felt. Let me take you to your cabin."

Star didn't want to go below. She couldn't face the confines of her small room, especially now. She longed to believe Grady's explanation, but . . . "No. I can't. Not yet. I . . ."

Grady stroked her hair. Star pressed her cheek against his chest. The strong rhythm of his heart calmed her. When her trembling stopped, she lifted her head to thank him. Her mouth opened, but his gaze left her unable to speak. What had started off as a comforting embrace suddenly turned intimate. Her gaze devoured his; her breasts, pressed flat against the hard wall of his chest, tingled with awareness.

"Grady." Her surroundings faded. Nothing mattered right then except the blanket of desire co-cooning them from the rest of the world.

His head lowered. Her heart pounded, matching his. His lips, smooth, soft, and warm brushed over hers, like a whisper of wind caressing her skin. His tenderness ignited delicious swirls of desire within her.

Then he pulled back. For a long moment, they stared at one another. His eyes, were dark with passion.

Her mind screamed that this was not wise, yet she would not listen. She gave herself to the moment. She slid her hands up the hard contours of his chest and stared at his mouth, her tongue slipping out to moisten lips gone suddenly dry.

As sweet as a summer breeze, Grady's breath teased hers, tormented her until his lips parted hers in a soul-searing kiss that was at the same time as tender as a mother's caress. Star quivered at the bold taste of his mouth, aching for more. Lifting herself up on tiptoe, she wrapped her arms tightly around his neck, pulling herself harder against him in her need for more.

Grady's control shattered when he felt her desperate need that matched his own. There was no hesitancy or shyness on her part, only need. A deep, burning desire flowing from her to him. His mouth possessed hers, tasted what she so sweetly offered. Her moan urged him to deepen the kiss. At once he plunged inside, unable to hold himself back. The hunger of a starving man consumed him, and nothing mattered except this kiss, this woman and the rising passion surrounding them.

Pain and pleasure burst through him simultaneously, causing his blood to pump furiously and fill the empty places deep in his soul. He needed her, as much as he needed air to breathe and food to eat. Her fingers tangled in the hair at the nape of his neck and tugged. His own hands went up to the back of her head and her hair cascaded over them. His desire grew. The blood pumping through him gathered and pulsed in time to the massage of Star's fingers in his hair.

Her tongue boldly entered his mouth. His hands stilled on either side of her face, silently begging her to continue her explorations, before sliding down her back to rest along the gentle curve of her spine.

She moaned again, collapsing into him and bestirring him from the drugging kiss. Breathing hard, he stole one final taste, then released her, breaking off the kiss. He stared down at her. Gone was the pain and fear that moments ago he had been determined to chase from her. Desire and need had replaced her haunted look.

Threading his fingers through the hair at the back of her neck, Grady bent his head nearer. He hadn't meant to kiss her just then, but something had exploded between them. He rested his forehead against hers. What had he done? He'd promised to protect her, to keep her safe. Only now did he realize that he might very well be her biggest danger. "I apologize, Star. My behavior was improper."

He felt a tremor run through her, and she touched her own lips briefly before she clasped her hands in front of her. She pulled away.

"It was as much my fault as yours. I needed you to touch me. I wanted it." She was giving him an excuse, and while her eyes begged him to accept it, to believe it, he couldn't use her state of mind to justify his own lack of control or judgment. He'd wanted her. For weeks, he'd thought about nothing but kissing her. Her and no one else.

Loneliness hadn't caused this. He'd been alone many years, and not once had he felt this driving need to be with or to touch someone. He hadn't yearned for soft hands in his hair, or a gentle mouth moving beneath his. In nine years he hadn't needed to kiss a woman like this, as if his life depended on it. And to feel all this now, this strongly, scared him. He'd loved once, and lost the woman of his heart.

He tried to pull forth the familiar sense of guilt that always came when he looked at an attractive woman; that sense of being unfaithful to his dead wife had always prevented him from pursuing another woman. Until now. This time, it did not come.

This time, there was only Star and, because of her, a deep, raging need for fulfillment. Being alone no longer appealed. He was hollow inside, a shell of the man he once was—and it was clear. He yearned to share life, love and laughter with this woman who made him feel complete. He wanted it all—and it was more than Star could give him.

He trailed the back of each hand down her cheeks. His hands fell to his side and he backed away. Could he love again? Was it possible after all these years, that he'd finally healed? He didn't know.

One thing *was* clear though; before he went any further, he had to be sure he could survive the debilitating grief of loss. Right now, he wasn't sure he could. Until he was, he had to keep his distance.

"I have to go below and make sure everything is ready for disembarking in the morning." And like the coward his sister had once accused him of being, Grady ran.

"See that? I told you they liked each other," Renny gloated from her hiding place on deck.

Tucked into the small cubby beside her, Morning Moon whispered, "But your father left. I don't think they liked kissing each other."

Renny wiggled. "But they have to like it. If my father falls in love with your mother, they'll get married. Then you'll be my sister for real. And your mother would be my mother."

Morning Moon tilted her head, whispering, "And your father would be my father."

Renny grimaced. "Yeah, I guess he would. Too bad for you."

"Your father is very nice, Renny."

"Wait till he yells at *you*. Come on, we'd better get back to our room before your mom does."

Creeping out, Renny stood, then nearly screamed in fright. Zac stepped out of the shadows to block her path, crossing his arms across his massive chest. "Lose somethin', Miss Renny?"

With her heart thudding in her chest and her blood pounding in her ears, Renny glanced around frantically. She'd forgotten about her father's friends wandering around. If Zac told her father she'd left the cabin—disobeying again—he'd probably yell at her and ban her from the horses again. "Oh. Uh, Zac, we were just going to bed. Morn—ah, Matilda was just worried about her mother being up here all alone."

Beside her, Morning Moon looked puzzled. "That's not—" She broke off with a squeal of pain as Renny stepped on her toes.

"Well, now, Miss Renny, it looks like she's fine."

"Yep, Star is fine. We're fine. You're fine. So Matilda and I'll just head back to bed." She backed away. As one, the two girls turned and ran for their cabin.

Renny wasn't sure, but she thought Zac's soft laughter followed.

Chapter Eight

According to Grady, St. Louis merchants controlled the Missouri River trade in the mid-Mississippi valley. Steamboats crowded the harbor, some docked, coming in or heading out. Black smoke from countless smokestacks left a gray haze over the city. Rows of warehouses and wholesale establishments lined the streets near the busy levee, while hotels and shops thrived in the retail business district. In the concentrated industry sections, factory chimneys proudly spewed smoke, signaling employment and prosperity. Beyond stretched solidly built neighborhoods.

The pulse and power of the city thrilled Star as much as it frightened her. To her inexperienced eye, the whole area seemed a mass of confusion. Aside from steamboats docking and others waiting, there were hundreds of drays, wagons and carriages rushing along at all speeds. She turned in a slow circle. As she struggled to take it all in, her breathing quickened. From the busy harbor with boats coming and going to the wharf teaming with activity, she could only stare in stunned disbelief. She wiped her forehead with her sleeve, forgetting about the white handkerchief in her reticule. The hot, muggy weather that had followed them down the Missouri warned of summer's approach.

But the heat didn't seem to bother those around her. Men of all colors, sizes and shapes strode from ship to wharf, unloading or loading cargo, their bodies gleaming with sweat. Around them, finely dressed passengers came and went, some pushing and shoving while others strolled lazily about, as if they had all the time in the world. Many spoke languages she didn't understand and wore clothes illustrating the diverse cultures and religions Captain Billaud had spoken of during their evening meals.

Star studied the women. Some wore fine gowns such as her own, yet others, such as the group of women she saw huddled between two nearby buildings, were clothed in dirty rags. Her gaze sought out the men, then. They were garbed in hats, coats and pristine shirts. The gentlemen carried walking sticks and contrasted drastically with the workers. She could tell them apart, for the latter dressed in baggy trousers, ripped shirts and shoes with flapping soles.

The rich and the poor. The concept confused her, though this was obviously what Grady had talked about when discussing the pursuit of wealth. It was wholly strange to her, as her people all dressed the same. If her family had more furs or hides or food than they needed, they shared with those who did not. No one went without food or decent clothing. Once more, she turned in a slow circle and took it all in: people, buildings, boats, horses, carriages.

Across a street made of rounded stone, people came and went from warehouse buildings the size of which Star couldn't fathom. A boy ran past, laughing gleefully. Close behind, four others gave chase, their faces red with anger, their fists bunched and waving. A horse pulling a black carriage clattered past. Inside, a woman and man sat, staring blankly, oblivious to the commotion outside.

"Oh, my. Oh, my." Star pressed a hand to her fluttering stomach and glanced down at her daughter. Morning Moon's eyes were wide.

"What's wrong, Star?" Renny asked, hopping from one foot to the other.

"I never imagined." Her voice trembled.

Renny glanced around, puzzled. "Imagined what?"

Star held her hands out helplessly. "Everything. All this."

Grady joined them, putting a reassuring arm around Star's shoulders. "Remember, child, Star and Matilda have never seen any of this. Think how you felt when you first arrived in their village."

Her bluish gray eyes widened. "I was scared. It was so different." She paused, then gave her father a meaningful look. "But Night Hunter and his family were nice to me, so I got used to it. Then Striking Thunder found me—and he gave me horses so I wouldn't miss Emma so much." She frowned, her eyes narrowing, as if she were trying to view it from their guests' perspective. "I guess I'm just used to this. You'll get used to it, won't you, Star?"

Star laughed somewhat nervously. "It might take me a while." Her gaze sought something familiar—green trees, grass, a patch of land not crowded, anything. Her eyes could find no such thing. "This is so . . ." Words failed her.

"Citylike," Grady supplied, his lips twitching with humor.

Star could only nod.

"Are you scared, Matilda?" Renny took her friend's hand.

Morning Moon's eyes shone with the same sense of wonder, but there was an added gleam of excitement. She bounced from one foot to the other and giggled with an eight-year-old's easy acceptance of change. "No. But I would not want to have to find my way alone to your house. When do we go? I want to see your bedroom of pink and white."

Renny wrinkled her nose and eyed her father. "I hate pink and white. I want my room to be blue or green."

"Let's get home and settled first, child. Then we'll see about redecorating." He turned to Morning Moon. "And as for your question, we'll be ready as soon as Charles Manning arrives with a carriage. He's what we call a lawyer. He has managed my property for me while I've been away." He turned back to Renny.

Renny gave him a blank look. "Where are my horses?"

Grady turned his daughter to face the scouts. The three brothers were holding the reins to the horses they'd brought with them—both Renny's and Grady's. The little girl opened her mouth, but her father stopped her. "Come on. I'll take you over there. You might as well make yourself useful and hold the reins so Zac and Zeb can take care of unloading the rest of our luggage."

Star sat on one of the trunks, content to observe. To her left, a man carrying a large wooden crate on his shoulder brushed past. As he stubbed his toe on a loose stone, he swore, his curse filling the air as the crate crashed onto the ground. It broke open, and several items flew out and shattered into tiny fragments.

"You clumsy oaf!" A well-dressed gentleman swore as he salvaged what he could of his shipment and checked the rest. "Lucky for you, only two vases broke. Now get this into the warehouse. And be careful." The man's boots crunched on the pearl and blue bits of colored glass.

He tipped his hat to her. "Sorry, ma'am—" His voice broke off when he noted the color of her skin and the darkness of her eyes. His expression went from polite indifference to something much warmer—and most unwelcome. It was the look she'd encountered on board the *Annabella* with Bobby Smith. Star met the man's pale blue eyes proudly, ignoring the chill that ran up her spine. At last, he stalked away, and she sighed with relief. She was determined not to let him ruin her new beginning.

Standing, she paced, careful to avoid the broken glass scattered on the ground. Glancing down, she saw a much larger piece wedged between two trunks. The shade of blue reminded her of the stranger's eyes. Bending down, she picked up the palm-sized fragment, curious about a red design that was glazed onto the side.

Grady's voice caught her attention and she turned. "Charles should be here soon. I wired him from St. Joe that we were arriving. I hope he had a chance to see to the opening and airing of my house."

Star dropped the cool piece of pottery into her reticule, wondering why all of a sudden she felt chilled. Star smiled at Grady, her eyes tracking the activity around them. "I'm sure it will be fine—"

A sudden high-pitched scream rent the air.

Whipping around, her heart in her throat, Star spotted a woman fighting three rough-looking men across the street between two warehouses. As she watched, the woman was slammed against the building. The girl's cries faded.

Without thinking, Star picked up her skirts and bolted across the street, dodging between two teams of horses.

"Star, wait!" Grady called. "Come back!"

But Star rushed forward without thinking. "Stop. Do not hit her again!" Her anger flowed through her, making her fearless. Positioning her body in front of the woman slumped against the brick building, she glared at the three men.

One of them—short, wiry and with a scar marring his face from the edge of his nose to his jaw—stepped close to her. He rubbed his hands together. "Well, what have we here? Looks like we's in luck today, boys. Not one woman for the boss, but two."

The other two took up positions on either side of Star, who crouched before the moaning girl. She palmed the knife she kept strapped to the inside of her calf. Ever since her encounter with Bobby, she'd made sure she carried it.

"Stay back!" she warned, moving into the defensive crouch her father and brother had taught her.

The short man moved forward, tossing his knife from one hand to the other. "Come 'ere and fight me, pretty baby." With a smile, he put his knife away and held out his hands. "Look, no weapon. Just you and me. I like a woman with spirit." The others jeered and urged him on. Star braced herself for his lunge.

Seeing the spot Star was in, Grady hurried over. "Touch her and you're a dead man," he warned coldly, drawing a revolver and holding it steady,

"Move away." His heart pounded, and blood roared in his ears. The other two ruffians still had their knives drawn. If they both lunged at Star, she wouldn't be able to fend them off. Worse, he might accidentally hit Star if he tried to hit them.

The leader drew his knife again. "Looks like we have company, boys." He motioned for the other two to flank him. "This don't concern you, *sir*." He spat at Grady's feet, sneering at his uniform.

"Oh, but it does. That woman is in my employ and under my protection."

"Yeah, but the blackie ain't. She belongs to our boss. Tell yer *woman* to quit interferin' lessen she gits herself hurt."

Behind Star, the sobbing woman struggled to sit. Suddenly, the woman lifted her head and cried out, "*Non!* I am free. These men kidnapped me and my family. Please, *monsieur*, do not let them take me. They sold my husband and son and will sell me." She whimpered, frightened. "I am a *free* woman," she repeated, her French accent musical, despite her fear.

Grady lifted a brow. Her speech was not that of a field slave; it was educated, refined. He addressed the leader of the ruffians. "You kidnapped a free woman?"

"She ain't free." The scarred man took a step back, toward Star, but she shifted her position, her knife hand steady. The look of deadly intent in her eyes made them nearly black. He stopped. "Ya can't believe a nigger. She's a runaway."

"You lie," the woman said.

Grady frowned. If indeed the young woman had run away, he could not stop these men. His gut clenched at the thought of turning this frightened woman over to this group of villains. "Can you prove you are free? Do you have papers?"

The woman shook her head, then winced and put her hand to her temple. "*Non*. When we were taken, our papers were stolen from us."

"Don't ya believe her! She can't prove nothin'."

Grady kept an eye on the belligerent leader, who suddenly seemed very nervous, as if he had something to hide. "Who was your master?"

"Monsieur Gregoire. I was the nanny to his daughters until they married. He died two months ago, and we were given our freedom and money to start a new life. That too was stolen." Her voice turned bitter.

The three men looked nervously at the gun in Grady's hands. "Look, we have our job to do. We'll just take her and go. We don't want no trouble."

A sudden voice sounded behind them. "On the contrary, gentlemen. If this young woman is telling the truth, there will be proof. I knew Mr. Gregoire. It should be easy enough to verify her story. All we have to do is obtain a copy of his will and talk with his children." The voice paused, ominously. "And if she is indeed free, then there will certainly be trouble—for you."

Grady heaved a sigh of relief at the voice. It was that of Charles Manning. Behind the lawyer, another man—some concerned citizen—had also stepped into the alley. A small pearl-handled pistol was in his hand. Feeling encouraged, Grady spun and smiled coldly at the scarred leader of the woman's attackers. "Shall we let the law decide this?"

Outnumbered, and suddenly looking unsure of themselves, the three men backed down the alley, then turned tail and ran. When they were gone, Grady hurried to Star's side. His hands shook as he pulled her up. "Are you all right?"

Star nodded. "I'm fine, but—"

Grady, still shaking from the danger she'd put herself in, exploded. "Are you crazy? You could have been hurt! What made you do such a foolish thing?"

At his words, Star narrowed her eyes. "You would have me turn my back on this poor woman? Did you not see what those men were doing?"

"You didn't have to rush over here and put yourself in danger! Damn it, Star, this is the city." He stopped, realizing that where she came from, violence was a part of everyday life. She was more adept at handling it than most. He dropped his hands. "You *scared* me."

She rested her head on his arm. "For that, I am sorry. In the future, I shall try to warn you before I rush to someone's rescue. Can we get a clean cloth? This poor woman is bleeding."

Knowing this was not the the time to impress upon Star the danger of the city, Grady handed her a clean handkerchief. Then, ascertaining that the woman's wounds were not life-threatening, he rejoined Charles who was talking to the citizen who had appeared with the pistol.

"Name's Todd Langley," the man said, thrusting his hand forward.

Grady shook it. "Grady O'Brien." He jerked his head toward Charles. "This is my attorney, Charles Manning. Thanks for the help."

Todd and Charles shook hands. "My pleasure." Todd swung his hands behind his back. "Bad business this. It's always awful to see ruffians beating on women, no matter what color. You folks just arrive?"

"Yes." Grady nodded, then turned to Star. He wasn't sure he liked this man. "Ready to go?"

She glanced over at him. "We can't leave her here."

Langley stepped forward. "Seeing as you're new in town, I can take her to see Doctor Williams. He's not far from here."

"That's kind of you," Star began, "but I'd like for her to come home with us. She'll need a place to stay." Her gaze begged Grady to give his permission.

Grady glanced at the battered black woman. "What is your name?"

"Hattie, monsieur." She met his gaze without flinching.

"Hattie, are you telling the truth?"

"Yes, sir. My husband, my son and I were set free."

"That should be easy to verify," Manning volunteered. "I can check that out. It looks like a good thing I was here."

Grady nodded. "All right, Charles." He turned to where Langley stood. "Thank you for your offer, but it looks like we can handle it from here."

The other man nodded and then turned to head off down the walk. "Y'all take care now." Giving him a wave, Grady, Star and Charles helped Hattie over to where Zac was watching over Renny and Morning Moon. The luggage was piled nearby.

Star's daughter ran forward, her long black hair streaming out behind her. "You are unhurt?"

"I am fine, my daughter."

"You sure were brave, Star." Renny's eyes were round with awe.

Grady cuffed Renny gently. "She was foolish," he said, but his voice dropped an octave, and he couldn't hide the pride leaking through. "Brave, but foolish." With that, he strode off and oversaw the loading of their possessions.

*   *   *

During the drive from the wharf, Star tended the deep gash on Hattie's forehead as best she could. When the coach stopped, she glanced out the window. They were stopped in front of a large white house.

Renny bounced off the seat. "We're home, Star. This is where we live." She jumped from the coach. "Come on, Matilda." They ran to the house. The front doors opened and a servant waited on the top step.

Grady jumped down. He reached in and held out his hand for Star.

Star gulped and stared at the enormous white house with green trim. Four round columns as wide as tree trunks framed the wide front door. Her awed gaze roamed over a sloping roofline, windows of several different sizes and shapes, sharp angles, intricate curves and details carved into wood unlike anything she'd ever seen. "This is where you live?" The sizes of the buildings they'd passed since leaving the wharf should have warned her, but nothing could have prepared her for this grandeur. Compared to Wolf's cabin, this was unimaginable. Her head twisted from side to side as she tried to absorb her surroundings.

She stepped down onto a street wide enough for at least four or five coaches abreast of one another. Between her and the house, a neatly tended lawn edged with spring blooms, full shrubs and tall trees gave the front of the house a somewhat pastoral setting. But the house itself defied all description. Star tipped her head back, trying to take it all in at once. Glass panes set in sharp-angled windows on either side of the house caught and reflected the midmorning sunlight.

Suddenly, a door onto a landing framed by black

wrought iron, high above the front door swung open. Renny and Morning Moon stepped out. Renny leaned over the edge, but Morning Moon stayed back. "Come on, Star! Come see my room."

Morning Moon waved from her safe distance. "*Ina!* You must come see. It is pink. Lots of pink. And Weshawee's sleeping room is as big as she said. All our family could fit inside of it."

"I'll see Hattie settled," Charles said, gently leading the woman toward the house.

Grady offered Star Dreamer his arm. "Welcome to my home, Star." Behind them, Zeke and his brothers arrived in the wagon bearing a mound of trunks and their horses. "Shall we?"

Star nodded and allowed Grady to lead her up steep steps to where the servant stood, stiff and silent in a dark blue and white shirt. His matching jacket had shiny gold buttons and trim.

"I am Jeffers, your footman," he introduced himself to Grady. "Mr. Manning hired me, sir."

"Thank you, Jeffers. Ask the maid he has hired to bring tea and refreshment to the drawing room."

"Right away, sir."

Star listened to the exchange with half an ear. Eager to see the inside of the house, she stepped inside—and into another world. Her mouth gaped open.

The foyer was huge. A staircase curved upward before her, and as she looked about she found four tall doors to her left, two to her right and another set in the back wall.

A small round table stood to her right, holding a huge vase of flowers. Other arrangements sat on a long, narrow table leaning against the staircase. Everywhere she looked, there was furniture. Some of the pieces had white cloths atop them, others a thin white stone fitted to the table shape. On every surface, objects were arranged.

Everything was as Renny and Emma had described. Star bent down to touch the dark, gleaming floor. It felt cool to her fingers. Standing, she grazed the smooth walls with her gloved fingers. From the waist down, the walls were brown. Above, they'd been painted a creamy white. A wide band of a darker brown, painted in an intricate design over the pale wall, separated the two. Along the ceiling and floor, polished wood added warmth to the room's decor.

"I never imagined," she said, turning to Grady. "I feel so small and insignificant standing here." She glanced up at the ceiling high above her, awed by the chandelier and the ornate molding.

"This is the foyer." Grady smiled, hanging his hat on a brass hook set into a tall wooden object to their left. "I think it is meant to make guests feel that way."

Between two doors to her left, Star spotted a large piece of furniture. It had a mirror in the center and tiny shelves on either side. She glanced in the mirror and shook her head. "Your people must really like to study their images," she said.

Her cabin aboard the *Annabella* had boasted a mirror, as had the dining room and the grand salon. Since she'd never been terribly concerned with how she looked before, it took her by surprise to see her reflection so often.

Beside her, Grady's laughter rang out. In the glass wide eyes—her own—stared back at her. She grinned and spun around. It was fun to study one's own image, she admitted, but one should not do so for too long. She swept her gaze around the room once more. More objects of various size and color sat on nearby shelves and begged to be picked up and examined. But she would do that later.

The sound of pounding feet and calls for her to hurry warned of the girls' impatience. Grady gripped her elbow. "Come on. Let's go upstairs. Then I'll show you the rest of the house."

Taking a deep breath, Star placed one hand on Grady's arm and the other on the smooth wood of the banister and climbed. Richly detailed carpeting made their steps silent. At the top of the stairs, before the landing and after, two vases nearly as tall as children sat in the curved alcoves.

To her surprise, although Grady had predicted it, as soon as they left the landing and could no longer see below, the house became less ornate. The dark, decorated band along the wall turned to a plain solid color and the carpet was one of blue hemp.

Star found herself oddly pleased by that.

Grady wandered through the downstairs after leaving Star in the kitchen with Thomas, the cook, three young maids, Jeffers and Hattie. Of all the rooms he'd shown her, the kitchen fascinated her the most. She'd looked in every drawer, cupboard and bin at least twice, exclaiming at the amount of food to be found. She'd even opened the oven doors and made the cook, a nephew of Charles's own, explain how the stove worked.

Of Renny and Morning Moon, Grady hadn't seen either little girl in an hour. They were still in their bedroom.

Zeb, Zeke and Zac were out in the carriage house, settling in the horses and seeing to the condition of his carriage and wagons.

"Ah, peace and quiet." He sighed, eager for some time to sit and absorb the fact that he was home at last.

Home. His home. Passing a closed door down the hall from the den, he hesitated. Then, slowly, he opened it. From the doorway, his gaze followed a beam of sunlight streaming inside from a tall window down to the rug before the fireplace.

He swallowed hard, suddenly besieged with memories. He recalled cradling his wife in his arms as they sat before a roaring fire. She'd always hated the use of wood stoves; she loved to watch the flames lick at the logs of wood in a fireplace. She'd loved it so much, she'd even painted the fire screen that still sat before the hearth.

This had been her sitting room, the place where she spent most of her time—sewing or entertaining her closest friends. Off to the right, a sliding wooden partition separated this room from the den. Taking a deep breath, his gaze went to the painting above the marble mantel.

"Margaret Mary," he whispered, staring up into the misty-green eyes. The portrait captured their love, laughter and mischief. Examining it, Grady saw the similarity between Renny and her mother. Now, from across the room, the woman in the painting smiled tenderly down on him.

Nine years had passed since he had set foot in this room, laid eyes on her beauty, but it still felt like yesterday. The last time had been just before he'd fled, and he'd come inside to beg her to forgive him for leaving their daughters behind.

He entered and waited for the pain, the raw welling of grief, the despair to overwhelm him. Sadness and regret filled him, for what had been denied them both, but nothing more. He held his breath and waited. The terrible pain didn't come.

Shocked and a bit shaken, he realized that his devastating pain was gone. Grief had been a part of him for so long, he wasn't sure how to react without it. Had something so simple as coming home taken the pain away? No. With sudden insight, he realized that things had changed long before he'd stepped back into his home.

But when? When had he ceased to feel the anger, resentment and pain that simply thinking about Margaret Mary used to bring forth?

Since meeting Star.

The Indian beauty's image glided across his mind. Then he saw both women, compared them. Each was so different, each had so much to offer. Star's petite frame, sad smile, haunted eyes and quiet nature contrasted sharply with Margaret Mary's larger-than-life persona. Maggie had boasted love of life, easy laughter and a wonderful way of filling a room—and the hearts of all those around her—with music and laughter. But Star did that for him.

Grady tensed, expecting a return of the guilt, of the feeling that he was betraying his deceased wife's memory by bringing another woman into her house. Indeed, something in his heart moved, but not what he expected. A wall crumbled, releasing long-held feelings, allowing fresh air to circulate in his soul. He felt light, free. And suddenly unsure of himself.

Stunned by his revelations, he backed away. He'd loved Margaret Mary. Theirs had been a once-in-a-lifetime love. He'd loved her during the years of their marriage and for nine years following her death. He'd vowed on her grave that if he couldn't have her, he'd have no one.

But had things change?

Though he'd known he was attracted to Star, that something about her drew him, he'd been sure that once he stood here, in this very spot, it would fade before the love and happiness he'd known with

Thrill to the most sensual, adventure-filled Historical Romances on the market today…

FROM 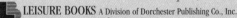 LEISURE BOOKS

As a home subscriber to the Leisure Historical Romance Book Club, you'll enjoy the best in today's BRAND-NEW Historical Romance fiction. For over twenty-five years, Leisure Books has brought you the award-winning, high-quality authors you know and love to read. Each Leisure Historical Romance will sweep you away to a world of high adventure…and intimate romance. Discover for yourself all the passion and excitement millions of readers thrill to each and every month.

SAVE AT LEAST *$5.00* EACH TIME YOU BUY!

Each month, the Leisure Historical Romance Book Club brings you four brand-new titles from Leisure Books, America's foremost publisher of Historical Romances. EACH PACKAGE WILL SAVE YOU AT LEAST $5.00 FROM THE BOOKSTORE PRICE! And you'll never miss a new title with our convenient home delivery service.

Here's how we do it. Each package will carry a 10-DAY EXAMINATION privilege. At the end of that time, if you decide to keep your books, simply pay the low invoice price of $16.96 ($17.75 US in Canada), no shipping or handling charges added*. HOME DELIVERY IS ALWAYS FREE*. With today's top Historical Romance novels selling for $5.99 and higher, our price SAVES YOU AT LEAST $5.00 with each shipment.

AND YOUR FIRST FOUR-BOOK SHIPMENT IS TOTALLY FREE!*

IT'S A BARGAIN YOU CAN'T BEAT! A Super $21.96 Value!

LEISURE BOOKS A Division of Dorchester Publishing Co., Inc.

GET YOUR 4 FREE* BOOKS NOW— A $21.96 VALUE!

Mail the Free* Book Certificate Today!

Get Four Books Totally
F R E E* —
A $21.96 Value!

(Tear Here and Mail Your FREE* Book Card Today!)

PLEASE RUSH
MY FOUR FREE*
BOOKS TO ME
RIGHT AWAY!

Leisure Historical Romance Book Club
P.O. Box 6613
Edison, NJ 08818-6613

AFFIX
STAMP
HERE

Margaret Mary. But it hadn't. Instead, what he'd felt for his wife had faded. He had the sudden urge to weep, but he fought it off.

Was he falling in love with Star? *No!* His mind rejected it even as his heart lifted at the thought. It was impossible.

But you kissed her. You enjoyed it. You wanted more, he accused himself.

The taunting voice in his head betrayed him, brought forth memories of their kiss, the feel of her lips moving beneath his, the sweet taste of her on his tongue. An intense hunger struck, leaving him shaken, weak. Passion had flared between them, but they had restrained it. How would it be if they both gave that passion free rein?

Incredible. Wild. Consuming.

"No. It was just a kiss," he whispered. *Just a kiss.* It had been a temptation brought on by the romantic setting; stars, water and the gentle rocking motion of the deck beneath their feet, all had contributed. And her beauty had been irresistible.

"It was nothing more," he said again, louder this time. But the volume couldn't erase the truth. Star was a gentle woman who saw with more than her eyes. Her wisdom and insight combined with her humor and bold outlook on life had already endeared her to him . . . or more.

Like the coward he was, he ran—back to his den, away from the emotional onslaught. There, in his domain, he would rebuild his barriers.

As he shut himself inside, he ran for the cabinet. *Ah, thank you, Charles!* The man had kept him stocked. Pouring an inch of brandy into a snifter, he took a sip.

Zeke's voice drew him from his worried contemplations. "Ma'am, you can't just barge in on the colonel!"

161

The door burst open with the huge scout falling into the room. A tall, thin, determined woman had shoved past him as if he were no more than an annoying gnat.

"Grady! I didn't believe it when Cook said she'd heard you were back."

"I tried to stop her, sir." Zeke eyed Hester Mae with a baleful glare.

Hester Mae hurried toward Grady, her arms outstretched as if to embrace him in greeting. He moved behind his desk and sat. "Good afternoon, Hester Mae. I'll handle it from here, Zeke." Grady gave the man a motion of dismissal.

He wasn't up to dealing with his unwanted visitor, yet he had no choice.

Hester Mae moved closer to his desk. "Why didn't you send word of your arrival? I could have met you, and seen to your house." Her shrill voice held a note of censure.

"My solicitor saw to it." He poured another glass of brandy and indicated the chair positioned to one side of the desk.

Hester Mae sat on the edge of the chair, but as the sound of running feet pattered above her head, she jumped up and clapped her hands to her scant bosom. "Ah," she cried, "my nieces have returned! You found them!" She turned, watching the door.

"Do forgive me, Grady. I had no idea they'd run off so foolishly. Had I known, I'd have stopped them, of course; of that you can be sure. I do hope you scolded Emma for her impetuous behavior." She stopped to draw in a breath of air.

Grady steepled his fingers, recalling just why Emma had left the way she had. "Emma did what she thought was right. I understand that you were threatening to take Renny from her."

Hester Mae whirled around, her face turning an

unbecoming shade of red. "I was trying to do what was best for the child. Emma was too young to handle Renny. You weren't here. Someone had to take care of matters."

"You never wrote me."

"You made it clear that you wanted nothing to do with your daughters."

The truth stung, and it silenced him for a moment.

"You *knew* how much I wanted to raise them, yet you denied me. None of this would have happened if you'd just let them live with me."

"None of this would have happened had I remained home to do my parental duties," Grady said softly.

Hester Mae dismissively waved a gloved hand at him. "No one blamed you, Grady, dear. Why, even after all these years, it's difficult for *me* to come here." She wiped her eyes with a plain white handkerchief. "I still miss Margaret. Not a day goes by where I don't think of her. And to know that her two precious daughters had run off into needless danger near broke my heart. If anything had happened to them—"

Leaning back in his chair, Grady stared into his brandy. He swirled the caramel-colored liquid, then took a sip. "I accept the blame. I should never have left, but the past is over and done with. I am here now."

"Of course, Grady dear. Of course you are." Composed now, she approached him. "And now that you no longer have your sister to oversee your household, I shall be more than happy to assist. I will see to the hiring of your staff and come each day to make sure your household is run smoothly. And of course, I'll be here to help both Emma and Renny while you go about your business. In fact, we should talk about Emma—and the need to find her a husband."

Grady stood and rested his fingertips on the smooth surface of his wooden desk. "I won't require your assistance, Hester Mae. Everything has been taken care of." Well, he still had to hire a housekeeper and butler yet, but he could manage that. Charles had already seen to the cook, a footman and three maids.

Affronted, his sister-in-law drew back. "Well, if you insist. But about the girls. Renny will need a governess, and—"

Grady held up his hand, its unspoken order silencing the woman. Being blunt would be the quickest way to end Hester Mae's visit. "Emma did not return with me. She has recently married. As for Renny, I've already hired a companion for her. So you can rest assured, everything is taken care of here, Hester Mae. Thank you for your consideration, but it is unnecessary. Now, it's been a long day—"

Hester Mae gaped at him. "Emma married? How? To whom—"

"Papa, come see our room!" Renny and Morning Moon suddenly burst into the den. Grady's daughter skidded across the polished wooden floor and careened into her aunt.

"Whoops, sorry." She stepped back, saw who the visitor was, then glanced sideways at her father. "Uh-oh. Told you so."

Hester Mae's eyes were riveted on her niece. She went down on her knees. "You are so like your mother, Ranait. How about a hug for your aunt?"

The little girl moved tentatively forward and allowed her aunt to hug her. The woman gushed. "I'm so glad you are back safely. I was *so* worried.

You must come visit and tell me everything that happened."

Renny smiled hesitantly, glancing from her aunt to her father. Grady kept silent, unwilling to expose the child to his memory of past difficulties with his sister-in-law. When he saw Renny reach into her pocket he came around the desk, quickly guessing her intentions. "Renny, I don't think—"

He was too late; Renny held out her rats. "Look, Aunt Hester. I have two pets now. Their names are Anna and Bella. Want to hold them?" The rodents' twin noses and long white whiskers twitched.

Nose to nose with the animals, Hester Mae screamed and backed away, nearly falling in her haste to put distance between them. "Ranait! Get those filthy creatures away from me."

Renny backed away, looking uncertain. Grady noticed Star standing in the doorway, biting her lower lip to keep from laughing. He wanted to, himself, until he noticed his daughter's hurt expression.

Hester Mae's gaze bounced from Renny to Morning Moon, then settled on Star Dreamer, for the first time becoming aware of the other woman. Grady had hoped Star wouldn't have to come face-to-face with Hester Mae before having a chance to get used to her surroundings, but there was no possibility of avoidance now. He came around the desk and pulled both girls to him. "Hester Mae, this is Matilda Cartier, of the Nebraska Territory."

He held out his hand to Star, urging her to enter and deliberately uniting the four of them for Hester Mae's benefit. "And this is Matilda's mother, Star Cartier. She has graciously agreed to watch over Renny and see to the household." *And thereby removed any need for you.* He struggled to hide his distaste for Hester, though it would be a cold day in hell before he allowed her any foothold in his household.

Stunned, Hester Mae's gaze traveled from Star to her daughter. White lines appeared around her pinched lips, her eyes narrowed with anger, and she gripped her gloved hands tightly in front of her. "And, Emma? Where is she? I must congratulate her on her marriage and welcome her home."

Renny rocked back on her heels, leaning against her father. "She didn't come home with us. She's married to Star's brother, Striking Thunder. He's a Sioux chief and a brave warrior with lots of horses."

Hester Mae's mouth moved, but nothing came out. Grady bit back his groan. What was the point in making up a new name for Star if they were going to announce that she was an Indian princess?

In the back of his head, Grady felt sure that Renny had deliberately set out to shock her aunt in retaliation for her adverse reaction to her beloved pets. His daughter had the same gleam in her eye as Margaret Mary had often shone when riled—and like with her mother, Grady knew chastising her would do little good.

"Is this true? Margaret Mary's daughter married a savage heathen? Like these two?"

"Careful, Hester Mae. Star and her daughter are family, and they are here under our invitation."

Hester Mae laughed uneasily. "Much has happened, I see. There is so much we must catch up on. My husband has just returned home from one of his little trips. *You and Renny* must come to dinner tonight."

"Not tonight, Hester Mae. Another night, perhaps."

The excuse, while understandable, seeing as they had just returned home, must have sounded hollow, for fury glittered in Hester Mae's eyes as she picked up her skirts and sailed out the door. Moments later, the front door slammed shut.

Renny edged around Star, but Grady stopped her. "Not so fast, young lady. You and I are going to have a nice little talk." Star and Morning Moon left the room.

Chapter Nine

Hester Mae stormed through her front door, startling the footman who'd hurried to open it. She tossed her hat, gloves, reticule and coat at the poor man, then slammed the heavy oak door shut, gaining a small measure of pleasure at the thundering crash that echoed through the large entryway.

From a doorway down the dark paneled hall, a short, stocky man with hair going silver at the edges and a neatly trimmed goatee peered out. "Must you make so much noise, Hester? I'm trying to work."

Hester Mae glared at her husband. Baxter Olsen looked disgustingly healthy, which only fueled her fury.

Without replying, she shoved past him and stormed into his domain. Going to the sideboard, she poured herself a shot of whiskey and downed it. "Leave me alone, Baxter."

He leaned against the door frame, his eyes sharp

as he took in her agitation and shaking fingers. She gripped the shot glass tightly, fighting the urge to throw it at his head. Instead she glared at him, for once perversely glad she was taller by several inches—not that it had ever mattered to him.

His bright blue eyes took on a nasty gleam. "Judging by your fouler than normal temper, I'm guessing you've seen Grady?"

Hester Mae sucked in her breath. "How did you know he's home?"

Baxter shrugged. "I spoke to him down at the wharf."

Splashing more whiskey into her glass, she put it to her lips, welcoming the smooth heat burning her throat. "And you said nothing to me, knowing how worried I've been?"

"I figured I'd give the man a chance to settle in without having to contend with you. If he was less than pleased to see you, I can't blame him. He's made it perfectly clear that you're not welcome in his home. When are you going to accept that, Hester Mae?"

"When hell freezes over, you damned old goat. Those are my nieces. I have the right to see them." Remembering Renny and her rats and Emma's supposed marriage to a savage, broke her tenuous hold on her temper.

With a low shriek of anger, she threw her glass into the fireplace. The sharp shattering of breaking glass was satisfying, knowing she'd destroyed another of her mother-in-law's precious crystal glasses. Glancing up at the painting of the woman's formidable face, she silently cursed the old biddy. The woman had, until her dying day, made life in this house a living hell. When Baxter was gone, that damn painting was going into the fireplace.

Susan Edwards

Baxter smiled grimly but said nothing. He went back to his desk and sat down.

Hester Mae paced. "I suppose you also know about that woman—that savage and her brat that he brought back with him?"

"Yes. Pretty little thing. Can't blame the man."

A sudden, utterly distasteful thought occurred to her. "What if that child is his bastard? What if he's been bedding that woman?"

"I'd shake his hand and tell him he was a lucky devil."

"Well, I won't have it. That's immoral, I say—as bad as allowing my dear, sweet Emma to marry some savage! Something must be done."

"Ah, Grady did mention something about the birth of his first grandchild come fall." Her husband smiled thinly.

Hester Mae sank into a chair. "My Emma, my baby with child. And he left her out there without proper medical care. My God, the man's lost his wits. Whatever would Margaret Mary have said?"

"Your sister would have been happy for her child." Baxter regarded his wife with a look of pity, but his voice had hardened. "You will leave them alone, Hester Mae. If I hear you've caused any trouble, I'll cut you off. You have caused that poor man enough trouble already. I'll have no more."

Jumping up, Hester Mae paced, her mind in turmoil. "You don't understand—"

"No, it's you who doesn't understand. Their affairs are none of your business."

"But Margaret Mary was my *sister*," Hester Mae whispered, fighting to keep from breaking down in tears at the unfairness of this. Her baby sister, her beautiful, gentle, sweet and kind sister had been taken so cruelly from her. The sister who had overshadowed her, but for whom Hester had overcome

170

her own sickly gawkiness to protect. And Margaret Mary had loved her for that protectiveness, almost as much as her parents had appreciated it. How could she stop now?

"I mean it, Hester Mae! Leave that family alone."

Hester Mae's angry strides took her to the door. "You don't understand, Baxter. You've never understood. All you care about is your business, making money."

Baxter stood and leaned forward, his palms flat on his desk. "Money you seem to have no trouble spending, wife. As for not understanding, I beg to differ with you. I know you far too well. Now go upstairs. I have work to do."

Hester Mae paused in the doorway. "More letters in the hope of abolishing slavery? What wasteful work, Baxter—but work is all you're good for, isn't it? Too bad you never sired any children to carry on your precious business. Believe me, it will give me immense pleasure to sell it!" She glanced at the painting. "As will burning that portrait of your mother."

Baxter's voice was icy. "Then perhaps I should talk to my solicitor. I'm sure Charles would be happy to change the terms of the distribution of my estate in the event of my demise."

Furious, Hester Mae slammed the door behind her.

Baxter lowered his head into his hands, listening to his wife stomp up the stairs. Another door slammed. What had gone so wrong in their marriage? Though not a love match, he'd asked Hester Mae to marry him after his first wife died, believing she'd be a suitable wife. She'd been older, mature, relatively smart, and, more importantly, she'd never been a simpering, addle-headed girl. And her family's wealth and status had equaled his own.

Spotting the whiskey bottle on his desk, he recapped it and put it away. She was drinking too much again. During his three-day absence she'd consumed nearly half the bottle. Pulling out his brandy decanter, he stared at it with narrowed eyes. Hester Mae hated brandy, yet there was a significant amount gone. Opening his cigar box, he noted two were missing.

With a set expression, Baxter went to his desk and wrote out a letter. Calling one of his servants, he instructed the man where to deliver it. He hoped his friend still recalled the fact that he owed him a favor.

Stalling, not ready to face a night alone in her newly assigned bedroom, Star wandered through the downstairs with a lamp held high. She still marveled at all Grady's furniture, the house's wall and window coverings and the richly patterned rugs beneath her bare feet.

In the kitchen she grinned. What a room! Though she'd already explored it completely, she couldn't stop herself from doing so again. She opened each of the cupboards, though the bin table was her favorite piece. On one side, it held flour, the other, potatoes and rice.

Maybe she could find a nice cup of tea to help her sleep. She eyed the pie safe. Maybe a slice of that too. Tempted, she opened the door and sighed at the desserts just sitting there. She'd sampled her first at dinner.

She took a small scone, then proudly poured water from the kettle. It was still hot from earlier. Thinking of Hattie, Star prepared a second cup and slipped down the corridor into the back of the house. Hattie had been given a room there, for she refused to take one of the guest rooms upstairs. The cook occupied the room next to Hattie's.

From the basement, she heard male laughter. Grady's scouts had also refused to sleep upstairs, preferring to come and go through the rear servants' door. The two maids and footman had tiny rooms on the third floor.

It seemed odd to Star to have a staff to take care of the house chores. The fact that Grady also planned to hire a number of others left her reeling. If there were going to be so many people—a dozen for the house and outside staff—what was left for her to do?

Knocking on Hattie's closed door, Star balanced the tea tray and waited for permission to enter. When given, she entered. The woman was roughly Star's age and she lay on the bed. The white bandage wrapped around her head contrasted sharply with her skin, which was the color of newly tilled earth. One eye was swollen shut, and blood had crusted her lower lip from a gash. Dark, ugly bruises bespoke beatings, some several days old.

"I thought you might like some tea." Star set the tray down and helped Hattie sit. The woman gave a hiss of discomfort. "I added some herbs that will help ease your pain. I brought more salve too."

Star held up the teacup, urging the woman to drink from it.

"Thank you." Hattie's dark eyes swam with unshed tears. "You saved my life today. How can I ever repay you?"

"Rest and heal."

Hattie leaned back against the pillows and closed her eyes. "They think me a slave, but I am not. They stole my family." Her voice echoed with despair.

Star set the teacup aside and soaked a strip of cloth in warm water infused with healing herbs.

While on board the *Annabella*, she'd heard passengers discussing slavery. It seemed this was one horrible tradition that Indians and whites shared. She knew many tribes turned captives into slaves, though her own tribe usually did not. However, there was a difference between the traditions. For the Sioux, the slaves taken were not just of one race. They were taken in battle—from any who opposed them. It didn't matter whether the captive was Indian, English, Spanish or French.

Star didn't understand how an entire race could be enslaved just because of the color of their skin. It seemed terribly unjust.

On that thought, she left Hattie to rest. At the foot of the grand staircase, she noted a faint light coming from down the hall—Grady's den. She hesitated, unsure of her welcome.

Would he resent her intrusion as Renny seemed to believe? The little girl had seemed to think the room was meant to be entirely off-limits. Moving silently, she peered in. Grady was seated at his desk, staring off into space. Her own sense of loneliness gave her the courage to step inside.

Ever the gentleman, the colonel stood. "I thought you'd gone to bed already."

"I took Hattie some tea." She paused. "What will happen to her? Where will she go?"

"If she is indeed free, she can go where she chooses. If she is a slave, the law says she must be returned to her owner."

"That is wrong."

"Yes, it's wrong." Grady reached out and tucked a strand of hair behind her ear.

The warmth of his fingers sliding across her skin sent tingles of awareness through her. To combat her urge to lean toward him and beg for more of his soothing, yet disturbing touch, Star walked past him. At the window, she stared out into the night. Grady joined her, his palms warm as they rested on her shoulders.

"I'll do what I can to help Hattie," he said softly.

"Thank you." Grady's selflessness wrapped Star in a cocoon of hope that things might work out. Then she shook herself. She was leaning on him far too much. Still, her body longed to relax and fall back into the sheltering warmth of his arms. There, she knew she'd be safe. A yawn overtook her, Grady's presence overcoming the stress of the day.

His hands began to massage the tension from her body. Beneath his touch, Star gave in to her need and leaned back into him with a sigh. It seemed so natural, so right. Tomorrow she'd worry about being strong. Right now she was much too exhausted. Closing her eyes, she gave herself over to the magic of his fingers easing the tightness from her neck and shoulders.

"I should check on the girls, in case my daughter has difficulty sleeping," she murmured. She felt guilty to feel this good.

Grady led her gently to the couch. It was set beneath another window to one side of the fireplace. Morning Moon slept at one end, and Renny sprawled on the other side. "They're fine."

New appreciation for this man who wanted so much to love his daughter and make amends for his past errors curled through Star. She hoped he'd find the happiness he deserved, even envied him a little. She spoke softly, so as not to wake the girls. "Renny was so sure you would refuse to allow her in here."

Grady leaned down to stroke the tangle of red curls around Renny's face. He stood, and the love in his heart shone in his eyes. "Because of the past, my daughter expects the worst from me." His voice broke. "Unfortunately, I can't say I blame her."

Leaning over, he scooped the girl into his arms. At the slight disturbance of her friend, Morning Moon lifted her head and smiled sleepily at her mother.

"Weshawee has such a nice house," she murmured.

Star held out her arms. "Yes, it is a nice house. Let's get you to bed." Morning Moon wrapped her arms around her mother's neck and her legs around her waist. Star pulled her daughter close, love swelling in her heart. She had so much for which to be grateful. Even if she'd lost her husband, she still had her children. As she climbed the stairs behind Grady, she thought of her son, Running Elk. How she missed him.

What fun he'd have in a place the size of this house. There were so many rooms and places to hide. And the stairs; he'd love to run up and down them—then slide down the banister as Renny did. She carried her daughter upstairs, the rough hemp carpet silencing her steps.

After tucking in Morning Moon, Star kissed the child good night then moved to the doorway where Grady waited. Leaving the door partway open, she let him walk her to her room. As they passed one room—Emma's, Grady had said earlier—Star glanced over her shoulder. On the other side of the landing, another long corridor boasted several rooms reserved for guests.

At last they reached her room, and Grady opened the door. Star entered. The chamber was beautiful, but she wasn't used to sleeping in total solitude. In her tribe, and in her family, nights were a time of closeness. Many evenings she'd lay awake listening to her children breathe, and to her husband's quiet snores. They had always been reassuring sounds.

Even on board the ship, she'd shared her cabin with the girls. But now, she was faced with sleeping alone—in a strange bed. Seeing no choice but to enter, she stepped inside. The bed, a huge four-poster with a canopy and heavy drapes, intimidated her. Perhaps she might sleep on the carpet in front of the wood stove.

Grady had explained earlier that this room had been designed for use by his wife—it was apparently common practice for husband and wife to have separate rooms—but she had never used it. His voice had been sad when he had explained that Margaret Mary had never used the room, preferring to share one with him. Both of their girls had even been born in his large bed.

Instead, this room had become for guests. His sister, when she'd come to stay and care for Margaret Mary during her difficult pregnancy, had used the room.

Star was glad to know that Grady's wife had been like that. Why would any man and wife spend the night in huge separate beds all by themselves when one bed was more than big enough for two?

Grady spoke up. "Don't hesitate to wake me if you need me. I know this is all strange to you." After an awkward silence, he stuck his hands in his pockets. "Well, we'd best get to bed. We'll need to get an early start if we plan to go to the market in the morning as you wanted."

Don't leave me alone. The words tried very hard to burst from her lips, but she held them back. She wasn't a young child in need of a parent's comforting embrace during the dark of the night. She was a grown woman.

A grown woman full of doubts and fears of being

alone, especially when nightmares haunted her dreams and visions came unbidden.

She stepped back, forcing herself to be calm. "Yes. It's late. I'll see you in the morning." She watched as Grady left, closing the door behind him. Star pressed her palms against the smooth wood. She'd never spent a night truly alone. This was going to be a long one.

Entering the master bedroom, Grady faced the ghosts of his past. He hadn't set foot in the room since the day Margaret Mary died.

The maid had turned back his sheets, and a bed warmer sat on the wood stove for him to rub between the sheets before getting into bed. A small lamp on the table beside the bed dispelled the gloom, but not the memories shadowing his mind: Margaret Mary sitting on the edge of the bed, brushing her long red locks, counting the strokes. How he'd loved her hair. In his mind's eye, he saw himself taking the brush from her hand, drawing the bristles through her hair, using his fingers, reveling in the soft, silky strands flowing over his skin.

She'd turn, smile and beckon him with her eyes. Together, falling onto the bed, they would make sweet, gentle love. After, they'd talk long into the night, her voice, her touch the last thing he'd remember before falling asleep, confident that he'd awaken with her beside him.

But death had stolen her from him, cheating him of so much. Wearily, he approached the bed and took several deep breaths. How could he possibly hope to sleep in that bed? Perhaps he should just go downstairs and sleep in the den.

Taking the lamp, he fled the room, all the while despising his cowardice. Downstairs, he paused, tempted to find a bottle of scotch or brandy to ease the pain coiling inside him. Earlier, in the parlor, he'd been amazed to find his anguish had lessened. But in the bedroom, it'd been too much. His hand closed over a bottle, then opened and fell back to his side. It would be so easy to turn to alcohol for solace, but so wrong. Leaving the den and temptation behind, he strode into the kitchen.

To his surprise, he found Star and Hattie at the stove. Both jumped guiltily when he entered. Then, with a knowing smile, Star poured more milk into the pan. "Would you like some warm milk? I couldn't sleep, and neither could Hattie."

Ruefully, he eased down into a chair at the worn table. He should have known both women would have trouble. It had been a stressful day for all of them.

Hattie edged back to the door leading to her room. "I shall go back to bed now."

Grady stopped her. "Join us, Hattie."

Her eyes widened. "Oh, no, sir. I can't. It wouldn't be proper."

"I disagree. You are not a servant or slave in my household. You are a guest." He stood and pulled out two chairs.

Hattie hesitated, then smiled shyly while Star carried over mugs of steaming cocoa. Once seated, the threesome sipped their warm drinks. A slight noise drew three pairs of eyes as the swinging door opened. Renny and Morning Moon stepped into the room.

"What are you two doing up?" Grady asked.

Morning Moon walked over to her mother and put her hand on her arm. "I went to your bedroom and you weren't there."

"And I woke up when she did," Renny added. "We didn't want Star to be alone 'cause she's never slept in a room all to herself." She sniffed and looked longingly at the cups of cocoa.

Star smoothed the hair from her daughter's face. "You are right. I could not sleep, but I will learn."

Renny leaned her forearms on the table and swung a leg back and forth. "Maybe we could sleep with you for a few days until you get used to it. Your bed is big enough."

"Renny . . ." Grady began.

"No. It's all right. I'd like that Wesh—Renny." Star, proud of using the stove, stood to prepare another pan of warm milk.

With Renny's sleepy chatter, the tension quickly broke. Soon they were all talking and laughing. Grady sat back and soaked in the love and warmth of each of these people who were now his friends. Laughter had returned to his life.

Margaret Mary, you'd have loved this. His gaze fell on Star's sleepy features. *You'd have loved Star, and you'd have championed Hattie.* A sense of rightness suddenly filled him. This night would remind him that new memories were waiting around the corner. Not to replace those of his wife, but to add to those of his life. They were all to be part of the same collection. Some were to be shelved and never looked at; others, like tonight, were to be taken out and remembered whenever loneliness assailed him.

When yawns finally overwhelmed their laughter, they all headed back to their beds. Star and the girls went to her room, Grady to his. This time, though, he forced himself into his bed, grateful as exhaustion took over. Unbidden, his mind filled with images of Star. He fell asleep remembering the feel of her in his arms and the kiss beneath the stars that he should forget but couldn't.

Sometime in the early morning hours, a weight

on his feet woke him. Pushing up on his elbows, he blinked and stared, then smiled. There, curled at the foot of the bed, lay his daughter. She was huddled in a ball, and she moaned, obviously cold. Thankful that he'd worn his nightshirt—in case Star needed him during the night—he slid from the bed, shivering in the cold.

Lifting Renny, he tucked her into bed, on her mother's side, then climbed back beneath the warm cocoon of heat. Stretching sleepily, Renny snuggled deep. Opening her eyes briefly, the girl murmured, "I love you, Papa."

"I love you too, sweetheart." Happiness burst forth and lulled him into a deep, restful sleep.

"What do you mean, she got away?"

In the darkened alley the two men, one tall, one short, twisted their caps between nervous fingers. "She hit Barney and got out of your cellar. We went after her, but she made it to the wharf. When we tried to nab her, she started screaming. Some nosy squaw tried to stop us. We could'a taken care of her, even gotten ya another woman ta sell, but some other gents came along."

"Damn." Leo paced. "That woman would have fetched a hefty price on the block." His body tightened with lust. *After I'd had my fill, of course.* The woman had been pretty and, unlike most women her age, birthing a child hadn't ruined her body. Leo turned his furious gaze on the men he'd hired to watch over his slaves and help transport them.

"Get her back. The Dragon won't be happy to learn of this."

At the mention of the man Leo worked for, the two men backed away, eyes wide. "But we don't know where the gents took her!"

Leo grabbed one man by the front of his shirt.

"Then you'd better start searching." He twisted his fist in the material, choking the bungler. "And when she turns up, you two idiots will grab her—without attracting attention. Do you understand?"

"Yes, boss. . . . We'll find her."

Heading back for the warehouse, lost in thought, Leo nearly ran into the one man he didn't want to have to face.

"You lost her." It wasn't a question.

Leo didn't bother to make excuses. "She escaped, but we'll get her back."

The Dragon came forward, his eyes glittering above the beard concealing his features. "See that you do. That one would have fetched me a nice price." He handed Leo a slip of paper. "Start your search here."

"What's this?" Leo looked at the address on the paper.

"It is where you'll find my slave. And Leo, she *is* mine. You're not to touch her."

Leo held back a protest. Normally, the boss didn't care which of the women Leo used before they were shipped off to plantations or brothels.

"I want the squaw, too." The voice deepened.

A bead of sweat trailed down his back. Leo licked his lips and watched the man's hands to be sure he wasn't going to go for a weapon. His boss's temper could explode without warning. He remembered all too well what happened to the last man who'd let down the Dragon. He had been found floating near the landing.

"Get them for me or else." With that, the Dragon melted back into the shadows and was gone.

Leo stalked away. Furious, he stormed back to one of Baxter's warehouses and into its office. Hunger drove him. All day he'd pleased himself with plans to enjoy the slave before the Dragon shipped her and the other young women off to a brothel. Now he was left with a raging hunger burning in his groin. *Hester*. She was the answer. He'd go to her. Before he'd gotten out the door, he paused, his mind clearing.

"Damn." Baxter was back home from his trip. Seeing Hester tonight was out of the question. It was too risky with his boss home.

Leo paused. Maybe not. He was in the mood for danger tonight. Returning to the main part of the warehouse, he tore into some of the sealed boxes and ransacked the office. Then he left, a plan well formed in his head.

Searching, Leo found a lad huddled in an alley with a ratty blanket wrapped tight around himself. Leo kicked him awake.

Scampering to his feet, the lad backed away. "Whaddya what?"

Snagging the boy, Leo kept his face hidden in the deep shadows. "Got a job for you. A message to deliver."

"Wh-what's the pay?"

Tightening his hold until the boy struggled for breath, Leo whispered, "Your life. Fail me, and I'll hunt you down and kill you. Got it?" There was no point in paying street trash when one could intimidate them. The lad nodded and quickly ran off with the message. He would tell Baxter that someone had broken into his warehouse.

After a moment, Leo followed. When he arrived, he saw the old man leaving the house with the boy in tow. Leo slipped upstairs, surprising Hester Mae in bed.

"Leo, what are you doing here? My husband is *home*."

Need pounded through his veins, along with deep disappointment at not having the newest slave to slake his lust. Leo unbuttoned his pants. "I saw to it that he was called to work."

He pulled a narrow strip of cloth from his pocket. Hester Mae's eyes widened. He knew she didn't like dominance play, but she wouldn't refuse him. Her old goat of a spouse hadn't bedded her in years, so she accepted whatever Leo demanded. He was always careful not to hurt or scare her, though. For now. When Baxter died and she married him—and he got all the money—then he would show her what true dominance was.

After gagging her and tearing off her clothing, Leo bent her over the foot of the bed and entered her roughly. As he pounded out his frustrations, her muffled squeals of pleasure drove him over the brink. But his satisfaction didn't last long. He was a master without a plantation or his own business. He had no power of his own, but soon that would change. Someday, this house and Baxter's shipping business would belong to him. Then he'd be the boss, and never again would he have to take orders.

As he pulled back, Hester Mae stood and removed the cloth from around her mouth. She stretched her arms overhead and yawned. "You'd better go before Baxter gets back."

Leo found himself filled with an inexplicable rage. As if he would take orders from a woman! He grabbed Hester, forcing her to her knees, then shoved his still-hard manhood at her. "Who's the master, bitch?"

Hester Mae gave him a hurt look. "You've had your fun, Leo. You know I don't like it when you act like this. And you know I don't like to . . ."

Leo smiled wickedly. "If I leave now, I won't be back. But it's your choice, Hester Mae." Starved for sex and affection as she was, Leo knew she'd comply. She always did.

As her mouth closed around him, he imagined the pleasure he'd get when he was free to make her do what his slaves did. The thought of seeing real fear in her eyes brought him to a violent release. Yes, soon he'd show her and everyone else who was in charge. And if she gave him any trouble, he knew a perfect place to stash her away.

Chapter Ten

Star woke to ribbons of sunshine streaming across her face. Blinking, she glanced at the windows. Sheer curtains billowed gently inward with the breeze. She'd left the window open before going to bed so she wouldn't feel so closed in. Rolling onto her back, she stretched out her feet, then pulled them back when she encountered the cold mattress.

She smiled. How quickly she was becoming spoiled. The cold had never bothered her before. Now she snuggled deep in the drowsy coziness of her bed, loath to rise. She gave herself a few precious moments to absorb her surroundings.

Above her, instead of blue sky peeking in through a smoke hole, an ornately detailed ceiling drew her admiration, as did the wall covering in tiny pink roses and green scrolls of leaves. Heavy drapes in a pale pink hue hung to the side of each window, and a darker shade covered the floor. Her gaze followed dancing dust motes as she absorbed her new, plush surroundings.

Rich, gleaming wooden dressers, a large wardrobe, a desk with carved, wooden legs, two chairs and a low table near the fireplace with a white mantel furnished the bedroom. Sitting, she hugged her knees to her chest and rested her cheek on the soft material of a feather-stuffed comforter.

At a soft knock on her door, she called out, "Enter."

One of the maids, Katie, slipped inside carrying a tray with tea and some sort of sweet pastry. She set it over Star's lap. "Breakfast will be served in two hours in the morning room, ma'am." The maid went to the wood stove and stoked it to life, adding a fresh log. Then she filled a teacup with warm water from a large pitcher.

Staring at the tray, Star wanted to protest. Being served in her bedroom reminded her of how the Smiths had been ordered to their cabin to eat in solitude. But after protesting so many unaccustomed actions of the staff yesterday, and facing their looks of horror, then having Renny or Grady tell her this was how things were done, she held her tongue.

Tears of helplessness came to her eyes. She'd talk to Colonel O'Brien later. There had to be something useful for her to do. Unwilling to hurt the maid's feelings, she sipped her tea and nibbled on a scone while Katie took a gown out of the wardrobe and shook it out in the dressing room.

Star waited until the maid left the room before getting up. She straightened the bedclothes and pulled up the neatly folded white counterpane at the foot of the bed. It was a small rebellion, but one that made her lighter of heart.

With one finger, she traced the large rose motif

in the center of the blanket, then went into the dressing room. There she availed herself of the chamberpot behind a screen, then washed, using water the maid had poured into a small bowl nearby. This was one thing she hated: washing from a bowl. Later she'd find out where to bathe. Learning that most people did not bathe often had shocked her. Her own people washed daily, no matter the temperature or weather.

Katie returned to help her dress. It was an arduous process. Feeling exhausted though the day had barely begun, Star made her way to the kitchen, where she found Hattie sitting at the bin table, kneading dough. "Good morning, Hattie," Star said.

Hattie turned, her movements slow and stiff. "*Bonjour,* Mrs. Cartier." Hattie bobbed her head.

Star wrinkled her nose at being formally greeted with her mother's name. "Hattie, I'd like it if you just called me by my first name, Star."

One of Hattie's dark eyes widened. The other might have, if it hadn't still been nearly swollen shut. "Oh, no, ma'am. It wouldn't be proper." Her agitation made her accent thicker.

"Is it not my choice what I am to be called?" Star felt annoyed.

Hattie thrust out her lower lip in thought, then winced. It was split in the center, and one of her cheek's was swollen. "Ah!" She shook flour from her hands. "I will address you as Mrs. Star." She tried to smile, but it turned into a distorted grimace.

Star grinned for her. "That's better. Now, what can I do to help?"

Thomas, a tall, dour man, the O'Briens' cook, who was nephew to Charles Manning's, whirled around, his thick, bushy black brows lifted in hor-

188

ror. Star backed away. "Don't tell me. I'm not supposed to cook, either."

Hattie tried to hide her amusement. "Why don't you go on into the morning room, Mrs. Star?"

"What about you, Hattie? You should rest."

"Don't fret, Mrs. Star. I'm just a bit sore and bruised."

Before Star could suggest she was a bit more than bruised, she found herself gently directed from the kitchen into a bright dining room with sun streaming in through gleaming windows. Wondering what to do, she breathed a sigh of relief when Grady and Charles joined her. Though the two men were of a similar size, and the attorney looked truly distinguished with his silverish brown hair, sharp gaze and neatly trimmed beard, it was Grady who held Star's gaze enthralled.

The man before her was the same one she'd spent most of her waking hours with during the past two months, yet he was different. He was now dressed similarly to Charles, yet the lack of military attire didn't lessen his commanding presence. He wore an air of authority with the same ease he wore his new clothes. But it wasn't seeing him in different garb for the first time that held her breathless and transfixed.

It was his face. She'd suspected that if he shaved, he'd be a handsome man, but she'd had no idea just how attractive. Now she knew. His freshly shaven face was strong, commanding. His features were sharp, yet held an intriguing hint of softness. His jaw jutted out, its line clear, the skin smooth. His chin was square, yet in the center, to her surprise and delight, he had a deep cleft that softened the harshness. An image of her dipping her thumb into that small dimple played out in her mind.

She gripped the towel in her hand tightly to still

her trembling fingers. Amazed, her gaze traveled upward, lingering on his cheeks, which were a shade paler than the bridge of his nose and forehead. His gaze was on her and alight with amusement, as if he knew his changed appearance affected her. As it did.

Her pulse sped up. The stark white shirt, neat cravat tied at his throat and low-cut waistcoat and trousers of the same shade brought out the blue in his eyes and the fire in his hair. He filled the room with a strong sensual magnetism that made her want to go to him, wrap her arms around his neck and beg him for another sweet kiss.

She'd always found him attractive, but now he was heart-stopping. She stared at his mouth, drawn to him as the dawn must follow the night. Recalling their last night beneath the stars only two nights ago, Star again felt his lips on hers. That night, she'd learned their shape and feel by touch. Now, with no facial hair to hide his mouth, her gaze traced their firm contour at will and recalled how he'd tasted and felt. Deep creases bracketed his mouth, and for just a moment, as if he too was remembering, his lips parted.

Hers followed suit. Her gaze met his, her tongue slipping out to wet her lips. The look in his eyes warmed her already overheated body. There was no doubt he too was remembering their brief but potent kiss.

Grady cleared his throat, broke eye contact and pulled at his collar to direct his lawyer to a chair at the polished cherry-wood table. Then he asked, "Where is Hattie? Is she able to join us?"

Star took several deep breaths to clear her mind. "She's in the kitchen with Thomas. I was not needed." She couldn't keep the hurt from creeping into her tone.

Grady smiled and seated her. "I'll talk to him. Right now, we have some things to discuss with Hattie. I'll fetch her." He returned a few minutes later with the woman in tow. A maid followed with coffee.

"Go ahead, Charles," Grady invited.

The solicitor took a sip of his coffee and nodded in appreciation. "Strong and hot. Just the way I like it. Thomas was trained well by his aunt." He turned his attention to the papers before him. Taking the top sheet, he pushed it across the table to Grady. "Hattie is indeed a freed slave. As are her husband and their thirteen-year-old son." He smiled when Hattie slumped back in her chair with relief. "It wasn't hard to get copies of the will," he said gently.

The freedwoman scooted her chair forward and rested her arms on the table. Tears fell from her eyes and ran down her cheeks. "I was so afraid no one would believe me."

"Well, I have new papers for you and your family. And I will also keep a set for safekeeping." Charles passed an envelope to her.

Star watched as Hattie picked it up with shaking hands. "If she was free and she had papers that said so, why were those men trying to capture her?"

"Ah, Mrs. Cartier," Charles began. "I'm afraid there are folk who don't believe people of color have the right to be free. And there are unscrupulous, greedy men who care only for the profit they make when they sell slaves. Unfortunately, these men don't care whether a man, woman or child is already legally freed. To some people, a human life means only money."

"That's terrible!" Star looked at Grady "What about her husband and son? Can you find them?"

Grady reached over and patted her hand. "I'll hire the best men to start searching." His gaze switched to Hattie. "I can't make any promises, though, Mrs. Dumont."

Holding the precious papers to her breast, Hattie drew a deep breath. "*Merci*, Colonel O'Brien—for all you've done. I will send word to you after I find a place to stay."

Star gasped. "Hattie! You are not well enough to go anywhere. And where could you go where you would be safe? We can't allow you to leave and place yourself back in danger."

"It's nice of you to be concerned, Mrs. Star, but—"

"Mrs. Cartier is right, Hattie," Charles began. "There's a ring of ruthless men who have been kidnapping and selling free slaves to the highest bidder—mostly plantation owners down south. I've spoken to the police, and they say that these men are very dangerous. Their leader goes by the name of the Dragon."

Charles's eyes grew distant, his voice lowered, filled with pain. "I myself lost a servant several days ago." His brow furrowed. "The police think he ran away, but he would not have done so. I hired this man fifteen years ago. He was free to quit anytime, and I paid him well. Lord, he was practically a member of my family. Not for one moment do I believe he ran away. I believe he too was a victim of these kidnappers—and I won't rest until I've found him."

"It's too late," Hattie whispered miserably. "You'll never do it. My husband and son were shipped out two days ago. There are too many plantations to ever find them."

"Why weren't you shipped out as well?" Grady asked, drumming his fingers on the table.

Hattie lowered her head and hugged herself, her fingers clenched around the envelope with her papers. "I was to be sold to a brothel, as were two other women. The men, boys and older women were shipped off to work on a plantation. I don't know where," she whispered. She lifted eyes filled with remembered agony and fear.

Grady leaned forward. "Tell us what you can, Hattie."

Gripping her cup, the woman bit her lip. "The three men in the alley were the ones who grabbed us when we were on our way to Kansas. They took us to a house, I think. I got out by hitting one on the head, but they came after me. I ran then, but they caught me. That's when madame came to my rescue."

"Can you find your way from the wharf back to the house?"

Hattie shook her head. "I was so scared, I just ran. It wasn't far from the wharf, but I couldn't tell you what it looks like. I was blindfolded when I was taken there, and they kept us in a dark cold basement.

"I wish we'd taken those ruffians to the police when we had the chance," Charles said, looking disappointed.

For just a moment, Star remembered the despair and sense of death she'd felt when they'd passed that steamboat a few days ago. She shuddered, fighting the pull of the vision. It wanted to overcome her, to show her—

Grady's warm fingers slid over her hand and gripped her tightly, keeping her from sliding into the darkness. "What is it, Star?"

Could Hattie's family have been on that boat? The time was right. Star opened her mouth to remind him of her vision, then stopped herself. What if she was wrong? She'd felt death. Had it been Hattie's husband or son, or the servant Charles had lost? Or had it been just as Grady had said—a death unrelated to this horrible tale? "Nothing," she said, smiling weakly. She'd tell him later, in private.

He frowned but didn't press her. Pulling free from him, she turned back to Hattie. "Until this Dragon is caught, you can't leave. Stay with us. It isn't safe for you to be out on your own."

Hattie's rich, coffee-colored eyes filled with pride. She drew herself up. "No. I have no money to pay my way. And I will not accept charity."

Star turned to Grady. "You said you were going to hire a housekeeper."

Grady looked startled. Across from him, Charles coughed, but then Grady smiled at Star and turned to the freedwoman. "What a wonderful idea. Would you consider employment, Hattie? As Star mentioned, I do need a housekeeper."

Hattie sat straight, her mouth hanging open. "I've never been a housekeeper before." Awe filled her voice, and hope lit her eyes at the thought of such an honored position in such an elegant dwelling.

"You'll know more about running a household than I do." Star grinned. "Tipis are very small and we Sioux have very little. Please say yes, Hattie. You're the first friend I've made since I arrived in St. Louis. I don't want anyone else."

The woman smiled slowly, then grimaced with pain. "*Merci*, again. I am honored, Mrs. Star." She glanced between Charles and Grady. "Are you certain?" At their nods, she rose. "Thank you as well. I'll go check on our meal, then."

"That's settled," Grady said when she was gone, rubbing his growling belly in response to the smells coming from the kitchen. "Where are the girls? Star, can you go call them?"

Hattie appeared again from the kitchen. "They

came in much earlier and ate, then went out to the stable." A maid followed with a cart laden with steaming platters of pancakes, bacon, sausage, eggs, toast and many other items Star couldn't identify.

Smiling, Star stood to help, but Hattie's frown made her resume her seat. All at once, the three scouts rushed in, presumably drawn by the aroma of food.

With one look at the men, Hattie squealed in horror. She held her apron over her nose. "Out! Out until you've bathed," she ordered, ushering them back toward the kitchen.

Zeke held up his hands in horror. "A bath? Not on yer life."

Hattie stepped back and rested her hands on her hips. "Then, you don't eat."

Zeb sniffed. His stomach rumbled loudly. "Colonel," he beseeched, poking his head from the kitchen.

Grady, Star and Charles exchanged grateful looks that Hattie was willing to lay down the law. "Looks like you boys will have to do as she says if you want to eat."

Hattie shook her head, holding her nose and grumbling as she ushered the men into the kitchen. Just before the door closed behind them, Star heard one of the men yell out, "Yer not touchin' my hair."

Grady chuckled, then groaned with pleasure as he tasted his food. Charles followed suit.

Though she enjoyed the meal, Star found it vastly amusing and entertaining to watch Grady. She shook her head. Men were the same, no matter their skin color. They all took enormous pleasure in a good meal. She'd learned a long time ago that when her mother wanted something from her father, all she had to do was fix his favorite meal, then make her request when he was too sated to argue. Her own husband hadn't been any different.

Grady scowled at her. "What?"

She turned her attention back to her own full plate. "Nothing."

Wiping his mouth with his napkin, Grady leaned back and patted his stomach. He sighed. "Food is one of life's greatest pleasures."

Chuckling, Charles eyed the heaping platters of food, rubbed his belly, then tossed his napkin down with a sigh of regret. "Maybe I should take Thomas back, Grady, old man."

"Not without a fight you won't."

Charles sighed and stood, gathering his papers. "Then I shall have to visit often. That boy knows how to cook."

Grady pushed away from the table too, and before Star could do the same, he was there, pulling her chair back for her. "Shall we get ready to go to market?"

Star smoothed her skirt. "I'm eager to see what it is like," she admitted. After hearing so much about the place where you could go to purchase goods, Star was eager to view the scene for herself. The idea of just sitting around in rooms, no matter how nicely appointed they were, didn't appeal to someone used to hard work from the time *wi* greeted the dawn until *hunwi* rose to rule the night. Inactivity had been the hardest part of being confined to the steamer.

And the thought of spending another day directly in Grady's company thrilled her, though she tried to convince herself he was doing this just because she was a stranger in a new place. But the truth was, she'd gotten used to having him at her side all during the long trip down the Missouri River. She'd dreaded arriving in St. Louis, fearing he'd go his own way and leave her to simply care for his child, as they had agreed.

Following the two men out, Star let her gaze roam the back of Grady's tall figure. She worried at how quickly this kind, gentle man had filled the lonely void in her life. For reasons she couldn't understand, she felt closer to Renny's father than she'd ever felt to her husband. She'd loved Two-Ree and, in his own way, he'd loved her, but they hadn't shared the strong bond of friendship that she and Grady had developed. She'd never before felt that she'd missed anything during her marriage to Two-Ree, but she had known their feelings for one another weren't the same deep love her parents shared. Now she was beginning to see how much more there could have been.

Two-Ree had treated her as most warriors did their wives. He'd given her children, protected and provided for them and was there to offer silent comfort when her visions haunted her nights. But rarely had they spent more than a few minutes conversing during the day. Star now looked forward to those times she could just talk or listen to Grady.

Star found she liked the close bond of friendship she and Grady had developed: the walking together, sharing meals, talking. Even when they sat in silence, she never felt alone.

Heading up the stairs to prepare herself for the trip to market, she glanced down and met his gaze. Awareness shot between them. Need and desire flooded her belly. Star sidestepped him one stair up, then turned and hurried the rest of the way, warning herself not to fall in love with him. This was crazy, these feelings very dangerous. Once he and Renny settled their differences, she and Morning Moon would either return home or make a new home for their family elsewhere. The last thing Grady needed was to complicate his life with a woman cursed by visions—and one whom he could never present to his society because of her Sioux blood.

But as she continued up the stairs, she knew when the time came, walking away would not be easy.

Nearly two hours later, Star and Grady stood in the foyer. He paced, while Star fidgeted with her full skirts and pulled at the gloves on her fingers. "What is keeping the girls?" he muttered. At the foot of the stairs, he shouted, "Ranait! The carriage is waiting."

"Coming, Papa."

"How do your women stand all this clothing all day, every day?" Star muttered, glaring at her fingers, then checking the position of her hat in the mirror.

Grady watched her fuss over her appearance—adjusting not for looks but comfort—and pictured her as she'd once been: clothed in her simple Indian garb. How did it feel to wear so little every day? He couldn't imagine wearing only a breechclout or even just breeches outside his bedroom, and the sudden desire to experience the simple pleasure of the wind against his bare skin surprised him. The sound of running interrupted his contemplation. Ah, well, he mused. It would never happen. Not even when he returned Star to her people at the end of summer. He was too well-bred. Men of his station did not give in to such impulses. *A shame*, a voice in his head said.

"Renny, we are waiting!" he called, tapping his foot impatiently, and wishing his daughter would hurry down the stairs. His eyes widened, then narrowed as he saw a blue blur sliding down the banister. Swearing beneath his breath, he jumped forward and caught his daughter before she went flying. He set her before him. "Since when do we slide down the banister, young lady?"

Renny assumed her rebellious pose: arms crossed, jaw jutting forward, a glare in her eyes. "Emma always let me."

Grady didn't believe her for a minute. "Young ladies use the stairs, and they *walk* in the house. You will conduct yourself in a manner befitting your upbringing."

Renny pouted. "I told Emma you'd be mean." Tossing her braided hair, she tore open the door and ran out of the house.

Grady wondered if every day would be filled with these quicksilver mood changes. He'd thought for sure when he'd found Renny curled at the foot of his bed last night that she'd begun to realize she needed him. But it looked as though they still had a long way to go.

He turned to Star. "Ready?"

She adjusted the red bow in her daughter's hair, then sent the girl outside to the carriage. "Yes. What about Hattie?"

Grady frowned. The woman belonged in bed or resting, but she'd insisted on coming along to see to supplies personally. Before he could go check on her, the door directly opposite the front door in the foyer opened. It led to the porch at the back of the house, where the servants did a lot of their work and relaxing. "Good; now we can go—"

Words failed him when he caught sight of Zeb, Zac and Zeke. They had followed Hattie into the foyer. Not only had all three men bathed, but their beards were trimmed and combed, and their hair was brushed and tied back. Their clothing still reeked, however. Grady suspected one of Hattie's reasons for going to market was to make sure the three brothers got new clothing.

"Well, I'll be damned!"

"Ah, come on, Colonel, don't go makin' no big deal, okay?" Zeke glared at the woman who had forced cleanliness upon him.

Hattie shrugged. "Your choice. It makes no difference to me if you eat or not. Fetch the wagon. We are going to need to purchase many supplies, and you're not riding in the carriage with Mr. O'Brien and Mrs. Star smelling like something that crawled into a hole in the ground and died." She shoved them out onto the front porch.

Behind him, Star giggled. Grady smiled, then held out his hand. Together they burst out in laughter as they left the house. Outside, the carriage awaited. It had been cleaned and polished, and Jeffers held open its door, then climbed into the driver's seat.

Grady and Star sat on one side, with the children across from them. Renny chatted to Morning Moon as the carriage followed the border of Lafayette Park. Inside, well-dressed gentlemen and ladies strolled along its verdant grounds or sat on benches. There was also a pond, which attracted many citizens, both wealthy and poor, young and old.

As their carriage entered the park at a gallop, two boys cut in front of it. Renny craned her neck to watch. "When can *I* go riding?" Excitement chased away her poutiness and her eyes shone eagerly.

"Perhaps tomorrow," Grady said, pleased when she nodded happily and started pointing out places of interest to Star and Morning Moon.

The two Sioux were in awe. And though he hadn't seen the city in nine years himself and was amazed at the astonishing growth that had taken place, Grady enjoyed seeing it all through Star's eyes. As they passed three-storied elegant mansions; working-class neighborhoods with tiny, two-story brick buildings and front porch stoops; storefronts promising all manner of goods and streets filled with horses, carriages, wagons and people going about their daily business, he tried to imagine the thrill of seeing it all for the first time.

But it was the marketplace that would truly put the wonder in her eyes.

Soulard Market teemed with vibrant life. The morass of humanity and noise was incredible. Vendors shouted and waved their goods at passing shoppers. Some beat on metal tins to attract customers. Crated chickens set up a din of their own, while pigs in pens squealed. Good-natured arguing and shouting competed with the greetings of friends and laughter. Groups of men in suits, tall hats and walking sticks engaged in earnest and serious conversation while their wives shopped, gossiped or discussed the latest fashions.

"What do you think?" Grady asked Star. He had her hand firmly on his arm to keep them from becoming separated. The girls were in front of him with Hattie. Zeb, Zeke and Zac, behind him and Star, were still grumbling about meddling women.

Star blinked. "What?"

Grady chuckled and bent his head to speak directly into her ear. "What do you think of the market?"

The feel of his lips brushing against the sensitive area below her ear made Star shiver. It was a moment before she could speak. "I've never seen anything like it, though all these people remind me of the end of summer, when all seven councils of the Sioux come together."

"—Grady O'Brien, is it really you?" The sudden voice came out of the blue, and Star glanced around for the speaker. She saw a large, matronly woman hurrying toward them. Beside her, Grady swore softly beneath his breath. She met his gaze with a silent question.

"I apologize in advance," was all he had time to say before the woman descended.

"Why, it is you, Grady. You've returned after all these years! Splendid! Mr. Hamburg and I will have to have you and your delightful daughters over. My own darlings have both wed. Oh, there is so much to catch up on." The woman stopped to regain her breath, her gaze traveling to Star. Her smile of welcome faded.

Beside her, Grady stiffened. "Mrs. Irma Hamburg, may I present Star Cartier of the Nebraska Territory? She is recently widowed, and she and her daughter are my guests."

"Oh?" Her expression of shock turned to one of sly interest. "There is much to catch up on, I see. I shall have my husband call on you."

Star noticed the change in the woman's eyes and voice. She recognized it, having had to deal with it on board the *Annabella*. While most of the passengers had become friendlier after the initial shock of seeing an Indian woman dressed in the latest fashion had passed, some had never thawed.

Grady cupped her elbow. "We really must be going, Mrs. Hamburg. Give your husband my best."

The woman smiled suddenly and a gleam came into her eye. She waved frantically at someone behind Grady. "Yes. Well, I must be going as well. It will be most interesting to have you and . . . Mrs.

Cartier over one evening." She bustled off, calling out a name.

Star glanced over her shoulder and saw the woman greet two others. All three turned to peer at her and Grady.

"Well, you've just had the misfortune of meeting St. Louis's worst gossipmonger. Your presence in my household will no doubt be the latest news for her and her cronies to spread."

When she'd left her tribe, Star had had no idea how her presence would affect Grady. After two months on the steamboat, she had a better idea. "I am sorry, Grady."

His brows rose. "For what?"

"I had no idea others would view you in this manner."

Laughing, he took her arm and pulled her onward. "If you think a few gossiping magpies can harm me, or put a pall on my day, then you are mistaken. People like Irma Hamburg are boring, witless and have little of worth to do with themselves. Forget her. She can't harm either of us."

Star knew that wasn't strictly so. She'd gleaned enough of the culture she was stepping into to know that her actions and presence had a definite effect on both of them. But for Grady, she put her troubled thoughts aside and gave herself over to the day—one that proved to be the most wondrous and overwhelming she had ever experienced.

She wandered from stall to stall, choosing strangely shaped and colored vegetables she'd never before seen, breads in fresh loaves and blocks of cheese. Some of the items Grady purchased didn't look so appealing to eat. She wasn't sure she'd find them to her liking, but to please her employer, she promised to try the new foods. The smells of aromatic coffee beans, smoked meats, ripe fruits, colorful flower stands and exotic spices competed with those of livestock, perfumed bodies and the odors of overly warm bodies all pressed together.

By midafternoon, hunger drove the group to sampling various displayed sweets, meat pies and cheeses. As they sat to do so, people passed, some smiling, some not. They all acknowledged Grady; and his previous absence seemed well known by many of the most elegantly clad citizens. There came a blur of invitations to dinners and promises of visits. When at last one final couple stopped before them, Star braced herself for the familiar once-over that had been making her self-conscious all day.

It didn't come. The woman, after being introduced smiled warmly. "How nice to meet you, Mrs. Cartier."

The woman's name was Rachael Browning, and as the two men exchanged news, she chatted about her four young children. Renny and Morning Moon ran over to them, Hattie in town. Zeke, laden with purchases, followed too.

"Why don't you and the two girls come to lunch on Thursday, Mrs. Cartier? Renny and Emma have been frequent guests for many years. Our parents were old friends of Grady's own."

"I'd like that." And she did look forward to it— as much as she now looked forward to returning home. They all rose and went back into the market proper.

After a while, the sights, sounds and crush of shoppers became too much. The mass of humanity had shoved her forward from one shouting vendor to another. Worse, voices here always seemed insistent, demanding, merging into one. Hands waved items for sale in front of her; young children held out trinkets, shouting prices, striving to be heard.

At last, in a tobacco vendor's stall, everything blurred.

There were too many colors, too many people. Too much noise. Too many demands.

From inside the stall someone bumped her, knocking her back out into the street. She tried to get back to Grady but felt as though some force was holding her back. Blinking against panic, she stood on tiptoe, desperate to catch Grady's attention, but he was caught up in purchasing the tobacco she'd picked out to take home with her come summer.

A cold wave slammed into her back. Icy fingers gripped her upper arm. She couldn't breathe. Glancing down, she saw a hand, its fingers wrapped around her arm, holding her, pulling her away from the crowd. Away from Grady.

She turned her head. Cruel pale blue eyes, bored into her. The rest of the man's features were concealed by a thick brown beard. The edges of her vision darkened.

Evil.

Darkness.

She heard his voice. "You took what was mine. You'll be sorry."

Anger, fury, hatred—she felt them all, *billowing from this man*.

Star shook her head in denial as her assailant's face contorted, turned hideous. He was a monster who watched with satisfaction as she sank into a dark void.

Chapter Eleven

Star woke to a pounding in her head and the frantic calling of her name. Confused, she opened her eyes, blinking against a stabbing shaft of light. At the blinding pain in her head, she moaned. Turning her head, she covered her eyes with her hand and tried to gather her scattered wits.

What was wrong? The last she remembered, she'd been trying to select tobacco for her father. Brief flashes of images returned, then it all came back to her: the blue eyes, the cold fingers gripping her arm and the sense of something horrible, before everything had gone dark. She tried to turn her head but it hurt.

"Star. Thank God you're all right. You fell and have a nasty bump on the side of your head."

Fingers tenderly smoothed her hair from her face. Her eyes teared when she removed her hand. Above her, Grady's face came into focus. The golden-red of his hair haloed around his head in the bright light, and the warm, dusky blue of his eyes soothed her. She relaxed. She was safe. The sound of a shade being drawn came, and the bright light dimmed. She tried to sit, but the movement sent waves of agony through her head.

"Don't move," Grady commanded, his lips pinched. "I'll have you home in just a few minutes—as soon as the others return."

Star realized they were sitting in his coach, and he had her cradled in his arms. Feeling weak, she did as he ordered, sinking into the warm haven of his chest. Beneath her ear, she heard the throb of his heart pumping. His fingers combed tenderly through her hair and his words rumbled in her ear as he spoke. "I shouldn't have turned my back on you. You're not used to the madness that often-times prevails at this market."

Star opened her mouth to tell him that she'd been pushed, grabbed and knocked down, but blazing eyes—cruel eyes full of hate and anger—replaced Grady's features. Sucking in her breath, she cringed from the imaginary creature who seemed to snake and twist around her mind. She saw no body, but the face alone was enough to frighten her. She'd never seen anything so hideous. She shuddered.

"Grady—" Calling out to him broke the spell.

Grady cupped her face. "Shh. It's all right."

Star focused on the gentle caress of his fingers on her skin to combat the pain in her head and the fear in her heart. She'd just had a vision—no—two of them. Tears burned the backs of her eyes.

At the arrival of Hattie, Morning Moon and Renny, Star insisted on sitting. Grady helped her up and Hattie fussed over her. Renny watched, for once silent. But the worry in her daughter's eyes made Star lean back into Grady's soothing embrace. She might be able to hide the effects of the vision from everyone else, but not her daughter.

What had she done? She'd thought to escape the gift of Sight, but since the night before their docking, it had quickly been proven that her attempt to do so had been futile. It had followed her from the land of her birth, a predator stalking its prey. She had been foolish to think that the Spirits could not go where the white man reigned.

As much as she longed to deny it, she couldn't. Worse, the question of her vision raised its ugly head: who was in danger this time? Herself? Hattie? Both of them? The voice had promised revenge. What did this new enemy want?

Though she'd turned her back on the Spirits, Star suddenly found herself begging them to watch over her. Her and everyone she loved.

Once they reached his house, Grady carried Star into the sitting room, ignoring her protests that she could walk. He needed to hold her, needed that reassurance that she was all right. How quickly things had changed. The day at the market had started with such joy and anticipation. Watching Star absorb the color and flavor of St. Louis had given him such pleasure. The wonder in her had filled him, allowed him to relive it all over again.

But in one instant, everything had changed. One moment she'd been beside him, sniffing tobacco, contemplating which plants she wanted to purchase as gifts for her father when they returned to her people in the summer, and then she was gone. Why had she collapsed like that?

Setting her gently on a dark rose settee with scrolled wooden trim, Grady knelt in front of Star Dreamer, his gaze skimming over her pale features, lingering on her eyes. They were wide and haunted—an expression he remembered well. Only now did he realize how much he'd grown used to seeing humor and an almost childlike excitement and wonder in her soft, dark eyes, such a change from the woman he'd first met. He was terrified to think she might again be sad.

"Just rest. I blame myself for forgetting that you're not used to the city and such crowded areas."

She shook her head. "It's not your fault, Grady." She leaned back and closed her eyes. Her thick black lashes fluttered. Fresh tears slipped from the corners of her eyes. "My family was right. I can't run from what I am."

Before he could ask what she meant, the new housekeeper rushed into the room, her small black face wreathed with worry lines. She clasped her hands together. "How about some tea, Mrs. Star?"

Grady smiled at the woman. "Tea sounds wonderful, Hattie. How about bringing some broth as well?"

Hattie hurried out, her voice echoing back into the small room as she ordered Zac and Zeke to hurry and bring the supplies from the carriage. Star smiled weakly. "I have a feeling those poor men will regret coming home with you."

Relieved to hear the humor in her voice, Grady pulled over a footstool and sat. "Truth to tell, I think they like it. No one has ever cared about them. They've been on their own since they were boys. Hattie will earn their loyalty—as you have— because she too cares."

After a long silence, Star plucked at her skirts. "Emma told me a lot of what to expect from your city and the manners of your people. You do not have a household that is normal for this city or your position, do you? You have a Sioux compan-

209

ion to watch over your daughter, three trappers and a housekeeper whom most would never trust with such responsibility. It will be hard to find a butler who will also accept both Hattie and myself, won't it?"

Grady rested his elbows on his knees and steepled his fingers beneath his smooth chin. "I am fortunate to be surrounded by people I care about and trust with my life, and my daughter's." His gaze softened. "I value loyalty and friendship more than the opinion of society. I always have."

Reaching out, he ran the back of his hand down the side of her face and followed the gentle slope down to her chin. His fingers came away wet from her tears. He longed to find the words to put a smile back in her eyes. "What more can a man ask for?"

Love and a wife. The words hung between them, though maybe only in his head. Now that he was back where he belonged, it was the next logical step for Grady. Even so, he wasn't sure what made him think the words. Just because they'd shared a kiss didn't mean there would ever be more between them. Yet he couldn't imagine life without her. What would happen if he took her back to her people as they'd planned? Would she choose to remain while he and Renny returned to his home?

He saw her glance down and huddle deeper into the cushions. She curled her feet beneath her and nervously played with her fingers. Making her uncomfortable was the last thing Grady wanted, but he couldn't deny the truth. He wanted this woman's love. Only then would his life be complete. The more he thought about it, the more right it felt. But perhaps now wasn't the time to press his case. He reached forward to grasp one of her hands.

She looked up at him through troubled eyes. "I'm

fine, Grady. You don't need to sit with me. I'm sure you have other things to do."

"Nothing at the moment." He hesitated, worried. She'd hit the ground hard. Maybe he should call in a doctor. First, he'd see how she responded to tea and food. And a fire. Though the day was warm, her fingers were like ice.

Standing, he went to the door and called for Jeffers to light a fire. Guilt sat heavily on his shoulder. He paced, unconsciously clasping his hands behind his back.

Star frowned at him, her gaze tracking him from one side of the sitting room to the other. "It wasn't your fault, Grady. It was—" She broke off.

Grady noted the fear that entered her eyes before she fixed her gaze on an intricate piece of woven hair his wife had fashioned into a wall hanging, framed and hung opposite her.

"It was what?" he prompted.

Troubled, she stared at him. He sat again and waited.

"I don't think my fall was an accident."

"What do you mean?" Grady recalled the look of terror in her eyes just before she'd fallen. "Someone pulled me from the stall, then shoved me." She didn't meet his startled gaze.

"Are you sure?"

She looked at him, her eyes full of despair. "I saw him, felt him. His eyes, cold, full of hate. When he touched me, I felt death."

Stunned, Grady felt a sudden fury. "Who was it? What did he look like?"

Star covered her face with her hands. "I don't want to remember. I don't want this to happen. Not again. Please, no more visions."

Grady moved to sit beside her so he could touch

her and lend her his support. "You had a vision? I thought you said—"

"Both," she interrupted. "Someone grabbed me, then pushed me. The vision was coming, just before I hit my head. Then, in the carriage, it came."

If only he knew more about her visions; he wished he'd asked more questions of her family and learned what to do when she had these spells.

Star tipped her head back, strained. She looked hopeless. "The visions aren't going to go away, are they? I left home for nothing."

Trying to ease her tension so he could find out more, Grady said, "Well, I wouldn't say that. You're doing me some good."

"Judging from the reactions of your peers, I'm not sure. I may be more trouble than help. And now this." Releasing a long breath of air, Star tried to smile but couldn't. "In my heart, I've always known."

The deep despair in her voice tore at Grady. If only he could help her. He knew she fought and resented her visions, and after witnessing the effect they had on her, he couldn't blame her. That brought him back to what had happened earlier. What had she seen at the market? Who had tried to harm her, and why?

"I'd like to help. Even though I've never known anyone with your abilities, Star, I can't deny what I've seen with my own eyes. I owe you more than I can ever repay for saving my daughter's life. I'm a good listener if nothing else," he invited.

One of the maids came in with tea, a bowl of broth and a plate of sliced bread and cheese. After setting the tray on a marble-topped table, she left quietly, closing the door behind her. Grady poured two cups of tea, added sugar to Star's, then resumed his place beside her. He handed Star the drink. She cradled the warm cup of tea in her hands, her fingers flexing around the porcelain.

"Drink it. It will help," he urged. He waited patiently until her cup was empty, then replaced both of their cups on the tray.

"Now tell me what's going on." He took her hands in his.

Star's lips trembled, as if she was not sure how to begin. "Something will happen."

"*What* will happen?"

Her eyes filled with bleak despair. "I don't know. It's too soon. The visions will worsen as the event nears."

"Go on," Grady encouraged.

Tightening her grip on his hands, Star's gaze begged him to believe, to understand, to help her. But could he believe her words? "I saw a monster today. I felt his anger and hatred. I heard his voice. Darkness and death surround him. Someone will die—I have felt that twice now." Uncontrollable sobs tore through her.

Grady's heart hammered. His protective instincts rose to the surface. This fragile woman needed him. He would not fail her. Scooping her into his arms, he cradled her close. One hand stroked her arms and back while he murmured softly into her ear. Together, they'd piece this puzzle together. She didn't have her family to help her get through this—just him. That thought scared him.

Of their own accord, his eyes sought the mantel and Margaret Mary's portrait. From the angle at which he sat, it looked as though her eyes were watching him. He waited for the stab of guilt, the slice of pain to wash over him. He was embracing another woman in front of her.

But there was nothing. Only regret. Maggie had

been young, full of love and laughter. So full of life. They should have raised their family together, grown old together, but fate had decreed otherwise.

He brushed the silky strands of hair from Star's face, stroking her head and combing her locks through his fingers. He feathered his lips across her forehead and continued to murmur softly to her. When her sobs at last subsided and she lay exhausted in his arms, he pulled out his handkerchief and wiped her face as if she were a small child. She took the linen from him, blew her nose and clutched it to her.

Tenderness welled inside him. "Better?"

"Yes."

"Liar." He said the word gently.

"What am I going to do?"

Grady tried to recall the first time he'd met her, how her family had dealt with her when she'd been so distraught about his daughters being in danger. "Do your visions always come true?"

"Yes."

"Could you change the outcome?"

"Yes. If I learned the meaning in time." Her voice hiccupped. "My grandmother was able to, at least."

Grady rubbed his cheek against the top of her head. Her hair had long since lost the pins holding it off her neck. He liked the way it fell, framing her face. "Then you and I will have to figure out what the Spirits are trying to tell you."

"And if we don't, someone will die." She gulped air into her heaving lungs.

At his prompting, she described the man who'd grabbed her and repeated what he'd said. Grady thought it made perfect sense.

"That's the first clue! It means your visions have to do with Hattie and your intervention in saving

214

her." That knowledge, while giving him warning, was bad news. It meant Star was now a target. The thought that she was in danger chilled his soul. When he told her, Star did not discount his assumption.

He watched her absently rub her upper arm. Gently, he unbuttoned the cuff at her wrist and shoved the full sleeve up. When he saw finger-sized black bruises marring her honey-brown skin, he felt as though someone had knocked the wind from him.

Thinking back on all Star had said, his mind focused on the steamboat, when she'd had the vision as they entered the city. She'd felt death there. That steamer had left St. Louis the same night Hattie said her husband and son were shipped out. Along with Charles's servant, was his guess. Perhaps this all was related to today's incident.

Determination hardened him. Without saying a word, he slid the material back down her arm. Calm blanketed the fury inside him as his military training took over. This was war. "No one will die."

Star pushed away from him, using her fisted hands planted on his chest to hold herself away. "If it's meant to be, no one can stop it."

Her utter hopelessness strengthened Grady's vow. He would best death this time around. He'd lost too much to it already. "If we have warning, we can prepare."

"How do you prepare for death, Grady? How can anyone be ready to lose a loved one?" Her dark eyes swam with fresh tears.

The words hung between them, stark and raw. People died every day from illness or murder,— even childbirth. Like Margaret Mary. And though the doctors had warned him, tried to prepare him, her death had devastated him when it came. Nothing and no one could have adequately prepared him for that moment.

Star dropped her head to his chest. Grady's hands slid up her arms to cup it, to hold her to him. He rested his cheek on the top of her head for a moment before he gently forced her to look at his face. His lips once again grazed her brow. "By not accepting it. By doing all we can to prevent it. I couldn't save Margaret Mary. No one could. I realize that now. And from what you've said, nothing you could have said to your husband would have prevented him from riding to war.

"But this is different. We have hope. We have time and warning. We'll fight it, Star. Together."

Her hands crept up his chest and wound around his neck. "Help me."

Their heads moved closer. "I will," he whispered, his mouth touching hers, her breath mingling with his.

Raw need exploded between them. Grady wrapped his arms around her, and Star gripped him hard, her fingers digging into the corded muscles along his shoulders. His lips slanted over her mouth. Hers parted, begging for his touch, his kiss.

Star felt herself swimming in a pool of desperate need. She wanted this man, craved his strength and iron will. He'd fight death for her. For the children. But could he change the outcome? She had no idea who would die. Not knowing both scared her and relieved her.

With a low cry deep in her throat, she put visions, hatred and death from her mind. Right now she needed life. She needed to feel. And kissing Grady brought to the surface passions she'd never known resided inside her.

Her senses swirled, hunger clawing through her

despair. She moaned and slid her hands up the hard column of his neck, then along the outline of his jaw.

Grady's hands roamed up and down her back, moved to her head, his fingers tangling in her hair. She aped his movements. She loved the feel of his hair, thick, soft and long.

Lifting her head, he leaned forward, holding her firmly as his mouth followed the line of her jaw and moved to her throat. Then he pulled away. For a long moment they stared at one another, their ragged breathing drowning out the sound of a ticking clock on the wall, each of their hands resting on the other's shoulders, as if not sure whether to push away or come together in fury.

His eyes, soft and smoky with desire, devoured hers. Slowly, as one, they moved back into each other's arms. This time, the kiss was hesitant; it was as if each was afraid of the turbulent emotions and the fiery possession that had swept them up in this burning desire. Grady again pressed his lips to her forehead, her eyes, the bridge of her nose, then hovered a breath away from her lips.

Star tipped her head to one side and leaned down to kiss his chin, her tongue dipping into the dimple there. He shuddered as she did. Planting tiny, soft kisses along his jaw, near his ear, Star trailed her mouth over the hard planes of his sculptured face before returning to his mouth. But she didn't kiss him there. She waited.

Time stood still as they took turns exploring each other with their lips and tongues but their mouths stopped short each time. A brief lick here. A tiny nibble there. Until finally, Grady flicked his tongue along the corner of her mouth. Star bit gently and tugged at his bottom lip with her teeth. A brief touch followed, then a short parting to allow their breaths to mix and entice.

When they finally kissed again, it was slow and sweet. Star wasn't sure which she preferred: this langorous melding of souls or Grady's demanding mastery. Both called out to her. She yearned for all this man could give her.

That need grew and filled her. It frightened her. "Grady—"

"I know. I know." He pulled her close and held her, her breasts pressed to his hard chest. "I shouldn't have kissed you, but you're in my blood. You're my bright star. My *bright star.* You saved me and showed me life is worth living and fighting for. I won't lose you."

Something squeezed her ribs. Her heart ached under the pressure. She lifted her head and covered his mouth with her fingers. "No. Don't love me, Grady."

A pained expression crossed his features. His hand shook as he cupped her face and feathered his fingers over her features. "It might be too late."

Star couldn't breathe. She pushed off his lap and struggled to her feet, her limbs tangling in her long skirt and layers of petticoats. "I didn't want this to happen. I can't love. Not ever again. I won't risk it." Her voice rose, her lungs felt heavy, refusing to draw in air.

He couldn't love her. She couldn't love him. This couldn't be allowed to happen. Death hovered on the horizon. Someone close to her was in mortal danger, and there was no guarantee that her visions could save them. It didn't matter if it was her or someone else. If anything happened to her, then Grady would suffer another loss. In fact, both times that she'd felt the premonition of death had been in Grady's presence. *It could be him. She might be in danger, and he could die protecting her.*

"No!" she cried. More frightened than she'd ever been before, she ran from the room.

Grady followed Star to the doorway and heard her running up the stairs. Pausing, he glanced over his shoulder toward the mantel. In the waning after-noon light, Margaret Mary looked as sad as he felt.

"Don't love me," Star had said.

It was too late—too damn late.

Sagging against the wooden frame, he glared over at the curving staircase. Margaret Mary was his past. Star was his future. She'd given him back his nights, chased away his nightmares and given him hope. She brightened his days, made him feel alive.

"Don't love me," she'd said. He closed his eyes. Someone had to. *He* had to. His life had changed forever the day he'd met Star Dreamer. Like a vision, she'd woven her way into his life and bound him to her.

Straightening, he knew that neither of them was ready emotionally to make a commitment. Too much baggage had to be gone through and dealt with. Too much anger, despair and guilt still created a chasm.

"Papa?"

Grady glanced up the stairs. Two worried faces stared down at him. "Yes, Renny?"

"Is Star all right?"

"She's fine, sweetheart. She needs to rest, though, so I want you and Matilda to play quietly. And, Renny . . . I'm going out for a while. I'd like you and Matilda to stay in the house while I'm gone."

"Yes, Papa."

Grady donned his hat, then went in search of the

scouts. He ran into Zac in the kitchen. He wore new denim pants, suspenders and a flannel shirt. On his feet, he sported new boots.

"Well, well, well. You don't look half-bad cleaned up." Not only that, he looked fifteen years younger. Grady would bet the brothers weren't that much older than he—maybe in their early forties, instead of their fifties, as he'd originally figured.

"Gots ta eat. That woman even took our clothes and burned them," he announced, disgruntled.

Seeing disguised pride, Grady knew Zac was enjoying the attention. "Where are Zeb and Zeke?"

"Zeb's out in the stable. Zeke is in there." He hitched his thumb over his shoulder to indicate the pantry.

Grady heard the other man talking to Hattie. "Get him and meet me at the stables. I need to speak to all three of you." At Zac's nod, he left the house.

Finding Zeb, Grady asked him to saddle his horse. He declined the use of a buggy. Waiting in the carriage house, he paced. In the far corner, Margaret Mary's old phaeton sat, and next to it, also covered in a think layer of dust and spiderwebs, his Dearborn coach looked woefully neglected. Another thing waited for him to do: purchase a stable of suitable horses.

"What's up, Colonel?" Zac and Zeke joined him.

"Is Mrs. Star all right?" Zeke looked worried. The three brothers had quickly adopted Hattie's title for her.

Grady's jaw dropped when he got a good look at Zeke in dark pants, a white shirt and a snug-fitting jacket. He wore white gloves on his hands too. He looked uncomfortable with Grady's scrutiny.

Zeb entered, then, and that stopped Grady from asking the man what he was dressed up for. It was too early for a supper engagement. "She's fine. But listen. I want one of you with her, Hattie or the children every time they leave the house."

Zac scratched his ear. "What's up, Colonel? What's you afeared of?"

Pacing, Grady told the three brothers what had happened at the market and his suspicions that it was tied to Hattie's kidnappers.

Zeke flexed his hands. "Ain't nobody gonna harm any of them, Colonel." With that, he left to return to the house.

Taking the reins of his horse from Zeb, Grady patted the animal and gazed thoughtfully after Zeke. "Where's your brother going now?"

Zac smirked. "To take up his post."

"Post?"

"As butler," Zeb said. Pride shone in the man's brown eyes.

Grady whistled. "Who hired him?" Zeke was not exactly butler material. His friends' sudden silence cued him. "Zac, you and your brothers are not my servants."

"Reckon we'd rather work fer you than anybody else, Colonel."

Grady eyed the twins with curiosity. The idea of these men wanting to remain with him warmed and pleased him beyond measure. "And what positions have you two claimed?"

Zeb shuffled his feet. "I always did like animals and being outdoors." He eyed the various means of transportation. "I figure it can't be too hard to learn to learn to drive these—and Mrs. Star will need a driver. I figure I can do that and some other stuff 'sides, like making sure your grounds are just as fine as those of them neighbors of yours."

Grady slapped the large mountain of a man on

the back. "I accept your offer to be driver and head gardener. Zac?"

Zac's face turned beet red. "Heard you have need of a valet, Colonel?"

Grady wasn't sure whether to laugh or cry at the absurd notion of Zac pressing his clothing, but as with the other two, he accepted Zac's offer with a slap on the back. He would deal with the situations as they came up. "Welcome aboard, men."

Zac escaped back to the house, leaving Grady staring after him. Well, that was settled. With the exception of a few servants for the cleaning and upkeep of his estate, he had his main staff positions filled. Not a conventional staff, he admitted, but the only people he wanted. The corner of his lip twitched. Zac as his personal valet? That was downright hilarious. Yet there wasn't a man he trusted more with his life.

A slight noise coming from behind the Dearborn stopped him from mounting his horse. Frowning, he scanned the area. He didn't see anything. About to turn away, he saw a rat scurry out from behind a wooden crate.

A hand reached out to grab the rodent.

Grady straightened and clasped his hands behind his back. "Ranait O'Brien! Front and center!"

Covered with bits of straw and layers of dust, Renny emerged from her hiding spot with a wooden box cradled in her arms. She skirted him, staring up at her father with wary eyes. Her pet rats peered up at him too, from over the edge of the pocket in the girl's apron.

"What do you think you're doing? I told you to stay in the house."

"I was just—"

"Disobeying as usual. When I give an order, you *will* obey, understand?"

"But—"

"But nothing! There is no excuse for this wanton display of disobedience. You will go straight to your room and remain there until tomorrow. As further punishment, there will be no ride in the park tomorrow."

"Papa!" Renny's lips trembled.

Grady felt anguish at punishing her, but he was tired of waiting and hoping for simple obedience. "Perhaps next time you will think twice before you disobey. Go."

Tears streamed down the girl's cheeks, but she didn't argue further. She ran for the house, the box clutched in her arms and her hand over her pet rats to be sure they didn't bounce out. Grady ran a hand tiredly over his jaw. He hated to be harsh with her, but she had to learn to do as she was told. Mounting, he left.

Chapter Twelve

Clutching her precious box under her arm, Renny dashed into the house through the kitchen. She ran past Hattie, Zeke and Cook, wanting to reach her room without anyone stopping her. Tears blurred her sight, making her trip on the stairs. In her bedroom, sobs tore from her. "I hate him. I want to go back. I want Emma!" She threw the box that had gotten her into trouble onto the bed, reached down into her pocket to scoop up Anna and Bella and set them back into their cage. Then she flung herself facedown on her bed.

Morning Moon joined her. "What's wrong, Weshawee?"

Renny lifted her head. "Father is so mean, and he broke his promise to take us riding tomorrow."

"Why?" Morning Moon sat down and crossed her legs, resting her back against the footboard.

"'Cause I went to the carriage house." Renny turned over and hugged a pillow to her chest.

"You disobeyed him? Why? He told us to stay in the house."

"I only went out for a minute . . . and it was before he left," she muttered. "I just wanted to get this box before he left, but before I could get back into the house, I heard him coming, so I hid 'cause I wanted to surprise him. Then Bella got loose. That's when he caught me." She sniffed and wiped the tears from her face with the back of her hand.

"He didn't have to be so mean! He wouldn't even let me explain." That bothered her more than being in trouble for disobeying—and he had said to stay indoors while he was gone. That made her mad too. He hadn't left yet. She hadn't done anything wrong.

She glared at the box lying next to her on the bed. Angry all over again, she shoved the box away. It fell onto the carpet with a muted clunk. "I was going to give that to him, but not now. I won't give him anything, not ever again." She flopped down onto her back. "I wish me and Emma never went to find him!"

Morning Moon tipped her head to the side. "But Weshawee, if you and Emma hadn't gone to find your father, Emma wouldn't have married my uncle and we wouldn't be sisters."

Her friend's words gave Renny pause. "Sometimes you're real smart, Morning Moon. I am glad we got to meet. You're my best friend. And my sister. I just wish he'd stayed away."

Looking serious, Morning Moon objected. "It is good you found your father, Weshawee. He needs you, and so does my mother."

Renny narrowed her eyes and slid off the bed. She stared down at her box, then kicked it out of sight beneath the bed. "Well, I don't need him." She ran out of the room, down the hall and around a

corner to another set of wide but steep stairs. They
led to the third floor, where there were three small
rooms for servants. This set of stairs, used only by
servants, joined the back ones. She climbed and
stopped on the landing.

From the third floor, another set of stairs led to
the attic. She glanced up at the dark area and de-
bated. She needed to be alone, and the attic was
one of her favorite places to hide. On her left, there
were four small rooms, two in the front, two in the
back, all for servants or storage. Keeping things
symmetrical, the same space existed on Renny's
right. There, however, instead of four rooms, there
was only one large chamber. She slipped inside
what had once been her mother's studio.

Closing the door behind her, Renny stood there.
She loved this room, for it received both morning
and afternoon light from windows installed along
the front and back walls.

A thick layer of dust now covered the bare floor
and the few pieces of furniture in the sparsely furnished room. There were two chairs, one small table and a long worktable, a paint-splattered stool
and two easels, one with a half-finished painting
on it. The servants were not allowed in this room.

Everyone must have forgotten its existence—except her. She wandered around, peering into the
two small storage closets where her mother had
kept her supplies. On one worktable, several
stained towels lay where they'd been carelessly
tossed, as if the painter had been planning to come
back and finish covering the displayed bare canvas
with soft, muted colors.

Tears trickled down Renny's face and splattered
onto the floor, sending puffs of dust upward. She
moved and sat down, her back against the wall. In
front of her, spread out by her own hand, beams of

light poured over and illuminated the half-dozen pictures.

Her mother's paintings.

Unframed. Forgotten.

Renny drew her legs up to her chest, hugged them and rested her chin on her knees. One portrait was of Emma playing on the grass with two dolls. She looked to be about the same age as Renny, or younger. Those same dolls now lay on Renny and Morning Moon's bed. Her gaze slid past painted scenery of the park across the street. There were several other canvases of trees, grass and flowers. Those didn't interest her. Her forlorn gaze came to rest on her favorite work, one showing two horses.

Both animals were absolutely breathtaking. They frolicked across green, rolling hills. In the background, two riders on other mounts, a young girl and her father, sat in their saddles beneath a distant tree, its spreading boughs giving them shade from the bright sun as they watched the animals race for freedom beneath a bright blue sky. Dots of flowers added color to the lush painting.

Renny loved this work, wanted it for her own, but had always been afraid to ask. Still, if no one remembered this room or these paintings, then she could come up here and look at them whenever she wanted to. And she could pretend those riders were her and her father riding in the park together.

"But they weren't!" she cried. They would never be her and her father. The thought that he would never come to like her, let alone love her, left her feeling terribly sad. She didn't mean to be bad. She just wanted him to like her as much as he liked Emma.

"Renny?" Morning Moon poked her head into the room. "Do you want to be alone?"

"No." She sighed. "You can come in. But shut the door so no one knows we're in here." Morning Moon joined her, sitting beside her, their shoulders touching.

"Did your sister paint those?"

"No. My mother. But Emma is a good painter too." Renny was glad that her sister had never used this room. Renny hadn't even known this room was up here until she had gone looking for a hiding place the day she broke Aunt Ida's favorite flower vase.

Since that day, Renny had come here often. This room was all she had of her mother.

"I wish I could paint like my mother and Emma."

"I know which one is your favorite." Morning Moon pointed to the horses.

"Yeah." Renny sighed. "I wish I could have it."

"You have not asked?"

Wrinkling her nose, Renny snorted. "No. *He'd* say 'no,' just to be mean. Then he'd take it and hide it so I could never see it again."

Frowning, Morning Moon shook her head. "You let anger rule your thoughts, Weshawee. Your father is not a mean man. He loves you."

"Yeah, and he needs me, right?"

"Yes."

"What if I said I didn't care?"

"You would lie to yourself?"

Renny scrubbed her eyes with the back of her hands. Sometimes having a friend as smart as Morning Moon was a pain. "No. But, I don't want to need him. What if he leaves again?" She voiced her worst fear. "I'm not very good at listening and I break things. What if he gets sick of me and leaves?"

"He won't."

"How do you know?"

Morning Moon smiled softly. "He won't," she said simply.

Unconvinced, Renny drew circles in the dust on the wooden floor with her finger. "We'll see. At least I have you and your mother. Star never yells."

Remembering how unfair her father had been, how angry he'd been to find her in the carriage house, made her sad all over. If only her rat hadn't gotten loose, he'd never have known she'd sneaked out. Then she could have given him her special gift—one she'd saved and waited her whole life to give him.

Through her anger and pain, she recalled what she'd overheard. Her father believed that someone had tried to hurt Star at the market. Was it true? If anything happened to Star, Renny wouldn't have anyone.

"How much can you see of the future, Morning Moon?"

Morning Moon stared out one of the windows. "I see some things."

"Like what?"

"I've seen my mate."

"Yeah, you said that a long time ago." Suddenly curious, Renny turned her head to look into her friend's eyes. "Do you know yet what he looks like?"

"A little. He has black hair."

"All Indians have black hair." Renny slumped back against the wall.

"He's Indian, but he's not like my people. He dresses and acts different."

"What about other things."

"Like what?"

"Bad things. Like what your mother sees."

Morning Moon reached across and took hold of Renny's hand, strangely adult. "I cannot tell everything I see, Weshawee. Some things have to reveal themselves."

But Renny wasn't asking about that. She was more worried about Hattie or Star, but she didn't ask. She wasn't sure she wanted to know if anything bad was going to happen to Star. She eyed Morning Moon curiously. "It doesn't bother you to see things?"

"No. My gift will someday serve my people." She stood. "Come. Let's go see if Cook will let us have some cake. I like cake. A lot."

Renny hopped up, grinning. Then her smile faded and she slumped back down. "I can't. I'm supposed to stay in my room." Neither made mention that Renny wasn't in her room now.

"I'll sneak you up some."

"Okay." The girls exchanged grins. They were sisters. They'd always take care of each other.

Long after the household settled down for the night, Star returned to her spacious, plush bedroom and settled on the seat built in beneath the large window to await Grady's return. She wrapped a quilt around her shoulders to ward off the slight chill. A spring storm was brewing, relieving the air of the hot mugginess that made it difficult to breathe. The coolness coming off the pane of glass actually felt good.

She stared at the strange-looking clock on the mantel of the fireplace. A brass statue of a woman formed its base. Balanced on her hand, the clock swung with the face on top and the part that made the hands go around on the bottom. She found the gentle pendulum motion soothing, even if she still hadn't figured out how to use the machine to tell the time. To her, it was just a pretty piece.

A carriage coming down the street drew her attention. It passed the house. *Not Grady*. She yawned but fought her tiredness. She had to talk to him about Renny before she went to bed.

The poor child was so distraught over what she saw as an injustice, she'd refused to come down from the third floor. She'd also refused to eat from the tray Star had brought up to her. Star couldn't leave the child on the cold floor all night. Though she knew if she'd demanded, not asked, Renny to return to her room, the girl would have obeyed, Star understood that Renny, at odds with her father, needed to feel close to her mother. That was why she was in Margaret Mary's room. So Star would wait up for Grady. Unfortunately, that gave her time to fret and stew over their last kiss.

Resting her head against the wall, she wondered what she was going to do. She'd never anticipated falling in love with the colonel. Startled, she reared up.

In love?

It couldn't be. She couldn't love Grady.

How could attraction and respect and admiration have turned to love without her being aware of it? That it had happened at all frightened her very much. She'd never before felt this way, and that confused her more. She'd been married, had two children by a man who'd treated her well, valued her and protected her, yet what she felt with Grady was like nothing she'd ever known.

Her marriage to Two-Ree had been one of mutual respect and friendship, as many of her people's marriages were. But that was all.

With Grady she felt different. She felt cherished and vulnerable, needed and needy—and stomach-churningly fearful now that she knew the true danger of loving, not only to her heart but to her sanity.

She'd warned him, down in the sitting room. His words, *"It may be too late,"* echoed in her mind and heart. Desperation made her jump up and pace. What was she going to do? She didn't want to hurt him, but she could not risk love. The memory of the devastation of seeing Two-Ree's death beforehand in a vision seized her, reminding her of the premonitions of death that had followed her to St. Louis.

The reality that it could happen to Grady frightened her. "No," she moaned, cursing her gift. Why did it follow her and torment her so? Why was it growing stronger with each passing year, when before her marriage to Two-Ree, it hadn't been nearly so potent?

Once more she experienced the sensation of standing on the edge of a cliff, a bottomless pit. One strong gust of wind would send her spiraling downward. Instinct warned her to step away and protect herself at all costs. Survival—her own—might very well depend on listening to that voice of reason.

She couldn't afford to love Grady or allow him to love her. Wasn't it bad enough to fear her parents', brothers' and sisters' deaths? Or those of the children born into their family? Yet she accepted that she could do nothing to prevent visions of those closest to her.

"But no one else," she whispered, hugging her knees to her tightly. "No one else." Somehow she had to harden her heart and protect her soul from the pain of possibly losing this man she loved. This love had to be denied, banished, driven away.

Her eyes lifted to the glittering heavens. Her questions echoed back down at her. *How do I block the light in my soul or the joy in my heart? How can I turn away my soul mate?*

With stunning clarity that had nothing to do with her gift of sight and everything to do with the longing of her heart, Star faced the truth. She'd known from that very first vision—that of flying with the eagle, of being one with the great bird—that she and Grady were meant to be. They'd merged, become one, as a man and woman did when they became husband and wife. She'd felt safe and cherished. The spirits had revealed her future in those visions. Grady *was* her soul mate; she felt sure of it. He was the one she was meant to love and live side by side with until death claimed them.

In the midst of her heart-stopping self-revelation, the edges of her vision darkened. "No. Oh, no," she moaned, gripping her head with both hands. Her heart raced and she held her breath. And this time, the darkness did not claim her completely. A shadowy shape formed—Grady's, as he held out his hands to her. Nothing more.

She waited, fearing the worst. As unexpectedly as it had come, the image receded. But rather than relieving her, the vanishing left her on edge. Pain sliced through her heart, cleaving her in two. Was she to protect her heart and mind by avoiding Grady, denying herself the love he offered, or risk eventual heartache?

Pressing her fingers to her lips, she closed her eyes, reliving the passion, the warmth, the gentleness of his kiss. She flushed with anticipation, yearning for, needing his touch, his tender caresses, his kisses. She needed him. His love. Standing, she moved slowly toward the door connecting her room to Grady's.

The choice was hers. Safety and loneliness for the rest of her life, or love and joy. And loss.

Her fingers wrapped around the doorknob.

She opened the door and stepped inside.

She chose love. She wanted Grady, wanted what he so freely offered. And by accepting his love, she'd be free to give her own in return.

Glowing light from the lamp on the table beside his bed penetrated the gloom of the room and chased away the shadows in her heart. She sat on the edge of his bed and smoothed her palm over his pillow, imagining his head resting there, her fingers combing through thick, golden-red strands of hair as his blue-gray eyes turned smoky with desire. And his mouth was full and soft, parting, begging her to lean down and touch and taste it.

The image of him there, with her, was so strong, so powerful, that heat pooled between her legs. Star moaned and hugged the pillow to her breasts, wishing he was there.

"This ain't the cargo listed on the manifest." The substitute captain of *Freedom's Fancy* frowned and studied the shipping papers.

Leo shifted his gaze, one eye on the rough-looking crew and the other on two men down on the wharf, guarding his cargo of slaves. "There's been a change."

The captain shook his head. "I'm going to have to clear this through Mr. Olsen."

Damn, Leo thought. What rotten luck to have the regular master of the steamboat out ill. Baxter had found one of his other men to pilot the steamboat until the captain was well again. And everyone knew how Leo's employer felt about slavery.

Leo snatched the papers, folded them and tucked them into an envelope. "Mr. Olsen is out of town. I'm in charge, and I have a customer willing to pay—and pay well—to have this cargo delivered safely. Your job is to pilot the damn boat, not pry into business decisions. Now, do you follow orders, or do I relieve you of duty? There are other captains who will be more than happy to take your place." Leo knew the man had seven children to support.

"But Mr. Olsen has never transported slaves before." The captain looked unhappy and uncertain.

Sweat broke out along Leo's forehead. If only he'd been informed of the change, he could have called off the shipment—but it was too late now. There was too much risk taking them back to the abandoned house on the outskirts of the city. He peered into the darkness beyond the wharf. Time was of the essence.

"Decide now."

"Maybe I want to keep my job." The captain paced nervously.

"You'll be paid extra for this run. The money's good. What does it matter what the cargo is? It's all about money. For Baxter, for me and for you." Especially for him.

At last, the captain acceded. Relieved, Leo ordered the five women to be taken down to a room belowdeck. Three men escorted the shipment on board. One man held the arm of a young woman who stumbled.

"What's wrong with that one?" Concerned, the captain stepped forward.

Leo slid in front of him. "She gave birth two days ago and lost the babe. I'll see them settled."

Leo followed his cargo, saw them herded into one small room. Gripping his riding crop, he smacked his hand with it. Each of the women was lined up against the wall. Each wore baggy sacking.

The first woman he came to cowered. He grinned and grabbed her jaw. At fifteen, she was the youngest, and a virgin. "You'll fetch me and the boss a nice bit of cash." He leered, reaching out to fondle her breasts before moving to the next woman.

The next two shrank from his touch. He'd enjoyed them several times already, before turning them over to the Dragon. The fourth woman was old. No plantation owner would want her, nor would the brothel. But for right now, she was useful. She held up the fifth woman, the one who'd slumped against her and was moaning.

Leo shoved the filthy hood off the hidden woman's head. Blond hair cascaded forward, covering her face and sliding soft as silk against his arm. He caressed it, then yanked. The dazed blue eyes blinked. Drugged, and bound beneath her cloak, her moans and fearful cries were muffled by the gag. "And you are my prize."

This one would fetch him more than the last two shipments combined. And best of all, she was his—as was the money she'd fetch. "Keep this one drugged," he ordered. The two men he addressed would see his cargo to its final destination: a brothel on the fringes of the western frontier whose madame paid well for young girls, especially virgins, and didn't care if they were willing or not.

Leaving one man inside the cabin to make sure the prisoners caused no trouble, he locked the door to keep everyone else out. Relief swept through him. Everything was going as planned. Come morning, long before Baxter returned, *Freedom's Fancy* would be gone. He'd always been secretly amused at his choice of ships to transport slaves. He handed the second man the key. "No one but you is to go in there."

"Yes, sir. We'll git 'em delivered." The man rubbed his hands together. "When does we git our pay?"

Leo brought the whip down hard onto the man's thigh. "When the cargo is safely delivered, and not a second before. Bring back a a letter from Madame Olivia." Then he left, certain that everything would go according to plan.

Lost in his own thoughts of the money he'd make, he started when a dark shadow emerged from an alley and stopped him. "Any trouble?" it asked.

"None, boss." Leo didn't mention the switch of captains. Why bother? He'd taken care of it.

"What is wrong with the one slave?"

"Nothing. Just trying to get the captain's attention." Leo kept his voice carefully neutral. There'd be hell to pay if this man realized two of Leo's own young slave girls had been released so he could ship them in place of those who had escaped. He would eat the loss in the money, though. The Dragon always got the biggest share, but he always made some cash, and the blond girl would more than make up for the difference.

"Well done, Leo." The Dragon, heavily bearded and wearing a large, thick overcoat, handed him a leather bundle.

Leo measured the thickness, peeled back the leather and counted the bills inside.

Soft laughter followed. "You don't trust me?"

"No."

"Ah, you're a wise man."

"Just wait until I own Baxter's business. Then we'll be able to ship more often. Maybe we should arrange an accident."

"Leo, my friend, you're thinking again."

Leo, caught up in his own plans, missed the dark edge to the Dragon's voice. "I could marry Hester Mae and have it all." For he wanted it all: the house, the business, the status. And even Hester Mae, though marriage to her wouldn't stop him from taking his other pleasures where he pleased.

"*All*?" The voice had turned quiet. Deadly.

Leo swore to himself. "You know what I mean. I'd have the business and you'd have your transportation."

"For a fee, of course."

"Same as now."

"I see. I will take care of Baxter when the time is right, but for now, we will not do anything rash. Your day will come, my friend. We have more important things to see to first. I want Hattie back. And I want the squaw." His voice turned rough. "Get them for me. Understand?"

Leo stuttered, "Y-yes, boss. We'll get them."

"Don't let me down, Leo. And don't be in such a rush. You must be patient." With that, the slave lord slid back into the shadows and disappeared down the alley.

At the Blue Horn, a gentleman's club, Grady set his empty glass down on the table with more force than needed. "Slavery is wrong! I fear there will be war before all is said and done."

"People have the right to own slaves. And the South will fight to keep that right." Todd Langley, overhearing their conversation earlier and recognizing them from the other day at the wharf, had joined Grady and Charles. The man was a businessman who owned his own importing company. He set his own empty glass down, then beckoned over a young serving woman. She wore a low-cut blouse that revealed all but the tips of her overly generous bosom every time she deliberately leaned over him to gather empty glasses.

"Another round." Langley's hand trailed high beneath her skirt. She winked.

"No more for me," Grady said, put off by the blatant sexual play as Todd reached up to fondle one of her breasts. The man had seemed pleasant enough when he'd joined them, but he was quickly beginning to wear on Grady's nerves, what with his narrow-minded view of the world.

Charles refused another drink as well, and when the young servant sauntered away with swaying hips, he returned to their previous conversation.

"Humans were not meant to live in bondage, their children taken from them, their mates sold and shipped off at the whim of some cruel master. Free men should not have to fear being captured and sold against their will." He jabbed his finger at Todd. "I will stop this! When I discover who is behind this—when I find this Dragon—I will expose him and see him rot in jail."

Grady laid a stilling hand on his friend's shoulder. Like him, Charles publically denounced the practice of auctioning off slaves in the courthouse and the presence of agents in the city working for a dozen dealers. And the injustice of free slaves being forced back into slavery, and having no rights because they weren't considered citizens, infuriated him.

"At least we saved Hattie—and because of her, we now know when the rest were shipped out. It shouldn't be too hard to learn which steamer took them and where. That will lead us to who."

Todd's eyes flashed with anger as he drowned his whiskey in one gulp. "A waste of time, if you ask me. *Niggers* were brought to this country to serve. That's the way it's supposed to be . . . and no one is going to take away my right to own slaves."

Grady eyed Todd with a mix of disgust and disappointment, wondering why the man had even bothered to help defend Hattie against her kidnappers. He was just like so many others in this city. If Grady hadn't been there with Star, would Langley have walked off and left the woman to her fate?

Probably. It seemed everyone here turned a blind eye to the abuse of slaves. The path the country was taking, thought Grady wearily, could only lead to bloodshed.

Noting the lateness of the hour, he stood. He hadn't planned on staying out so late, but he and Charles had spent the afternoon talking to pilots and workers on the wharf, trying to trace the steamer that had left the night the *Annabella* arrived. Charles stood as well. They would find no answers here. Together the two men left, leaving Todd to flirt with the serving woman.

Chapter Thirteen

Grady rode through the dark streets, his mind on the results of his and Charles's search. Overall, it had been a good day. He had no doubt that they would soon know the whereabouts of his solicitor's manservant and Hattie's family. Money talked. And Grady had made sure each person he and Charles had spoken with knew they were willing to pay well for information.

Nearing home, he spurred his mount faster, suddenly eager to return to those awaiting him. It didn't matter that they would be in bed, for they were there. He was no longer alone. After nine years of wandering, never belonging, he'd come home. He didn't ever plan to leave again.

Unless war broke out. Then he would have to fight for what he believed in. After talking to people all day, he could already imagine a war between the South and North, pro-slave states against those who wanted freedom for all. But that would mean family against family, friend against friend.

Already, arguments of rights, escalating skirmishes along the Missouri and Kansas borders and talk of war were rampant. The Dred Scott case—a slave who was suing in the courts for freedom—was yet another example of the turning tide.

And that tide worried Grady—especially heading as it was for war. He'd seen enough battles, and had given a good share of his adult life to the military. Now all he wanted was peace, time to learn who he'd become and figure out what he wanted to do with the rest of his life. For the first time, his military career meant nothing to him. He had a daughter to raise. And a woman he wanted to spend the rest of his life loving.

A woman who doesn't want me to fall in love with her.

Tipping his head back, he stared up into the night sky. A few pinpoints of light peeked out from the incoming clouds.

Star Dreamer. She was his star. She had shattered his darkness, filled the empty void his life had become and left him with an overwhelming desire to live again. He wanted to reach out and touch her, and not just her body, but her soul. He wanted *her*. All of her.

Arriving home, he wasn't surprised when Zeb met him at the carriage house and insisted on seeing to his horse, despite the late hour. The man wanted to be helpful. He gratefully handed over the reins. Wondering if the other two brothers were waiting up for him, he shook his head as they appeared. He dismissed both.

"Lord, it's been a long day." The market, Star's ordeal, their kiss, all seemed like it had happened years ago rather than hours. Wanting nothing more than to forget everything, to climb into bed and sleep, he started up the stairs, then hesitated, his eyes shifting to the sitting room. He stepped inside without bothering to turn on a lamp. Clasping his hands behind his back, he stared at Margaret Mary's portrait.

The kiss he and Star had shared in this room had destroyed once and for all the grip his past had on him. He stopped in front of the mantel, knowing it was time to take Maggie's portrait down and get on with his life. Strange, how good it felt to let go of the pain and anger. Only since returning home had he realized he'd been so angry that she'd died and left him.

She left me.

The words burned in his mind. *Margaret Mary left me.* As had his parents.

With sudden insight, Grady finally admitted to himself that he'd been hiding from himself all these years, running from the pain of grief. He'd never been able to deal with his own anger and feelings of betrayal that those he'd loved had always left him. His sister Ida had been right when, so long ago, she'd accused him of running.

The army had been the perfect place to hide, to deny all emotion except grief. But anger was a part of grief, and the part he'd refused to acknowledge. Until now.

He rocked back on his heels, stunned by the self-revelation. Love had been the answer all along. Love for his daughters. Love for Star.

Love had made it possible to accept Margaret Mary's death, to rejoice in the daughters she'd given him and let go of the rage that had filled him for so long. Love had made it possible for him to forgive her for leaving him.

"Forgive *me*, Margaret Mary," he whispered. "I thought you'd betrayed me, just as my parents did when they died. Your death seemed the final betrayal. I ran. When you needed me to be strong, I let you down . . . and I'm so sorry." He'd turned his back on their children.

Once he was back in the army, it'd been easy to pretend that his absence from home was temporary. Just one more assignment. Now, after a lifetime of running, he yearned for a future filled with love and hope. A future with the woman who'd brought light back into his life and given him back his dreams. No more running.

Now it was his turn to give Star back her dreams. Then they could hope for a future together. But how? There had to be a way to banish the demons that were slowly destroying her.

"God rest, Margaret Mary. You'll always hold a special place in my heart." Though he couldn't see her, he felt a warm glow inside. He knew his decision would have pleased her. Feeling light of heart, he left the room and headed up the stairs. Halfway up, he spotted a small figure huddled next to the wooden banister at the top.

He stopped just below Morning Moon. "Child, what are you doing up so late?"

Troubled dark eyes held his. "Renny is sad. I was waiting for you."

Grady sighed. It hadn't taken but seconds after Renny ran off for him to regret his harshness and realize he hadn't handled the situation well. He wasn't in the military anymore, and expecting a child to obey blindly all the time wasn't realistic—especially if that child was Renny. And truthfully, she wasn't a willfully bad or disobedient child.

But where did he draw the line? Her own safety was at stake, and until he knew more of what was happening, he had to do what was necessary to protect her.

You could have told her why, a small voice scolded.

She's a child, he argued.

A child who knows a good deal of what's going on. His stomach clenched at the sudden realization that she'd overheard everything he'd said out there in the carriage house. Why hadn't he thought of that earlier? Now she'd had all evening to worry and fret over the danger he suspected Star and Hattie were in. He sat down heavily on the stairs. "I shouldn't have yelled at her. I should have given her my reasons." *I should have made sure she knows I'll protect her and Star and Hattie. And Morning Moon.*

Morning Moon looked up at him with wide eyes. "Do you know why I asked you both to stay inside? Did Renny tell you what she overheard?"

"No. But I know my mother's had visions."

Grady took a deep breath. "You know she's worried about you having them too. Have you?"

She met his gaze boldly, suddenly looking much older and wiser than her eight years. "There is danger. I sense it."

"Have you talked to your mother about it?"

"No. It would only upset her." Morning Moon lowered her eyes.

Grady reached out and tipped her small, rounded chin up. She looked so much like Star Dreamer, it was a little disturbing. "Child, you might hurt her far more with your silence. You are not protecting her. She needs to know." He held up his hand when she protested.

"It won't be easy. Facing our fears and being truthful is scary. I more than anyone else know this to be true. But until we face facts, we cannot come to terms with ourselves and change. Talk to her."

Morning Moon sat in thoughtful silence for a

moment. Then she smiled. "You are wise, father of Weshawee. I will talk to *ina*. She worries. But this was meant to be. My gift will serve our people someday."

"All right. Good girl. Now, up to bed."

Morning Moon nodded and pulled a broken wooden box from behind her. "Weshawee wanted to give you this. A gift."

Grady recognized the box as the one Renny had fled with from the carriage house. He hesitated to take it. "Maybe she doesn't want me to have it now."

Serious eyes held his. "It is meant for you."

Taking the small wooden box, he noted the freshly broken lid and side. It looked as though it had been thrown or kicked. With self-loathing at what he'd inadvertently put his daughter through, Grady clutched the gift. Without saying a word, Morning Moon got to her feet and left him.

Back in his den, he lit a lamp so he could see clearly and removed the box's lid. It was stuffed full of papers. One by one, he pulled out letters and drawings. As he went through them, glancing at some, reading others, the years slid past. Each piece in the box reflected Renny at a different age. Down at the bottom were drawings, some no more than lines scribbled on paper—Renny's first endeavors, saved no doubt by his sister.

There were also small stones and other tiny treasures. She'd saved them all, and had planned to give these treasures to him. He leaned back in his chair, feeling awful. She'd probably disobeyed him to get her box from her hiding spot in the carriage house, and for that he'd yelled at and punished her.

Guilt ripped through his heart. Leaving the den after dousing the lamp, he hurried up the stairs and entered her bedroom. His hands were clammy as he silently made his way to her bed. Originally, after seeing Morning Moon, he'd planned to talk to his daughter first thing in the morning. Now, it couldn't wait.

"*Renny is sad.*" Star's daughter's words tore at him.

He moved to Renny's bed. His heart lurched when he found it empty.

Sensing someone, he whipped around.

Morning Moon watched him from her bed on the other side of the room. She pointed at the ceiling. He furrowed his brows in confusion—until he remembered. "Of course," he said softly, heading for the door. "Thank you."

"Renny needs her father." The words were soft.

That gave him pause. This girl had lost hers. "And what about you?" He'd never given thought to her loss or the pain with which she must still be trying to deal. He felt selfish and self-centered for not considering that.

She smiled in a way that reminded him of her mother and raised the gooseflesh along his arms. "Renny is my sister." With that odd statement, she climbed beneath the covers.

But the implication wasn't lost on him. Because of her closeness to Renny, she regarded him as a father. He felt honored. Grady lit the lamp on the bedside table, then carried it with him to the door. Morning Moon's sleepy voice stopped him. "She really likes the horse painting."

He laughed. Would that make everything up to his daughter? A painting? "You are as wise as your mother, young lady." With that, he climbed the stairs slowly to the third floor, his mind whirling, trying to sort out everything that had hit him in one short day. And how his life would change. If he managed to convince Star to marry him, he'd have two daughters—and a son. He paused on the landing, liking the image that brought to mind.

Stepping into Margaret Mary's studio, Grady held the lamp high. Renny lay huddled along the wall beneath a quilt. An untouched supper tray lay next to her. Several canvases drew his attention. He'd forgotten all about them. Squatting, he studied them, smiled sadly at the one of Emma, then shook his head at the painting Morning Moon had mentioned.

Setting his lamp down, he scooped his daughter into his arms. She stirred, yawning sleepily, then opened her eyes. "I didn't disobey—exactly," she said. "You hadn't left yet, and you said I had to stay inside while you were gone. Are you going to yell at me for not staying in my bedroom?"

Grady blinked. "No, sweetheart. Never again."

Renny sighed and giggled. She wrapped her arms around his neck and snuggled close. "Yeah, you will."

He chuckled, too, then. "Yeah, probably so. But only because I love you. Never, never forget that, child."

She opened her eyes, then glanced around her. "You're not mad 'cause I came up here, are you?"

"Of course not. You can come up here any time you want."

Renny yawned again. "Truly?"

An idea formed in Grady's mind. "Truly. After I hire someone to clean it. Deal?"

"Deal."

"Come on. Let's get you tucked into bed. You feel like a block of ice."

"Okay."

Lamp in hand, he carried her back to her bed and tucked her in. Then he headed for his own room. As he sat on one side of his bed, a soft sigh from the other, startled him. He spun and stared.

There in his bed, snuggled beneath the thick pile of quilts, Star Dreamer lay asleep. Leaning over, he shook her gently. "Star?" Leaning over, he smoothed the silky strands of black hair from her face and ran his fingers down along her jaw.

She stretched, then smiled up at him. "You're home. Did you find Renny? I didn't want to leave her up there, but she didn't want to come down."

He smiled. "Yes, she's in bed. But what about you? What are you doing in my room . . . in my bed?"

She sobered, her gaze intense. "I belong here."

Grady's heart raced. Her words soothed the ache in his heart. *She belongs here, with me. Today and tomorrow. Forever.*

But no matter how much his body longed to take what she offered, he couldn't. Not yet. "I'm not sure having you here is such a good idea. I want you, make no mistake, but you have to be sure, Star. Very sure," he finished, then waited.

Stay, his mind begged. *Stay. Love me. Be mine forever.* The plea from his heart and soul reverberated loudly within him, but he didn't dare scare her away by saying the words aloud. How he wanted her to stay the night, and the next and every one thereafter—yet he had to be sure she knew to what she was committing herself.

"I need you. And you need me," she answered, shifting onto her side and moving toward the center of the bed—closer to him.

"Star—"

She lifted her hand and pressed her fingers to his lips. "I'm sure, Grady. I don't want to be, but I *am*."

Taking her hand in his, he kissed her fingertips, curled her fingers over his and rubbed his jaw with the backs of her fingers. "I love you, sweetheart. We belong together." And with that he closed the gap between them.

Her eyes were wide, dark with turbulent emotion. "What I feel scares me, Grady."

Bursts of sunshine reached into the dark corners of his soul, warming him from the inside out. "Loving you is the scariest thing I've ever done. Facing the enemy in battle is nothing compared to admitting that I love you."

"What if—"

Reaching out, he silenced her doubt with a gentle kiss. "No what ifs. We have each other. That's all we need. There are no guarantees. We both know that. Let's just take each day as it comes. I love you, Star. With all my heart and soul, I love you. Nothing else matters. We stand together, united."

Tears gathered in her eyes. She pushed the covers off and rose to her knees. She removed her nightdress in one smooth motion.

Grady sucked in his breath. Soft light bathed her body in a golden glow. His blood heated, pooling in his groin as his gaze dipped to linger on her breasts: small, gently rounded, with twin dark nipples. He watched as the tips tightened and peaked.

Swallowing hard, his eyes lowered, following the smooth slope of her body downward to her narrow waist and onward over the gentle swell of her womanly hips. There, his gaze lingered on the dark patch of curls nestled between her legs. His hands twitched with the need to cup her, to feel her warm, moist heat. Her knees parted slightly, and he could see the faint outline of her nether lips. His fingers longed to slide through the springy curls and find the sensitive heart of her. His body swelled with desperate need.

Willing himself to go slow and not rush, Grady

stood, facing her as he removed his shirt, shoes and socks. He hesitated, watching Star closely. She wet her lips—his own had gone dry too—and as her gaze roamed over his body, his skin tingled as if she'd kissed every inch of him. When her eyes lowered to his fingers, poised on the buttons at his waist, he undid each one, drawing out the moment of divesting himself of his trousers. He could hear her intake of breath.

Suddenly, his desire demanded he continue the sweet torment. He had to touch her as he'd dreamed of doing, now. Seconds later, he stood before her, naked. And when she held out her arms, he didn't hesitate. He joined her on the bed, kneeling in front of her, gathering her close until they were pressed together from thighs to chest and breast. But Grady made no movement to lie them down. Instead, he wrapped his arms around her and reveled in the meeting of their naked flesh.

Star sighed with pleasure as Grady's arms closed around her, enveloping her in his strength and scent as his heated skin made contact with hers. Her breasts ached and swelled against the hard wall of his chest, and the feel of his pulsing manhood against her belly increased the ache between her legs. Moisture gathered where the ache throbbed deepest. She moaned with such need, she felt embarrassed, and lowered her head to his chest.

"What's wrong, sweetheart?" He tipped her head up.

"I've never felt this way. I want you so much, it hurts *here*." She pressed her hand to her lower abdomen. Her hand grazed his swollen length. He shuddered and took her hand, placing her palm along it.

"I hurt with my need for you as well, my sweet, lovely, bright Star."

She gently cupped him, her finger caressing his velvety tip, smoothing the moisture beading there. "Bright Star. You've called me that before." She liked the name, it held a certain shared wonder for her.

"You brought light back into my life. Through your eyes, I've found love and laughter once again. You saved me, gave me hope for the future." His hands crept up to cup her face. He kissed her.

Star moaned. There was no gentle teasing in this demanding assault. Passion took over. Her hands wrapped around Grady's neck, pulling him close. As she opened her mouth, his tongue thrust inside. She suckled. He groaned and retreated. Following, she took from him, stroking his tongue, sliding along the inner flesh of his mouth, sinking under waves of building passion.

As one, their hips moved. The mattress moved beneath their knees, and Grady's hands slid down her back and cupped her buttocks. He pulled her tight against him. She rocked there, seeking to be even closer. Moving one of her legs outside his, he thrust his thigh hard against her. She cried out and shuddered, fighting the urge to let herself go. But her body, stroked to a feverish pitch, needed release. She cried his name, breaking off their kiss. His lips trailed down her throat and one hand slid down over her belly, making her catch her breath.

Then his hand cupped her, pressed down hard, and she could only grab his shoulders and hold on. Her own harsh, ragged breathing filled the room.

"Find release, Star," he begged. He slid one finger into her moist folds and grazed the swollen heart begging for his touch. He stroked it with one hand while his other supported her lower back, his fingers digging into the flesh of her buttocks.

Star could do nothing but what he asked, for her body could stand no more. His breath tickled her ear as his mouth found the sensitive area behind it and along her neck.

Her hips circled frantically, his fingers matching her movements, driving her faster, pressing her harder, leaving her no choice but to follow him up the path to pleasure and pain—and release.

Gasping, she thrust her hips forward one last time and felt herself explode into fragments of shuddering ecstasy. Incredible color burst around her. Still Grady stroked, coaxing wave after wave of ecstasy from her throbbing flesh until, spent, she sagged against him.

Grady lowered them both to the mattress. "God, you're so beautiful." He stroked tenderly from her hip to the gentle swell of her breast, then cupped it. She noticed that she filled his palm, her size perfect. Bending his head, she felt him taste her, his tongue circling the peak of her breast before his lips took the dusky nipple into his mouth.

Her gasp of pleasure shocked her. His hand cradled and caressed her other breast. Then he took his time licking and sucking the straining tip until both of her breasts were wet with his kisses, her puckered nipples erect and hard.

Star's fingers gripped his head, her fingers massaging his scalp, tangling in his hair. He lifted his head. Strands of his hair hung down and brushed against her breasts. He kissed her slowly, but his passion could not be contained for long. Nor could hers. Frantically Star urged him over her, her drawn-up knees falling wide. He needed no further invitation. Supporting himself on his hands, he leaned down to brush his lips over each breast as he maneuvered his body.

"I can't wait much longer, bright Star," he said. "I need you, now."

But Star didn't want him to wait. She wrapped her legs around his waist, drawing him inside by tipping her hips. He slid into her.

With him buried deep within her, Star convulsed around him. She was near to finding release again. He moved slowly and she moaned, but then the storm of need broke. Their mouths locked, tongues thrusting and retreating in time to the sudden frantic movements of their hips.

Star dug her fingers into Grady's shoulders, feeling her body tensing, tightening with each hard thrust. Every time he withdrew, she cried out, then moaned in pleasure when he surged back inside. Her legs tightened, keeping him from withdrawing completely. His mouth left hers. She arched her back and again, felt his teeth scrape against her sensitive, swollen nipple.

"Grady," she cried.

"Yes, love." He was moving hard and fast now, demanding she follow him. In. Out. Faster and faster until Star could barely breathe.

"Now!" he gasped, his voice hoarse, his eyes squeezed tightly shut as he threw his head back. With one last thrust, his body stiffened and pulsed deep inside her.

"Yes." She sobbed, arching up, her body convulsing around him, drawing his length deeper, holding him as tremors wracked her body, sending her higher until she too stiffened. The ecstasy of joining with him, becoming one, sharing a climb to the peak of joy held more wonder than she'd ever known. Again, her body spasmed as if there was no end to her pleasure. And she didn't want one; she wanted to savor this incredible moment, the bright stars bursting behind her closed eyes.

Finally, her body calmed. Grady collapsed on top of her. They kissed; lazily, tiredly, letting each other know without words what the joining meant to them.

Still united, Grady smiled down at her. "I love you, Star Dreamer."

Running the pads of her fingers over the contours of his face, Star felt tears slip from the corners of her eyes. She loved this man, wanted to say the words but was afraid. "I—"

He stopped her with a kiss. "We have time. When the time is right, when you have to say those words to me or burst with it, then say them." He sighed even as he flexed his hips, causing another tremor to roll through her. "I suppose you should return to your own bed."

She tipped her head, both relieved and on edge. "Why?"

"So our daughters don't find us sleeping together."

Star tightened her hold on him. Whites held different views of love than her people. This was not the same as it would have been at home. By her own people's beliefs, she and Grady would be considered married now. Many times, couples defied parents by running away together, and when they returned, they were considered husband and wife.

But that was not so in Grady's world. And despite her love—and having admitted it to him—she wasn't sure she could take that next step. "I don't want to leave. Not yet."

Grady's smile grew in the candlelight. "There are many hours before I have to tuck you back into your own bed. In the meantime, I'm not the least bit tired."

Near her, Star felt his hardness grow. Her own center throbbed anew. "Neither am I," she answered. She sighed when he bent his head to her breasts once more.

Chapter Fourteen

Hester Mae paused in the entryway to check her appearance in the gilt-framed mirror before leaving the house. Using both hands, she adjusted her hat, setting it at a slight angle. Satisfied, she drew on her gloves, then hesitated once more to study the image in the glass.

She leaned forward, smoothed a faint crease in her forehead, then turned a critical gaze to the tiny lines fanning out from each corner of her eyes. When had time stamped its passage on her face? The forties, she mused, were not kind years to a woman. But at least she had her figure. Though no children. Desperation combined with unfulfillment slid through her, deepening the creases on the sides of her mouth and thinning her lips.

"Hester Mae, let's go. I'm late." Baxter strode back in through the front door.

Turning from her unhappy image, she followed her husband out to their waiting carriage. When the buggy stopped in front of his warehouse, Baxter handed her the reins and climbed down. "I won't be home tonight."

An opportunity to see Leo. Yet the prospect of her lover didn't thrill her as it once had. She was tired of the man, and his demands. All he cared about were his own needs. He would come tonight, no matter how she felt. With a sigh, she wished her husband would stay home. It seemed as if he'd only just returned from a trip. "Leaving again so soon, Bax? You had better watch out, or the neighbors will think you've got a mistress tucked away somewhere."

Baxter lifted a brow. "Would you really care, Hester Mae? You've made it clear you abhor my presence."

To her surprise, the thought that he might have a mistress bothered her—a lot. She stared down at him from her perch in the carriage, noting how he suddenly looked his age. Sighing, she looked away, wishing that things had worked out better between them.

"No doubt. Because you'd worry over what the neighbors would think," he finally answered himself, sounding tired and sad.

She sighed. "Maybe we should never have married. Why *did* you marry me, Baxter? Neither of us has made the other happy."

"Do you really want to know?"

Suddenly afraid, Hester Mae chewed on the inside of her cheek. She'd always assumed her father had put pressure on Baxter, the son of one of his acquaintances, to take pity on her. "Why?"

"I thought you'd make a good wife and mother. You were mature, not some simpering, empty-headed girl who cared only for balls and being invited to the right homes. And after my first wife died, I was lonely."

She laughed hollowly. "That hasn't changed, has it, Baxter?"

He stared off toward the harbor. "I promised your father that I'd take care of you."

Her throat clogged. "You have taken care of me, Baxter." He had. He'd provided for her, and though she might consider him to be tight-fisted, she had never lacked for the things a woman of her social position needed.

"But I haven't made you happy, Hester Mae."

Drawing a deep breath, she turned to look at him. "I suppose it's not your fault you couldn't give me children."

"If you'd already had a dozen, perhaps you'd have been happy and content with a man nearly old enough to be your father." He ran one hand over his thinning hair and gripped an envelope in the other. He stared at it, then dropped both arms to his sides. "Do you want me to set you free, Hester Mae? I will. I can buy you a house and see you provided for life. I'll have Manning do up the paperwork."

Startled, she turned in her seat. Once she'd have jumped at that. Even yesterday. But today? She wasn't sure.

Squeezing the reins tightly in her gloved fists, she shook her head. "I don't know." Her life was so empty; she just didn't know what she wanted anymore.

"We'll talk when I get back."

Hester Mae nodded, then left. She drove aimlessly, thinking. If she hadn't married Baxter, what would her life have been like? Not much different than now, perhaps. She'd already been a spinster, and her chance of having made an acceptable marriage had passed her by. Baxter had given her the opportunity to be a wife.

But she'd failed in that role. And now, like her father, Baxter was disappointed in her. Knowing that she was lacking shouldn't have the power to hurt her—not anymore—but it did.

The old pain returned. Her father had wanted a son. He'd gotten Hester. If she'd been beautiful or clever or talented like her sister, things might have been different. But she'd been plain, gawky and painfully shy. A big disappointment to her parents. And now Baxter too.

So where did their marriage go from here? Children might have bridged the gap between them, given them a common interest, but they didn't have any. Now what? Did she want Baxter to set her free? She thought of Leo. She'd be free to marry him, but that didn't appeal. She and he really had nothing in common, and if she was honest, it was the attention he gave her that she sought—and the lovemaking. But he didn't provide what she needed most—companionship.

Left with no easy answers, she turned another corner. She'd planned to visit her niece after dropping Baxter off at the warehouse. The thought of encountering Grady's animosity or his savage governess nearly made her change her mind, but she stiffened her back. It was up to her to make sure her sister's child was being taken care of.

Without warning, a small girl in a ragged dress darted out from an alley in front of her horse and froze. The child screamed. Hester Mae screamed then too, and yanked hard on the reins. Three boys who were throwing rocks at the little girl skidded to a stop, took one look at Hester Mae and ran back the way they'd come.

Furious with the youths for their meanness, Hester Mae dropped down in front of the girl. "Are you all right?"

Sniffling, the girl—somewhere around five years old—nodded. She reached up to touch the back of her head. Blood smeared her small fingers. Her eyes, a brilliant blue, glittered with unshed tears.

"Why, you're hurt. Those boys should be whipped." Hester Mae planned to find the ill-mannered ruffians and give them and their parents a piece of her mind. What was this city coming to?

Meanwhile, this child needed tending. She took one of her new embroidered hankies and dabbed at the child's head, parting hair a shade between light brown and blond that hadn't seen water in months. She shuddered to think about lice, but she needed to see how bad the gash was. "It's not too bad," she said, relieved.

Big blue eyes stared up at Hester Mae.

"It's all right, sweetheart," she soothed. "I won't hurt you. What's your name?"

"Aggie, ma'am."

"Well, Aggie, let's get you home to your mother. She must be worried."

Aggie's lower lip quivered. "My ma's gone."

Hester Mae stood and held out her hand. "Then show me where you live, child." Taking the tiny, frail-feeling hand in her own, they walked around Hester's carriage. Hester Mae lifted the child, shocked at the feel of her ribs. The girl was far too thin.

With the child pointing out the way, they soon arrived at a small building. Aggie led her inside, up five flights of stairs, and down a long corridor that smelled of stale alcohol, greasy food and urine. Open doorways revealed tiny apartments. Noise flooded out into the hallways: babies crying, frustrated women shouting at noisy children, barking dogs. The girl stopped before a closed door. From inside, Hester Mae heard the wails of a baby.

Knocking, she stepped back and waited. A young woman opened the door. In her arms, she held a screaming, red-faced infant. Several other children of various ages peeked around her skirts.

"What do you want?" The woman had to shout to be heard over the racket.

"I've brought Aggie back. I'm afraid she's hurt. Not badly, though." Hester Mae explained what had happened. "She's too young to be running around out there unsupervised." She couldn't help the note of censure. Did this woman not care for these children? Did she not realize how fortunate she was to have them?

"See here, ma'am, she ain't mine. Her ma died birthin' this here boy. I'm only lookin' after her and the babe until someone comes to claim her. I got six of my own to tend to."

"What about their father?"

"Spent all his time in jail and finally got himself killed 'bout six months ago in a brawl."

"Are there no relatives?"

"Look, I ain't got the time or money to search for any. I thought I could take them in, but looks like I'll have to turn them over to the church or an orphanage. Me and my husband just can't feed and clothe two more."

Staring down at Aggie's sad features, Hester Mae felt the first stirring of maternal protectiveness. She opened her reticule and withdrew several bills. "I'll have my husband's attorney see what he can do. I'll be in touch. This should set food on your table for a few days."

The woman's eyes widened. "This is so much!"

Realizing just how fortunate she was, how much she had, Hester Mae shook her head. "No, it's not.

I'll have fresh milk and bread delivered later today." She hesitated, hating to leave Aggie. But before she did anything, she had to talk to Baxter. If she stayed with him, would he be willing to adopt Aggie and her brother? Her hungry gaze settled on the infant.

"Could . . . I'd like to hold him—if I may?"

The woman, some of her worry and fears set aside, smiled and handed over the boy. "Come on in."

Hester Mae stared down at the squalling baby. She rubbed his tiny back, thrilled when he stopped crying. Holding out her hand, she—with a baby in one arm and Aggie clutching her other hand—stepped into the small, cramped apartment. Surrounded by eight children, Hester Mae felt as though she'd entered another world.

Baxter settled himself in his office. Though he had a lot on his mind and a confrontation to deal with, he couldn't help playing over that last conversation with his wife. In all the years of their marriage—nearly twelve years—they hadn't ever talked about their future, or what the other wanted. Theirs hadn't been a love match, but he'd truly been fond of Hester Mae—at first. But her disappointment and disillusionment had prevented love from growing and taking root.

She blamed him for her childless state. Women often measured each other by their families, and her lack of children had always been a source of bitterness between them. He didn't blame her for assuming the problem lay with him—after all, he was so much older—but he knew the truth. And the one word that would clear him would destroy her—so he kept his secret.

Pulling several sheets of paper from the envelope

he'd been carrying, he reread the report from the man he'd hired to follow her. He'd suggested she drop him off this morning because he'd planned to bring her into his office and confront both her and Leo. But after their conversation out front, he couldn't. She was young; maybe she needed more than he could give her. He couldn't blame her for that. And still, though he'd offered to release her from their marriage, he didn't want to lose her.

He slid the papers back into the envelope and tossed it into the back of his desk drawer. He'd burn them later. How could he accuse her of infidelity, take her to task for it, when he'd had his own affairs over the years? "What a sorry pair we are," he murmured, praying it wasn't too late to make things right.

The one thing she wanted he could give her, but by confessing, it could very well spell the end of their marriage. Pulling out another missive, this one delivered yesterday, he reread the message. Beatrice, his mistress, had died three days ago. Their children were on their way to him.

He'd told Hester Mae he was leaving town, but he wasn't. He had planned to settle his children in another house he owned—one Hester Mae knew nothing about—and spend the night there. He still had to hire a nursemaid for them. Or he could ask Hester Mae to accept them and raise them in place of the children her own body could not give her.

Hearing a door bang, he saw Leo walk past. A glance at his pocket watch confirmed that the man was early. "Leo, I'd like a word with you," he called out.

His employee entered and took the seat Baxter indicated.

"*Freedom's Fancy* returned to port this morning with engine trouble." He paused, noting the man's slight widening of the eyes before he composed himself. He didn't say anything.

"Imagine my surprise when the captain asked what I wanted to do with the cargo of runaway slaves on board." Baxter slammed his fist on his desk. "What did you think you were doing?"

Leo shifted in his seat. "The money was good. The customer was desperate and willing to pay."

Baxter glared at Leo. "I don't care about the money, and you know it. You went against my policy." He paused. "You're fired."

Leo jumped up. "You can't fire me. You need me!" Fury and disbelief were evident in his voice.

Baxter picked up his pen, dismissing him. "I'll hire someone else." He began writing an advertisement for the paper. When he glanced up, Leo was still standing there in stunned disbelief. "Leave the premises. And, Leo . . . stay away from my wife."

Leo knocked over the chair in his agitation. "Hester Mae loves me, not you, you sorry excuse for a man!"

Baxter ignored him, which infuriated the man further. Leo walked to the door but didn't leave, so Baxter kept writing. Knowing he wasn't going to leave easily, he lifted his head, ready to threaten him.

Baxter's eyes widened when he saw Leo staring down at him with hatred. The man held a large white statue of a woman that had sat on the shelf in his office. He raised it.

"You're not going to ruin my plans!" Leo shouted. "I'm tired of being poor and having everyone else tell me what to do. It's my turn."

Baxter held up his hands to deflect the blow but wasn't fast enough. His attacker had the advantage of height and the weight of the statue. The stone caught him on the temple. Pain radiated from his head as he slumped forward. Blood dripped into his eyes. His last thought was of Hester Mae and his children. Too late, he thought.

Blackness swallowed him up.

When Star woke in her own bed, alone, she stretched, feeling pleasantly sore. Wondering where Grady was and eager to see him, she dressed without waiting for the maid.

A knock on the connecting door made her smile. She opened it.

Grady pulled her into his arms for a quick kiss. "I promised to take Renny riding this morning. How about if you and Morning Moon come?"

Star rested her head against his shoulder and smiled. "No. This is your time with your daughter. I have much to do here."

Grady nodded. "How will I manage all day without you, without this?" His kiss grew more demanding.

"By thinking of tonight." Star slipped her arms around him. Not one to pass up an opportunity to kiss the man she loved, she deepened the kiss until he was breathing harshly. She ground her hips against him, then stepped back, enjoying this new sensation flowing through her.

Grady leaned against the door. "You're a cruel woman to lead me on and then make me wait, Star. Now I can't go downstairs."

"But I can."

With a wicked grin, Star shut the door and left her room, feeling happy and carefree. She put from her mind her fears of the future.

Going downstairs, she saw to the children. When Grady came down, they enjoyed a lighthearted breakfast in the morning room, with Renny chatting about the upcoming ride in the park.

Though both father and daughter tried to talk Star into accompanying them, she held firm. To her surprise, Morning Moon also declined. As soon as Grady and Renny left, her daughter came around the table, her gaze serious and determined.

"I'd like to talk to you, my mother." The words were spoken in Lakota.

Sighing, Star knew the time had come. Her daughter was right, and her personal happiness had made this discussion all the more imperative. It was time for them to talk about their respective gifts. Standing, she held out her hand and led the way into the family parlor. There they could relax and talk, undisturbed.

As Star sat down, Morning Moon climbed into her lap. "My grandmother has given her Sight to me."

"I know." Star struggled to keep her fear from her voice, but Morning Moon smiled reassuringly and stroked her mother's cheek. "Do not be afraid for me, *Ina*. It is meant to be."

The girl's calm acceptance allowed Star to relax. As a young child, Star had never felt comfortable with the Sight. Yet her own daughter showed none of her mother's fear of the unknown. "It does not frighten you?"

"Sometimes. But it is the way of the Spirits. And someday, I believe my gift will save our people. This I know to be true. They have chosen me. I will bring honor to our tipi."

"Yes, my daughter. The Spirits have chosen wisely, for you are brave, and worthy of their gift." Star hugged her daughter close, grateful for the calm acceptance Morning Moon exhibited toward her gift and her future. Why could she herself not enjoy the same pride and peace in such a great gift? Usually, its owner was regarded as *wakan*—great, powerful, all knowing. Yet in her heart, Star knew she didn't want that honor.

Morning Moon turned and hugged her mother. "As you are *Ina*. Our grandmother watches over us, and she is proud."

How Star longed to believe that. Smoothing loose strands of hair back from her daughter's face, she smiled. "I am glad you are happy with this. You will come to me if you are frightened?"

"I will first seek council of our *wicasa waken*."

Star sighed. "As you must, my daughter. Remember, I am here if you need me." In the Lakota way, Morning Moon would first seek council from their holy man. Then their chief. Losing that little bit of control hurt, but Star accepted that her little girl, with her mother's and grandmother's gift, was growing up fast. She could fight that no longer.

Standing, she took her daughter's hand. They had a couple of hours before Grady and Renny returned. She eyed the kitchen. Cooking on the stove fascinated her daughter. Perhaps they could do that together.

Morning Moon seemed to sense her intention. "I would like to bake more of those round cookies, but Hattie will not welcome us right now. She is cleaning."

Star laughed, feeling lighter of heart now than in a long while. "We shall have to wait until later, then."

Two hours later, baking cookies forgotten, Star and Morning Moon were talking and laughing freely as they each worked on their beading and quilling. The intricate designs in the carpets and wallpaper provided new and interesting patterns to copy. Morning Moon's was a simple dark blue with gold scrolls, while Star was trying to copy the carpet in the dining room—one of rose, pink and burgundy flowers.

The ringing of the front bell interrupted their work, and Zeke's footsteps shook the floor as he rushed to answer it. Hattie poked her head into the parlor and shook her head.

"I haven't ever seen a man more unsuited to be a butler."

Star and Morning Moon laughed. "I think he'll do fine." She glanced at Morning Moon. "Shall we go see who is here?"

They made their way into the foyer. Zeke met them, his expression dark.

"Who's here, Zeke?"

"That woman. Wants to see Grady. I told her he ain't here, but she insists on waiting."

"Where is she?"

"I put her in the front parlor." His expression plainly said that wasn't where he wanted her to be.

"I'll go see her." Though to see Hester Mae was the last thing Star wanted, she also knew that for Grady's sake she had to act the gracious hostess. People of society would expect that of governess. She stopped Zeke. "Ask Hattie to send in tea . . . and maybe some of the tarts the cook baked."

"Yes, Mrs. Star, though it seems a waste to serve them things to that woman."

Star hid her smile and stepped into the formal parlor. Hester Mae stood near the window, staring out. "Good day, Mrs. Olsen," she said. At the sound of Star's voice, the woman drew herself up to her full height.

"I've come to see my niece." The request was belligerent.

Star nodded, unsure of what to do. "Renny and her father have gone for a ride."

"I'll wait." Her expression dared Star to disagree.

Indicating that Hester should sit, Star moved into the room. "You are welcome here. I've sent for tea and refreshment." Watching the older woman take a chair and fold her hands primly in her lap, Star hesitantly took a seat across from her.

Hattie carried in a tray and set it on the table between Star and her guest. "Would you like anything else, Mrs. Star?"

"Thank you, Hattie, no. This will be fine."

"Call if you need me," the housekeeper said, then exited.

"What does that woman think I'm going to do?" Hester Mae snapped.

"Cause trouble. Try to take Renny, perhaps."

Hester Mae paled. "That was a long time ago. I was out of my mind with grief." Her hands shook as she pulled out her hankie. Star saw a stain of blood on it before the woman could shove it back. Noting another stain on Hester Mae's gloves, Star frowned.

"What happened? Are you all right?" Concern softened her voice.

Hester Mae pursed her lips. "Do you care?" She looked uncomfortable, as if she were about to bolt.

Unsurprised by the woman's bitterness, Star gentled her voice further. She was not a part of the bad feelings between Grady's family and this woman. "You are Renny's aunt."

"And you are Grady's—" She closed her mouth, with a snap, then sighed. "Forgive me. It's been a difficult day. Suffice it to say, I am concerned about Renny's upbringing."

"Renny is loved by her father, and myself."

"I love her too." The words ended on a sharp inhalation of breath.

Star eyed the woman's agitation with worry. Was she unstable? Should she have Zeb go find Grady?

She didn't dare leave this woman alone. Wishing she was anywhere but where she was, Star decided to try and soothe Renny's aunt before the girl and her father returned from their ride. "Yes, I believe you do."

"All I want is to see her, to spend some time with her. It's not too much to ask." Hester Mae's chin quivered.

No it wasn't, Star thought. Beneath the gruff exterior, she sensed sadness. And something else. Pouring two cups of tea, she slid one across the small oval table to her guest.

The woman reached for her cup, then brought it back over her lap. Her fingers shook so hard, tea sloshed over the rim. She laughed without humor. "When I left the house this morning, I was determined to come visit my niece. She is, after all, family. But"—she shook her head and closed her eyes—"but I truly don't wish to cause trouble. I'd like to see her, take her on outings and to go shopping . . . but if Grady wishes me to never see her again, I understand. I haven't given him much reason to think well of me."

Star sipped her tea, considering all she knew of this family. "You loved your sister very much."

"Yes, and *she loved me*."

Those simple words told Star much. Again her gaze fell to the stains on the woman's gloves. She pointed. "What happened?"

Hester stared down at where Star indicated. Her voice turned soft with yearning. "A child was hurt. I helped her and took her home." She leaned her head back. "The child has no parents or family that I know of. The woman who is caring for her and her infant brother plans to send them to an orphanage." Hester Mae's eyes softened. "I held the boy, and now I want them both. They have no one to love them."

Before Star could reply, she heard Grady and Renny come in. Hester Mae kept talking; apparently the floodgates had opened.

"All I ever wanted was to have children of my own. And when the years passed leaving my arms empty, I tried to find contentment in loving my sister and her children. But it wasn't enough. Watching her with Emma just magnified what I didn't have. And when she became pregnant with Renny, a desperate need grew inside me until it drove those around me away."

"There must have been a way to—"

"Adoption?" she cut in. Shaking her head sadly, Hester Mae dabbed at the corner of her eyes with a corner of a lace-trimmed handkerchief. "No. Then, I didn't want some other woman's children. More foolishness on my part. Until today, I didn't think I could love anyone else's children except my sister's. But when Margaret Mary died, Grady didn't trust me to raise them." Hester Mae sighed. "And with good reason. I wanted children so badly, needed to be a mother, that I was willing to take his from him. But today, when I held that baby, and that sweet little girl clung to me as I was leaving, I realized how wrong I've been, and how many wasted years have passed. I hope someday Grady will forgive me."

"I believe he will," Grady said, entering with Renny beside him. His gaze met Star's.

She smiled at him to let him know everything was all right. "Hester Mae has come to visit."

Hester Mae stood, her teary-eyed gaze moving from brother-in-law to her niece. "I'd like to be allowed to visit my niece, Grady, but I will understand if you decide not to allow it. I will abide by your decision."

Clasping his hands behind his back, Grady inclined his head. "I, too, have made mistakes. I should never have left my children. Leaving them was wrong and had I stayed, we might have been able to work out our problems. Relations between all of us might have gotten better. My girls have forgiven me, so it's only right I forgive you as well—along with granting permission for you to visit. If Renny is agreeable, you may do so."

The girl leaned against her father's thigh. "I'd like that. And I'm sorry for scaring you with my rats. I didn't know you'd be spooked like that woman on the boat." Her eyes widened then, as if she'd said too much. She winced as her father's fingers squeezed her shoulder, but they shared a knowing look.

"Perhaps you could show them to me again. From a distance," Hester Mae offered.

"Why don't you take your aunt up to see your room, child? As I recall, her taste in decorating is impeccable."

Renny's eyes lit up. "Really? My room is pink and white, but I hate it. Papa says I can choose my own colors. I want blue and green."

Hester Mae's eyes misted over. "Thank you, Grady."

"Everyone deserves a second chance, Hester Mae. I'll have someone take care of your horse and buggy."

Zeke poked his head into the room. "Already taken care of, Colonel." With a satisfied grin, he took the tea tray from the parlor.

When they were alone—Renny, her aunt and Morning Moon had left the room—Star went to Grady. "You were generous."

"No more so than you, my love. You've given me a second chance at love and my daughter. It seems only fair to give Renny's aunt one as well."

"Morning Moon spoke to me today."

"Ah. She's a wise child. What did she say?"

Star drew a deep breath. "She does not seem to hate her gift as I do. She accepts it. She even seems sure it will serve our people one day."

"That is good, isn't it? Now you can stop worrying about her." Grady took her hands in his and kissed the backs of them.

"She doesn't understand—"

"I think she does, love. Perhaps it is you who doesn't. Let go of your fears for her. Let's see what the future holds. The best thing you can do for her is to be there when she needs you. I've learned that. Now come here and kiss me. I've missed you."

His words were wise. There was little she could do but deal with her own visions. And she didn't want to do that, not now. She went willingly into Grady's arms. "It's only been half a day."

"That's far too long to be apart, don't you think?"

"Much too long." Star leaned into him and lifted her head. A commotion at the door broke them up before they could indulge in kissing, though. Someone had come through the front door and was shouting for Grady. As they went out to the foyer, Charles ran up to them.

"Charles, what's wrong?" Grady drew Star alongside him.

"I need to speak to Hester Mae. She said she was coming here, but I didn't see her buggy out front."

"It's in the back. She's upstairs with Renny."

"I've got bad news. Someone tried to kill her husband!"

A loud gasp came from the top of the stairs. "What happened?" Renny's aunt ran down the stairs, the two girls following. "Where is he? Is he all right?"

Charles stepped forward. "He's at the City Hospital, Hester Mae. It doesn't look good. He took a hard knock to the head."

Hester Mae stumbled and cried out. "Take me to him."

Grady turned to Star. She nodded. "Go." Grady led Hester Mae out the door and into Charles's waiting carriage.

Renny came to Star and took her hand. "Will he be all right?"

She recalled her visions of death. Someone would die, but was it Renny's uncle? How did he tie into this whole thing? Suddenly she just knew he did.

She shuddered and glanced down at her daughter, her own gaze questioning. This was the first time she sought to see if Morning Moon had any knowledge, and it felt strange.

Morning Moon shook her head. "The future has not revealed itself to me, but the danger has not passed."

Her words chilled Star to the core, yet she realized there was no fear in her daughter's voice. No despair. Just calm acceptance. It seemed Grady might be right about Morning Moon; the girl was wise.

Turning to Renny, Star said, "We will just have to wait." She put an arm around each girl, and together they headed into the kitchen to await further news.

Chapter Fifteen

Across from Grady's home in the park, a bearded man sat on a bench, presumably enjoying the spring day. Yet the Dragon was anything but relaxed. He had a score to settle. No one interfered in his business without learning his wrath.

A patient man, he knew all he had to do was wait. Soon, he'd have the slave back as planned, and she'd go to a brothel after he had his fill of her. Both she and the Indian bitch would learn soon enough that it didn't pay to anger him.

Around him, women strolled past with their children. Across the way, two dogs raced over the wide expanse of green grass, their tongues lolling out of the sides of their mouths. His keen eyesight missed nothing, especially the sight of a young black girl walking briskly along with three young charges. Speculating, he studied her slim frame, slender neck and full lips, then dipped his gaze back to the swell of her breasts. She was young, not much older than the eldest girl in her care, but she was old enough for his needs—and right now, he needed distraction.

The youngest child, a boy, ran back to his nurse. She bent and hugged him, ruffling his hair.

Thrown back in time, the Dragon recalled other hands—dark hands—doing the same to him when he was but a boy: ruffling his hair, rubbing his back when nightmares woke him, teasing him with a swat when he'd raided the sweets.

He'd trusted her, loved her—*and suffered because of her*.

The Dragon stood, his breathing rapid. Never again would he trust a Negro. They'd pay. They'd all pay for what they'd done to him. He stepped back onto the path, intending to follow at a safe distance and see where the girl lived. This one might do, at least until he had back the one named Hattie. Coming toward him, a carriage rushed past and stopped in front of Grady's grand white house. A man jumped out. The Dragon frowned when he recognized the suited form of the solicitor running up the walk.

He'd have to get that other girl later. She lived close by, surely.

He crossed the street to get closer to the O'Brien house. Swinging his walking stick, he noted a large man out front, wearing a flannel shirt and kneeling on the ground, pulling weeds, whistling as he worked. The Dragon didn't dare get any closer. He sauntered in front of the house, his steps slow and measured, as if he didn't have a care in the world. He moved just far enough that a thick wall of shrubbery hid his presence. Stopping, he peered through the shiny green leaves.

Moments later, the front door burst open. The

colonel and his solicitor rushed out, each holding on to a woman's arm.

"Why would someone try to kill Baxter?" he heard her cry out.

One brow lifted. Someone had tried to kill Baxter Olsen? Frowning, the bearded man watched the three enter the coach; then it left, as quickly as it had come. Moving as fast as he dared, the Dragon reentered the park.

Removing his beard and coat, he mounted his horse and rode for the wharf. At last, he reached his destination: Baxter's warehouse. There, he dismounted and walked toward a young policeman guarding the door. He tried to enter but was barred entrance.

"State your business, sir."

The Dragon lifted his brow. "I've come to see Mr. Olsen regarding my cargo. It was due in port three days ago."

The young officer shook his head. "Sorry, sir, but Mr. Olsen has been taken to the City Hospital."

Affecting shock, he asked, "What happened?"

"Someone tried to kill him."

The Dragon widened his eyes. "Are you sure? What happened? Do you know who was responsible?"

"No, sir. Mr. Olsen was found by his attorney. It happened before the workers arrived, but it's my guess that he fell afoul of a robber."

"That's terrible." The Dragon paused. "Will he be all right?"

"Don't know, sir. Pretty bad knock to the head. And with his age and all . . ."

Shaking his head in sympathy while striving to hide his fury, the Dragon asked, "Is Mr. Dufour about? I really do need to learn whether my cargo has arrived. He might know the status." And he would most certainly know the truth of what had happened. There was no doubt that Leo was behind this. He was trying to make Hester Mae a widow much sooner than the Dragon wished.

"Yes, sir. He's here. Arrived after we did." He glanced over his shoulder. "Ah, there he is now. But you'll have to wait until we are done questioning him and the rest of the workers. I suggest you come back in a few hours."

Nodding, the Dragon left and found a place to watch. At last, the police left, and he slipped the beard back on and entered the dark, cool building. He found Leo in the office, staring out at a small window overlooking the alley.

He closed the door softly as he entered, but the snick was enough to alert Leo, who turned and blanched. The Dragon pulled a gun from his pocket and leveled it at him.

"Good, you're afraid. You should be after the stupid stunt you pulled today. I thought I told you not to rush things."

"B-boss," Leo stuttered. "The captain of *Freedom's Fancy* returned to port with engine trouble. That old bastard Baxter found out about the slaves and fired me. I had no choice. But it's all right. No one knows, so nothing's changed."

"Fool! Everything's changed. You've ruined *everything*." Fury at what this inept man might have cost him made him see red. It was Leo's carelessness in the first place that had put this shipment in the hands of an unknown riverman, and now there was no way to unload the slaves without drawing attention to himself.

"I had to do something," Leo whined.

"You blundered again. You should have waited, come to me. Thanks to your panic, I've lost my cargo." Fury, barely leashed, coursed through him.

"You listen to me and listen well. We are going to salvage what we can of this mess. I'll make the arrangements this time. As no one knows you were fired, you'll remain here, on duty. And you'll keep me informed as to what happens to my cargo. And, Leo . . . no more making your own decisions."

"Y-yes, boss." The man wiped his hands down the front of his pants and licked his lips nervously. "What about Baxter?"

"I'll take care of Baxter. I suggest you go console your lover. As soon as her husband is dead, you must convince Hester Mae that you two should marry straightaway."

"But we can't marry until she's gone through her period of mourning. What will society think?" Leo sounded both eager and afraid.

The Dragon lifted a brow and waved the revolver. "If she doesn't want to marry you, we'll find a way to force her. Either way, you and I will become partners within the fortnight."

"Partners?" Leo looked horrified.

The Dragon grinned and rammed his gun hard into Leo's stomach. "Any objections?"

"Uh, no. None at all." His voice shook.

"Good." As Leo heaved a sigh of relief, the Dragon felt a reminder was necessary. "Leo? If you try to run or cut me out, I'll hunt you down and make you sorry. Remember, I know what you look like, and you don't know who I am. Understand?"

"Y-yes, boss."

"Good. Now walk me out."

As he did, the Dragon kept the gun hidden but trained on Leo, just in case the man tried anything foolish. He had no choice but to keep this fool idiot alive for now. But soon the man would pay for his stupidity with his life.

*   *   *

Grady and Charles sat on one side of Baxter's hospital bed while Hester Mae sat on the other, her hand clutching her husband's to her breast. She alternated between sobbing and begging him not to die.

Grady added his prayers for the man's safe recovery. He'd always liked and respected Baxter—and had felt sorry for him. Only now did he realize he should have also felt some measure of compassion for Margaret Mary's sister. He'd been fortunate to find love—not once, but twice. He was a lucky man indeed.

At last, he and Charles left, though not before making sure Hester Mae knew where to get hold of them.

As they drove back toward the wharf, and the place where Baxter had nearly met his demise, Charles told Grady that Olsen had wanted to see him in his office early that morning. If Charles had not arrived, Baxter might have been dead before anyone else had ventured into his office.

When the two men arrived at the warehouse, they found one of Baxter's employees arguing with a ship captain. His name was Leodegrance Dufour, Charles said as they approached, but he didn't know why the riverman's words were making the man so angry.

"I want them slaves off my ship," the captain was saying.

Leo paced before him. "You'll have to wait until another ship comes in and can take them to their destinations. I don't have anywhere to put them."

Grady and Charles exchanged startled glances. They stepped forward, Charles identifying himself as Baxter's solicitor. "What is this about slaves on board one of Mr. Olsen's ships?"

Leo glared at him. "This doesn't concern you, lawyer. I'll handle it."

Grady lifted his brow and addressed the captain. "Considering the state of Baxter Olsen, I think the police might be interested in his cargo. It's a well-known fact that the man doesn't support slavery. What's one of his ships doing, transporting slaves?"

Stepping forward, Leo jabbed himself in the chest with his thumb. "I'm in charge whenever Mr. Olsen is away. I authorized the cargo. The pay to return runaways is too good to ignore for stupid beliefs about equality. This is a business, and I made a business decision." Leo stared them down as if daring them to object.

"The money? In Olsen's books? How did you account for it? I'd like to see the paperwork." Charles said.

For the first time, Leo looked uncomfortable. "Those are company records and not open to you, sir. Mr. Olsen has not authorized me to give anyone any papers—including his solicitor. Now, if you gentlemen don't mind, I have work to do."

With that the tall man strode off, leaving the captain cursing a blue streak. Grady turned to him. "I'd like to see those *runaways*, Captain."

Though obviously eager to unload his cargo, the man hesitated. Charles stepped in. "As Mr. Olsen's attorney, I authorize full cooperation and accept full responsibility, Captain. If you'd feel more comfortable, we can have the police there as well. I suspect this might be a cargo of freed slaves kidnapped to be resold into slavery."

The captain paled. "Hey, I was told they were runaways. I don't know anything else." Agitated, he ran his hand through his thinning hair, leaving the strands tangled and standing on end.

"Then you won't mind if we question them and learn if it is so, will you?"

"No—no, of course not. And if you're Mr. Olsen's attorney and willin' to take responsibility, you can figure out what to do with 'em."

Arriving where the steamboat was docked, Grady glanced up and grabbed Charles's arm. He pointed to a man pacing along the deck; it was one of those who'd chased Hattie down the alley the day he and Star arrived.

"Praise be," Charles muttered, glancing around. "Looks as though we are going to have some answers at last." With the captain leading the way, Grady put his hand on his revolver. Since the day someone tried to harm Star, he had taken to wearing his gun.

Together, he and Charles approached the man, moving stealthily up behind him. The ruffian turned, but he and Charles each quickly grabbed an arm.

"Hey, git yer hands off me," he sputtered. "I ain't done nothin' wrong."

"Try kidnapping," Charles said. "Remember the woman you were trying to grab? Turns out she was telling the truth. She is a free woman."

The man's eyes widened momentarily, then narrowed slyly. "That's not what the boss said." His eyes shifted from side to side as he searched for an escape.

"And who is this boss of yours?"

The man clamped his lips tight.

The captain jerked his head toward the stairs. "There's another man down there, locked in the room with the slaves."

They tied up the thug, then Grady searched him. He found a key. Dragging their prisoner to and then tying him securely in the captain's quarters, the threesome headed downstairs. As they passed two crewmen, the captain ordered them along.

Unlocking the door, Grady flung it open and stepped inside, his revolver drawn.

"Hey," a voice shouted. A man struggled to his feet, reaching for his weapon.

"Don't even try," Grady warned, recognizing him as well from that day in the alley.

The captain ordered the two crewmen to take care of the ruffian while Grady and Charles checked on the slaves. Five women were slumped against the walls. After careful questioning, Grady learned all but one old woman had been freed, she and a young girl who lay in the old woman's lap. Grady bent down to wake her, to learn from her own lips that she too was a free woman.

He pulled back the hood of the unconscious woman and stared in numb disbelief. It was a blond-haired girl, and her breathing was shallow. Too shallow. Her skin was pale, the same dingy gray-white of the walls. Grady felt sick. "There's more to this," he whispered to Charles. Even the captain looked shocked.

"Leo said this woman had just given birth to a baby. I swear, I didn't know she was white."

"Leo knows more than he's telling," Charles stated grimly.

Grady turned to the old black woman. She had bruises on her face. "What is *she* doing here?" He motioned to the blonde.

The woman's swollen lips firmed. Blood leaked from a deep cut but fire lit her dark brown eyes. "They's gonna sell her—her and them younger women to a brothel. I heard 'em talkin'. Me, I's too ol'. They thinks ta sell this ol' woman to some new massa, but I knows they's gonna kill me." Her fleshy lips quivered. "I has a massa—he treats

Tassa nice. They stole me." She reached down to smooth the hair from the blond girl's face.

"I 'spect her parents must be worried sick. Sick," she whispered, shaking her head as she stared down at the girl.

Grady turned as two police officers entered. He introduced himself and Charles, then explained everything that had happened.

The officer, a middle-aged man, smacked his fist into his palm as he stared at the white girl. "I've heard about the Dragon, but I figured it was just another story. No one could ever prove there was anything like this going on." He looked ill. "That child can't be much older than my own daughter. If this Dragon is responsible, we'll find him."

Grady watched as his friend picked up the unconscious girl. Charles was furious. "Now that a white girl is involved, you'll do something . . . but when I reported a missing servant who just happens to be a freed slave you couldn't bother to find the time to search!" He glared at the officer, then addressed Grady. "I'm taking this girl to the City Hospital. She's in a bad way."

"I's goin' with her," the old slave declared, making it clear no one was taking the girl out of her sight.

Grady waved aside the officer's protests and personally vouched for his friend. As soon as Manning left, he considered the four remaining women, noting their frightened yet hopeful faces.

"I'll arrange for a place for these women to stay until Mr. Manning can identify them and confirm their freedom. Then, I think a talk with that Leo Dufour is in order."

By the time Grady arrived home, it was late and he'd done everything he could. He'd found a church to take in the women until Charles could deal with the legalities. Leo still maintained he had been told the cargo was of runaway slaves, and he said he couldn't tell them who'd paid him to transport them. He was lying, of course, but until Grady had more proof, there was little he could do.

And as the women had been bound for a brothel, there was little hope that Charles's servant or Hattie's family would be found there. Perhaps the two men now in police custody could be convinced to divulge their whereabouts. Right now, they apparently feared the wrath of the Dragon more than anything.

Disheartened by the discoveries of the day, Grady leaned against the front door and eyed the stairs. He longed to go to Star, but one whiff of his clothing told him he needed to bathe first. The small cabin on board the *Freedom's Fancy* had been filthy. His clothes stank.

Zac and Zeke came into the hall, stopped, their eyes bulging. "Lordy, Colonel, but you stink somethin' fierce!" This came from Zac. "I'll heat you water for a bath."

Though exhausted, Grady chuckled. "This from someone who doesn't believe in bathing or washing clothes?"

The two brothers had the grace to look embarrassed. "Living in a fine house calls for changing one's habits."

Grady followed Zac to a room off of the kitchen where his large copper tub waited, wondering what the brothers were doing up but grateful anyway.

The bath was heavenly. Thirty minutes later, he felt human again. The scout handed him a snifter of brandy.

"Thanks, Zac."

"Don't go gettin' sloppy on us, Colonel. Jest doin' my job."

Feeling incredibly fortunate to be surrounded by people who were not only loyal to him, but for whom he held the utmost respect, Grady headed up the stairs. As scouts, these men were the best. But only a few weeks ago, he'd have laughed if someone had suggested hiring them as household help. Once again, they were proving their worth. Grady couldn't imagine surrounding himself with cold, distant strangers, as he once had done. In his room, he went eagerly to his bed. He felt a stab of disappointment upon finding it empty.

Checking the connecting door, he found it was unlocked. He stepped into Star's room. She was sound asleep in her bed. Deciding not to wake her even though he wanted the comforting warmth of her embrace to erase the horrors of the day, he returned to his room, undressed and climbed into bed.

Hester Mae, bone-weary and emotionally drained from spending the day and most of the evening at her husband's side in the hospital, stepped down from the carriage. "Thank you, Charles."

Her husband's solicitor rubbed his eyes and sighed heavily. "Get some rest, Hester Mae. I'll come by for you early. I want to go back and check on that poor young lady."

Hester Mae stopped him from climbing back into his carriage. "You don't have to be so kind to me. Heaven knows I haven't done anything to deserve it." How she'd have made it through the day without this man's support, she didn't know. Once he'd returned with that young blond girl he'd stayed, alternating spending his time with Hester, the girl and the slaves, until the blond girl's frantic parents at last arrived. They'd been searching for her for some time.

"I think we can put the past behind us, Hester Mae. Right now, your husband needs you. Be there for him."

Be there for him. She sniffled, wiping the corner of her eyes. "It may be too late."

"No. Bax is strong. He'll make it." Charles smiled reassuringly.

Hester Mae's answering smile wobbled. "Stubborn is a better word."

"That too, Hester Mae." With that, he climbed back into his carriage and tapped the roof with his cane.

She waited until the conveyance faded from sight before moving up the long walk to her front door. Sighing, wishing she didn't have to enter the dark, empty house and face the bleakness of her past, which had haunted her all during the silent hours spent at her husband's side, she paused.

"About time you got home, Hester Mae," a voice said as a dark shadow rose from the porch.

Startled, Hester Mae nearly fell back down the steep stairs. "Leo! What are you doing here?" She glanced around, but there wasn't another soul in sight. Her neighborhood slept, as she longed to do.

"Ah, my love, what a touching display of concern you gave. I thought you'd *never* get home. We have all night, and soon we'll have forever." He grabbed her and kissed her, his mouth moving hungrily over hers, his fingers digging hard into her buttocks. His enthusiasm put her off, and where once she had found his alternating mastery and flattery pleasant, she now found him dull.

"No, Leo. Stop." She shoved him away.

Looking annoyed, Leo frowned. "What's wrong?" Feeling guilty for her part in their affair, Hester

Mae tried to be gentle. "It's over, Leo. I'm sorry, but if Baxter survives, I want a second chance to be a better wife to him."

"What? No!" Leo reached out and grabbed Hester Mae by her arm. "Don't be ridiculous! The man is as good as dead. He won't survive. Do you know how hard he was hit?" He yanked her hard against him. "And if he isn't dead, we'll have to finish him off. Then, Hester, it'll be just you and me. Together, as we planned."

Once more Leo started groping her, and something sharp and cold stabbed at her insides. With horror, Hester slapped his hands away but couldn't free herself. "You! You're the one who tried to kill Baxter today."

Her lover laughed. "He had the nerve to fire me . . . and warn me away from you. He knows, Hester Mae. He knows about us. So you see? I had to do it. I did it for you . . . for us." He lifted his head. "And don't tell me you hadn't been waiting for the old bastard to die so that we could marry."

He bent his head to nibble on the soft flesh of her earlobe. His breath, hot and desperate, sent chills through her. "I did it for us. For you," he repeated. "I can give you what he can't, *ma cherie*: children. Lots of them." His gaze, shadowed by the night, begged her to understand and accept him.

Closing her eyes against the stark truth, Hester Mae acknowledged Leo's hurtful accusation and her own shameful role in the day's events. But that had been before; before her talk with Baxter in the carriage, before she found the two adorable children who needed a home. And now Leo's actions might have ruined everything.

"There's a difference between dying naturally and murder. I never asked you to kill my husband, Leo. But thankfully, you *didn't* murder him. He's alive—and he'll survive. She paused, tearful. "Now, go! I learned today that I love my husband, and in a way, Leo, I have you to thank for that. Spending all day in that hospital made me take a good long look at myself and my life. I didn't like what I saw, and I hope Baxter will forgive me." She pushed Leo away and reached behind her for the doorknob.

"No! You're ruining everything," Leo shouted, reaching out for her.

Hester Mae turned the knob. "Don't come here again, Leo." She quickly slipped inside and locked the door behind her, ignoring his shouts and threats and pleas. After several minutes, she heard him stomp down the stairs.

Tugging the gloves from her fingers, she stared around. The fight with Leo, learning he'd tried to kill her husband—*for them*—left her shaking. How many times in the past few years had she walked through those double doors and wished she were no longer married? Too many. And today she'd nearly gotten her wish. Her knees buckled. She laughed, the sound humorless. "Oh, Baxter. What a fool I've been," she sobbed softly, falling back to lean against the doorway.

She didn't want her marriage to Baxter Olsen to end. For better or worse. In sickness and in health, she would go the distance.

Removing her hat, she stepped toward the stairs. She'd get a few hours of rest, then head back to the hospital.

Halfway up the stairs, her maid called up to her.

"Mrs. Olsen, you're home."

"Yes, Clare. I won't need you tonight. You may go to bed."

The maid looked uncomfortable. "But, ma'am, you've got company."

Hester Mae frowned. All the downstairs rooms were dark. "Who is it?"

Before the maid could answer, a short, plump woman bustled out of the parlor, her traveling dress wrinkled and her hair rumpled. She'd been asleep. Hester Mae descended the stairs. The woman handed her an envelope. "They be sleeping in there." She jerked her thumb over her shoulder. "I done me duty now, so I'll be on me way."

"Wait," Hester Mae begged, confused and too worn out to be dealing with any of this. She stared at the envelope. "Please, tell me what's going on. Who are you?"

"I be the children's nurse—um, I mean, I used to be their nurse. Got me own family to look after, and I can't look after these no more. Me husband is out in back with the carriage, waitin' for me. We wants to head back to our house right away."

"What children?" Hester opened the envelope. In the dim light, the words were hard to read. She hesitated. The letter was addressed to Baxter.

From the parlor came a soft, frightened cry, followed by bare feet slapping against the wooden floor. Hester Mae turned. Standing in the doorway, a dark-haired little girl blinked and rubbed her eyes. She was joined by another child, a boy with touseled black locks.

The woman, now wearing a threadbare coat, pointed. "The girl is Edith. She's four. And the boy is Adam. He just turned two." She strode to the door with hurried steps.

Hester Mae ran after her. "Why are they here?"

The woman turned pitying eyes on her. "Their ma died. I was asked to accompany them to their father. As he didn't see fit to come meet us at the dock tonight, I asked questions and learned where he lived. Now they are here where they belong, and

I've done what I was paid to do. They are none of my concern now."

"These are Baxter's children? There must be some mistake." She turned to stare at the brother and sister standing silently, watching her. The little boy stuck his thumb in his mouth while the girl gathered him close to her.

"No mistake, ma'am. It's all there in the letter." The door closed, ending any hope Hester had of trying to learn more from the woman.

Hester Mae hadn't thought there could be any more surprises this day, but how wrong she'd been. In the parlor, she lit a lamp and skimmed the letter. The truth pounded in her head. Baxter had had a mistress who'd borne him two children.

The ugly truth slammed into her. Her inability to conceive hadn't been Baxter's fault. And she'd blamed him for years. The fault lay with her. She was infertile. Another flaw reared its ugly head. Voices of the past sounded in her head, whispering that she was stupid, awkward, plain and odd. Now they added barren to their chants. She couldn't even bear children. As a woman, she was a failure.

Hester Mae closed her eyes, wishing her sister were here. Margaret Mary had loved her, hadn't cared that she'd been too tall and ugly. Her sister, graceful as a bird, beautiful as a china doll and so full of vitality, wasn't here, though. No one was. She was alone. So alone. She sank onto the settee.

From the doorway, Clare appeared to usher the two children up the stairs to a guest room, leaving Hester Mae staring at the letter. She slapped it against her palm.

Oh, they were a pair, all right, she and her husband. And it was a good thing he'd survived, because right now she was angry enough to finish him off.

Chapter Sixteen

Orange and red flames burst from the windows and the wooden roof, leaping high, sending billowing gusts of black smoke out into the air to obliterate the brick building. Star turned in her sleep, moving across the bed to the far side, as if she could run from the dark dream. But the heat from the fire followed, burning as if it were real.

She tossed and turned, her fingers clutching the sheet she'd drawn over her face. The smoke shifted, took shape. As if looking down on the scene from the sky, Star spotted a blurry group of women huddled together, with smoke and flames surrounding them. They had nowhere to run. They were trapped. They called out to her, held out their hands, beseeching her to save them.

"No!" she cried, staring in horror at the trapped people. From this distance they seemed familiar, yet between the smoke and her wavering vision, she couldn't see them clearly.

She didn't want to see them clearly. She was afraid.
Look, she commanded herself, but it was too late.
The smoke had obscured them. She tried moving
closer. Through the clouds of billowing smoke she
flew. She had to try and stop the tragic deaths in
her vision from becoming reality.

She fought wave after wave of smoke and heat.
The closer she got, the louder were the screams.
Female screams. Children's screams. She shuddered. Before she could reach them, a winged creature slammed into her; talons as thick as her arms
grabbed her, kept her from going to the women.
She fought.

Low laughter, mocking and menacing, drowned
out the screams. Cold blue eyes filled her vision,
and the form holding her took the shape of a snake.
It had a bestial face and wings.

Star screamed, over and over. Then, as it had in
past visions, the shape of an eagle appeared in the
sky. It swooped down, but hesitated between coming to her rescue or that of the women who were
trapped by the flames. The eagle's form shimmered
and shifted until it became Grady. He stood before
her and the snake creature, then ran toward her,
shouting for the vile beast to release her.

A shot rang out. Grady fell, blood blossoming in
an ugly circle across his white shirt.

High above them, the screams continued. The
face of her daughter appeared. "Save me, Mother.
Save me!"

Star's heart raced. No. Not Morning Moon! *Save*
her. Save her, she screamed. *Save them all!*

Star turned to fight the death grip the creature
had on her arm. "Let me go," she sobbed, over and
over. The hands dragged her from the place of
death. . . .

A voice called out to her. The blackness faded to

blinding light. She reached for the figure, sought the voice pulling her through the darkness of her vision.

"Star! My love, wake up."

Opening her eyes, she nearly screamed into the darkness.

"Shh, it's all right. It was just a dream." Grady's soothing voice washed over her.

Star trembled and held on to him. Her heart raced and she was cold. She shivered, her teeth chattering. "Not a dream, a vision." She sobbed.

Grady pulled back. She clutched him tighter. "Don't leave me."

"I'm not leaving." Grady scooted her over and climbed into bed beside her, then drew the covers over them. He gathered her close.

His scent and the warmth of his bare flesh surrounded her. She buried her face against his shoulder and slid her legs between his as she sought the hard feel of him against her. On board the ship with the two girls, she'd adopted the white woman's nightdress, but here, in her own room, she preferred to sleep as she had at home—in nothing. The warm feel of naked flesh sliding against naked flesh gave her comfort as nothing else could. She needed Grady, needed his toughness, the strength of his arms around her, the feel of his rock-hard chest to hold. Yet, she couldn't get close enough to blot out the horror of her vision.

His large hands roamed up and down her back, clasping her shivering form tightly.

Star, her gaze still wild and filled with terror, drew her head back from where she'd buried it in the hollow of his shoulder. She reached up to kiss the hollow of his throat, her teeth nipping lightly. Then she fiercely pulled his mouth to hers. "Love me, Grady. Love me now." She wrapped her legs around his hips, pulling him on top of her, refusing to let him go.

"Do you want to talk about it?"

Grady's breath tickled the sensitive skin below her ear. Exhausted, Star shook her head. "I can't." After the savage loving—he'd read her silent desires and brought her to a powerful release—she couldn't bear to meet Grady's eyes. She'd never acted in such a manner. She'd been totally selfish in her lovemaking.

"Star?"

"I'm sorry," she cried.

"For what?" Grady brushed the tears from her face.

Star's lips trembled. "I used you. That wasn't loving."

Smiling, Grady traced her lower lip. He seemed both awed and amused. "It was incredible. It was wild, with no pretense. Natural." He laughed. "You know, for most animals, the mating act is violent."

"But we're not animals." She tried to bury her head but he wouldn't let her.

"Ah, but we are. Beneath the social-climbing and gossipmongering, beneath the veneer of our society, we're just animals. I'm surprised you can deny it." He laughed. "But what are you worried about? Did you hear me complaining?"

"No, but—"

"Then, no more. Tell me what prompted it."

Star sighed. "Not tonight. In the morning." She couldn't bear to relive her vision. She needed time to sort it out.

Strong fingers brushed along her jaw, slid up into her hair and held her close. "Will keeping it to yourself prevent it from coming true?"

Star groaned. It wouldn't, and that was the truth

of the matter. She didn't want to acknowledge that he might die . . . or someone else might. "Oh, Grady, I'm so frightened." She burrowed her head beneath his chin.

"Of what?" He brushed his lips across her temple.

"Fire. Death. Losing the ones I love. Losing you." And she would, if she couldn't warn him not to come after her. He had to save the others. She lifted her head. She had to warn him. Tonight . . . Now. She'd hesitated once and lost her chance to warn her husband. She'd not make the same mistake twice. And she new she didn't have much time.

Grady held her tenderly and stroked her arms. "I know how much this upsets you. We'll talk in the morning . . . if that's what you want."

Star sat up and faced him, feeling cold and bereft. "No. *Now*. You must know. There's going to be a fire. There are going to be women and children . . . trapped."

Grady sat up and drew her up with him. "Where?"

Star closed her eyes and tried to place the burning building. "I don't know." Her voice broke. "I don't know. There was too much smoke." She clenched her fists in frustration.

"Come here."

Star allowed Grady to settle her in front of him with her back resting against his chest. His bent legs cradled hers, his arms wrapped around her, their fingers entwined. They were linked together as one. She and her eagle.

"Relax; lean your head back and breathe slowly."

Obeying him, Star freed her mind, allowing the images to replay.

"What do you see?"

"Women and children trapped by fire. And you."

At the recalled sight of him falling to the ground, she tried to break free, but Grady held tight. His strength infused her. She released her breath in a shudder.

"The women: how many and where are they?" His voice remained low, soothing.

"I don't know. It was too blurry, there was too much smoke. They were screaming." Squeezing her eyes in concentration, Star sought details but they evaded her.

"What else?"

Frozen in time, the image before her taunted her, as did the evil gaze of the monster holding her, preventing her from going to help Grady. She opened her mouth to tell him, then hesitated. If he knew she'd be in danger, what would he do? Would he come after her or save the others? With certainty, she knew he would come after her and fight the monster—and those trapped by the fire would die . . . with him.

Turning, Star straddled Grady's lap and cupped his face in her hands. "If you have a choice between saving me or those women and children, you must save *them*. One of them is my daughter, and the other must be yours. Save them. I don't know why I feel this, but you must promise to listen to me."

He hesitated.

"Say you will save our children."

As if in great pain, he closed his eyes. "I promise."

She sagged against him. "I'm so frightened, Grady. What if those women die? Or our children? What if something happens to you?"

"Nothing will happen to me."

"How can you say that?" Her heart contracted.

"I've been given a second chance at love. No— we've been given a second chance, and I won't let anything destroy it." Grady reached up and drew her head to his. Their breath mingled. "We will take it one day at a time."

Moving beneath her, his body reacting to the sensation of her pressed against him, he cupped her breasts. "Take me in you, my love, my bright Star. Let me feel you. Ride me, and let us soar with the stars." He slid down onto the bed, lying beneath her.

Star's heart thudded painfully within her chest. She couldn't lose this man. Ever. Nor could she ignore her own desire to be one with him.

Grady gripped her buttocks, lifting her and bringing her down on him hard. She sheathed him, impaling herself deeply. Star's thighs gripped his hips and they remained still for a moment, savoring the newness of the position, building their passions with only their lips and tongues.

She bent her head down and he plunged his tongue into her mouth, teasing her with the rhythm they each longed to match with their hips. She tried to move, to initiate the thrusting that would drive them both through the heavens, but he held her tightly against him. She moaned, and without moving her hips, she flexed the pulsing walls surrounding his swollen flesh. He gasped and broke the kiss.

Star laughed softly in his ear, then traced its shape with her tongue before returning to his mouth. Beneath her, Grady squirmed and moaned, his breathing harsh. Burying her fingers in his hair, she bore down on him. She'd discovered quite by accident, by listening to his sounds of pleasure, that he liked this.

She squeezed tight around him, drawing him in and holding him within her. He tried to break the kiss and pulled at her hips, but this time she plunged into his mouth, stroking and dipping her tongue in time to her inner muscles closing around him. She developed a rhythm that had them both pulsing with lust.

Her moans grew as her need built. Her hips rocked, her buttocks clenching with each sweet pulse. Faster. *Harder*.

"No more. God, no more!" Grady's fingers clutched her waist and lower, his fingertips brushing against her sensitive inner flesh. Yet he didn't pull her away. Instead, one hand slid around and found that part of her that needed touching, and his head lifted up. He opened his mouth and latched onto one breast.

His fingers stroked and pressed, his mouth suckling until in a burst of frantic need, Star cried out and lifted her hips.

"Yes, my darling Star. Now! Harder." He rose to meet her and when they again were fully joined, the storm broke. He gripped her hips, she clutched his shoulders, and they began a frantic tempo, pounding into each other with wild need.

She gasped with each deep thrust, and he moaned beneath her. Then she found release, and he did too. They rode wave after wave of sweet ecstasy, and at the end they were both left trembling.

Sweat drenched their bodies as they collapsed against each other. "I love you, Star. I love you," Grady murmured.

Star threaded her fingers through his. "You are the warrior of my heart. Together we are one." Somehow, she had to remember that. She and her eagle. Flying together. Always one. Forever.

That was the one thing that would see her through.

* * *

Voices woke Grady around seven. He slid from Star's bed, slipped into his room and donned his robe just as a knock sounded at his door. He opened it. Zeke stood there, obviously woken from sleep.

"Your lawyer is here to see you, Colonel."

Keeping his voice low, he nodded. "Tell him I'll be right there."

He washed and dressed quickly and found Manning waiting for him in his den, pacing. "What is it, Charles? Is it Baxter? The girl?"

"No. I think I've found the plantation where Maurice and maybe Hattie's family were taken."

"Where? How?"

Charles grinned. "I spent the night looking through Baxter's papers. Leo got sloppy, and I found some manifests taped to the bottom of a desk drawer. There are four plantations south, and several brothels north, all along the Mississippi River, each listed as a destination for the shipment of slaves. The night you arrived in the harbor, there was only one plantation name with a shipment. I have a steamboat waiting to take us down the Mississippi to Alabama. It leaves in less than thirty minutes." He put his hat back on.

"Let me get my coat. And I have to inform Zeke where I'm going. We'll take Zac with us. We might need some help." Grady left the den and thought about Star, wondering if he should wake her before he left.

Turning, he found her awake and coming down the stairs. She wore the same blue dress she'd donned the first time she'd worn the clothes of his daughter. His eyes roamed over her in appreciation.

"Grady, what's going on?" She joined him and Charles in the foyer.

"I have to leave. We may have found the plantation where Hattie's husband and son were sold. But I don't want to say anything to her yet, just in case we're wrong."

"Oh, I hope you're not," Star whispered. Her eyes darkened and her mouth pinched with worry. "Grady, please be careful."

"I will. I'll be back as soon as I can." He reached out to cup Star's face. Behind him, Charles slipped quietly out the front door.

Grady drew Star to him and kissed her tenderly, quelling his hunger. "I love you, Star. And when I get back, I'm going to ask you to marry me. I'm warning you here and now, so you can think about it."

"Oh, Grady—" Tears misted her eyes, but he also saw fear and worry. "Don't ask that of me. Not yet. I'm not ready."

"Do you love me?" He searched her eyes for his answer.

"Yes," she whispered.

She loved him, yet he still saw fear and uncertainty in her gaze. "Please think about it. Just do that. Don't deny us this chance we have at happiness. It's taken me so long to realize again what's important. . . . I want to have that."

"The cost may be too great." Her eyes swam with tears.

"Sometimes you have to take a risk in order to reap great rewards. Think on that." God, he didn't want to go. He hated leaving her like this, especially after last night. But he had to. "I'll be back as soon as I can."

Star reached out to slide her fingers through his hair. She brought her lips to his. "Grady, be careful. I can't lose you, married or not."

Grady kissed her hard, conveying his own fears

and emotions. "You won't. Remember that."

Charles poked his head back in. "Let's go, old man, or we'll miss the boat."

Grady nodded and stepped away. He longed to tell her again that he loved her, to beg her to say the words aloud to him, but he didn't want to add undue pressure to his proposal. Instead, he left her standing there in the large foyer by herself.

Riding quickly, he and Charlie arrived at the wharf with several minutes to spare. Riding past piers where men ran like ants to unload or load cargo, they were forced to slow down in order to avoid running down workers and passengers.

Just before they got to their boat, a voice hailed them. Grady halted his horse and turned in his saddle to see Todd Langley sauntering toward them. Frowning, Grady waved Charles on. "You go ahead, stop the ship. I'll catch up." He dismounted out of politeness, then turned to the businessman. "You're not leaving, are you?"

"My friend thinks he found where his servant was sold."

"Ah. Good for him. Don't let me keep you, then." Todd stepped back and waved his hand in farewell as Grady swung back up into the saddle. "I know we had a bit of a disagreement, but I wish you well. I hope you find Hattie's husband and son as well."

Nodding his appreciation, Grady made his way to the steamboat.

"You fool!" the Dragon roared, the sound echoing through the large, nearly empty warehouse.

Leo backed away and bumped into an open crate. He glanced down and cringed at the sight of a tall vase depicting a painted serpent whose body wrapped around the white vase. "It's not my fault."

He skirted the crate, not wanting anything between him and the door.

"Then whose fault is it, you damned idiot? Everything was progressing just fine until you tried to kill Olsen. Now we've lost everything."

Nervously, Leo watched the bearded man pace. Somehow he had to fix things or he'd wind up floating in the river. "We can still kill him."

"And what of the woman?"

"I can take care of Hester Mae. She'll come around." He made himself sound far more confident than he felt.

The Dragon pulled out his gun. "You've done enough."

Leo eyed the door, desperate. "We'll force her . . . then take her to that brothel you sell the other women to. No one will know. We'll still have it all."

The Dragon smiled and advanced. He reached down and stroked the smooth surface of the vase. "You're right. I can still have it all." He set his revolver down.

Leo felt a wave of relief, until he saw his boss motion to someone behind him. He whirled around. Two beefy men grabbed him by the arms.

"I warned you not to hold out on me," the bearded man was saying. "I know about the white girl and the old woman. You got greedy, Leo. And you messed up, too." He looked at the men holding Leo. "Get him out of here. You know what to do."

Then the Dragon picked up his coat and left the warehouse, leaving Leo to struggle futilely for his life.

Chapter Seventeen

Grady wanted to marry her, was the first thing Star thought as she watched him leave.

The words both thrilled and scared her. Overcome by emotion and fear, Star paced through the downstairs rooms, for once unaware of the gilt mirror in the entry, the tables of all sizes topped with fascinating works of art, the rich colors and intricate designs in the plush carpeting.

In the sitting room that had once belonged to Grady's first wife, Star gazed up at the features of the beautiful woman holding a place of honor above the mantel. Rather than feel threatened by this woman's portrait, she felt a sense of comfort. Grady had known love and happiness, and the knowledge that he wished to pursue the same with her filled her heart with joy.

He loved her. And though she hadn't spoken the words aloud, she loved him as none other. He was her soul mate, the one man who'd touched her so deeply that she ached for him whenever he was away. Against her will, their love had sprung from friendship and companionship; it had grown into a soul-searing need to be together. Without him, Star felt lost and alone, adrift, with no log to hold on to as life's current swirled and carried her into dangerous waters.

Though still frightened of the consequences of her visions and her gift, in Grady she'd found a rock. Someone to cling to, to ease her fear. He believed in her and gave her strength. Yet was she strong enough, brave enough, to take that next step and marry him?

She wandered and paced—in one doorway, out another, winding her way from one end of the house to the next, ignoring Hattie and the other servants as she searched deeply within herself. Could she let go of her fear of losing him? Could she risk becoming Grady's wife even if it meant losing him? It was far too late to stop the love, but binding their souls further scared her. Before, she could tell herself that it was all over at the end of the summer; she was to go back to her people. But now?

The very thought of leaving Grady brought forth a wave of pain so great, it nearly doubled her over. In that instant, she had her answer. For better or worse, she was already bound to this man. They were committed—not by words binding them in marriage, but by a love that joined their souls more tightly than anything.

Staring at the rich burgundy carpet at her feet, suddenly the colors darkened and the pattern faded. An image of dark-skinned men and women bound by chains blurred her vision. They faded once more, but frightening visions seized her mind. A horrific red creature, scaly like a snake, with a long, pointed tail and a mouth full of sharp teeth reached out to grab her. It laughed, spewing hot, angry flames. So horrible was this creature, she knew it could not exist—yet she'd seen it somewhere. She was sure of that.

Putting her hands to her head, she wanted to cry out, to call for Grady, but he wasn't there. No one was there to help.

Don't fight. Breathe. Don't be afraid of this. This is a gift, not a curse. Your daughter is not afraid, so you can also handle this.

She heard Grady's voice, heard the soft murmurs he'd whispered to her during the dark of last night as he'd coaxed her into talking. She hadn't even realized how much he'd eased her mind, until now—until her subconscious mind whispered back his words.

She relaxed, sitting on the floor, and didn't fight the vision. This time, instead of allowing the vision to frighten her and block all rational thought, she pulled it into focus, then tried to remember where she'd seen this creature. Grady's life and that of the women she'd seen in last night's vision might depend on her learning that.

There was a wild beauty to the creature. Around it. As if it was something to be prized. The vision faded from her mind, and she resumed her pacing, staring blankly at objects gracing nearly every surface. Small porcelain figures, painted glass eggs, statues, vases filled with fresh-cut flowers. But none of them sparked her memory.

Then she stared at one tall, fragile vase. Picking it up carefully, she felt the coolness of the glass— and remembered another container. Putting it back, she ran up the stairs to her room. There she searched through her drawers for the reticule that matched the dress she'd worn the day she'd arrived in St. Louis. She opened it and dumped the contents out onto her bed.

There! A small piece of broken glass lay facedown, its white underside gleaming in the patch of sunlight on her bed. Picking it up, she turned it over and drew in a sharp breath. On it was the tiny image that had frightened her in her vision. It was the same creature.

She recalled the day she'd arrived, the crate falling and breaking open, the beautiful pieces hitting the ground and shattering. This piece had been flung near their trunks and bags, and when she'd found it, she'd been intrigued enough to keep it. She'd meant to show it to Grady and ask him about it. She'd forgotten.

She studied it anew. The creature reminded her of a snake but was much more hideous and repulsive. Yet there was a savage beauty to it. Perhaps Hattie or Zeke could tell her what it was. And perhaps it was the key to unlocking the message of her visions.

Downstairs, she hesitated. A sound coming from the stairs behind her warned her to move and move fast. She jumped just as Grady's daughter flew off the banister. "Renny!"

"Oops, sorry. I didn't see you there."

"And what if it had been one of the maids with something valuable . . . and breakable?" she scolded.

"Oh. I didn't think of that." Renny looked shamefaced.

Star softened. "I know. You must begin to stop to think, or else your impulsive nature will land you in trouble." She held out her hand. "Do you know what this is?"

Renny's eyes widened. "Hey, it's a tiny dragon. Where did you find it?"

A *dragon.*

The word chilled Star. She felt sickness and dread coil within her. Her chest constricted. Grady and Charles were searching for a man who called himself by that name. Star knelt in front of Renny, her grip on the girl's shoulders almost painful. "Are you sure?"

The girl nodded. "Yep. Lots of shops sell stuff like this."

"Thank you, Renny." Star stood.

The Dragon.

Images hovered at the edge of her consciousness. She tried to call them to her. There were more, many more, and she needed to remember them.

"Star!"

Startled, she blinked. Renny and Morning Moon stood in front of her, Renny hopping impatiently up and down. "What?"

"I asked if you would take us to the park for just a little while. We want to go feed the ducks. Matilda's never done that."

"I don't think we should leave the house with your father gone."

"Ah, we'll just stay in sight of the house. He said he'd take us, but now he's gone." Renny's lip jutted out. "He's always leaving."

Star sighed. Perhaps the fresh air would do her good. "All right, but not for long. Let me go tell Zeke where we are going."

Walking into the kitchen, and finding the cook, maid and Hattie sitting at the bin table going over menus, she waved them to remain where they were. "I'm looking for Zeke."

"He went to the market." Hattie rose.

"Hmm. I'm taking the girls across to the park for a short walk."

Hattie bit her lip. "Are you sure it's safe? The colonel gave orders for no one to leave the house unescorted until he returns."

"We won't be gone long, Hattie."

Outside, Zeb stopped her as well. He was working and didn't look pleased when Star refused to wait for him to accompany her. She pointed across the street. "We won't go far. The park is crowded. We'll be fine. . . . We'll stay in sight of the house."

"All right, but I'll be out here where I can watch you."

With the girls skipping on ahead, they crossed the street. Under the cool shade of the tall trees, Star breathed in deeply.

Renny turned suddenly. "I forgot to ask Cook for bread crumbs for the ducks. I'm going back to go get them."

"Be quick—and Renny, could you grab my gloves?" The items were a nuisance in Star's opinion, but she had no desire to shame Grady and dress inappropriately. Both girls ran back and disappeared around the side of the house. Star sat on a bench behind the wrought-iron fence where she could watch for them to return. Roses climbed over and along the fence, providing a nice, secluded spot to sit and reflect. A tall shade tree kept the sun off her. She adjusted her hat.

Enjoying the warm breeze on her cheeks, she watched Zeb go down on his knees in front of some bushes along the side of the house. He'd left the patch that he'd been planting so he could position himself to watch her. Though he appeared to be working, she knew he hadn't taken his eyes off her.

She waved to him. Who'd have thought he'd be in his element working soil? Of all the brothers, his chosen position seemed to fit his personality perfectly. It turned out he'd always kept a garden—at the base and in the mountains.

Star turned her thoughts to her home and family, then to her son. In less than two months, she was supposed to board another steamer bound for home. Her decision loomed: accept Grady's proposal and return here to marry him, or return to her old life.

Leaving had taught her that she couldn't hide from what she was. No matter where she went or what name she used, she was Star Dreamer, a Sioux Indian—and with that came her heritage, including the gift of the sight. If she accepted Grady's proposal, she'd have to leave the land of her people. Was there somehow a way to merge the two cultures into one? Could she have both?

Her mother and Emma had each given up all they'd known for a new life. Could she?

She closed her eyes briefly, torn between love and fear of the future. She thought again of her visions. Something was going to happen, and she and Grady were involved. Was it too soon to be thinking of marriage? Would Grady lose his life in battle as Two-Ree had? Like Two-Ree, Grady was a warrior—he would constantly be in danger. She knew she had to expect that. So where did that leave her? But she might be able to help him survive. Her grandmother had—From the corner of her eye, she noted a large black carriage pull to a stop in front of Grady's home.

Who had come to call? Curious, she stood. From her angle across the street, she saw the driver, a large man, jump down. The carriage door opened and another man, his face hidden by a large, bushy beard, exited, pulling a woman down with him. She stumbled, but he grabbed hold of her. The driver came to her other side and held her arm. To her surprise, Star saw it was Hester Mae.

Frowning, she hoped there wasn't bad news

about her husband. Picking up her skirts, she prepared to cross back over to greet Renny's aunt. But when two more men alighted, she hesitated. Their stances and furtive glances made her fall back into the shadows. Something was wrong. Why was Hester Mae here, and who were those four men?

She watched Zac walk down to the carriage to great the visitors. The bearded man stepped forward. Zac stopped. Even from where she sat, Star heard his curse. To her horror, one of the other men held a gun trained on the scout. Then they all walked down the side of the house toward the rear entrance. The bearded man turned to watch the street as he walked.

Star cringed in her secluded seat. Even from this distance, she recognized him. He was the man from the market—the one who'd grabbed her and shoved her. Her heart pounded and her mouth went dry. With certainty, she knew he was the Dragon.

When he disappeared, she stood. Her girls! Hattie! The servants.

There was no way for her to warn them.

Renny grabbed several slices of bread, then sneaked out two tarts, hiding them beneath the bread. Hattie came up behind her and shooed her away. Grinning, she left through the doors leading to the dining room where she showed Morning Moon her stash.

Her friend licked her lips. "Cook gave you tarts?"

"Nah, I took them. Much more fun than asking." Renny giggled. "Let's get a napkin to wrap these in and then we can go feed the ducks—and us." Sauntering nonchalantly back through the kitchen, she headed for the rear door, eyeing the cooling sweets on the tray. Hattie stopped her with the shake of her finger. "If you want a sweet, *cherie*, please ask for it."

Shamefaced, Renny sighed. "Yes, Hattie." The housekeeper's voice when she scolded sounded like music as her French accent came alive. Smiling over at Morning Moon, Renny decided she just might have to make Hattie scold her again, so she could hear that same lilting tone.

They ran down the porch steps and headed back around the house. Suddenly, Morning Moon grabbed her arm. Her eyes were wide as she stared toward the side of the house they were walking toward. "Renny, we need to hide."

It only took one look at her friend's features for Renny to realize something was wrong. Then she heard voices. They were deep men's voices and following, came the muffled cry of a woman. She didn't know what was going on, but if Morning Moon said they needed to hide, they would.

"Come on." Renny pulled her beneath the porch. Through a small crack between planks, she saw two men shove Zeb around the corner of the house. One of them hit the scout over the head and his limp body fell with a muffled thud.

Renny barely covered her own mouth in time to keep from crying out. Then she saw two men holding her aunt's arms. One of them had a gun. A man with a beard yanked on her aunt's hair, causing Hester Mae to cry out. "You'll get us into the house, Hester, or I'll kill you here and now."

"You won't kill me. You need me." The woman sounded scared despite her brave words.

"Then I'll kill those girls." The bearded man laughed when Hester Mae's shoulders slumped.

"Much better, my dear." Loud steps sounded above Renny's head as the group climbed the steps and entered the kitchen.

Renny listened as her aunt opened the door. A loud shout followed by the sound of a gun going off made both girls fall to the ground, terrified. Above them, the floor shook mightily. Both girls retreated to the far end of the porch.

One of the men yelled out, "No one else here, boss. The squaw and them brats is gone."

In a rush, Renny remembered what her father had said the day he'd caught her in the carriage house. These men were after Hattie and Star. She had to do something to save them!

"Damn. I want that squaw." The voice came from above Renny's head on the porch. "Where are they?"

Hattie's voice trembled. "They went shopping."

"You better be telling me the truth, you no good Negro." The man's voice was ice cold. Hattie cried out and the porch shook. Something fell—hard.

"No! Leave her alone," Hester Mae called out.

The man laughed. "You like her so much, you can share her fate, Hester Mae—after you and I marry."

"You won't get away with this."

"Who's going to stop me? Your husband? I don't think so. Leo started the job, but I'll finish it." Renny bit her lip at the sound of the man's laughter.

"You're a real bastard—" A loud slap joined the sound of the older woman's soft weeping.

"Get them servants tied up and make haste." Steps receded back into the kitchen. The cries faded. Furious that these men were hurting the people she loved, Renny knew she had to go warn Star and get help. She motioned for Morning Moon to follow her. The porch wrapped around to the other side of the house and to a door that led into the servants' quarters. The two girls exited from beneath it and ran around to the front of the house, peering cautiously at the empty carriage out front. Now what?

"My mother. We must warn her." They ran for the street, but the terse voices of the men and the crying of the women growing closer warned Renny there was no time to cross to the park without being spotted. And if those nasty men saw them, they'd get Star Dreamer.

They had to hide until the bad guys left. It seemed her aptitude for finding hiding places would pay off. She grinned at the thought, though she knew the situation was awful. Hurrying, she ran to the rear of the villains' carriage. "Come on. We'll see where they take my aunt and Hattie. Then we can get help."

She climbed in, folding herself down in the floor area in front of the seat. Morning Moon squeezed in too, and Renny pulled the lid down. Long moments later, she felt the carriage shift as the men entered. As she heard crying, she realized two of the maids were also inside . . . along with her aunt and Hattie? Suddenly they were moving. Lifting the lid an inch, holding it tightly so it wouldn't fly up, she saw Star frantically hurrying toward them.

Chapter Eighteen

Star waited until the Dragon's carriage turned the corner, then she ran across the street and around the back of the house. She found Zeb sprawled on the grass, unconscious. Placing her ear against the mountain man's chest, she breathed a sigh of relief that he was breathing. With no time to lose, she ran into the carriage house and selected one of Renny's horses. They had been trained by her people, and so she would trust them in her time of need. But with all her petticoats, she couldn't mount.

Uncaring that she was destroying her garments, she divested herself of the hampering material, her shoes and her stockings. She had forced herself to be white too long. Grabbing the small knife she still kept strapped to her thigh, she slashed the fabric of her skirt up each side. With that, she mounted, using her hands and knees to command the horse.

Once out on the street, she paused. Everywhere

she looked, she saw carriages. "Now what?" she said to herself, then thought. She recalled the tiny dragon painted against a blue background. *Water.* The harbor. She needed to find someone to give her directions.

She found a gentleman in the park and asked him. He told her, then eyed her bare legs with interest, but Star didn't care. She was tired of pretending to be someone else . . . and of being afraid. She was a Sioux princess . . . and she was proud of that. She swung away from the surprised gentleman and urged her animal into a gallop.

Having set off in the right direction, after a bit she spotted the carriage. Doing so, she slowed and stayed hidden from the driver's view. This was it. This was the situation in her vision. Somehow, she had to stop those men before it was too late.

Fire? A burning building. How would they end up in that? She prayed to the Spirits to watch over the women and show her what to do to save them. Grady was gone and there was only her. She could go for help, but who would she ask? She couldn't risk the time it would take to explain. She stayed with the carriage.

When it turned into an alley, Star had to go past. She didn't dare follow. Instead, she rode around the block. When she returned and peered back down the alley, she saw the carriage parked along the back—empty. The buildings here sat close together, and nearly back-to-back with the ones behind it. To which of the four had Hattie and Hester Mae been taken?

And the girls too. Star had to get them to safety. But before she could dismount and go in, one of the men exited one of the buildings—just as Renny peered out of the carriage.

*   *   *

On board the steamboat, Grady paced, eager to be on his way. The sooner they found Maurice and Hattie's family, the sooner he'd be back home with Star. Why had he mentioned marriage so soon? Had he frightened her off? Fear clenched his stomach into a knot, and he decided maybe it was for the best he would be gone for some time. That would give her time to think.

You're running, again. He heard his sister Ida's words in his head.

No. I'm going to find Hattie's family and stop this Dragon, he answered her.

Sighing, he rubbed the back of his neck to ease the tightness. He was running from Star's possible rejection, though. He was giving her time, a chance to escape. If he was courageous, he would have demanded an answer from her.

The need to leave the ship and return to Star, overwhelmed him. He needed Star. He needed to make sure she was safe.

Now where had that thought come from? She was safe in his house. Though he'd brought Zeb with him, the others were there to protect her. So why did he suddenly feel as if something was wrong?

Listening to his instincts had kept him alive more than once during his military service. Falling back on years of training, he separated the emotional scene of leaving Star from the worry prickling at the back of his neck. Something important niggled at the back of his mind. Something he wasn't considering.

"Something's wrong," he murmured to Charles. Both men stood at the rail, waiting for the captain to weigh anchor.

"I'm sure it's just a short delay. We'll head out soon," Charles commented absently, assuming

Grady was speaking of the boat's delayed departure.

Grady gripped the rail and leaned on his arms. "No. Something else." He tapped his fingers along the side of the smooth, varnished wood.

"None of this is right, O'Brien, old man. When I find this Dragon, I will personally see him behind bars for what he's done. I just hope we can find Maurice and Hattie's family. God knows how many more were taken and sold back into slavery or locked away in brothels."

Grady remembered the sick feeling he'd gotten when they'd learned the scope of the Dragon's activities. Recalling the condition of the blond girl, and how the police were now willing to take action, also made him feel ashamed and angry that justice wasn't equal for all. And while that wasn't something new, it had never hit quite so close to home before. The hypocrisy of his society was galling. This came down to wrong and right. Every man or woman or child was entitled to justice. And here in St. Louis, it seemed the only justice was for whites.

"You're just anxious to find Hattie's family and get back to your woman, that's all." Charles eyed him with speculation.

"That's it!" Grady snapped his fingers and grabbed Charles by the arm. "He knew we were looking for Hattie's family!"

"Who?"

"Langley. Todd Langley. He wished me luck in finding Hattie's husband and son. How did he know about them?"

"We must have mentioned it the other night at the Blue Horn."

Grim, Grady shook his head. "No. You mentioned Maurice, but I never mentioned Hattie had a son. Just family, yet Langley knew! Outside of the

319

captains I've questioned and the authorities, I've not spoken to anyone about Hattie's son or husband."

Grady paced.

"Maybe someone—one of the captains—told him."

"Why? That's not something that would come up in casual conversation." Recalling that Langley ran an import business added the last piece to the puzzle. "How would he know unless he was the Dragon?"

"Not likely, old man." But Charles narrowed his eyes. "Although he is pro-slavery."

The words hung between the two men. "I think it is worth doing some further questioning." Finding Zac, the three men left the steamboat and ran along the wharf. It didn't take but a few questions to learn which warehouse belonged to Todd Langley's importing business.

Shoved into a small work area in the back of the warehouse, Hester Mae glared at Todd Langley, the Dragon. "You can't get away with this."

The man laughed. "Wrong, Hester Mae. I already have. And as soon as I finish off Baxter, you'll marry me. If you don't, I'll kill all of those women with you watching. And I promise it will be a slow death for each of them."

The gleam in his eyes warned Hester Mae that he'd enjoy doing it. "Let them go. You don't need them."

She cringed and turned her head as Todd lifted his hand to strike her. But, instead, he caressed her face. Then, like a striking snake, he grabbed her chin and forced her to look at him. "Why, Hester Mae, like you, they'll fetch me a nice sum from any one of the brothels I sell them to. And don't think

I won't sell you. Once I have your husband's shipping business, you're history. Like your lover."

Hester was surprised that she felt a brief twinge at hearing of Leo's death.

The Dragon continued. "Men out along the western frontier are eager for women. And some don't care if they are willing or not. In fact, some *like* a woman who'll fight." The gleam in his eyes warned that he was one of those men.

"You're disgusting," Hester Mae spat.

He laughed. "Yes, my dear, I am." He turned to Hattie, who cowered. "And you—I should beat you right here and now for all the trouble you've caused." He grabbed her by the hair and tossed her to the floor. Removing his belt, he stood over her.

"Maybe I'll just kill you, to show everyone I mean business. Besides, everyone knows the only good Negro is a dead one. Ask my pa. He married one. And *I* suffered for it! I was an outcast growing up." He grew thoughtful. "Still, the old man learned his lesson when he caught her in bed with another man. Killed them both and then he killed himself. All that pain for nothing." He brought his belt down, hard, striking Hattie's legs.

Hester Mae screamed and tried to stop him, but one of Langley's thugs grabbed hold of her. The two Irish maids from Grady's household staff were clinging together, sobbing softly.

"Now it's my turn to cause the pain." Langley lifted his arm again.

"Hey, boss, we got a problem." A tall, thin man entered the back room of the warehouse. He held on to a squirming Renny and Morning Moon. "Found these brats out back."

Hester Mae struggled against the man restraining her. "Renny, oh God! Don't you lay your filthy hands on her!" She stepped hard down onto the arch of the man who was holding her. He released her with a howl of pain, hopped back and knocked over a crate. Hester Mae lunged forward to grab Todd, but he dodged and snagged Renny by the scruff of her neck. "Watch it, Hester Mae, or the brat will be the first to go."

"No! Don't hurt her. Don't hurt her," she cried, backing away.

Grinning with malicious enjoyment, the Dragon pulled out his knife. "Perhaps you need a demonstration, Hester Mae."

The expression in Renny's eyes chased away her frantic fear and fueled her fury. No one treated her niece, her sister's child, in this fashion. Her gaze swept the small, dark, windowless work room for a weapon. As Renny twisted away in her struggles, distracting Todd, Hester Mae grabbed an old, smoking lantern. She tossed it at him.

It hit Langley on his shoulder, bounced off and fell onto the floor, then shattered. Flames shot out, eagerly licking at the straw littering the floor. As they hit an overturned crate filled with dry straw for packing, a loud whoosh sounded. A wall of flames shot into the air.

With a yell, the Dragon released Renny with a curse. The flames forced him to jump back. Frightened of the fire, the man holding Morning Moon released her. With a shriek, he ran out the back way to save himself. Hester Mae grabbed her niece and the Indian girl.

Langley backed away and pulled his gun, blocking their escape. "Stupid bitch, you've ruined everything I've worked for! Now you can die in the fire you started."

Hester Mae knew that, separated from them by the flames, Langley would shoot them if they tried to go out the front door. "Oh, Lord. I've made it worse," she cried.

"No, look," Hattie cried. She had been flung to the ground and was unguarded.

Hester Mae glanced at Hattie, then to the stairs to which she was pointing. She shoved the two girls toward safety. "Go. Quickly."

Renny and Morning Moon bolted for the steep stairs, followed by the two maids. As soon as Hattie ran up the stairs, Hester Mae turned to save herself. Behind her, Todd's screams filled her ears.

A bullet whizzed by her. Hester Mae glanced back briefly and saw Langley trying to come after them through the flames, but they were too hot, and spreading fast.

"You'll die. All of you!" the Dragon screamed. He aimed, his grin malicious. At the impact of the bullet, Hester Mae fell against the rail. Pain radiated up her chest and shoulder. Thinking of only Renny, of saving her niece, she pulled herself up the stairs. Then everything went black.

Chapter Nineteen

Star ran around the block to find the front entrance. If she went in the back, she'd only get herself captured—then she'd be of no use to anyone. By the time she reached the front, a crowd had gathered, her worst fears realized. Billowing smoke was escaping broken windows high above the ground. Around her, alarms sounded all along the wharf.

Star's heart leaped into her throat as she shoved and pushed, making her way to the front. *No!* Over and over, she denied that it was too late. Smoke continued to gush out of the building she'd seen Renny and Morning Moon hauled into. She ran for the doors.

Hands held her back. "You can't go in there."

"I have to. There are women and children in there." A hush fell around her.

Opening the door, blinding smoke and heat forced her back along with the others crowding around her. Sobbing, she tried again, but it was futile. No one could get in. The building was engulfed.

"Star!"

At the sound of Grady's voice, she fell into his arms and sobbed, "I failed. It's too late."

Grady's face paled, his lips pinched tightly together. "No. We won't give up. Let's check the back." Grady grabbed her hand and pulled her around the building.

Windows burst and flames shot out. There seemed no way in.

Suddenly, they heard cries. Star whirled around, searching. She glanced up. "The roof, up there. They are safe," she cried with relief. "But not for long."

"Look for a ladder." Around the corner, they found one attached to the back wall that led to the roof. Grady started climbing. Star pulled her skirt between her legs and tied it around her waist so she could climb unencumbered and followed. "Hurry."

Three rungs up, she felt something icy-cold grab her ankle. Glancing down, she screamed. Cold blue eyes burned into hers. Then a face, red with fury and covered with raw, angry blisters—distorted, melted from fire until he had became the monster in her visions—appeared. The Dragon. She screamed, kicked and gripped the rungs, but he yanked her down.

"This is all *your* fault. You've ruined me." He threw her to the ground. His hands went around her throat. "All because of one—"

Star, from the ground, saw Grady glance down. He hesitated, glancing from her to the roof, which could collapse any minute. She looked up at him, pulling Langley's clawing fingers away and managed to scream: "Save them. Save our children! Save my daughter." *Save my people*.

The words burned inside her head. In that moment, while Star struggled against the Dragon, she knew she'd finally found the answer. The reason she'd been tormented for so long with the gift.

Morning Moon and her easy acceptance of her own gift was the one who'd save their people some day. Star's gift to her people was her daughter—and by saving her, she would be saving them. When her daughter had told her this was meant to be, she'd thought the child was just parroting what she'd heard others tell her mother. Now she knew better. And she also knew she had to free herself and help Grady save the girl. That too was clear. In her vision, it had taken both of them.

Star fought even as her chest tightened and her eyes bulged from lack of air. Her fingers frantically searched the ground for a weapon. At last, they closed around the sharp piece of broken glass that had fallen from the pocket of her day dress. She brought her hand up and sliced one sharp edge down the Dragon's face.

He screamed and reared back, giving her the chance to draw in much needed air and shove him off her. Rising, she ran for the ladder. He followed. She leaped up the first two rungs, but as she climbed, she glanced down and saw him gaining on her.

He reached out and grabbed her foot again. "No!" she yelled, trying to kick him away. And then he was gone. Below her, Zac and Charles had pulled him to the ground. Breathing a sigh of relief, she climbed as fast as she could. A window to her left exploded with heat. Her skin stung from fumes. Fire shot out as she climbed past, preventing anyone else from climbing up. Charles fell back, for he was trying to follow.

"Come on," Grady yelled, helping her over the top of the roof. They found the girls, Hattie and the maids. Hester Mae lay slumped beside them. She'd been shot. Grady searched the roof, which was in poor repair. Finding two long planks used to haphazardly cover a hole in the roof, he motioned for Star to give him a hand. "Come on. I think they might reach across to the next building."

He glanced down between the buildings. Their presence on the roof had been noted, and men were scrambling up the ladder on the other building to help them. By the time he and Star had pulled the boards to the edge, three men were waiting.

Making quick work of forming a bridge, he lifted Renny up. "Go."

Renny nodded, until she looked down. Then she grabbed hold of her father and froze, her gaze riveted on the long fall below them. Grady tried to get her to move, but she refused to let go of him. She whimpered. Star wasn't sure what to do.

Then, Morning Moon climbed up on the edge of the building. Fearlessly, she stepped onto the plank. "Come on, Weshawee. It's just like crossing a ravine on a fallen tree."

Renny slowly met her friend's gaze, then held out her hand. Together, the two girls crossed to safety. The two maids followed after a stern order from Hattie. Then Hattie went.

"Grady, what about Hester?" Star knelt down beside the unconscious woman.

Bending, he slung her over his shoulders. "I'll take her, then come back for you."

Praying the planks would support the weight of two adults, he told Star to hold on to the plank on her end. The men across from him were doing the same. Three-quarters of the way across, Star heard the plank groan. With a desperate lunge, Grady jumped. Hands grabbed at him and pulled him over the ledge. The boards gave way beneath his feet. He barely made it, but he did. The others had caught Hester.

He leaped to his feet and stared back in horror at the empty space between the buildings. Star watched all this, now trapped.

Horrified, Star watched flames leap up on the roof of the building she was on. It was now on fire.

Relieved that at least Grady and the girls were safe, Star searched for a way off the roof. The heat beneath her bare feet was becoming unbearable. Tears streamed down her face.

And suddenly, in that moment, she knew she'd risk it all to tell Grady she loved him. She would marry him. She'd been acting silly, afraid to love and making reasons to avoid it . . . reasons to avoid loss. But now she'd never get the chance to show him. It was too late.

At least she'd saved him and the children. Now she could die in peace.

Across the way, her daughter climbed up onto the edge of the roof. Grady's arms were holding her securely. She lifted her hands out to her side. "Jump, *ina*. Fly—like the eagle!"

Fly like the eagle?

Fly with the eagle.

Grady! He was the eagle. He would catch her— just like in her visions. But she would have to trust them. She ran to the front of the building to the wide brick ledge that ran the length of the warehouse. Slightly wider than the plank, it would allow her to get a running start. She *would* do this. Her vision had given her the knowledge that she could.

Just like a fallen tree over a ravine, she thought, smiling at her wise daughter's words. And though the distance between buildings was farther than she'd ever jumped, what choice did she have? To stay here meant death. And she wanted life. With Grady.

Taking a deep breath, she ran and jumped, praying for the Spirits to give her wings.

They gave her something better.

Grady.

Leaning over the building, he reached out and plucked her from the air. The roar of blood in her ears drowned out the gasp of the crowd below. He clutched her as she half-dangled over the edge of the building and, saved, Star laughed and cried. Just as he had in the visions, Colonel O'Brien had been there to catch her when she fell.

Chapter Twenty

It was a ragged, filthy, but happy and relieved group that walked through the front door of Grady's house. Zeke and Jeffers ran to greet them. Jeffers had a nasty welt on his head but proclaimed he was fine.

Water for baths was heated and they all changed clothes. Then, after an early meal, they gathered in the family parlor before a warm fire.

"You were brave today, Matilda. You weren't afraid." Renny eyed her friend with new respect as she cuddled one of her rats.

Morning Moon giggled when the second rat climbed from the back of the settee to her shoulder. "You were brave too, Renny."

"But I was afraid." She wouldn't look at her father.

Grady knelt in front of her and lifted her chin with his finger. "I was scared too, child." More scared than he'd ever been.

"Truly?" She moved into his arms.

Grady held her tight. "Absolutely. I've never been so scared in my life. I thought I might lose the people I love the most."

Renny hugged him tight. "I love *you*, Papa."

"I love you too, child." He pulled away and cupped her face between his large hands. "I was wrong to leave all those years ago and will never leave again. I should have said that long ago. Will you forgive me for abandoning you?"

"Yes, Papa." Renny smiled happily.

They embraced. Tears ran freely down Grady's cheeks. Finally he pulled away. "Now, how about you two going up to your room to rest? It's been a long day."

"Oh, Papa, must we?" Renny pouted.

"Yes." He tried to be stern but couldn't. Before he relented, Morning Moon came to his rescue.

"Come on, Renny. They want to be alone."

Renny's eyes widened; then she grinned. "Okay, we'll rest for just a little while."

Grady swatted her on the way out. Such impertinence! When he and Star were finally alone, he went to her and lifted her into his arms. Then he sat back on the settee. He glanced at her bandaged feet. The burns she'd suffered likely still hurt. "How do you feel?"

"Alive." She snuggled into him. "Grady?"

"Yes, my love?"

"I'll marry you."

He pulled away. "What?"

"I love you. I realized today that life without love isn't worth living. I don't know how long either of us has, but I want to spend whatever time the Spirits allow me with you."

"I love you, Star—my bright, shining star." Grady lowered his head and kissed her. He tried to stop after just a brief touch, but Star would have none of it.

She slid her hands into his shirt, past where she'd undone several buttons. He was about to cup one breast when a flash of brown caught his eye. A whisker-twitching rodent sat up on its haunches and stared at him with beady eyes. He pulled back.

Looking over, he saw a hand reach through the slightly open pocket doors that separated the sitting room from the dining room.

Before he could shout his daughter's name, Renny's head peeked out and her mouth curved. "You were kissing. Does this mean Star's going to be my new mother?"

Epilogue

November 1857

"They're here," Renny shouted, sliding down the banister.

Grady caught her, and Star was pleased to note he didn't scold. Zeke, with his hair cut short, his face shaven and dressed as any butler, opened the door with Renny dancing eagerly beside him.

Three children ran in, and the noise level escalated; the youths had all started talking at once.

Hester Mae and Baxter followed. In Hester Mae's arms she held a seven-month-old baby. Once in the family parlor, Star held out her arms. "How is baby James doing?" She took the infant from her new sister-in-law.

"Teething something terrible." Hester Mae complained.

From the hall, Star heard Grady's daughter call out, "Come see my new room. It's blue and green and doesn't have any pink or white. Aunt Hester helped me choose the colors." She was likely trying to impress her cousins.

Star and Grady exchanged smiles. They'd turned Margaret Mary's painting studio into a bedroom for Renny, complete with her mother's portrait and the horse painting. Emma's portrait now graced the area above the mantel in Grady's den. Morning Moon had decided to keep Renny's pink and white room.

Star sat with a sigh, cradling the baby boy in her arms. Underneath it, her own unborn child greeted his cousin with a swift kick in the diapered behind.

Baby James let out a yowl of protest. Everyone laughed.

"How are you feeling, Hester Mae?" Star asked. She had to admit the woman looked wonderful. Becoming a mother to Baxter's two children, and to the two they'd adopted, agreed with her.

Star and everyone else in the room glanced at Hester Mae's protruding belly. After a long convalescence from the bullet wound, and the hectic pace of adjusting to four children, they'd all been surprised at the fact that she'd conceived.

Beside her, Baxter hovered, ready to see to her needs.

"Tired, but wonderful. I can't believe after all this time, it finally happened."

Star was glad. There was nothing like feeling life grow inside you.

Minutes later, Charles and his wife arrived, accompanied by Maurice. The man, who had been rescued quickly after the collapse of the Dragon's slave trade, went into the kitchen to visit with the rest of the staff.

"How's the trial coming?" Grady asked the lawyer.

"Langley? I think the jury will certainly find him guilty," Charles said. "After all, he admitted to killing Leo in front of witnesses."

Talking about the Dragon turned to the subject of slavery.

Hester Mae cleared her throat in warning. The three men went on to a more acceptable conversation for mixed company, though Star thought it was an important topic.

Still, content to just sit and watch, Star thought of the last six months. They'd spent nearly six weeks with her family, welcomed Emma and Striking Thunder's firstborn son into the world, then returned to St. Louis. But soon they'd leave and start anew in the territories. Grady had decided to put his knowledge to good use and wanted to act as an agent in negotiations for peace. His friends in the army, though hopeful that he would return to active duty, had agreed to work with him. Star was glad. It would allow her more opportunity to visit with her family.

Loud whoops sounded from the stairs, followed by shrieks. Seconds later, Aggie and Alice rushed into the room screaming. Behind them, Running Elk, wearing only a breechclout, gave chase.

"Matthew!" Star clapped a hand over her mouth in part to hide her laughter. Running Elk had yet to make the adjustment to the wearing of clothing. And at six winters, he had also learned the joy of shocking those around him.

Grady stood and scooped him into his arms. A young black boy, around thirteen, and tall and gangly, ran into the room hot on the boy's tail. He stopped in front of her husband, holding a small shirt and trousers. He rolled his eyes at the half-naked Indian boy.

"*Ma mère* is going to be angry," he said, "if she comes in here and catches you running around without any clothes."

Grady handed Matthew to Hattie's son. "Here, take him up and get him dressed properly."

The boy slung Matthew over his shoulder. "You sure are a bad one, Monsieur Matthew."

At last, Zeke announced that the meal was ready, and they gathered in the dining room. For Thanksgiving, Grady had insisted everyone eat together. The only moment of silence came when Grady said grace. After that, the noise rose in volume.

Across the long, food-laden table, Star gave thanks for her wonderful family and friends. Life couldn't be better. Not only had she and Grady been blessed with new life, but for the last six months, she'd slept dreamlessly. No visions at all. For that she gave thanks.

Sometimes she pondered the reason, and wondered if the visions would return, but somehow, she knew they wouldn't. They'd served their purpose. Each vision had led her up the path to save her daughter—and that had fulfilled her gift to her people. It was going to be easier from here on out.

Yes, life was good. She had much to be thankful for. She met her husband's blue-gray gaze across the table with longing. She had the sudden urge to tell him that she loved him. Noticing that the pitcher of milk for the children was nearly empty, she stood and waved Hattie back to her seat. "I'll get it."

Grady stood as well. "Looks like we could use more wine."

Hester called him back. "There's another bottle—"

Renny's voice cut her off. "He knows, Auntie. He just wants to go kiss my mom."

Laughter and good-natured teasing followed them out to the kitchen.

When Grady swung her around and kissed her, Star sighed and wrapped her arms around his neck. His hands slid down her sides. "I love you, Star O'Brien."

"And I love you, Grady O'Brien."

"Think they'll miss us if we sneak out?"

Star giggled. "For shame," she scolded, though she wished they dared. She slipped out of his arms and sent him a teasing, hungry look. "You'll just have to wait until they leave. Now behave." She turned in a slow circle, searching the kitchen.

"Now, what did I come in here for?"

Grady couldn't resist. He slipped his arms back around her waist and kissed the side of her neck. "For this."

Dear Readers,

I hope you enjoyed Grady and Star Dreamer's story. Writing about and getting to know these two lost souls touched me deeply and strengthened my belief in the healing power of love.

In July 2001, look for the story of Star Dreamer's sister as my *White* series continues with *White Dove*. Sparks will fly as the Sioux maiden meets up again with Jeremy Jones. For excerpts and reviews, check out my website at http://susanedwards.com or write me at:

Susan Edwards
P.O. Box 953
Tracy, CA 95378-0953
(SASE greatly appreciated)

LAIR OF THE WOLF

CHAPTER TWELVE

CONSTANCE O'BANYON

Lair of the Wolf also appears in these *Leisure* books:

COMPULSION by Elaine Fox
includes Chapter One by Constance O'Banyon

CINNAMON AND ROSES by Heidi Betts
includes Chapter Two by Bobbi Smith

SWEET REVENGE by Lynsay Sands
includes Chapter Three by Evelyn Rogers

TELL ME LIES by Claudia Dain
includes Chapter Four by Emily Carmichael

WHITE NIGHTS by Susan Edwards
includes Chapter Five by Martha Hix

IN TROUBLE'S ARMS by Ronda Thompson
includes Chapter Six by Deana James

THE SWORD AND THE FLAME by Patricia Phillips
includes Chapter Seven by Sharon Schulze

MANON by Melanie Jackson
includes Chapter Eight by June Lund Shiplett

THE RANCHER'S DAUGHTERS: FORGETTING
HERSELF by Yvonne Jocks
includes Chapter Nine by Elizabeth Mayne

NORTH STAR by Amanda Harte
includes Chapter Ten by Debra Dier

APACHE LOVER by Holly Harte
includes Chapter Eleven by Madeline George

On January 1, 1997, *Romance Communications,* the Romance Magazine for the 21st century made its Internet debut. One year later, it was named a Lycos Top 5% site on the Web in terms of both content and graphics!

One of *Romance Communications'* most popular features is The Romantic Relay, an original romance novel divided into twelve monthly installments, with each chapter written by a different author. Our first offering was *Lair of the Wolf,* a tale of medieval Wales, created by, in alphabetical order, celebrated authors Emily Carmichael, Debra Dier, Madeline George, Martha Hix, Deana James, Elizabeth Mayne, Constance O'Banyon, Evelyn Rogers, Sharon Schulze, June Lund Shiplett, and Bobbi Smith.

We put no restrictions on the authors, letting each pick up the tale where the previous author had left off and going forward as she wished. The authors tell us they had a lot of fun, each trying to write her successor into a corner!

Now, preserving the fun and suspense of our month-by-month installments, Leisure Books presents, in print, one chapter a month of *Lair of the Wolf*. In addition to the entire online story the authors have added some brand-new material to their existing chapters. So if you think you've read *Lair of the Wolf* already, you may find a few surprises. Please enjoy this unique offering, watch for each new monthly installment in the back of your Leisure Books, and make sure you visit our website, where another romantic relay is already in progress.

Romance Communications

http://www.romcom.com

Pamela Monck, Editor-in-Chief

Mary D. Pinto, Senior Editor

S. Lee Meyer, Web Mistress

Chapter Twelve

By Constance O'Banyon

Lady Meredyth was so stunned by all that had happened that she couldn't fit the fragments together in her mind. How could Garon believe the lies spun by Sir Olyver? How could he believe that she'd ordered the release of his enemy and then set him against her own husband? She paced the room, trying to decide what action to take. For the moment, the marauders were the immediate danger and her first concern. Only after they'd been safely dispatched could she address her problem with Garon.

Her gaze fell on the mug of mead Dame Allison had left on the side table, and she lifted it to her lips, thinking it might help to clear her mind.

At that precise moment, Dame Allison entered the chamber and, seeing what her lady was about to do, knocked the mug from her hand, sending it clattering across the room. "Had you swallowed a dram of that mead, you'd have died in horrible agony." The old woman's voice softened. "You are the heart of our people, my lady, the last blood member of the proud Llewellyn family. You must survive!"

Meredyth felt burning anger toward the woman who had tended her faithfully for so many years. "Get you gone from my sight, old woman. There is nothing so distasteful as a valued friend who betrays a trust. You joined Sir Olyver against me, knowing that 'twas his hand that struck me down on the stairs and left me in the catacombs to die!"

"Sweet lady, 'twas not Sir Olyver who struck you. What happened to you on the stairs was my own plan gone astray."

Meredyth stared at Dame Allison in disbelief. "You have much to answer for. Tell me what you did, and quickly, or your throat will feel the point of my dagger!"

"'Twas Owain, who meant to overpower Sir Olyver on the darkened stairway, but by mistake he struck your dear head. When he realized what he'd done, he carried you to the catacombs to restrain you until Glendire was safe once more for you. Poor, misguided Owain was so distraught by what he'd done that he could hardly speak of it without crying. I had to change my plan, so I had Owen lead the Wolf's men to the catacombs to find you. But you were gone when they got there. It called forth a better plan than we'd expected, because you believed Sir Olyver to be the villain who struck you, and you convinced the Wolf that he was guilty. No one was so happy as I when the Wolf dispatched Sir Olyver to the dungeon."

Meredyth pressed her fingertips against her throbbing temples. "I don't know what you're saying. It's all a tangle. You come to me with this higgledy-piggledy conspiracy and expect me to believe you."

There was contrition in Dame Allison's expression. "If you believe nothing else, believe that I'd never allow harm to befall you. You will better understand why I involved you today when the liberators swarm through the castle to set you free."

Meredyth felt sick inside, as the truth was becoming clear to her. "If by liberators, you are referring to that rabble of ruffians who go about the countryside destroying and pillaging, you have become as addle-brained as they are. And how can you imagine that the marauders will breech the walls of the castle and win its freedom against an army of battle-hardened English troops?"

"The plan is to free *you*, my lady."

Meredyth stared at Dame Allison as if she'd lost her mind. "Free me from what? Know you that I could walk out the gates and free myself if I was of a mind to do so. No one keeps me a prisoner here. My duty lies with my husband and my people." Heavy sadness weighed on her delicate young shoulders. "My mother placed me in your care because she trusted you, and so did I."

Dame Allison reached for her mistress's hand, but Meredyth pulled away from her.

"You were more than my lady-in-waiting. You were my friend and confidante. But no more. Speak, old woman, and speak the whole truth, because I will know if you speak false."

Dame Allison seemed to age years before her eyes. "You know that Mott is my grandson?"

"Of course. But what has that to do with the marauders?"

Dame Allison's expression became fanciful, as if she were remembering something from long ago.

"In my youth, my lady, I loved and bedded a wild young man who deserted me when I told him I was with child. Your lady mother took pity on me and helped me hide my guilty secret. She allowed me to give birth to my son away from prying eyes, by sending me to another village for my confinement. You may recall Ruyen, who was your father's falconer for a time?"

"I know of no such man."

"Ah, well, you were yet young when he left. Ruyen was my son, but, unhappily, he had his father's wild spirit, and when he was old enough, he left Glendire to find his own way. But not before he got a kitchen maid in the family way. Frilla, poor girl, died giving Mott life."

Lady Meredyth was growing impatient. "Are you telling me that your son is one of the marauders now come to Glendire?"

"My son is their leader, my lady." There was pride in her voice. "With Ruyen's help, you will be free of the English dog who has enslaved you."

"Fool! Do you think I will allow your son to step one foot inside Glendire Castle, knowing what he's done to other villages? Do you not see that my people are better served under the guidance of my husband? Know this about me, Dame Allison—I will die, or kill, to keep my people safe. Go now and tell this to your son. And if you are wise, you will convince him to turn aside from Glendire."

Dame Allison's eyes took on a calculating gleam. "You don't know what you are saying. That Englishman has bewitched you. But he could not bewitch me. Even though the Wolf and Sir Olyver have joined forces for now, they cannot withstand my son's army."

"Your son's army is little more than a pack of predators who prey on our own people, as well as the English," Meredyth said in contempt. "They will not breech these walls, and they will never overcome my lord with his superior force. Go to your son and tell him he must turn aside!"

"I cannot do that, my lady. What you call predators are loyal Welshmen who have banded together to drive the English from our land. There are many among your own servants who will lead them safely through the catacombs and into the castle walls. Even a warrior as powerful as the Wolf cannot defend against front and back."

"Mother of God, Dame Allison, you are mad! If my husband dies today, King Edward will only send another to take his place. You have not helped my people. You would only help your son harm them." Meredyth shook her head. "It's all for naught, and many will die needlessly. Your son cannot win against seasoned, well-armed English troops."

Dame Allison's eyes were piercing and wild. "One Welshman armed with a sickle is worth ten Englishmen in full armor wielding battle-axe. We'll not give up until the English are driven back across the border like the cur dogs they are!"

Anger seethed through Meredyth, and she knew what she must do. "Only I can stop this madness." She felt the urgency of the situation. Even now she could hear the clashing of swords from the courtyard below. Reacting quickly, she moved toward the door.

Dame Allison quickly stepped in front of her, blocking her path. "I would have you remain in your chamber, where no harm can befall you."

Meredyth grasped the old woman's frail shoulders and forcefully moved her aside. "It will take more than you to stop me. It sickens me that you would even try."

Dame Allison feared for her lady's life. "What are you about?"

Meredyth spoke softly, putting her thoughts into words. "I must place my father's banner alongside my husband's, so that my people shall know that I stand with him."

Dame Allison's face drained of color. "You would display the Llewellyn colors alongside the Wolf's?"

"I shall, and I'll I wager my life that no Welshman will fight against my father's colors—not even your son."

"'Tis too late to stop the battle, my lady. It's gone too far now."

"Then I shall die trying. Relay this to your son—say that the lady of Glendire stands with her English husband. Say to him that if he slays my husband, he must slay me as well."

Dame Allison stared at Meredyth in disbelief. "You would die for that Englishman?"

"I would gladly die for my husband." She rushed through the door, her velvet slippers noiseless as she made her way down the stone steps and into the deserted Great Hall. The sound of battle was louder now, and she felt an urgency deep inside her. "Please," she prayed aloud, "don't let me be too late!"

Dame Allison could almost feel the displeasure of her long-dead mistress, accusing her of placing her daughter in danger when she had charged her on her deathbed to keep Meredyth safe. How she could ever have acted in a manner that would endanger her lady? She hoped she could stop her son, but she wasn't sure he would listen to her.

Lady Meredyth shoved a bench in front of the huge fireplace and quickly climbed upon it. Even so, she had to stand on tiptoe to reach her father's banner.

The red silk with the blue dragon folded about her like a caress as she leapt to the floor. Hurrying to the door, she uttered a hasty entreaty. "Forgive me, father, for what I do now. Forgive me for using your colors against our own people. I pray you understand. I trust you would approve."

Once outside, Lady Meredyth looked around frantically to locate her husband. What if he was already dead? With a feeling of relief, she spotted the black helm of the Wolf on the west wall walk, where the fighting was the heaviest. She had to warn him that he was soon to be attacked from within the castle walls.

Even as she hesitated, across the courtyard, the door of the lower storeroom burst open, and marauders surged through it from the secret catacombs below.

Lady Meredyth unfurled her father's colors and rushed toward the Wolf, who was still unaware that his enemy was at his back. She moved up the wooden ladder, past soldiers who paused long enough to stare at her in astonishment, but none tried to stop her.

Her eyes set on the man in the black wolf helmet, she did not see the deadly arrow hurled at her from below, but the impact of it sent waves of pain through her whole body. Weakness washed over her, and she dropped to her knees as blackness threatened to engulf her. One of the Wolf's men saw what had happened and rushed to her aid, but she stayed his hand and rose shakily to her feet. An unexpected silence fell across Glendire Castle as all eyes, English and Welsh, turned to Lady Meredyth.

Garon quickly ripped off his helm and threw it aside, taking a hasty step toward his wounded wife. But she shook her head, her eyes pleading with him not to interfere. The most difficult thing he'd ever done in his life was to stand there and let her come to him, knowing the pain it was causing her. But he realized what she was doing, and he could do no more than watch, though everything in him cried out to help her.

Meredyth knew that the reaction of her people would be determined by what she did now. She prayed for the strength to complete the task. Once her knees buckled, but she managed to stay upright by bracing her back against the limestone wall. Drawing in a deep breath, she took a hesitant step, which caused pain to engulf her. Despite the pain, she took another step, and then another, knowing she must not give in to the weakness that threatened to render her unconscious.

At last she reached Garon, and her eyes met his. "Please do not let me fall," she whispered. "And do not interfere."

He nodded, and his hand went to the small of her back, supporting her. He had seen men die in battle with extreme bravery, but never had he witnessed the valor he saw in his wife's actions today. He could not help her in this, although everything inside him cried out to do so. He felt her slight body shudder, and he placed his other hand on her arm to hold her upright. They both knew in that moment that there was more than their lives at stake; the future of her people, and his, rested in her small hands.

With difficulty, Lady Meredyth planted the red banner in front of her, and it blended with the Wolf's blue banner, like two hands intertwining. It was an act of love for him and for her people, and it brought tears to the eyes of many battle-hardened soldiers.

She began to speak, and her voice was so soft and weak that those who were far away had to be told what she said. "I implore you, my people, to lay down your . . . arms . . . and no harm . . . will come to you. I vow . . . this on my life. Know, you all . . . that this day I join the Llewellyn banner with that of the Wolf's. If you draw weapon against him . . . you draw weapon against me and the name Llewellyn."

At first there was the sound of one sword dropping. This was followed by another, and still another, and soon the clatter of abandoned weapons was almost deafening as it echoed against the stone walls of the castle. Not one Welshman, be he of Glendire Castle, or be he a member of the marauders, would draw sword against the last living person with Llewellyn blood flowing in her veins. Lady Meredyth had won. But many feared she had given her life for this peace, for blood stained the front of her gown, and it was apparent that she was having difficulty standing.

Garon's eyes misted, and he felt pride well within him for this woman who was his wife. Would he ever be worthy of the loyalty she'd shown him today? Surely God would not take her away from him now—death could not claim his love.

He spoke close to her ear. " 'Tis enough, heart mine." He saw the blood soaking the front of her gown and knew not how badly she'd been wounded. "I will take you in my arms and carry you below to tend your wound."

She shook her head. "First there is something I must do." She staggered backward, and he steadied her, knowing she would not be content until she had completed the task she had set herself.

"Yield to your health, wife. You have done more than could be expected of anyone."

Her voice was surprisingly strong as she spoke.

"Dame Allison, Ruyen of the marauders, and Mott, come forward so I may see you."

After much mumbling, the three stood below her, their hands crossed in front of them in a gesture of obedience. There was a look of arrogance in Ruyen's eyes, but Mott looked like a frightened lad. Dame Allison knew her lady better than anyone, and she knew what was to come. Shame riveted every nerve in her body, and she knew she deserved no mercy.

"Ruyen," Lady Meredyth said with anger, "let it be known by all here that I brand you as an outlaw. You are to be shunned by honest people and aided by none." Her eyes then went to Mott. "You, young man, are guilty only of doing what you were told. Learn from this mistake, and be more guarded in obeying orders you know to be unjust." Reluctantly, her gaze fell on Dame Allison. "What you did, you did out of love for me, but I can no longer trust you."

Dame Allison wiped tears from her wrinkled cheeks, feeling as if her heart would break. "I beg your forgiveness, my lady," she cried, falling to her knees and raising her hands in pleading. "I am much ashamed of what I've done. Forgive me! Forgive me!"

Meredyth's voice held a note of coldness. "You have my forgiveness if it brings you any comfort, Dame Allison. But know you this—to be betrayed by one such as your son is expected, but you, whom I loved and trusted—it is a grievous act indeed. Even though you betrayed me, I cannot bring myself to send you to your death. So go from here, and never let me look upon your face again. Take your son and your grandson with you, and all those who came through the catacombs to make war this day."

To his credit, Ruyen did not abandon his mother but helped her rise and escorted her through the angry crowd, where people shoved at them and mumbled harsh threats.

Meredyth turned to her husband, who had stood silent while she rendered her judgment. "Please, help . . . me. Do not allow my father's . . . banner to fall." With that said, Meredyth's strength gave out, and she fainted.

The Wolf lifted his unconscious wife in his arms while Captain Hanes grabbed the Llewellyn banner. "Carry the banner inside and bear it with much pride, Captain Hanes, for it has known great honor this day," Garon said as he gently carried Meredyth down the ladder while the crowd parted for them.

He knew heavy devastation. He could not lose her now, for if he did, he would be a man without a purpose, a man with no heart, a man with no reason to live.

As he passed with his precious burden, he noticed that Welsh yeomen, serfs, and servants, be they man or woman, were crying unashamedly as they reached out to their lady. It was obvious that they loved Meredyth. It was testimony to that love that not one had drawn sword against her today, not even the infamous Ruyen or his band of ruffians. The Wolf knew that the arrow that had struck her had not been aimed at her but had been a mischance shot, doubtless meant for his own black heart.

Lady Meredyth languished for days with fever, without regaining consciousness. She had no way of knowing that her husband never left her side during that time but held her hand and spoke to her softly of his love.

It was a dull, gray morning with a chill in the air when Meredyth awoke. Garon, looking haggard and unshaved, managed to smile and brush her tumbled hair from her face. "At last you have decided to join us, my lady-wife."

Her thoughts were muddled, and she licked her dry lips, wondering why she felt so weak. "What happened?"

Garon adjusted the coverlet about her breasts, taking care not to touch the bandaged wound on her shoulder. "You took on both English and Welsh and won, Meredyth. Minstrels will long sing songs of your heroism, and how you singlehandedly won the siege of Glendire Castle."

"I did no more than stand beside my husband," she said, raising her gaze to his. She looked for love in Garon's eyes, but as always, he was not a man to show what he felt. "You know now that I did not betray you?"

"I do," he said, tearing his gaze from her and standing. "I sent Sir Olyver and his men back to King Edward under heavy guard. I set my hand to a detailed description of his actions while he was under my command. Knowing Longshanks as I do, I feel certain that Olyver will not linger among the living overlong. The king does not suffer fools or disloyalty. Olyver was both a fool and a traitor."

There was a heavy silence as she waited for him to say more. Even in her weakened condition, she could feel her heart quicken at his nearness. She wanted to ask him how he felt about her, but she was overcome with sudden shyness.

The Wolf, mistaking her silence for indifference to him, bowed and departed, when what he really wished to do was go down on his knees and tell her of his overwhelming love for her.

* * *

A week passed, and Lady Meredyth did not see her husband. When she questioned the servants, they could only tell her that the Wolf had left the castle, but none knew where he'd gone.

As Meredyth grew stronger, she left her chamber and tried to go about her daily life, but she missed her husband, and she conjured up a dozen visions of what he might be doing. Had he gone back to England, weary of his Welsh wife? Was he in the arms of another woman, finding comfort and passion? Why did he torture her so by staying away?

It was two weeks later that Meredyth received word that her husband had returned to Glendire and requested that she join him in the courtyard.

It was a cold, crisp day, but the sun was bright, and there was not a cloud in the sky as Meredyth came outside. She was astonished to find so many people there, and further astonished to see the Wolf's Persian carpet spread as it had been the day she'd pledged fealty to him. She saw that her father's chair had been placed in the same place it had stood that day. As she approached, English men-at-arms and her Welsh yeomen made a line for her to walk through. The English priest who had come to the castle with Garon met her and led her onto the carpet and seated her in her father's chair. A hundred questions tugged at her mind. What could be happening? she wondered.

From within the crowd, Garon came forward, dressed in full armor, with his wolf's-head helm tucked underneath his arm. The look on his face was solemn as he caught and held her gaze. When he stood in front of Meredyth, he handed the priest his helm and dropped to his knees before her.

It was so quiet that only the cooing of a dove, nested in a nearby tree, could be heard.

Garon extended his folded palms to her, and she

looked puzzled. The priest whispered to her, and she reluctantly covered Garon's hands with hers.

Tears swam in her eyes as she understood the significance of Garon's gesture. Had there ever been a man to rival the Wolf in courage and tenderness? He had strength when it was needed, but he had a heart as well.

The Wolf spoke in a voice that carried to the farthermost corner of the courtyard, so all might know of his pledge. "I, Garon of Glendire and Saunders, enter into your homage and faith and become your man, by mouth and hand. I swear and promise to keep faith and loyalty to you against all others. To guard your rights with all my strength."

His eyes softened just the merest bit, and he stood, turning his attention to the others. "You have heard me pledge faith to your lady. Be it known that I will cause a decree to be set forth that every second son of the Saunders henceforth, and beginning with my line, shall bear the proud and noble name Llewellyn. I do this so a proud and noble house will not die but live on as tribute to my honored lady, and to bear testimony to the eternal love I bear her."

A loud cheer rippled through the crowd when their lady committed a very unladylike act. She stood and propelled herself into her husband's arms, pressing her lips to his cheek.

He chuckled in her ear and whispered, "Will you tempt me to ravish you before all those gathered here, my dearest heart?"

She looked into his eyes and saw the love reflected there. "You pledged me your love."

"Aye, that I did. And I would never tell an untruth in the form of a pledge."

"Did you mean what you said about our second son being a Llewellyn?"

"Aye, I did." He took her arm and led her across the carpet, toward the castle. "The sooner we start on our first son"—he raised a bold eyebrow—"the sooner we can work on the second."

She saw humor dancing in his dark eyes, but there was something more, as well. There was tenderness and love.

At the door of the castle, he turned back to the crowd. "There is a feast for all. Eat, enjoy, but you will have to excuse me and your lady. We shall not be in attendance."

As he escorted her up the stairs, she felt her heart pounding with anticipation. When they were in their chamber, he closed the door and held her away from him, his eyes drinking in her delicate beauty.

"Meredyth, I came to conquer and became the conquered. I know when I'm outmatched. I only hope I am worthy of you, my conquerer."

She smiled, nestling against him. "You are most worthy, dearest Wolf."

He looked deeply into her eyes. "Can you forget all the unpleasantness that's passed between us? Can you learn to love me?"

She smiled to herself. Never had she seen the powerful Wolf so uncertain, and she wagered no one else had either. "I have heard a rumor that wolves mate for life. Is that so?"

He looked at her, puzzled. "I believe I have heard this."

"Then I shall be your willing mate for life, my lord. Although I did not love you in the beginning, I have come to love you beyond all reason."

There was a triumphant gleam in his eyes when he lifted her in his arms and laid her on the bed, sending a disgruntled Beelzebub flying. "Mate with the Wolf, but love the man, my lady. Because it's the man who loves you."

Their coming together was fire and passion, with nothing held back, no doubts to haunt them. Each gave their body, as they had given their pledge.

From that day on, love would rule at Glendire Castle—the Lair of the Wolf.

WHITE WOLF

SUSAN EDWARDS

Jessica Jones knows that the trip to Oregon will be hard, but she will not let her brothers leave her behind. Dressed as a boy to carry on a ruse that fools no one, Jessie cannot disguise her attraction to the handsome half-breed wagon master. For when she looks into Wolf's eyes and entwines her fingers in his hair, Jessie glimpses the very depths of passion.

___4471-4 $5.50 US/$6.50 CAN

White Flame — Susan Edwards

Searching for her missing father, the determined Emma
O'Brien sets out for Fort Pierre on the Missouri River, but
when the steamboat upon which she is traveling runs aground,
she is forced to travel on foot. Braving the wilderness, the
feisty beauty is soon seized by Indians. Surrounded by
enemies, Emma learns that only Striking Thunder can grant
her release. The handsome Sioux chieftain offers her freedom
but enslaves her with a kiss. He takes her to his village, and
there, underneath the prairie's starry skies, Emma learns the
truth. The danger Striking Thunder represents is greater than
the pre-war bonfires of the entire Sioux nation—and the
passion he offers burns a whole lot hotter.

___4613-X $4.99 US/$5.99 CAN

White Nights
Susan Edwards

Eirica Macauley sees the road to better days: the remainder of the Oregon Trail. The trail is hard, even for experienced cattle hands like James Jones, but the man's will and determination lend Eirica strength. Yet, Eirica knows she can never accept the cowboy's love; the shadows that darken her past will hardly disappear in the light of day. But as each night passes and their wagon train draws nearer its destination, James's intentions grow clearer—and Eirica aches for his warm embrace. And when darkness falls and James stays beside her, the beautiful widow knows that when dawn comes, she'll no longer be alone.

Lair of the Wolf

Also includes the fifth installment of *Lair of the Wolf*, a serialized romance set in medieval Wales. Be sure to look for future chapters of this exciting story featured in Leisure books and written by the industry's top authors.

___4703-9 $5.50 US/$6.50 CAN

Dorchester Publishing Co., Inc.
P.O. Box 6640
Wayne, PA 19087-8640

Please add $1.75 for shipping and handling for the first book and $.50 for each book thereafter. NY, NYC, and PA residents, please add appropriate sales tax. No cash, stamps, or C.O.D.s. All orders shipped within 6 weeks via postal service book rate. Canadian orders require $2.00 extra postage and must be paid in U.S. dollars through a U.S. banking facility.

Name_____
Address_____
City_____State_____Zip_____
I have enclosed $_____ in payment for the checked book(s).
Payment <u>must</u> accompany all orders. ❑ Please send a free catalog.

Lair of the Wolf

Constance O'Banyon, Bobbi Smith, Evelyn Rogers, Emily Carmichael, Martha Hix, Deana James, Sharon Schulze, June Lund Shiplett, Elizabeth Mayne, Debra Dier, and Madeline George

Be sure not to miss a single installment of Leisure Books's star-studded new serialized romance, *Lair of the Wolf*! Preserving the fun and suspense of the month-by-month installments, Leisure presents one chapter a month of the entire on-line story, including some brand new material the authors have added to their existing chapters. Watch for a new installment of *Lair of the Wolf* every month in the back of select Leisure books!

Previous Chapters of *Lair of the Wolf* can be found in:

**To order call our special toll-free number 1-800-481-9191
or VISIT OUR WEB SITE AT: www.dorchesterpub.com**

Compulsion Elaine Fox

On the smoldering Virginia night when she first meets Ryan St. James, Catra Meredyth knows nothing can douse the fire that the infuriating Yankee has ignited within her. With one caress the handsome seducer has kindled a passion that threatens to turn the Southern belle's reputation to ashes—and with one torrid kiss she consigns herself to the flames. Ryan has supped at the table of sin, but on Catra's lips he has tasted heaven. A dedicated bachelor, Ryan finds that the feisty beauty tempts even his strongest resolve. In the heat of their love is a lesson to be learned: The needs of the flesh cannot be denied, but the call of the heart is stronger by far.

Lair of the Wolf

Also includes the first installment of *Lair of the Wolf*, a serialized romance set in medieval Wales. Be sure to look for future chapters of this exciting story featured in Leisure books and written by the industry's top authors.

___4648-2 $5.99 US/$6.99 CAN

Cinnamon and Roses
Heidi Betts

A hardworking seamstress, Rebecca has no business being attracted to a man like wealthy, arrogant Caleb Adams. Born fatherless in a brothel, Rebecca knows what males are made of. And Caleb is clearly as faithless as they come, scandalizing their Kansas cowtown with the fancy city women he casually uses and casts aside. Though he tempts innocent Rebecca beyond reason, she can't afford to love a man like Caleb, for the price might be another fatherless babe. What the devil is wrong with him, Caleb muses, that he's drawn to a calico-clad dressmaker when sirens in silk are his for the asking? Still, Rebecca unaccountably stirs him. Caleb vows no woman can be trusted with his heart. But he must sample sweet Rebecca.

Lair of the Wolf

Also includes the second installment of *Lair of the Wolf*, a serialized romance set in medieval Wales. Be sure to look for future chapters of this exciting story featured in Leisure books and written by the industry's top authors.

___4668-7 $4.99 US/$5.99 CAN